KT-527-260

THE QUEEN'S GRACE

NIGEL TRANTER

EDINBURGH
B&W PUBLISHING
1996

Copyright © Nigel Tranter
First published 1953
This edition published 1996
by B&W Publishing Ltd
Edinburgh
ISBN 1 873631 10 3

All rights reserved.
No part of this publication may be reproduced
or transmitted, in any form or by any means,
without the prior permission of B&W Publishing Ltd.

British Library Cataloguing in Publication Data:
A catalogue record for this book is available from
the British Library

Cover illustration:
Detail from *Catherine Parr*
attributed to Master John (circa 1545)
Photograph courtesy of
the National Portrait Gallery

Printed by Werner Söderström

THE QUEEN'S GRACE

AUTHOR'S NOTE

This may be called an historical novel, in that it is set against a background as historically accurate as the author's limited scholarship and research allow. Liberties have been taken with many historical characters, inevitably—but not wantonly, nor in a fashion designed to show them up in a role markedly other than that accepted by respectable historians. (Though even respectable historians differ.)

The fall of Huntly and the House of Gordon, the most powerful noble and the strongest clan in Scotland of Queen Mary's time, so little documented as it is, has long puzzled those interested. How did such complete collapse come about, in the short space of two months? The following story poses a possible solution—no more. A house divided against itself, and the dichotomy of a bastard clan—here is the stuff of tragedy.

This is fiction—though the issue would be worthy of more serious treatment. Its lack is my excuse—though no excuse is necessary, surely, for romanticising on the theme of lovely Mary, Queen of Scots. Her challenge will withstand less faltering pen than this.

Nigel Tranter

CHARACTERS

In order of appearance.
(Fictional characters printed in Italics.)

Patrick MacRuary Gordon, Laird of Balruary, in Glen Livet.

Black Ewan (Ewan Dubh), gillie, or body servant, to above.

Alexander Gordon of Glendoig, chieftain of a Gordon sept, and Seneschal or chamberlain, to Huntly.

GEORGE GORDON, 4TH EARL OF HUNTLY, Chief of Clan Gordon, Cock o' the North, Gudeman o' the Bog, etc., Lord High Chancellor of Scotland and Lieutenant of the North, principal Catholic nobleman of the country.

Sir Nevil Cleavely, unofficial envoy of Queen Elizabeth of England, to Huntly.

GEORGE, THE LORD GORDON, eldest surviving son of Huntly, and heir of Gordon. (Known as Seorus Og, or George the Younger, in the Gaelic.)

JAMES DOUGLAS, 4TH EARL OF MORTON, Head of the House of Douglas, later Chancellor, and eventually Regent of Scotland.

WILLIAM MAITLAND, OF LETHINGTON, the Queen's Secretary of State.

Mary Mackintosh, of Moy, an extra Maid of Honour to Queen Mary, eldest daughter of Lauchlan Mor, 16th Chief of Mackintosh and Captain of Clan Chattan.

MARY LIVINGSTONE
MARY BEATON   } Three of the Queen's Maries— favourite Maids of Honour.
MARY SETON

SIGNOR DAVID RIZZIO, the Queen's Italian secretary.

MARY STEWART, QUEEN OF SCOTS, Dowager Queen of France and heiress to the throne of England, only legitimate child of James Fifth.

SIR JAMES MELVILLE, a veteran courtier and statesman.

THE MARQUIS D'ELBOEUF
                              } de Guise uncles of the Queen.
THE GRAND PRIOR OF FRANCE

vii

JAMES OGILVY OF CARDELL, Master of the Queen's Household, and true heir of Findlater, disinherited by his father in favour of Sir John Gordon.

Master William Forbes, Protestant Minister of St. Nicholas, principal church of Aberdeen.

LORD JAMES STEWART (THE BASTARD), Earl of Mar, afterwards Earl of Moray, later Regent, illegitimate son of James Fifth and the Lady Margaret Erskine, half-brother of the Queen, and the power behind the Throne.

Donald Gorm Mackintosh, personal gillie to Mary Mackintosh.

Willie Gordon, Delmore, a Gordon freebooter.

SIR JOHN GORDON OF FINDLATER, 3rd son of Huntly, dashing gallant, favourite of his father, and famous as one of the handsomest men Scotland has produced. Succeeded to Findlater Castle by the will of Alexander Ogilvy thereof, who disinherited his own son James.

Angus The Boat, ferryman at Moy Castle, a prominent Mackintosh clansman.

DONALD OG MACPHERSON OF CLUNY, Chief of Clan Macpherson, one of the components of the Clan Chattan Federation.

FRASER OF FARRALINE, son-in-law to Cluny Macpherson.

WILLIAM DOUGLAS OF CAVERS, an officer in the Queen's forces.

Helen Gordon, Patrick's mother, widow of Hector MacRuary Gordon of Balruary, and once the object of Huntly's affections.

AGNES, COUNTESS OF HUNTLY, mother of Huntly's nine sons, daughter of Keith, the Earl Marischal.

LADY JEAN GORDON, daughter of above and Huntly, later wife to James Hepburn, the notorious Earl of Bothwell.

Father Roche, the Queen's private chaplain.

Daffing Davie Gordon, a familiar of Huntly's, thought to be an illegitimate brother.

I

POOR PATRICK GORDON, personable, swack, and just cocky enough to *be* a Gordon—little he knew. He was on a new road, and his comb, his cheek, and his broadsword, were all due to be reddened before the end of it. But did he know it, guess it, even sense a hint of it? He did not. Poor Patrick MacRuary Gordon of Balruary, indeed!

He whistled tunefully, in fact, as he went down between the birches, his buckled brogues tipping the turning green-gold brackens through which his mount swished stolidly, whistled away the last carefree bars of his youthful fine independence and innocence; for undoubtedly innocent Patrick was essentially, even though he had honourably killed his first man five years ago at the age of twenty, handfasted with a Mackintosh maiden who had proved a disappointment and gone back to her Speyside father before the year was up, and enjoyed such other amenities as might enrich the humdrum life of a stay-at-home Gordon gentleman. But in the things that mattered Patrick still retained his intrinsic innocence intact. And whistled.

At his thigh, shapely in its tightly-tartaned trews, his running gillie whistled too—but not musically. Well might he; with a hand twisted into the pony's mane he had run fifteen heather miles already at Patrick's side, down from the great brown hills of Glen Livet that cradled Balruary, and into this country of green knowes, and would run fifteen more if need be. Whistling breath was nothing new to Black Ewan, Patrick Gordon's foot gillie and shadow.

Neither was the track new that they followed—whatever might be the end of their road. The way to Strathbogie Castle was apt to be well known to all of the name of Gordon—and others too, in 16th-century Scotland. There were rumours that Mary the Queen herself was about to tread it. But it was not

1

often that a direct summons from the Chief came to Balruary, to set Patrick hurrying and whistling. A Gordon always hurried when Huntly summoned—even if he did not always whistle thereafter.

Through the legion of the small round hills, where the shaggy black cattle grazed in their hundreds amongst the already yellowing birches, the young men threaded their way, like the stream that they followed, to the accompaniment of the catchy Reel of Towie, the clop-clop of broad hooves, and the panting of breath. They did not fail to notice, either of them, that from the scattered turf cabins of the herdsmen that they passed, it was the women who came to gaze admiringly, throw a pleasantry, or skirl a tentative offer to the gallant dark lad in his fine tartans with the single eagle's feather to his bonnet—women only with an old dotard here and there. If it was no cause for whistling that two upstanding young men had to refuse their generosity, still it meant that the menfolk of the clan were gathering. The clan gathering—and Patrick Gordon of Balruary summoned by name to appear at Strathbogie Castle! The women could wait.

At length the hillocks dwindled before them, and they emerged from the green constriction to stare out over a wide valley, fair and fertile, flooded with the afternoon sun—the strath of Bogie. Threaded by a silver river, mantled with dark woods, patched with the gold of August corn, and dotted with turf cabins, stone houses, and tall towers, it stretched away northwards to join the still wider vale of Deveron, ever broadening between its guardian hills, Strathbogie of the Gordons, jewel of the North, envy of princes. And in the comely midst of it all, visible even at five miles farther north where Bogie and Deveron joined, the soaring walls and pinnacles and battlements of the Earl's castle lifted out of the pall of blue smoke from a hundred camp-fires. Patrick's chin cocked two degrees higher at sight of it, as was only fitting.

Since, of course, it was necessary to cut something of a dash down Strathbogie, the garron was tickled up with the point of a dirk, and Black Ewan perforce had to stretch his long legs wider still. The Reel of Towie was dispensed with—

though the gillie continued to wheeze a shade distractingly—
and the bonnet was adjusted to the correct angle so that the
broad eagle's feather projected as a suitable flourish above
the right eyebrow.

The strath was a-move with men, in large parties and
small—though none so small as Patrick's. All were heading
towards the castle, and though by no means all were dressed
so bravely as was Patrick, all were most adequately armed.
Making a point of passing them all, at the same time as
exchanging mannerly greetings, the young man under the
nodding-feather knew just a pang of regret that he should be
showing but the one gillie at his heels, and not a respectable
tail of armed men like these others; after all, Balruary could
have risen to twenty, and even more, at a squeeze. But the
summons had been to himself only, to present himself to his
Chief in his castle of Strathbogie forthwith. Innocent or not,
he was experienced enough not to seek to improve on that
order.

Across a dozen tributary streams, and through a score of
townships, they went, till, through the haze of smoke, the
great castle of Strathbogie—or Palace of Huntly as the Earl
would have it called these days—barred their way, its walls
thrusting above the reek, its red towers and turrets and bar-
bicans a challenge to the blue heaven itself—to say nothing of
lesser powers and potentates.

The seat of Gordon power stood on a triple mound above
the junction of the Bogie and rushing Deveron, with its castle-
ton separated from it by a wide green haugh of meadow that
lifted to the Lady's Pleasaunce. Today that green meadow,
normally a-graze with cattle, was black with men—an armed
camp. In their hundreds upon hundreds they filled the great
amphitheatre and overflowed in such directions as the rivers
allowed, a mainly tartan-clad mass, but with hodden grey to
it, and buff, and the glint of armour. The wall of noise that
arose therefrom, the shouts and songs of men, the skirl of
pipes, the neighing of horses, and the crackle of fires was a
heartensome thing—to friends of the Gordon!

Patrick's spirit responded fittingly, inevitably, to the colour

3

and challenge of it all, the clamour and bustle, the assembly of men, the flourish of stone. He picked his garron's way through the throng, and laughed for sheer wordless pride and satisfaction. At the horse's froth-flecked side Black Ewan laughed too, open-mouthed, silent—for he and his master were one. They climbed the steep hill to the gatehouse.

Armed guards, with breastplate and basinet over Huntly's new Lowland-style livery, held the black tunnel of the gateway arch, but they nodded, perhaps as much to the Gordon cock of his chin as to Patrick's proud eagle's feather and tartan, and let him through.

The great paved courtyard was as thronged in its way as was the grassy haugh below—but with a difference. Here was the quality of the clan, the lairds and gentlemen and captains that followed the Cock o' the North, a goodly company—but exemplifying amongst them, so much more clearly than amongst their men, the essential cleavage, the dual aspect, that was at once the strength and the weakness of the House of Gordon, the Highland and the Lowland partition. Very evident it was in that crowded quadrangle within Huntly's great castle, with the tartaned gentry of the mountains keeping well apart and to themselves, from the more numerous broadclothed and armoured lairds of the rich and fertile low country in the coastal plain, all naming themselves Gordon. But that was an old story, and no concern of Patrick's just then. Crossing the courtyard diagonally, to the massive towering keep, greatest in all Scotland, he dismounted and presented himself at the comparatively small iron-grilled doorway in the stair-tower.

Crossed pikes greeted him. "Who are ye?" a voice challenged.

"Patrick of Balruary, to see George of Huntly!" he answered, with no Lowland false-humility nonsense.

He heard the name Balruary passed back from mouth to mouth, echoing into the deeper fastnesses of that grim pile. And still the pikes barred his way.

Denying himself a frown, and turning to hand over his broadsword on its shoulder-belt to Black Ewan, and to busy himself with instructions as to his garron's care—that none might imagine a Highland gentleman to be kept waiting save of his own accord—Patrick did not look round again until his name was called.

He turned to find a slender exquisite standing between the pikemen, a wand of a fellow, younger than himself and even an inch taller—but with no substance to him—dressed ridiculously in long wine-coloured hose, slashed trunks, and canary silk doublet, after the foppish southron fashion, with a lengthy knitting-pin of a rapier sticking out indecently behind him to get in more honest folk's way. Patrick looked this apparition up and down at his leisure.

"*Dhia!*" he said. "And what are you?"

The other, already turning away, answered languidly: "My Lord's esquire."

"Esquire! Your name, I meant—if you have one!" That was rapped out in a manner befitting one of chieftainly as distinct from mere lairdly pretensions.

A little startled obviously, the elegant looked back. "Charles Gordon, Younger of Ethlick," he said, not languidly.

Patrick said nothing, but his snort was eloquent of what he thought of esquires and popinjay sprigs of Lowland lairdies, as he followed the other into the vaulted passage that led to the wide wheel-stair.

Indoors as out, the scene was one of bustle and stir—but purposeful stir. There was a great coming and going along dark passages lit by flaming torches of spluttering bog-pine, and the wide stairway was as throng as an ant-hill. Wafting along from the kitchens was the appetising fragrance of roast meats—only slightly spoiled by the eddying reek of the torches —and Patrick and his guide had to take their places on the hollowed stone treads of the stair behind somewhat distracted serving wenches tripping upstairs with great dishes of smoking beef and game. The distraction of these last, caused by their necessary efforts to keep the viands on the plates despite the prying and sportive hands of the numerous scions of Gordon who lined the wall—and who by no means confined their fingerwork to the victuals—transmitted itself in some measure to Patrick, who not only felt an empty stomach reacting

5

vigorously to the delectable aroma, but found himself looking down the almost equally delectable bare back of a young female whose bodice had been whipped loose to slip from shapely shoulders, while both her hands were occupied. The maids coming downstairs, empty-handed, were in a better state to defend themselves—such as were inclined. The general effect was a shade disconcerting to one straight off the heather. Huntly's retinue evidently cherished its comforts.

On a wide landing at first-floor level, where a harassed chamberlain was directing the flow of servitors, Patrick's usher handed him over to a spare elderly man, richly but soberly habited in Lowland garb, though a Highlander himself— Glendoig, Seneschal to the Chief.

"My Lord has been waiting for you this while back," he greeted, with a touch of asperity.

"I have travelled fast and far, Glendoig," Patrick answered, with no hint of apology. "You know the road from Glen Livet—or perhaps you have forgotten it?" That was shrewd thrusting, for the glen of Doig, patrimony of this tamed chieftain, itself opened off Glen Livet of the mountains.

The older man stiffened. "You are fit to see his lordship?" he inquired, looking Patrick up and down.

"I am always fit to see my cousin . . . and yours!" The Chief, according to patriarchal Highland usage, was all his clan's cousin.

Glendoig's narrow gaze rested on the other's brow and feather. "Your bonnet . . ." he reminded sourly.

"Comes off only to my Chief and my Queen!"

Thin lips compressed, the Seneschal shrugged, and moved through the press of folk and in at the wide doorway, Patrick at his side rather than his heels.

A tall screen of carved wood-panelling hid the doorway and landing from what lay beyond. Rounding it, usher and guest paused. Before them opened a vast and noble chamber, the Great Hall of the castle, stretching the entire length and breadth of the keep, lit by tall windows deep in the thickness of the walls, and also by both candelabra and torches. The contradiction of mellow candlelight and flaring bog-pine was displayed and proclaimed in every other feature of that handsome apartment—fine carpets side by side with animal skins on the stone-flagged floor, rich French tapestries cheek by jowl with tartan hangings, battle-axes and stags' heads on the walls, silver plate and Venetian glass sharing the enormous fifty-foot table that ran most of the room's length, with vessels of horn and beech, pipers waiting their turn to play when the lutists and lyrists should be done. Here was the uneasy marriage of the Highlands and the Lowlands, a wary match reflected in some measure in the garb and demeanour of practically all in that crowded hall, and not least in the figure that sprawled far at the head of the long table.

The Seneschal beat with his hand on a large gong that hung from the end of the wooden screen, and, as its deep boom rang out and shuddered into eventual silence, spoke into the consequent hush.

"Young Balruary . . . at my Lord Earl's summons!"

Patrick's dark brows came down in a black bar across his face—a thing not too difficult with the sort of features that he had. Young he might be, but he was not Young Balruary—as Glendoig well knew. Stepping over swiftly, he brought down his own fist on that gong—and cared not for the stoun it gave to his knuckles.

"Balruary himself, to see the Gudeman o' the Bog!" he cried, in amendment, into the echoes, and taking off his bonnet at last, strode forward up the room.

George Gordon, fifteenth Chief of his Name, Gudeman o' the Bog, Cock o' the North, Lord of Strathbogie and Enzie, of Badenoch and Aboyne, Knight of the Order of St. Michael of France, Lord High Chancellor of Scotland, Lieutenant of the North, and fourth Earl of Huntly, watched the advance of the bold lad with the saturnine face, through little shrewd eyes, whilst one strangely delicate hand toyed with the crucifix that hung from his waist beside the richly-jewelled dagger. He was a stocky gross man, heavy and corpulent, and as he lolled and edged and twisted in his wide chair, it was as at the spur of an urgent fretting spirit never at ease or at comfort within the great ponderous body. Of fifty or so years, heavy-jowled, with a wispy beard, the ruddy Gordon complexion congested and empurpled by overmuch blood, he looked what he was—a man who had lived to the full and denied himself nothing . . . nor had anything denied him. When he had dined with English Elizabeth's sire, Harry Eighth, there was little to choose between them, men said. Dressed carelessly, next to slovenly in flame-coloured satin doublet, stained lace ruff, slashed trunks and bursting hose, all incongruous beneath the voluminous folds of a great tartan plaid, his flat cap of black velvet sat the back of his head, weighed down at one side by a magnificent jewel clasping a bunch of cocks' feathers. Huntly remained covered before all men.

No sound was heard save Patrick's firm footfalls, no voice was raised, no servitor moved, until the Gordon should speak.

"Well, well, Patrick—your own self and none other I see!" the wheezy wet voice commented. "Welcome to Huntly, boy. Your mother keeps her health, I'm hoping?"

An involuntary sigh of relief rose from the gathering. Men had died for much less than this young man's gesture. Huntly was going to be patriarchal, the father of his people—at least, for the moment.

"She does, Huntly—and sends you her greeting," Patrick declared. And having established his due position in the sight of men, as was essential, he relaxed. "Myself—I am yours to command, Huntly."

"Aye, aye that's as well, lad—just as well," his Chief nodded, a trifle grimly. "For I've a ploy for you, cut to your measure. Come you, and sit by me here." And he waved that curiously elegant hand, crucifix and all. "Room for our Patrick."

At his left, men hurriedly made space at the Earl's side for this latecomer to his table, lords and chieftains as they were.

Patrick, flattered but ably concealing it, took his seat on the bench that flanked the table. "I was on the hill, up at the shielings, when your message came," he explained. "I came as fast as I might."

"Then you'll be hungry, boy," Huntly asserted affably. "Eat

you . . . if my poor fare pleases you. Ho—victuals for Balruary. Take your fill, Patrick—for you ride within the hour. We'll talk as you eat . . . that is, with the permission of Cleavely and you other gentlemen?" And the fat man raised an innocent eyebrow that deceived nobody.

Hasty agreement coming from all around, Patrick looked up, with interest, particularly at an elegant gentleman in black slashed with gold, on Huntly's right, spade-bearded and handsome, his every particular of dress as precise as the Gordon's was careless and untidy. So that was Sir Nevil Cleavely, Elizabeth's unofficial envoy to the Court of Huntly! Despite his excellence of appearance, Patrick eyed him with only doubtful approval. He was not sure that he welcomed his Chief's truck with the English—no new thing as it was.

"You would have me ride, forthwith?" he queried.

"To Aberdeen. I would have you in the town, at the Provost's lodging, before midday the morn. You'll do it fine."

"But . . ."

"Na, na. No buts to Huntly! It's a bare fifty miles, boy, and the going good."

"The Provost is in a hurry, for sure . . . ?"

"Tush, man—d'ye think Huntly bothers his head about a poor through-other body of a Provost—or any other man, forbye? 'Tis the Queen's Grace you're to be at, and none other—Mary o' Scotland."

"Mary Queen," Patrick gasped. "Me? To bespeak the Queen? You jest, surely . . . !"

"Yourself, yes—you sprig o' Reformed heather! God's grace —I jest not! You'll bear a message from Huntly to Mary Stewart—or better, two messages. And they must reach her before she leaves Aberdeen the morn's noon. Eat, you."

"But . . . why myself as messenger?" the young man questioned, through a full mouth.

"Why? Mary Mother—because you, puppy, like your obstinate and heretical father before you, are one of the Elect, the misguided few of my name and race to subscribe to the new, damnable, and Reformed Faith—so miscalled! You swallow whole the vomits of Knox and Buchanan and their black unsavoury crew!" The little pig eyes swivelled over to his right. "With condolences and regrets to Cleavely here, who has the misfortune to be similarly affected!" And the bloated body shook and quivered with a sudden spasm of its own silent brand of mirth.

Sir Nevil fingered his neatly-trained beard. "You jest with a catholic wit, my Lord!" he said, with the twitch of a courtier's smile, but his clipped voice was as stiff as his elegant back.

The Gordon lords, noting their Chief's humour, hooted and roared their laughter over this adroit feint at the Englishman, and at the promptitude of his reply, hoping for more. But Huntly, tearing a leg of grouse from a great silver platter before him, waved it for peace. Once again, and speedily, the lute and the singer could be heard.

"Aye, Patrick—as a worthy Reformed Gordon lamb, ye shall repair to the pack of Reformed wolves that surround our young Catholic Queen. Two words ye shall bear. One, as the Protestant messenger of the Lord Chancellor and Lieutenant o' the North, to the Crown . . . and the Bastard James Stewart that holds it in his grasping fist! And the other, as an honest man and a Gordon, to Mary Stewart the woman! And that you are of the Hieland persuasion, has its points."

Somewhat bewildered, Patrick furrowed his dark brows. "This smacks of statecraft, as I see it—courtiers' work! I see round your table, Cousin George, men versed in the like. Rothiemay. Bishop William Gordon. The Lord Ross. Why my own self, to make your double-talk? Send you one of them. Send your own son George that her Grace is said to smile on."

"God's death—fill up your cup, man, and see if it will liven your wits! All of these were in Aberdeen with me four days back—and will be less than welcome there again! The town is as throng as a bees'-bike with the minions o' the Protestant lords, and no known Catholic's life is worth a groat! But you—you are your father's son. Hector MacRuary bought you *your* entrance, six years syne!"

There could be truth in that. Six years ago, Hector

MacRuary Gordon of Balruary had died a Protestant hero's death in Aberdeen—albeit an involuntary one. Slain at the kirk door of St. Machars as he emerged from a preaching, by a hereditary and inveterate foe, Forbes of Tillygorm, who happened to be a Catholic, his demise had been seized upon by Reformers in need of a martyr. The name of Gordon of Balruary resounded throughout such of the North as had yet seen the light. If back in the Glen Livet hills, the felicity of it all had seemed less obvious, that would be the foreshortened view. Catholic Huntly himself was now demonstrating the same.

"So I am the only Gordon who may enter Aberdeen—is that the way of it?" Patrick exclaimed. "It's an ill day when the Cock o' the North may not ride into his own town!"

"As you say, Patrick—an ill day. A day that many will rue, as God's my witness! But all that will change, it will change. The worship of God is a chancy business—eh, Cleavely?"

"No doubt you are right, my Lord." Elizabeth's emissary raised expressive eyebrows. "But perhaps, if the Cock of the North had not ridden into Aberdeen with fifteen hundred cockerels at his tail last Lord's Day, there would be less need for young Master Gordon's services today! I said, at the time . . ."

"Wheesht, wheesht! We recollect your advice, Cleavely— and have no doubt but you meant it fair. But if we had ridden in with less, 'tis like we'd never have ridden out again!"

Warrantably nettled at being styled 'young Master Gordon' like some Southron page, Patrick spoke up. "My services are at Huntly's disposal ever—but I'd serve the better knowing the circumstance. Here and now I know nothing of what you would be at, of your policy, of where the clan stands. I had not even heard that the Queen's Grace was yet at Aberdeen. . . ."

"By the Seven Spirits—you hear little in that heather glen of yours, Patrick! It could be that I envy you!" Huntly sighed, belched loudly, and reached for another dish. "Fill up then, boy—and listen. Mary Stewart left Edinburgh two weeks syne, to make her first progress o' the bonny North. 'Twas said

11

'twas to be for her pleasure only, but she came well escorted! Whatever she may have come for, the rest o' the world—except only you, Patrick—kens right well that the Lord James, whom God rot, brought her up to ding doun the power o' Gordon! She has promised her ill-begotten half-brother the earldom o' Moray, the feckless quean . . . which earldom Gordon holds and will hold! Mar, the Bastard has already; the revenues of St. Andrews he has in one pouch, and the poor lass o' Buchan's in the other. But Moray he must have—and the Queen's loyalest subject and friend must be broken to give him it!"

"For shame . . . !"

"Well may you say so, Patrick. So Mary Stewart came to Aberdeen a sennight syne, with all the stinking pack o' hungry jackals James Stewart has coiled round her, and thither her good cousin Gordon, her Lieutenant o' the North, rode to greet her, with the keys o' the North, and the love of leal hearts. . . ."

"And a tail of fifteen hundred leal broadswords!" old Gordon of Rothiemay chuckled from Patrick's left.

"When the Queen had expressly ordered that you bring no more than *one* hundred!" Sir Nevil Cleavely reminded, supping his wine.

"Ordered?" Huntly barked. "Who orders Gordon? A message sent . . . and the Lord James spelt that message, I warrant! And one hundred, or fifteen—I never was the man for the counting!" He turned back to Patrick. "But there was the open Gordon hand of friendship and duty, the true clasp of the North. And how was it received? It was rejected, spurned. The jade is not even to visit us here at Strathbogie, though she must pass within three miles of us on her way to Inverness. She will lodge with any bonnet-laird in a rickle o' stones—but not with Huntly, who showed her mother, the Guise woman, what liberality meant! I swear by the Living . . ."

The skirl of a man-handled serving-wench from near the foot of the table, followed by a loud guffaw, drowned the rest of his words. And in an instant Huntly was transformed. Unwieldy body notwithstanding, he twisted in his chair and was on to his feet. Rising swiftly but necessarily clumsily, he knocked against the kilted servitor who stood behind his chair holding a dish of steaming game. The platter was jerked up, and some portion of its contents splattered over the plaid and doublet of the Earl. A single word Huntly spat out, and reached to grasp the hapless man by the wrist, dragged the arm over the high back of his chair, twisted it, and with one explosive wrench bore his great weight down on it. The snap of the breaking arm could be heard by all. Almost in the same moment, the yelping gillie was hurled to the floor, and his Chief stabbed a trembling forefinger down the room.

"That trull to the Deveron—quick!" he snarled. "And the cuddy who brayed, fifty lashes!"

At the quivered indraw of breath that rose from the company the Gordon swayed a little on small feet. "Now! Away with them!" he cried, and catching up his handsome silver-crusted drinking horn, gulped the last mouthful from it, and with eruptive violence hurled it from him, crashing down the length of that richly-laden board in the faces of the diners, spattering viands and liquor right and left. "When Gordon speaks, he shall be heard!" he panted, glaring down the chaos of his table.

Stony-faced, wordless, men stared before them in a tense silence broken only by the drip of spilt wines, the scuffling from the floor where the injured gillie swooningly dragged himself away, and the stout man's stertorous breathing, as for fifteen, twenty long seconds he leant against the table, head thrust forward, small eyes darting. Then, slowly, he sank back into his chair.

"Well, Patrick—where were we?" he wheezed.

The younger man swallowed what he found remained in his mouth. "I think . . . your message for me to carry to the Queen, Huntly," he said stiffly. He did not look at the Earl. That had been ill done. It might be the style of a Sassenach lord, but not of a Highland Chief. The Chief was the father of his people, not the despot. Moreover, lashes were not for the gentle—and any man sitting at the Gordon's table would be gently born. It was not Huntly's authority Patrick

13

questioned—it was the seemliness of the thing. The Lowland rot was deep set, to be sure. . . .

Chancellor Huntly's eyes narrowed, but whatever expression played about his fleshy lips, he wiped it off on the flame-satin sleeve of his doublet. "Aye—the messages," he agreed. And smiled, chuckled even. "Hear you, then . . ." He paused, and looked around him, and behind. The great room stayed all but silent. Converse was slack in resuming, and such as talked spoke in whispers. "Mother of Heaven—now a man may not speak privily!" he complained. "Heard you ever the like!" Huntly raised his voice again. "Ho! Pipers! Play you. Give me my 'Cock o' the North'."

And as the bagpipes emitted their preliminary groanings and wailings, the Gordon pushed back his chair, and still back, signing to the young man to rise and come to him.

"For your ear alone, lad—'tis not the word to trumpet to the world. Firstly, ye shall speak the Queen thus—that is, the Bastard James. Say that Huntly advises against any move into the North unless under Gordon escort. Say that Huntly has the word that the Laigh o' Moray is gathering against the Lord James and his Protestants, in fear that he should gain the earldom. Brodie and Rose and Buchan and Innes and Duffus are all in arms. It will be death to ride through Moray without the Gordons. The hill passes they must take, the back road to Inverness—and only Huntly can convey the Queen through them. She must come to Strathbogie forthwith, or turn back to the South, for her safety's sake. You have that, Patrick?"

"I have it, yes. The Queen, if she would travel north to Inverness, must come to Strathbogie and put herself under your protection, for Moray is in arms against the Lord James. She must travel through the hill passes, and only Huntly can put her safely through them."

"Aye. That will serve. Add you that the Lieutenant o' the North kens his North! That is to the Queen in Council, see you—in fact, the Lord James Stewart, miscalled Earl of Mar! That is simple—bairn's play. Heed ye—this is the bit. This ye shall speak privily in Mary Stewart's pink ear. Her choice, from Huntly—is it to be Scotland, or the Bastard? Her half-brother, or her throne—she mayna have both! Wheesht, man—wheesht! I have it on good authority that the lassie can't abide the man —and small blame to her! But she's feart o' him, and his Protestant wolves. Ye'll wait on her answer, Patrick. If she's flat for her brother, then ye'll just repeat the bit about the Laigh o' Moray being risen against Lord James, and her running her white neck into a noose if she allows the man with her. But she'll no' say that, Patrick—'fore God she'll no'! She darena take that line with Huntly in his ain North! She'll speak ye either fair, or canny. She'll no' speak flat against me. Either way, her ear's yours, and she'll heed the rest you have to offer."

Patrick Gordon gulped. "You . . . you would have me threaten the Queen's Grace . . . ?"

"Tchach! Not you, puppy—you are but the lips. 'Tis Huntly that speaks—and speaks for the lassie's good. Never fear, Mary will listen. She is no fool. Now, here is the meat of it. Huntly can give her the North—and therefore all Scotland . . . at a price! She will bring the Bastard to Strathbogie—and he will trouble her no more! If he will not come, then she shall take the passes under Gordon escort direct . . . and the hill clans will see that he comes not out! That is firstly. Secondly, Moray and Mar shall be Huntly's. Thirdly, she shall take to husband my fine son John o' Findlater—the Pope shall straighten out the tangle he's in with the Ogilvy woman with the flick o' a pen! A good Catholic marriage, a strong man behind the throne, and auld Scotland on her Catholic feet again!"

Where Patrick had gulped before, he all but goggled now. "*Dhia!*" he whispered. "You'd fly that high?"

Huntly elected to presume that his concern was with the religious implications. "Och man, never fear for your Reformers. Let men worship as they will, say I—so long as Holy Church guides the ship o' state. The Protestants are safe enough . . . so long as they keep their protesting to the pulpit!"

"But, Sir John . . . ! A third son . . . with a wife of a sort on his hands! And outlawed!"

His Chief's brow darkened. Criticism he did not love, and criticism of John, favourite of all his nine sons, he never would suffer. "Patrick," he grated. "I brought ye here to take Huntly's message—not to give Huntly your advice! When I need counsel I can seek it from more wily heads than young Patrick's o' Balruary!" He sat up. "You have eaten your fill?"

The other nodded, tight-lipped.

"Then off with you. You have your words? If ye gain Mary's ear—three points. The Lord James to be brought to Strathbogie, the earldoms o' Mar and Moray to be mine, and a marriage with Sir John." The Earl drew a ring from his finger, and held it out. "Take this. Mary will ken it—it was hers once. Go now . . . and use you what wit the good Lord gave you. You are Gordon's mouthpiece—the saints help us! And, Patrick MacRuary—for your bonny mother's sake, come you not back to Huntly empty-handed!"

Patrick bowed stiffly to that ominous dismissal, turned on his brogue's heel, clapped on his bonnet, and strode for the distant door.

At the screen a man waited for him beside the Seneschal, signed him through the doorway, and followed him out—a tall young-ish man, good-looking in a sombre thoughtful way, dressed quietly in tartan trews, leather jerkin, and plaid. Here was another George Gordon—Huntly's second son, and heir since Alexander had died ten years before, but by no means the apple of his eye. The Lord Gordon and his father did not always follow the same line—and in consequence men frequently found it expedient to keep their distance. Men said that there was insufficient of the rooster about this progeny of the Cock o' the North—Sir John of Findlater was of a different feather, of a truth!

"A word with you, Patrick MacRuary, if I may," he said.

"To be sure, Seorus Og," Patrick acceded, giving him the Gaelic designation.

"In the courtyard," the other suggested, and led the way down the crowded stairs. Unlike his sire, the Lord Gordon was a man of few words.

Out of the smoke-laden air, in the cool of the great quad-rangle, less thronged now that eating was general, they paused. The young Chief topped Patrick by barely half an inch.

"My father sends you on an embassy of weight, I think, Patrick," he said, slowly. "I would not ask you to break trust with him, but I have some slight knowledge of his mind, and fear that his intention bodes but ill for the Queen's Grace, for Scotland, and so for Gordon in the end."

"That is not for me to decide, Seorus Og. Wilier heads than mine . . . ! I am but Huntly's messenger."

"I know it. The messenger must deliver his message . . . if he may! But he might carry a second message . . . ?"

That was a question, and Patrick answered it by another. "Such a message would not have to counter the first?"

"Counter—no. But it might offer a better choice, I think—better for all, including the first sender!" The other eyed Patrick directly. "To some extent I put myself in your hands, believing you to be an honest man," he said. "My message is this—that the Lord Gordon has not forgotten the oath he swore to his Queen eight months syne. He urges that she shall avoid Strathbogie, and make all haste up through the Laigh o' Moray to the safety of Inverness Castle, of which he is the Governor."

"And the Laigh o' Moray risen in arms . . . ?"

"The Laigh is not risen."

"But, Huntly said . . . ?" Patrick swallowed his words. "Yes?"

He shook his head. "I am sorry, Seorus Og—I cannot carry your message."

"My message thus *does* run counter to his, then?"

"I cannot say. My loyalty is to my Chief, as you know . . . and him likewise believing me an honest man!"

"An honest man need not necessarily be a fool! And there are other loyalties than to a Chief . . . or a father! There is loyalty to Queen, and to country. They could be greater!"

Unhappily Patrick shook his head again. "I am sorry. Send another messenger. . . ."

The Lord Gordon sighed and, turning about, left him standing there.

A frowning—and less innocent—Highland gentleman went in search of gillie and garron.

II

IT was a pair of somewhat bleary-eyed and drooping horsemen that approached the towers and spires and huddled
gables of Old Aberdeen from the south bank of Don, in the
dazzling forenoon sunlight. They had taken it in turns to doze
in their saddles during the last ten miles or so, and now it was
only owlishly that they blinked at the smoke-blackened grey
granite double town, between the arms of its two great rivers
and backed by the limitless blue-green plain of the northern
sea.

Within the scorntily repaired town walls, the Old Toun,
that had been the ecclesiastical metropolis of the North, lay in
large measure deserted, its cathedral half a ruin, its Gordon
bishop's palace, the houses of its dean and prelates, its priories,
friaries, hospices, and all its chapels, no more than fire-scarred
rickles of stone and mute pointing gables, its statues and
imagery defaced and cast down, fonts used as horse-troughs,
holy-water stoups as street urinals—the whole a monument in
itself to Reforming zeal. Patrick, who had seen it all before,
many a time, scowled only sleepily, but roused himself to doff
bonnet on passing the door of the same St. Machars where his
father had died six years before.

Once within the narrow hilly cobbled streets and wynds of
the New Toun, however, the owlishness soon went. The place
was as throng with folk as was the stronghold of Strathbogie—
most of whom turned no welcoming eye on two tall lads
in the green-and-red tartan of Gordon. From windows and
vennels and close-mouths and booths, the citizenry looked,
tightened their lips and were suddenly silent, whilst on the
crown of the causeways the strolling, strutting, swaggering
men-at-arms, who seemed to be legion and had taken over
the town, stared, laughed, and even pointed—and made no
effort to open a way for the horsemen. The place was as

18

packed with idle and graceless humanity as a choked drain—
and the only tartan to be seen in the seething sink of it was
gracing the two Gordons.

Patrick's frown was fierce—but he cherished his patience
and prudence with both hands, however white-knuckled,
turning his steed's head this way and that, down this dark vennel, along that narrow lane, seeking to avoid the closest press
but heading deviously for the town centre. But presently he
was held, with no more alleys and side-paths available, and
the Gallowgate before him thick with the sauntering, idling
throng. For the time of day, it was an unseemly sight. So
many drunken before noon was a new thing for Aberdeen.

"Way, there!" he cried loudly, at last. "Make way. Passage,
to the Provost's lodging!"

He might as well have shouted at the waves of the sea.
Three or four of the nearest promenading paladins, two with
women on their arms even at this hour, turned to stare and
jeer.

"Hielant cockerel!" one cried.

"See whae's here—bog-trotters!" another hooted. "Heather
atween their toes!"

"Papist whoremongers, Jeanie," a third assured the young
woman on his arm. "Every bare-shankit one o' them." And
he spat with Protesting fervour, if only indifferent accuracy.

Patrick Gordon's hand jerked towards his sword-hilt, and
only halted there under the greatest effort of self-restraint. As
well that the spittle had not touched him.

So far, no other hands had reached for weapons. The
Lowland soldiery was merely being natural, not deliberately
seeking a fight. Being inexpert on tartan, they probably did
not recognise these as Gordons—and though their street-
women could have enlightened them, very wisely they held
their tongues.

"Gently, man—gently," a couthie Aberdeen voice spoke at
Patrick's thigh. Black-browed, he glanced down, to find a
plump elderly burgess standing just within a pend-mouth at
his side. "You're no' feart, a Gordon, to go dinging through
the toun, this day!"

19

"Feart? When is a Gordon feart, in Aberdeen or other-where? Is this a town, or a packman's wedding!"

"High-handed packmen!" the townsman observed. "And free wi' their wares, man. These are the Elect, I'd warn ye, Gordon!"

"I care not if they be the cherubim and seraphim—I am Balruary, with urgent tidings for the Queen's Grace!"

"Balruary, is it?" There was a new note to the man's voice—and though he touched his cap respectfully enough, the note was not one of increased respect. This was a recalcitrant of the Old Faith, evidently. "You are namely—but that will no get you through these ones."

"Will it not?" Patrick faced the front again, and raised his voice. "Ho, there! Aside—in the Queen's name!" he cried. "Make way for the Queen's messenger!"

A hoot of mirth was the best that greeted his words. Sundry advice was tossed back at him, little of it constructive.

"Can she no' wait for you, long-shanks?" one called, grin-ning. "She'll be a' the hotter wearying on you!"

"You jalouse you've got what she wants, the red-headed bitch, under those tartans o' yours, Hielantman?" another questioned, and set the woman skirling appreciatively.

"I told ye—a Papist!" the pious one cried. "Naming the name o' the Papist Jezebel herself!"

Patrick stared, astounded. He turned to Black Ewan, and then to the townsman. "What is this?" he demanded. "These . . . are they not the Queen's men? And they speak thus, of her Grace . . . !"

"Queen's men?" The burgess shook his grizzled head. "Waesucks—the lassie has nae men! No' a loon. Ill for auld Scotland that she hasna. These are a' the paid men o' her lords, the Lords o' the Congregation—the Lord James, Morton, Lindsay, Ruthven, and Glencairn, and the lave. They heed their ain masters—and nae soul else under Heaven!"

"But . . . their masters support the Queen?"

"Aye," the other said, heavily. "Ooch aye. I'ph'mmm. So they tell me!"

Patrick Gordon's eyes were being opened indeed. So this

was what Huntly had meant! Looking over the swash-buckling throng anew, he now perceived that they all wore some distinguishing colour—the livery of one or other of the great nobles who surrounded the young Queen and pulled the Crown this way or that.

He changed his tune, as need dictated. "I bear tidings for the Lord James!" he shouted. "Make way, in the name of my Lord of Mar! Passage to the Lord James."

It may be that the bulk of the retainers nearest to him were in other than the new Earl of Mar's employ—Ruthven's or Lindsay's, belike. At any rate, they displayed no access of respect nor concern. Worse, some in evident boredom even turned their backs on him—on Patrick MacRuary Gordon of Balruary!

The spate of furious words that surged to his lips was dammed back by a diversion rather than by any iron self-control. Out of a twisting narrow wynd that came down to join the Gallowgate almost opposite, issued a growing hullabaloo. Above the general din, this noise was different, deliberate, with purpose behind it. Something between a chant and a challenge, it swelled with monotonous but effective rhythm.

"A Douglas! A Douglas!" it sounded. "A Douglas! A Douglas!" And out from the wynd emerged eight or ten liveried and armoured horsemen, wielding pike-staves right and left. "A Douglas! A Douglas!" they repeated endlessly, to the entirely indiscriminate and impersonal swing of their poles. And before them, men, however assured, gave ground and pressed back hurriedly.

After the smiters rode a trio of gentlemen in rich half-armour, drawn swords across their saddle-bows. And behind these, and by himself, a squat figure on a heavy powerful charger, a man coarsely built, almost hulking, clad grotesquely in the puffed-out padded doublet, black velvet ribbed and quilted in gold, with the enormous built-up shoulders and billowing trunks of the day's most exaggerated mode, all adding to the toadlike impression of crouching squatness. With practically no neck to him anyway, the tall stand-up collar of his doublet and the starched folds of his ruff squeezing out therefrom, forced a bushy red beard outwards and upwards ridiculously. Together with the untidy thatch of rufous hair that projected from under an elegant high-crowned and plumed hat, it formed a fiery halo to a pugnacious ruddy face, round-eyed and bulbous-nosed. A noteworthy figure indeed by any standards, as many men—and women—knew to their cost.

"My Lord Earl of Morton," the burgess informed, sounded as though he might be going to spit, and then thought better of it. "On his road to the Council."

"Morton! So that is the Douglas! A red stirk, if ever I saw one."

"Hush you, man. . . ."

"Bah! If a Douglas stirk can bellow in the streets of Aberdeen, no man shall hush a Gordon! Yonder is the way to get through this rabble."

And with its notable screak, his broadsword was once more out of its scabbard. High above his head Patrick raised it, and then, digging his heels into his bay's flanks, brought the brand down in a great sweep forward and right up again, and forward and left. "Back, dogs!" he roared. "Out of a Gordon's path! A Gordon! A Gordon!"

There was a scatter of promenaders, a cursing and a woman's squealing. But no swords leapt out to bar his way— nor the persons of men, either. Into a round canter Balruary kicked his beast, its hooves striking sparks from the cobblestones At his heels Black Ewan swung his axe in an enthusiastic figure-of-eight. "A Gordon!" he echoed. "A Gordon!"

And before them a way opened, as to the prow of a tall ship. They had discovered the secret of traffic negotiation in Mary's Scotland.

Down in the wake of the Red Douglas they thundered, and at a better pace than he. Presently indeed, the rearmost file of my Lord's escort turned in their saddles to stare backwards. They might have felt called upon to do more than stare, had not just then their cavalcade turned in at a side-street, the Kirkgate, to make for the handsome former residence of the

Episcopal Chancellor, now the appropriate lodging of the Lord James Stewart. Patrick, heading for the Provost's house in Broadgate, clattered straight on. Morton and part of his train paused at his in-turning to view this tiny procession in some astonishment. The Gordons did not so much as spare him a glance—being much too intent on clearing their own path. Arms flailing, and shouting their name before them, they thundered on, out of the constriction of the Gallowgate into its continuation, the nominally wider Broadgate.

There, before an alarmed group of men-at-arms, horse-holders, lightly-armed officers and lairdlings outside the Provost's fine dwelling—that had so recently been the fine dwelling of Bishop William Gordon's favourite mistress, Janet Knowles, and her brood—he pulled up, saluted with his sword, Highland fashion, and sheathed it with deliberate ritual. From a dozen windows faces watched his spectacular arrival inter-estedly. Since not a few of the watchers were ladies, he doffed his bonnet gallantly.

"An envoy from Huntly, Cock o' the North, to the Queen's Grace!" he mentioned, swinging a long tartan leg over his saddle, leaping down, and throwing the reins to Black Ewan. Glancing neither to left nor right, he strode for the open doorway that was surmounted by the defaced stone arms of the bishopric impaled with Gordon—and no man sought to stop him.

The royal presence was not nearly so effectively guarded as had been that of Huntly—or of any of the Queen's lords, for that matter. Presently, without having to overplay his fine confidence, authority, and Highland pride, Patrick achieved the first floor, and was shown into a sumptuous apartment, part bedchamber, part study, where a tall thin dyspeptic-seeming man, dressed all in fastidious grey beneath a furred bed-robe, was in the act of rising from a great desk littered with papers. Glancing up, he showed a sallow smooth face, scholarly, fine-featured, high-domed, but with something strange about the mouth.

"Patrick Gordon of Balruary, with a message from the

Lieutenant of the North to the Queen's Grace and Council," the younger man introduced himself, forestalling any failure of emphasis on the part of the somewhat apathetic usher.

"Indeed! So that cock still crows!" the thin man commented. He held out his long slender hand palm open. "Very well—give me it, Master Gordon. You are just in time—I attend the Council forthwith. I am Secretary Lethington."

Patrick raised his heavy but so mobile brows. Secretary of the Realm, arch-plotter, confidant of princes, though he might be, William Maitland of Lethington should have known better than to name a Highland laird *Master* Gordon. "Huntly's message lies behind my tongue, not on a paper . . . Master Maitland!" he said tartly.

The other gazed at him—or, more accurately, at his un-doffed bonnet—entirely without expression for a moment, fingering his silky pointed beard. Then he lifted one shoulder in a frenchified shrug. "I might have known that Huntly was too wily a fox to commit anything to paper," he said, with a thin smile. "A messenger can always be silenced . . . or denied. The written word is a less, ah, tractable commodity!" And he chuckled at his own pun.

"Sir—you speak about my Chief, I'd remind you!" Patrick jerked.

"I speak about my old friend and collaborator, George Gordon," Mr. Secretary amended smoothly. "His message, sir?"

"It is for the ears of the Council—in especial, for the Lord James." Patrick was not going to trust this renowned schemer.

"I shall carry it to the Council."

"No. It is for the Lord James, his ear. So said Huntly."

Lethington frowned. "Young man, you are either uncommon insolent—or very foolish! My Lord James of Mar is in Council. You do not conceive that I can introduce you to the Council, do you? You give me Huntly's message—or it goes undelivered." He stalked over to a garde-robe, taking off his dressing-gown, to select and don a cloak of grey lined with silver. "I have no time to waste, sir—the Council awaits me, its Secretary."

"Then my instructions are to speak with the Queen's Grace," Patrick asserted steadily.

"And how will that serve you?" the other commented, almost casually, and turned on his heel, the cloak swinging, to open the door.

The younger man's brows rose. "I am to speak with the Queen," he repeated, stiffly.

The Secretary shrugged. "Michael," he called, raising his voice. "Take Master . . . h'm . . . escort Bal . . . Balrory, is it? . . . to her Grace."

Patrick stared after the departing man's elegant back, non-plussed. Nothing was as he had anticipated it. Apparently it was no problem to speak with the Queen of Scotland—but to gain the ear of her bastard half-brother, King Jamie's Mischance, was a different matter. . . .

Suddenly, from the end of the corridor, Lethington turned, to call back to Patrick's usher, a modish but depressed-seeming young man. "Michael—I have left the Darnaway papers with Balfour. My Lord will be wanting them. Get them from Sir James, and bring them after me to my Lord's lodging. With haste."

The esquire made respectful acknowledgement, and turned frowning to his charge. "This way," he said impatiently, and went off long-strided. Down a small winding turret stairway he led, and at the foot threw open a door beside which a halberdier stood yawning. "The Queen is in the garden, I think, with her ladies," he said, without even pausing in his walking. "You will excuse me, sir—I have important business to attend to."

The implication was very obvious. And he hurried off, leaving a Highland gentleman at something of a loss, to look from the sunny green of grass to the stolid halberdier, doubt-fully. The latter, picking his teeth, could hardly have been less concerned.

Patrick took off his sword and handed it to the guard, adjusted his bonnet to the required angle, took a deep breath—and marched through the doorway.

A Gordon heart for once quaked behind a typically dashing Gordon exterior.

The sight that met the poor man's eyes was not calculated to embolden him. Indeed, his marching faltered almost to a halt within three or four steps. It was, perhaps, the contrast to all that had gone before, the abrupt change of scene, of atmosphere and tempo, that took the wind from his sails. Here was a fair garden, bathed in the golden autumn sunlight, of lawns and flowers and fruit-trees and sanded walks, where a fountain played and not over-modest statuary postured. Bees hummed in the sun, carved peacocks spread their tails, and satyrs laughed at sirens and sundials both. Bishop Gordon had been a man of some taste and imagination. And like gorgeous butterflies in this sylvan sanctuary three young women flitted and darted and glowed. Laughing, singing, and running with wide skirts hitched high, they played with a coloured ball, while on the rim of the fountain's bowl sat a dark-eyed deformed half-man who twanged sweet melody from a lute. And a little way apart, on a carved stone bench, a fourth young woman sat, sewing at some needlework, and ever and anon lifting her eyes to laugh with, or at, the others—and this young woman had red hair.

Patrick Gordon, either unobserved as yet or ignored, swallowed, cleared his throat, and waited. It must be admitted that he was less well prepared to deal with this sort of situation than with the generality of contingencies with which he was apt to be confronted. Glen Livet and the Gordon country had taught him much, and his native wit, and good masculine instincts, had improved thereon. But Queen and Court ladies, especially skittish ones and very obviously shamelessly frenchified at that, tended to be outwith his comfortable range. Not that he was afraid of these laughing women—good grief, no!

As witness. Squaring manly shoulders, and hitching his plaid a little higher thereon, he strode out across the grass, directing his firm steps towards that seated needlewoman.

It seemed a long way, undeniably. The singing stopped, the leaping and the laughter died away—as well it might, beholding that black frown, that martial tread, and all the flaunting tartan—and if the lute-music still maintained, it seemed to have developed into a mere mocking twanging, to keep pace with his pacing, like tuck of drum. Patrick knew an intense if sudden hatred for that musician. He felt no flood of goodwill and warmth towards the staring smirking girls, either—he was sure that they were both staring and smirking, though he did not let his eyes glance once in their direction. Steadfastly he kept his regard fixed—not on the eyes and face, since that might have been presumptuous and unseemly—but a little lower, on the throat and neck of the red-headed young woman. And an admirable resting-place for any man's regard was that milk-white column and deliciously swelling bosom, cleft sweetly—even if less frankly exposed than those of her romping companions, who perhaps needed their exercise to keep warm in fashions designed for light Orleans rather than sober Aberdeen.

The young woman at the stitching plied her needle with unhurried application. Perhaps the fixity of the approaching man's gaze affected her just a little, for she turned a degree or two sideways on her seat—which profiling incidentally did no injustice to the area under regard, either.

Striding to exactly two yards from her, the man halted, swept off his bonnet, and dropped on one bent knee. As he did so the lutist plucked a single loud, long, and echoing string, and was silent.

"Madam," Patrick said, with rather more force than he had intended—that was the fault of the insolent ape with the lute. "I am Patrick Gordon of Balruary, your loyal, devoted, and humble servant."

For a brief moment there was silence. Patrick raised his glance higher. The young face that looked down at him, slightly flushed, was very beautiful. He knew that she was beautiful, of course—all the world knew that. The perfect oval of her face, framed in abundant vivid copper-coloured tresses, only just disciplined by a coif, was of a creamy whiteness, daintily and delicately freckled. Her eyes were large and deeply blue, her nose short and just slightly tip-tilted, her mouth red and generous and mobile. In her gown of royal blue, lace-collared, tight-bodiced, and swelling to wide skirts, slashed to

27

reveal the sprigged white satin of her kirtle, she looked every rounded inch a queen amongst women and a woman amongst queens.

But her voice was just a little breathless when she spoke. "I . . . I thank you, sir. But . . . you are too kind, too humble altogether, I fear. Rise, I pray you. I am sure I do not merit this, this . . ."

A trill of laughter, hastily quelled, came from the side, and four liquid notes were picked out on the lute-strings in dramatic comment. Then there was the rustle and flurry of skirts, and one of the other young women came running, to sweep low in deepest curtsy.

"Your Grace," she cooed, "the Hielands are prostrate at our feet, at last! Give them your gracious hand, Ma'am."

"Yes, yes. Your hand, Madam."

"Raise him up, your Grace. Embrace your wild Hielands!"

There was a tinkling chorus and a clapping of hands from the other two ladies.

Patrick stayed on his knee. It was the first time that he had ever suffered under the accusation of being too humble. But it might not be difficult to he humble before this woman and her loveliness. "You merit all that is within a man's power to offer, my Queen," he assured, and meant it.

"Bravo! Here we have a gallant indeed," the curtsying female cried. "A true courtier—and such are plaguey scarce north o' Tay, I vow! Your Grace must reward him!"

"I shall at least spare him your nonsense, Mary Livingstone! Sir, you will forgive . . ." The speaker's lilting voice tailed away, and slowly she rose to her feet, her glance far above his head.

Patrick turned his eyes also. The other young women were standing still now, facing away from him. The musician also was on his feet, a meagre creature. Inevitably the kneeling man looked round, right round.

Another young woman had come out from the house into the garden. Dressed all in white, she stood watching them, tall and slender—and she also had reddish hair.

As the newcomer started to move towards them, Patrick

clambered to his feet, a hot flame of anger burning within him—and on his cheeks. And as he came up, the girl beside him went down, like her colleagues, in a deep obeisance. But a hand was on the tartan arm of his doublet, the same that had split from wrist to shoulder . . . at his sword-swinging in the Gallowgate. She clutched tightly.

"Oh, I'm sorry. I'm sorry!" she whispered.

Patrick Gordon whipped his arm away, and swinging on his heel, stalked, blazing-eyed, to meet Mary of Scotland.

III

IT was a pity that the man saw little before him save the red mist of wrath and humiliation, for this lady too was lovely, lovely beyond all telling. Moreover, she was smiling, and hers was a smile that could totter both poets and thrones—her own included.

"Sir, sir," she called, over the greensward, and her voice was clear and strong. "Pray do not let me interrupt so touching a scene! Return to your lady. I vow 'twas the knightliest sight I've seen since leaving Edinburgh!"

"Not so, Madam." Patrick halted, jerked a very incipient bow, and came on. "It was a jest, only—and a poor one." And he eyed her, and all the world, bleakly.

"A jest? To kneel to your sovereign lady? Ah—shame, sir. Were I your Queen, I should demand deeper lealty than that! Is this our Mary's brave and gallant North? I thought, at last, I was seeing an ensample of it."

Patrick shook a brief but decided head. "Not so, Ma'am. I mean . . . your pardon, but what you saw was folly, a mistake. I mistook the—the colour of your hair!" That came out in a rush.

"Alack! My poor carroty hair again! I'll have it dyed, I vow! Then, at least, it would be less confusing . . . to her Grace, there." And she nodded, dimpling, towards the other red-head. "Would that not be wise, Majesty?" She swept a graceful genuflexion.

The man so far forgot himself as to frown, and a brogued toe tapped the turf, in what in other circumstances might have looked like impatience. He personally had had enough of this jesting and women's nonsense. If the Queen was in a mood for trifling and banter, deliberately continuing this unfortunate error—which had gone on too long by far, already —then she had better find another butt for her humour than

30

a Gordon! There was a plenitude of Court popinjays, no doubt.

"Your Grace," he said stiffly. "I seek the Queen's audience for an urgent matter of state—not for a play-acting!" Even in his present state of mind, he was mildly pleased with that.

For there was no doubt at all that this was the Queen. Without corresponding in any major respect to the general interpretation of the adjective queenly, there never was a woman who was more obviously and indefinably a queen. Young, boyish, and impulsive, she was admittedly—yet as assured, and proud, and very feminine, with all the experience of the ages to her. Soft, gentle, pliant—and yet somehow indomitable, somewhere even steely. Here was a woman that was contrast personified, true daughter of a hundred kings, in whose eyes every man thought that he saw the age-old plea to be mastered.

Looking into those eyes now, hazel flecked with green, Patrick swallowed, for all his summoned hardihood. He would not be able to look into them often, or for long, and retain his fine integrity, he perceived, in an unusual flash of insight. This woman was dangerous, he knew, dangerous to all men, and especially to men who could love danger—and the more so for being adorable, as few women born of men have been adorable. Here was no siren, no high-born courtesan, no Messalina who bartered body for soul, but the distilled essence of womanhood itself, exquisite, compassionate, magnetic yet unattainable, formed out of infinite beauty, infinite promise, and infinite tragedy. Such were Helen, and Dierdre, and Cleopatra, and Mary Stewart.

She was too much for poor Patrick Gordon. He had to lift his eyes quickly—or be lost. Nor did he have to lift them far, for she was tall, taller than the general run of women, but lissom and delicately made. He did not know it, as his eyes levelled, but he sighed.

Mary the Queen sighed also, frankly. At his lifted gaze? Perhaps. At the rejection of gaiety for the pompous claims of state? May be. Her eager bubbling spirit, rebuffed from without as often as from within, was apt to sigh.

31

"Indeed, sir? I am sorry to hear it." And she sounded as though she was. "This is a solemn land—and, heigh-ho, the state will be served . . . even in Aberdeen! Come." And crooking a slim finger, she swept over towards the bench which the man had so recently left. She was all a queen again as she did it, in her widow's gown of pure ivory velvet, her pearl-stitched coif, and high starched saffron ruff. She was nineteen years of age—and ageless.

At her slender gracefully-moving back, Patrick had never felt so wooden, so boorish—nor yet so anxious to be considered otherwise.

The young woman with the needlework would have slipped away at their approach, to join the others, but the Queen stopped her.

"Mackintosh, *ma chérie*—certainly it is for you to present this gentleman to us!" she declared. "We must have him presented, you know."

Flushing, the other girl paused, biting her red lip. "I am deeply sorry, Madam. I apologise—to your Grace . . . and to the gentleman. . . ."

"Your Grace—if fault there was, it was mine," one of the other young women called. "Mackintosh would have . . ."

"Hush, Livingstone! You will say your say later, I have no doubt—you always do!" the Queen chided. "But not now. Mackintosh, do not tell me that you were deputising for us with such devotion—without so much as discovering the gentleman's name and style? Is that all you have learned in two months, girl?"

"I . . . I . . . he did say, I think, your Grace. But I'm afraid . . ."

The man cut in on her pretty distress, with less sympathy than impatience, perhaps. "I am Patrick MacRuary Gordon of Balruary, with important words for your Grace's ear from Huntly my Chief," he announced.

"Ah—Gordon! I might have guessed as much," Mary observed, and promptly was the experienced woman of affairs, so that, though the others probably all were slightly older than she was, they looked the merest girls by contrast. "Well, sir," she said, seating herself. "And what has my Lord of Huntly to say to his Queen?"

Patrick glanced around him. "Madam—Huntly's words are for your Grace's ears alone!"

"So! And you fear that these chuckleheads might endanger it! You do them too much honour!" But the Queen flicked her beringed hand, smiling, and the young women withdrew a space, into what looked like very relieved whispering. "Davie—give us some music, the better to swallow this sober dose! And you, long lad—you had better sit by us, here . . . lest Huntly's weighty words miss our poor ears altogether and echo out into Aberdeen!" And she patted the stone bench at her side, drawing in a fold or two of white velvet.

The man hesitated. He did not know that he could trust himself so close to her as all that. Then her hand patted again, and peremptorily—and queens were to be obeyed, surely. He sat down.

From under one delicate upraised brow she eyed him. "Say on, Man of Gordon—and may you talk as dashingly as you ride through the streets of my town of Aberdeen!"

Patrick gulped. "You . . . saw?"

"There is nothing wrong with my eyes, sir!" And with the ghost of a smile, she let her glance rove over his lengthy person, near as he was, from black head to leather brogue. "I find the tartan . . . *très agréable*!" she said. "And now for my Lord Huntly?"

Patrick kept his face rigidly to the front. "Your Lieutenant of the North, and loyalest subject, sends two messages from Strathbogie, Madam—and they are different. One is for your own ear only. The other is for the Queen and her Council . . . but, mainly for the Lord James Stewart."

There was a distinct silence and then the Queen inclined her lovely head. "I understand you . . . even if you are less than flattering, sir. Pray proceed."

"I had expected to deliver the other, before this to you, Madam. It would be best, I think, to give you the meat of it, first . . . so that you may better understand the import of the second?" And at her nod: "Here is the message that is directed at the Lord James of Mar. Huntly, Lieutenant of the North, advises the Queen's train against any move northwards of Aberdeen, save under Gordon escort. He says . . ." Patrick paused only for a moment. "He says that the Laigh o' Moray, the lowlands of Garioch and Formartime and Buchan, is gathering against Lord James, who is rumoured to be seeking the earldom of Moray. Brodie and Innes and Rose and Duffus and the rest are in arms. If your Grace's train would travel to Inverness, as he has heard is your intention, you must go by the hill passes. And through them only Huntly can convey you safely. His advice is, to your Grace, and to the Lord James—come to Strathbogie forthwith, or turn back to the South."

His hearer drew a long quivering breath, but her voice was steady when she spoke. "Is that a threat, Gordon?"

"Not so, Madam. It is the advice of our Lieutenant and Chancellor—sent in deepest loyalty to your throne and person. Huntly considers himself your loyalest subject."

"You tell me so!" For a time she scanned his well-schooled profile, considering. And as he waited, the man already felt the first skirmishes of the battle of loyalties stirring within him. So soon. "My Lord of Mar will not thank you for that message, I think."

He looked at her, then. She had not voiced her own reactions. The impetuous vital girl was submerged in the calculating and politic monarch. She did not commit herself. Perhaps Huntly had been right, again—she might listen to his second message. Or some of it . . .

"Of that I know nothing," he assured her. "All I know is that there is a different word for your Grace's own ear—to Mary Stewart from her true Gordon, this one, as Huntly said it. Will you hear it, Madam?" Patrick suddenly remembered the ring, and reached into his doublet pocket. "My Chief sent this, in token," he said.

The Queen took it, and sighed as she held it in the cup of her hand. "*La belle France* . . ." she murmured. "I mind the day . . . Yes—Huntly served my mother passing well, and perhaps me also. I will hear his word."

Patrick cleared his throat. This thing was not going to be easy to say. "He words it with the greatest goodwill to yourself. He says, Madam, that you must choose. Between Scotland, and the Lord James. Between your throne and your half-brother. He says that your Grace cannot have both!"

"God's mercy—he says that, does he?" Almost she rose to her feet, her fists tight-clenched. "Huntly dares to speak thus! To me!"

"Out of his love for you, I am assured. He believes that the Lord James will have your throne from under you, illegitimate or no, one way or another." Hurriedly Patrick pressed on with what remained to be said, very conscious of the buffets that he was raining on this fragile girl that was his sovereign lady. Conscious too of the abyss between the two worlds, of which he was the unhappy bridge—the world of the mailed fist, of harsh fighting-men and proud chiefs and lords, and this gentle world of laughter and music, fair women and sylvan gardens. The contrast was too great, too sharp. The proposals that had seemed practical enough, however crude, in Huntly's martial hall, here seemed utterly inconceivable and offensive. So it was that he all but gabbled them.

"Huntly says, trust him. Trust Gordon. He can give you the North—and that means all Scotland. You can then restore the Old Faith. Three things he would have you do, the better to aid him. Bring the Lord James to Strathbogie—and if he will not come, take the hill passes with your train, to Inverness, under Gordon escort. Bestow on Huntly the earldoms of Mar and Moray. And . . . and bestow on his son, Sir John Gordon of Findlater, your royal hand in marriage. . . ."

"What! *Sacré Nom de Dieu!*" The Queen was up off the bench now, her eyes blazing. "Marriage, you said! Marry John o' Gordon! Me! Mary of Scotland! Are you bereft of your senses, man? Crazy-mad?"

The man rose to his feet, necessarily. "Your Grace's pardon—I can but give you the message. And Sir John of Findlater is a fine well-set-up young . . ."

"I would as soon wed the Devil, sir! I am Queen of this Realm, I am Dowager of France, and I am heir to England—

and Huntly would marry me off like one of his lairdlings' daughters!"

"I would remind your Grace that Huntly's mother was a king's daughter, though natural—your own aunt, Margaret Stewart. Sir John is your cousin, in some degree. . . ."

"John Gordon is a scoundrel, a felon, and an outlaw!" The Queen stamped a slender foot on the turf. "It is only six days since his own mother was here, praying me on her knees—yes, on her bended knees—to pardon her son, and release him from ward. And now, his father would have me take him to my bed!"

"You are passing hard, Madam, on a young man's cantrip, on a high-spirited tuilzie in the streets of Edinburgh. . . ."

"Cantrip!" she exclaimed. "Can it be that you know not what John Gordon has done? He has taken violent possession of the Laird of Ogilvy's castles of Findlater and Auchindoun, which were the rightful houses of my good servant James Ogilvy of Cardell, Steward of my Household. He has taken Ogilvy's own stepmother to himself, has 'married' her by some travesty of a union. And scarcely was I back in Scotland from France, than he and some of his Gordons created a brawl in the High Street of my Capital, seeking to kill the man he had so wronged, and seriously wounding my Lord Ogilvy of Airlie. When I had him warded in Edinburgh's Tolbooth, with the other rioters, he broke out therefrom, and ran loose here in the North. An outlaw, didn't he come hither to greet me here in Aberdeen, cocking his bonnet! My Lord James put him in ward again, and I gave it as my royal command that he should take to my castle of Stirling and be warded there, to await his due trial. But yestreen only, he has broken prison again, and his word likewise, and is fled into his Gordon hills behind a trail of blood." Like a flood, this recital had poured forth. "And this is the man whom my Lord of Huntly would have me take as my consort!"

Patrick swallowed, and ran a hand through rumpled hair. "It . . . sounds an ill tale, your Grace, truly," he admitted. "But there is that to be said on the other side, to be sure. The old Laird of Ogilvy disinherited his son James many years ago, and for good reason, naming John Gordon his heir to Findlater and Auchindoun. And James of Cardell had deserted his step-mother—who was a Gordon, see you! Moreover, Huntly says that the Pope will straighten out this marriage tangle with a flick of the pen. . . ."

"Mother of Heaven—am I then, who have the crowned heads of Christendom seeking my pillow, to be beholden to the Pope to make this sorry adulterer meet for my bed?"

"I cannot conceive that your Grace has the rights of it, entirely. . . ."

"What, sir! Would you argue with me—your Queen?" Mary Stewart drew herself up, a fine gallant figure of a lovely, proud and angry woman, her young bosom heaving right royally, her auburn head high, her delicate alabaster skin flushed with the throbbing of that blood which the poets swore could be discerned pulsing through her veins.

Before her, the young man bowed his head abashed, as much by the vehement force of her womanhood as by her imperious wrath. In his hands he turned his fine feathered bonnet in circles. At that moment he knew no satisfaction in himself—nor, for once, in the name of Gordon.

And then, suddenly, the storm was over. With a long tremulous sigh, Mary relaxed, and became her own prettily-assured self again. "*Ma foi*—what folly is this!" she declared, and found a Gallic shrug. "To upset oneself over an old man's havers. Your pardon, Man of Gordon, for an unseemly tantrum!" And she smiled on him.

And in that moment, he was lost. Deliberately she put her spell on him, and he was vanquished—as tougher men than he had been vanquished ere this, and would be to the end. Mumbling, stumbling with his words, he shook his head. "No . . . Ma'am . . . ! I beg of you . . . not so. My own self, it is, that asks forgiveness. . . ."

"Hush, sir. You are but the messenger. Yourself, you would offer me no hurt, I can see." A hand was even laid on his arm, his bare arm where his doublet sleeve was ripped. "Your name, sir? I regret I did not catch the first of it. How are you called—other than Gordon?"

"Patrick, Ma'am. Patrick MacRuary Gordon, of Balruary . . . and your Grace's very devoted and humble servant!"

"Good! Splendid!" She clapped her hands, in a gesture girlish as it was delightful—and calculatedly lethal. "I have one true Gordon now, at least! Or . . . must I share you with Mary Mackintosh, there?" and she turned, to skilfully end his private audience.

"Your Grace has more than one Gordon, I do assure you— but none truer, as all Heaven is my witness!"

"Bravo! But . . . was that what you said to yon Mackintosh?" she asked, laughing, and beckoned her watchful ladies forward.

They came tripping, a suddenly chattering bird-like throng— but with the red-headed Mary Mackintosh noticeably silent and to the rear. The Queen threw out her long arm. "Here they are—my chuckleheads! Beaton, Seton, and Livingstone— and, of course, our Highland Mary, my rival for your homage!"

"Not so, Ma'am. I mean . . . h'm . . . that was but a mistake."

"Oh—fie, sir! Ungallant! Mackintosh is hurt to the heart. Look at her!"

Covered with blushes, the lovely creature to whom Patrick had so foolishly knelt, looked down. She was different from the others, very obviously—quieter, less bold-eyed, bold-mannered, as well as bold-breasted, than these confident Lowland French-reared misses, though more satisfyingly rounded in her figure than any of them. Her confusion was so patent, her helplessness a challenge, and because she was apparently of his own Highlands, the man knew a sudden feeling of sympathy for her—moreover, undoubtedly she was beautiful with a warm glowing beauty that even the Queen could not rival.

"Had your Grace not arrived, this other lady would have held me on the crook of her finger, I have no doubt!" he declared—and as surprised to hear himself say it. Surprised too at the quick gleam of gratitude that came to him out of those deeply-blue eyes.

38

"Ha! So the man is but a weathercock, after all!" Mary Stewart cried. "I feared as much. When my back is turned, the Mackintosh will have him! Ah me—is there no constant amongst men?"

"None, Ma'am," the hoydenish Mary Livingstone assured. "They are all hunters only. The quarry is immaterial, the chase is all!"

"Even John Sempill?" the Queen asked, and there was laughter.

"There is *one* Gordon that would be constant, I think, Ma'am," the cool Mary Beaton put in tartly, to the aid of her friend Livingstone. "The Lord George burns his slow fires for you only!"

The Queen's face clouded, not at the open secret that the Lord Gordon was hopelessly enamoured of her, surely— for she was no woman to bewail her conquests—but at the reminder of his father's terms. "The Lord Gordon has a masterful sire . . . and a Hamilton wife!" she said shortly and turned away from her Maries. "See you to *this* Gordon's needs," she threw back to them. "I shall speak with him again, anon. Davie—inform Sir James Melville that I will see him now."

As the minstrel rose to do her bidding, the Queen paced away slowly to the other side of that sunny garden. Watching her, Patrick decided that despite all her ladies and her adorers and her courtiers, Mary Stewart was a very lonely young woman.

Waited on with mock attentiveness by three of the ladies, and with more sincerity by the fourth, the man sipped burgundy, disposed of two platters of biscuits, pined for more substantial fare, and held his own as best he could in the cut and thrust of distinctly edged word-play, broad as it was barbed—mainly on a theme to do with the potency or otherwise of the Cock o' the North. This was a new kind of pastime for that young man, and one at which he did not flatter himself that he shone so brightly as, for instance, he might at the not so dissimilar clash of sword-play. It was not the way that young women behaved in Glen Livet. Still, he parried where he was able, and even thrust on occasion, so that the Gordon cause went not entirely by default—and Mistress Mackintosh's freckles were submerged in a crimson flood throughout.

Presently David Rizzio, the Savoyard lute-player, brought Sir James Melville, a spare and dignified elderly man, who conferred with the Queen soberly and at length. Then two other gentlemen appeared, yawning as though this was the first of them that day, elegants these, outrageously over-dressed above and under-dressed below, who sauntered over to stare with arrogant wonderment at the tartan-clad stranger. With their candid scrutiny becoming quite inadmissible and un-bearable, Patrick was turning on them hotly, when once again a hand was laid on his arm.

"Your sleeve, sir," Mary Mackintosh said hastily. "It is shamefully torn. Sit down, and I shall stitch it."

He shook his head—and perhaps his arm, too—though his eyes never left those of the foppish newcomers. "No need," he said brusquely.

"Yes. I insist." She sounded breathless, but strangely deter-mined, and even pulled at him with considerable force. "I have my needle and threads here." And as he came reluctantly, frowning, she whispered: "Ssssh! Those are the Queen's French uncles—M. d'Elboeuf and the Grand Prior!"

"Eh? Oh . . . ummm. But . . . they are mannerless clowns, nevertheless!" he asserted, without any great moderation of voice.

"Hush! 'Tis only their foreign ways. Come you, and sit here, beside my needlework. I have a thread that will serve."

And so, perforce, Patrick had to sit on the stone bench again, one arm in the young woman's lap—since this was nowise the place to remove his doublet altogether, whatever advice the other ladies hurled at him—while the slow business of stitching the eighteen-inch rent proceeded, and the two Guise brothers attached themselves to the other Maries and drifted off chattering volubly in French and laughing, with sundry backward glances and nods.

In other circumstances, of course, the young man might

not have found fault with his immediate situation—such close proximity to a very personable female that his arm rose and fell to the strong tide of her breathing, that her rounded arm, making its own halo of tiny golden hairs in the sun, worked within an inch or two of a nose by no means unaware of the faint but heady scent of her abundant tresses—such situation was not normally to be sneezed at by an honest male this side of senility, whatever the effect of wandersome strands about twitching nostrils. But Patrick felt himself to be too patently thrust into this young person's arms, however enticing, and suspected guile if nothing worse—anyway, he preferred a modicum of privacy for this sort of thing. He kept a stiff back and a stern expression, as far as in him lay. His busy companion, red head down-bent, had nothing to say either.

It was the Queen who altered that. Glancing over Sir James Melville's gravely bowed shoulders, she caught Patrick's eye across the width of the garden, and pulled a grimace, impish, mocking, yet offering and seeking sympathy in one, and entirely shattering.

Flushing in turn, the recipient looked away hastily, and plunged into speech. "Er . . . you are of the North, Mistress?" he jerked. "Mackintosh? A strange trout to find in this basket!"

If she deplored the illustration in any way, the girl beside him showed no sign of it. In fact, she seemed to welcome the opening to break silence, and her soft Highland voice spilled words like a burn's music. "Yes. Perhaps. I went to Edinburgh with my father, to see her Grace. When he was sent to the Camerons in Lochaber, he thought it unwise that I should travel there with him. Because I was called Mary, the Queen took a kindly note of me, and said that she would bring me home in her train. She always has four Maries, as you will know, to wait on her, and Mary Fleming being ill, I took her place for the nonce. I leave her Grace at Inverness."

"Of which Mackintoshes are you, then?"

She hesitated just for a moment. "I am daughter to the Laird of Mackintosh, Captain of Clan Chattan," she said, in a rush.

Well might she hesitate to name that name to a Gordon.

41

Her father, Chief of Mackintosh and overall leader of the Chattan federation that included, as well as Mackintosh, the clans of Macpherson, Shaw, Davidson, Farquharson, and lesser septs, still smarted over the death of *his* father, who had been beheaded at Strathbogie twelve years before. The executed Chief, who had been Deputy-Lieutenant of the North, had fallen out with Huntly, and, tried by a Gordon jury, had paid the penalty. His son, though bound in man-rent to Huntly, three years later had turned against him during a decisive stage of a battle against the Lord of the Isles, causing Huntly's and the royal cause to fail. For that failure, Mary of Guise, who seldom knew her friends, had shrewishly imprisoned the Gordon. The Mackintosh had subsequently allied himself to Huntly's enemies, Argyll, Cassilis, and the rest. The Lord James, delighted, had swiftly drawn him into his net, and he was now proceeding against his hereditary foes of Clan Cameron with the Queen's letters of fire and sword. Not all of his name, nor of the Clan Chattan Federation, had followed his lead, but the business was a sore affront to Gordon pride.

"Holy Name of Mercy!" Patrick said.

Perhaps she sensed some hint of criticism or contumely in his comment. Perhaps she was over-sensitive. At any rate, she displayed a quite uncalled-for reaction—and a spirit that he had hardly suspected. "Perhaps you would prefer that I was Mackintosh of Dalnavert's daughter?" she suggested, more crisply than he had deemed possible.

The man blinked. It had been Mackintosh of Dalnavert's daughter with whom he had handfasted two years ago, and whom he had packed back to her father after the due twelve month's trial—to their mutual relief. Who would have thought that the Chief's daughter would have known anything of that business? He cleared his throat. "H'rr'mm. Not so," he said. "No, no."

"Anna, of Dalnavert, is niece to my father's Seneschal," the girl mentioned. "I hear frequent news of her."

What had she heard, then? What tale would Anna Mackintosh tell of him, that cold gimmer? "I have nothing to be reproached with in the matter," he declared stiffly. "We were but handfasted. She started no child, in the year—indeed, I . . . we found . . ." He stopped, floundering.

"Quite, sir—quite. Was I making any condemnation? Please to be holding your arm still, or you will be jagged!"

So there was silence again on that bench, whilst he held his arm, in fact his whole body, as though cast in iron, and her needle flew.

The second half of that seam was finished a deal more quickly than the first. And almost with the snap of the broken thread, the girl was on her feet, had dropped him the sketchiest of curtsies, and was away hot-foot almost before he had time to mutter some sort of thanks. The man stayed where he was, frowning at the Provost's daisies. He was unsure of himself in this women's garden, unsure of procedure in the royal presence, unsure of what to do now. He could not get up and leave, unannounced—and he had not yet obtained the Queen's answer to Huntly. He still had to deliver his message to the Lord James. And he was notably hungry, beyond the titillation of any biscuits.

Thus he was cogitating, keeping his eyes down-bent and carefully free of those of all women whatsoever, when a stocky solid man, plainly dressed, came through the same door by which he himself had entered the garden. Almost at once, this man's glance lighted upon Patrick, and he started and stiffened visibly, and then came striding across the greensward to the stone bench. Balruary looked up, to find standing before him, on legs wide-planted, a man of about forty, florid, prominent-jawed, and bull-necked.

"My eyes did not deceive me!" he grated, and jabbed a stubby finger at the ivy leaf that shared Patrick's bonnet with the eagle's feather. "That badge—the choking parasitic ivy! That is Gordon tartan. No man flaunting that weed and those colours should befoul good air . . . or the Queen's company!"

Patrick lifted on to his feet in a single lithe motion. "I think ye mistake, sir," he said softly, almost breathed. "They are Gordon—and men hold them in respect, or else . . . suffer!"

"I mistake not! Gordon they are—and accursed!" And the newcomer spat at Patrick's feet. "When decent men see such, they strike them down like the foumarts they are! How came you in here, sirrah?"

Both men's hands dropped involuntarily to where swords should have hung. Patrick answered with a sigh for the lack of it. "On my feet . . . and not as you, dog, will go out—on your knees!" And quick as thought the hand foiled of its sword shot out, fingers sank deep into the other's shoulder, and he jerked him forward violently. At the same time, his left foot thrust out, and over it the stocky man stumbled, to be forced down, while unbalanced, on to his knees indeed. It was a trick that Patrick had learned one time from a muscular friar who had found it useful for reluctant penitents. "Like that!" he finished, his downward pressure maintained.

The other was gasping his surprise, pain, and fury, when there was a rush of movement, and there was the Queen standing beside them, wide-eyed.

"What is this?" she demanded. "What buffoonery is this, in my presence? How dare you! Get up, James Ogilvy! And you, Patrick Gordon—unhand him!"

"I beg your Grace's pardon . . . !" Patrick began.

"This man is one of Huntly's traitorous crew!" the Ogilvy cried, clambering to his feet. "One of your Grace's enemies, parading in your very presence!"

"The Gordon is here as envoy of my Lord of Huntly, sir, as he has right to be," Mary Stewart said.

"Then a viper has right to your bosom, Madam! Where there is Gordon, there is treason!"

"Laird of Cardell—your spleen against the Gordon is known, and may have reason to it—but I would remind you that you are but Steward of my Household here! I will not be . . ."

"If you would hold your realm, Madam, you will trust Gordons different from this! Forsworn betrayers all, you will put them where they belong. . . ."

"Silence, sir! Will you outspeak *me*! You forget yourself, James Ogilvy! Leave our presence!"

Ogilvy drew himself up as though he had been stung, face empurpled, jerked his head in a bow that could best be described as vicious, glared at the Gordon, and then swung on his heel to stalk whence he had come. Three or four paces only he had taken when, without pausing, he threw back over his thick shoulder:

" 'Fore God—the Lord James will hear of this!"

The Queen's caught breath was not the only one that Patrick sensed in that sunny garden—and though he may have been wrong, he had the notion that it was less indignation than fear that underlay it all, not so much pain at the offence offered to the royal dignity as dread at a threat implied.

Patrick dropped on one knee before her, contrite. "Your Grace, I acted in haste . . . without thought. I am not used to ladies' bowers, see you. I crave your forgiveness, your indulgence. . . ."

Mary Stewart's sigh fluttered. "Ah, me—haste and lack of thought! Too many, it seems, act thus today . . . who should know better. Alack, alack for auld Scotland—she makes a sair load for a lassie's hands. But rise, Patrick Gordon—you are forgiven . . . though there will be more to be said, I fear, anon." And wearily, almost listlessly for that sprightly eager soul, she turned away, back to the tut-tutting sombre Sir James.

Patrick, looking after her drooping shoulders, felt compassion well within him. He had been the cause of sorrow to her—but unwittingly, unintentionally. For that, he would make amends, he swore. But others hurt her deliberately. How could men treat her so, whom all men could scarcely behold but worship? Obviously, both as queen and woman, men, many men, treated her harshly—this peerless generous creature that was made for devotion and adoration. How came it so? Here was a mystery, surely.

Glancing about him, he saw that it was as though the sun had gone from that pleasant place. A grey cloud and a chill wind had touched the spirits of all who walked and waited there. And that cloud and chill had been born, not at the folly and violence of his nonsense with Ogilvy of Cardell, but at the mention of a name—the Lord James. Was all Scotland to blench at the utterance of that name, the Bastard, King Jamie's Mischance? Not the Highlands, the clans—not Gordon, surely!

He waited.

45

IV

THE Council lasted longer than had been expected. The magistrates and good folk of Aberdeen were that day, with how much spontaneity and enthusiasm is debatable, providing a banquet for their Queen and her Court, timed for two of the clock. But at half an hour before that time, the Council still was sitting, and with no word or apology sent. The Provost, in something of a flutter, was taking it for granted that all must be postponed until the nobles were ready—though he had it that the meats would be a-spoiling—but Mary Stewart suddenly decided to assert herself, and announced that the banquet would commence as and when arranged. Was the Queen, and were her good citizens of Aberdeen, to be kept waiting for sustenance while a pack of long-tongued lords bickered? She would proceed forthwith to the banqueting-hall.

It was not only the Provost who gobbled and blinked and shook head over this rash and unrealistic decision. If nobody actually put it into words, the question was in all eyes—what was the Lord James going to say to this?

The problem of convoy and escort now arose. The Queen herself had no armed following; she had a Captain of the Guard—but the guard itself had to be formed out of the trains of one or other of the great lords, who alone could order and control them. The Captain of the Guard was the Lord John Stewart, Prior of Coldingham and Laird of Traquair, another of the bastards of James Fifth, and therefore half-brother both of the Queen and of the Lord James—but he was at the Council with his brother. None amongst the gentlemen and lairds who were unimportant enough not to be at the Council, had available sufficient following to convey the Harlot of Rome through the Protestant streets of Aberdeen thronged with the soldiery of the Lords of the Congregation. Such was the pickle of the Queen of Scots, in making this—

46

or any other—gesture. Obviously, she must wait for the Lord James.

Overhearing something of this discussion, Patrick Gordon, still in the garden and unfed, could nowise restrain himself. "I will cut a way for your Grace through this rabble!" he cried. "I opened a road here—with my gillie I will do the like for you!"

Though the gentlemen murmured, the Queen raised a smile. "I believe you would, my bold Gordon, having seen you at it. But such would scarce do, I doubt. No—I have a better way. We shall go afoot. Through this garden gate, Provost, over the vennel, and across the kirkyard of St. Nicholas at the back. That will bring us into that lane—yes, the School Wynd. And there we are, at the side of the Blackfriars." The former hospice of the Black Friars now served conveniently for municipal junketings. "Surely I have sufficient gentlemen to walk me that quiet route?"

After that, there could be little said. Even the Guise brothers were prepared to walk, treating it as an excellent cantrip that the finest blood in Europe should foot it across the backyards and lanes of Aberdeen to make a Queen's escort. Patrick Gordon, who knew the town better than any there save the Provost himself, went a little way ahead, in company with a French page.

This preternaturally solemn youth was a mine of information. It seemed that this banquet had been arranged only the previous night, as a matter of urgency, with the royal household running short of viands. They had all but eaten their way through Aberdeen, and had actually planned to travel north towards Inverness this very midday. But the escape from ward of Sir John Gordon of Findlater had altered all that. The Lord James of Mar, a cautious man, had deemed it inadvisable to move on through Gordon country until spies had ascertained whether Sir John was likely to cause trouble, and what Huntly his father was going to do. That was the wherefore of today's Council—and why the Queen's Grace did not attend it, it was whispered. The Queen did not necessarily accept the Gordons as her enemies, it seemed, as did the

Protestant lords—so she went not to the camarilla to plot their downfall.

It was to be conceived that this young Frenchman was enamoured of his adopted Queen rather than of her brother. Also, of course, he would be a Catholic. At any rate, he gave Patrick Gordon something to digest—till such time as he might set his teeth into more substantial fare.

The journey to Blackfriars, no great distance, was accomplished without incident—though with sufficient girlish laughter and high-pitched badinage to bring many astonished and disapproving faces to back windows. Entering Blackfriars by its side doorway, they surprised the assembled notability of the town by taking them in the rear. And on the tick of two, while the hospice clock still chimed from its belfry, Mary Stewart signed to a very doubtful company to be seated, and to an alarmed Provost to serve the repast.

The seating was a problem for most of those present, with the shadows of the Council lords looming large. A lot of space was left for them at the top end of the great table, extreme reluctance being evident on the part of the modest bailies and burgesses to be anyways near the upper half of the board at all. Some there were who had no difficulty, of course, about their places—the Provost, who as host sat on Mary Stewart's right, the Queen's ladies, who knew their places, and Sir James Melville and the like. Patrick Gordon, who was not the man to see the Gordon honour tarnished in any respect, was about to take the seat third on the Queen's left, when Mary Livingstone beckoned to him urgently to come and sit beside her. He was disinclined to accede—it was a shade lower down on the right side, and, moreover, would place him next to Mary Mackintosh also—but the Queen, noting her lady's pantomime, pointed Patrick imperiously thither. A shade stiffly, he obeyed.

"Waesucks, Gordon—would you make yourself a by-blow too?" that plain-spoken young woman demanded. "Those seats are reserved for her Grace's bastard brothers."

"Three of them?" Patrick wondered.

"Five," Livingstone corrected. "That is, at the moment.

48

Others there are, but they have fallen out with the Lord James. These ones are"—and she ticked them off on her fingers—"the Lord John, Prior of Coldingham; James Stewart, Commendator of Melrose; James Stewart Tertius, Prior of the Holy Rood; Robert Stewart, Earl of Orkney; and Adam Stewart, Prior of the Charterhouse of Perth!"

"*Dhia!* All brothers of the Lord James of Mar?"

"Half-brothers," she amended. "And each only a half-brother to the other."

"Mercy on us all!"

"King Jamie Fifth was a right puissant monarch!" the girl mentioned demurely.

The arrival of smoking victuals that made up in quantity what they lacked in variety, was the signal for a prolonged and powerful grace-saying from the minister of the reformed St. Nicholas, who dealt comprehensively with Popery, the lust of the eyes, the Monstrous Regiment of Women, and the damnation of all but the Elect, in a vigorous wrestling with his Maker, during which time the cookery cooled and congealed on the platters. However, it did rescue Patrick from the cross-talk of the Queen's Maries, against which practice was by no means perfecting his defence. Thereafter, concentration on the meats thus adequately blessed gave him some relief both from persiflage and quaking emptiness. It was nearly twenty hours since he had swallowed anything more satisfying than biscuits. He was at his second rib of beef, and wielding his dirk with undiminished enthusiasm, when there was a great commotion from the street below, the shouts of men and the clatter of hooves, and then the clank of armour on the stairway.

There was sudden quiet in the banqueting-hall. Many diners rose to their feet, expectant eyes on the wide doorway. Not so Patrick Gordon. He sat still, rib in one hand, *sgian dubh* in the other, and into the noteworthy hush he spoke loudly—albeit, it is to be feared, with his mouth full.

"Aberdeen beef is namely, your Grace—and worthy to be eaten hot! I would not let it spoil further!"

There was an audible gasp. The Queen, who since grace

had sat silent and preoccupied, toying with her food, looked up, irresolute only for a moment, and then answered back almost gaily: "You have the rights of it, Man o' Gordon! And a healthy appetite, I think! You at least do justice to our good Provost's fare." And there was a ring in her voice for all to hear.

"I broke my fast yesterday at Balruary under Ben Rinnes," he observed clearly. "I dined last night at Strathbogie . . . where I mean to . . ." He raised his voice; he had to, in an attempt to outspeak the noise made by a graceless pack of armed and armoured men, who burst in through the doorway, pushing and jostling as to who should be foremost.

"My Lord Earl of Mar!" the first shouted.

"The Lord of Morton!" another cried. "A Douglas!"

"A Lindsay!"

"A Ruthven!"

"My Lord Prior of Coldingham!"

"The Lord of Orkney!"

"A Kennedy, Lord of Cassilis!"

On and on the shouted tally went, and as at length it died away, and the stentorian heralds stood aside to admit their masters, out of the din and hullabaloo, Patrick Gordon's voice maintained, strong, calm-seeming, and unhurried. ". . . where I mean to break my fast the morn. I was a-horse all night, your Grace, and I jalouse I shall be the same *this* night. So I relish the Provost's beef . . . though I warrant you'll taste even better in the Castle of Strathbogie, Madam!"

Like stones dropping into a pool of silence, his words came, and having made a leisurely end, he bit deep into his meat.

The ranks of Scotland's nobility, crowded in near the doorway, stared and gaped and glared. In satin and velvet and broadcloth, in buff and leather and armour, they stood, as though transfixed. At the table, practically the entire company stood likewise, save only Mary Stewart, her French uncles, her ladies, and Patrick Gordon—and Sir James Melville, who was old and famous enough to sit still and smile thinly, sipping his wine.

Then, as the tension grew towards snapping-point, the Provost bustled out from his place at the Queen's side, a picture of civic agitation. "My Lords, my Lords," he cried, "I give ye welcome—hearty welcome. We are scarce started. Come, you. Her Grace was hungered . . . fresh meats shall be brought. . . . This way my Lord Earl. . . ."

Out of the press at the door, men started forward, and the Provost, a little man, was overwhelmed, lost in the surge of them, young and old, tall and short, fat and thin. Without actually running, they dived for that table and the highest seats thereat, elbowing and pushing, a stirring spectacle. Chairs and benches were unavoidably overturned, a little wine was spilt. Throughout, the young Queen sat silent, still-faced. Patrick divided his attention between the struggling lords and their sovereign lady, and marvelled.

"Hateful! They are brute-beasts!" a low voice said passionately at his side—and it was not the forthright Mary Livingstone who spoke, but the modest Mary Mackintosh.

Surprised, Patrick looked at her, and shrugged. "Just Lowlanders they are!" he pointed out.

When the battle for place and precedence had resolved itself, with the fiery-powed Earl of Morton achieving pride of place below the bastard Stewarts, and the scowling Lord Lindsay next to him, it was apparent that two men had not taken part in the scramble. They stood aside and apart, and the one that stood at the shoulder of and just behind the other was James Ogilvy of Cardell, Master of the Queen's Household. One chair, first on Mary Stewart's left, remained noticeably unclaimed.

Patrick glanced up from his platter, and found the eyes of both these men fixed upon himself. Ogilvy's remained so fixed, but the other's dropped hastily, almost furtively—which was strange, for they were very notable and prominent eyes, large, pale, and heavy-lidded. Apart from his eyes, the man was in no way an impressive figure. Slightly built, of medium height, and dressed in sober garb, he was without commanding presence—indeed, of a self-conscious and awkward carriage. His pale face was drawn down by a sharp black scimitar of

51

moustache that seemed to frame narrow lips down-turned in the same direction, and joined a thin slightly forked beard. He might have been an unfrocked priest of one of the less respectable orders, with something on his conscience. Could this be the great Lord James, whom all Scotland was to fear?

He came forward to the Queen's side, and though he looked down towards her, he did not look *at* her—the Lord James seldom looked directly at anybody. "Your Grace ought not to have come here unescorted through the streets," he said, and his voice was chill, unemotional, and level. That this should be the half-brother of the vital impulsive Mary Stewart, and the love-child of romantic King James Fifth and the passionate Lady Margaret Erskine, seemed well-nigh incredible.

"I had escort of several gallant gentlemen, brother," the Queen asserted. "And we came without hurt or hindrance, by back ways."

"Think you that was suitable for the Queen's Majesty?" the even censorious voice went on.

"My majesty suffered nothing—less than it would have done through a patient waiting on your lordships' pleasures!"

Expressionless, the Lord James looked away. "Our Council was prolonged only out of concern for the safety of your person and realm, Madam. It behoves you not to reprove our labours."

"Nor does it behove *you* to berate your Queen sir! Sit down, my Lord—this is a banquet, I would remind you, not a preaching!"

The other's eyes turned up towards the ceiling. "God forbid, Madam, that I should forget that there is a Higher Power than any earthly monarch! Gross appetite shall not prevail against Christian duty. I sit not until the meats be blessed." Slightly he raised that measured toneless voice. "Master Forbes—seek you for us God's grace and Christ's intercession."

"But . . . Master Forbes has already done so, and at length!" Mary protested. "The meats are blessed haunch, hip, and thigh."

"Yours may have been, Madam—but not mine! For ill

gluttony's sake would you have us imperil our immortal souls? On your feet, my Lords! Master Forbes—say on."

There was a great scraping of chairs and benches, and something like a groan—no doubt, of pious fervour—in which the young Queen's further remarks were lost. Actually the burgesses and magistrates at the foot of the table were up again more promptly than some of the new-seated lords—who possibly thought it seemly to dispose of their current mouthfuls first. Thereafter, the harshly vibrant tones of Master Forbes of St. Nicholas rose to fill the hall with thunderous assault against the very gates of Heaven, suitably drowning all sounds of residual mastication and mutterings. Not unnaturally on this occasion, the divine quite outdid his previous effort.

Throughout, Mary Stewart sat tense, her fingers tight-gripping the table's edge. Near her, the Guise brothers lolled and stared and yawned. The Queen's Maries took their cue from their mistress, and sat still and watchful. Patrick Gordon applied himself to his plate with no sign of repletion, while his glance roved—once to catch the Lord James's fish-like eyes resting on himself, and to sense no love in their pallor before they slid away.

The final salvo of homiletic assault had scarcely resounded from the rafters before the red Earl of Morton, standing almost directly opposite Patrick's seat, leant over and down, and crashed a great fist on the table. "A Gordon, and a papist too, I'll warrant!" he roared. "Stand, scullion, when your betters stand!"

"I am a Gordon, yes—and though no papist, I could almost wish I was one, here and now!" the younger man mentioned. "And when better than Gordon stands, I *shall* stand!"

"Soul of God! You damned insolent jackanapes! You'll speak not so to Douglas . . . !"

"My Lord of Morton!" the Queen's voice came down the table, high but strong. "The Laird of Balruary is here at my command. He is my guest. Moreover, he is the envoy of my Lord of Huntly."

"And that no mark of honour, i' faith! Madam, here is folly. . . ."

"Your seat, my Lord!"

Morton, blowing out his cheeks, looked to the Lord James for support. But that individual was now apparently engrossed in his victuals, eating with down-bent head and singleness of mind. He was a chancy man with his support at any time, even to his closest collaborators. Swallowing at least the verbal expression of his spleen, the Douglas tugged at his rusty beard, and subsided crab-wise to his chair.

Thereafter, in the serious business of eating, talk, and therefore temperature, dwindled, and the anxious furrows on the Provost's brow eased a little. Ogilvy of Cardell, who had left the hall before grace, now reappeared with Mr. Secretary Lethington, who bowed low to the Queen but addressed his remarks into the ear of the Lord James—who did not so much as glance at him. The Secretary's eyes found Patrick fairly promptly. He spoke at some length, and then found a place for himself beside Mary Beaton. In the absence of Mary Fleming on whom he had designs, he found the Beaton most to his seasoned taste.

The Queen, pushing her food away, talked in French to her Guise uncles with a somewhat forced gaiety, exchanging no word with the sombre half-brother at her side.

Abruptly, the Lord James rose to his feet, as though he had suddenly reached the limit of his capacity for the viands before him, belched satisfactorily, sketched only the genesis of a bow to his sister, and nodded to Ogilvy. Then he turned about, and walked quickly from the room.

The Master of the Household spoke up, stiffly. "With your Grace's permission, the Lord Earl of Mar would have speech with the Lord Huntly's messenger."

Mary inclined her head, but said nothing.

Patrick stood up, and moved round to the Queen's chair. "Madam, I have not had your answer to my Chief," he said.

"No." She sighed. "No. You will tell him that I shall consider his message—or part of it. Part of it only, you will understand!" At her fair temple he saw a pulse beat. "I will not . . . I cannot . . ." She paused. "More I cannot say." Suddenly she looked up at him. "You will tell him how I am placed, Patrick Gordon?" she said, and there was appeal in those lovely hazel eyes.

"I will, Madam, indeed. I would . . . I would that . . ." Patrick swallowed. "I am at your Grace's command, always." And he dropped to his knee.

She gave him her hand, and as his lips touched it, she gripped his fingers for a brief moment, tightly. "God-speed," she whispered.

Not daring to meet those eyes a second time if he was to hold his Gordon tongue, he swung round as he rose, and stalked long-strided for the door, in some turmoil of emotion. He recollected, however, to clap on his bonnet just before passing through.

Out on the landing, behind him, Ogilvy of Cardell's voice grated: "To your left, Gordon. And if you would know what is good for you, you will doff that bonnet!"

Patrick did not so much as look round, but marched straight into the anteroom indicated, a small panelled place, at the window of which the Lord James stood looking out.

"Huntly's messenger, my Lord," Ogilvy announced.

Another voice joined that of the Master of the Household at Gordon's back—the suave tones of the Secretary of State. "Her Grace seems to be a little distraught, my Lord. It may be that hers was a different message from yours. It might be wise to inquire. . . ."

"Leave us!" the man at the window said curtly, his back to them all.

Patrick heard the snap of bitten-off words from Lethington, and the smothered gasp from Ogilvy. Then quietly, almost stealthily, the door closed behind him, and he was alone with the man who ruled in Scotland.

"Well . . . ?" the flat self-conscious voice said, addressing the window-panes.

Patrick Gordon made his own tones level and deliberate—and found it no effort to do so. "George Gordon, Chief of his Name, Earl of Huntly, and her Grace's Lieutenant, sends this word for her Grace's Council. He has knowledge that the

Laigh o' Moray is gathering in arms against yourself and the Protestant lords, and advises against any move into the North save under Gordon escort . . . for the safety of the Queen's person. He says that the clans are risen all the way to Inverness, and that it will be death for her Grace's train to venture through the Moray lowlands. The only road is the back road, through the hill passes into Strathspey—and that road only Gordon can take you. Huntly says that if you would travel North, you must first come to Strathbogie, and put yourself under his protection. Or else, return to the South."

Apart from a further stiffening of that stiff back, he might not have been heard. There was silence in that little room. Only from the street below a muted murmur rose.

It might have been half a minute before the Lord James spoke. "Is that all?" he said.

Wondering, Patrick's brows lifted. "Yes. Save that Huntly was saying to mention that the Lieutenant of the North knows his North!"

"I'll wonder!" That was coldly said. "Certes, he does not know James Stewart!" There was another interval. "The Queen—you have given her this message, likewise?"

"Her Grace has the word, yes."

"In the same terms?"

"That is not for myself to be answering, sir."

The Lord James of Mar wheeled round and walked directly to the door, his thin lips tight closed. And still he did not look at the younger man. So surprised was Patrick at this abrupt and inconclusive end to the interview that the other had his hand on the door-handle before he could believe it, and protest.

"But . . . you have given me no answer for Huntly!" he cried.

"Your turkey-cock will know his answer in good time!" the Earl said, primly rather than grimly, and opening the door, passed out without another word. It shut carefully behind him.

Astounded, Patrick stared at the panelling, at a loss. Was this all? Was this the only result of his errand, of Huntly's message? Was the man coming back . . . ?

He waited, uncertain. But only for a few moments. Then

the door opened again, and Ogilvy of Cardell strode in, followed by six liveried man-at-arms. "Take that man, in the Queen's name!" he cried, and pointed.

Two halberds lunged forward at him, pinning Patrick into a corner of that tiny room. Unarmed, save for his dirk and confined with no space for manoeuvre, he was next to helpless. One halberd he gripped, seeking to wrench it from its owner's grasp, but though he pulled the fellow off his balance, the others were too much for him, Struggling, he went down under a confusion of blows. He grabbed hold of Ogilvy's hose-clad leg, and was reaching for his dirk with the other hand, when all Blackfriars seemed to crash down upon his head.

Oblivion received him.

V

PATRICK GORDON had never been, nor ever thought to be, inside the Tolbooth of Aberdeen—but he had no doubt whatsoever that it was therein that he recovered consciousness. Not that his whereabouts, at first, was a matter of vital moment to him—his stouning splitting head tended to restrict his interest. But as time went on, his immediate surroundings began to penetrate to a bemused perception—the bare stone walls, the high barred and unglazed window, the wooden bench on which he lay, the unclean cobbled floor. There were even chains attached to staples in the walling. This could be none other than the Tolbooth.

Righteous wrath boiled within him—but had to be kept rather crampingly damped down, unfortunately, lest his head burst open altogether. The same head did not seem actually to be broken—thanks perhaps to the excellent Gordon habit of remaining bonneted in the presence of all save chief and monarch—but it was comprehensively contused and swollen. Sundry other areas of his person likewise bore witness to rough handling. In the Queen's name . . . !

This was the Bastard's answer to Huntly, then? "Your turkey-cock will know his answer in good time. . . ." he'd said. Huntly was to get no answer, nor even his messenger back, until . . . what? If this was a sample of the Lord James's reaction, then obviously he was unlikely to bring the Queen to Strathbogie—for quite evidently it was he who would decide the royal itinerary, and not Mary. Huntly seemed barely to have grasped the extent of the Queen's helplessness. Nor assuredly would Mary be permitted to travel under Gordon escort. And certainly, these truculent lords would never consider returning to the South, as bidden. They had come north, whatever the *Queen's* intentions, expressly to overthrow Huntly and the Gordon power. What then?

They would never dare to attack Strathbogie itself, even with all their bravoes. What would they do, then? His head, in its present state, offering Patrick no answer to this problem of high strategy, he graduated to the less ambitious consideration of his own personal situation. How was he to get out of here—since to contemplate remaining where he was put was unthinkable? He had no weapons—his dirk even, was now gone. The Queen, surely, would never permit him to languish here . . . if she had any say in the matter! But would she even know? Would the Bastard, or any of them, tell her? Would she not think him safely on his way back to Strathbogie? Who would know of his predicament and his whereabouts? Black Ewan would find out. Therein lay his immediate hope. Ewan Dubh would follow him to the portals of hell, and beyond. Ewanie would find him. And in the meantime—since Patrick Gordon was nowise a man for sitting still and waiting on fate—he would see what the spoken word might achieve.

Getting somewhat shakily to his feet, he lurched across to the heavily iron-studded door, and beat on it, shouting—and with every beat and shout resounding viciously in his aching head, whatever impact it made outside.

"Aha! Guard—to me! A Gordon! Aha, there—a Gordon!"

Mercifully his uproar produced fairly prompt results—perhaps Aberdeen had not yet altogether outgrown its traditional respect for the name mentioned. At any rate, a small spy-hatch opened in the massive planking of the door at eye level, and a warily anxious face peered in.

"Wheesht, man—wheesht!" this apparition cried. "You'll no' win oot o' that by yowling. Dinna mak sic a stramash, or I'll hae to put you in the irons!"

"Irons! A Gordon . . . !"

"Och, jist that." The jailer rolled expressive eyes upwards. "Man—there's Andra Duthie, my ain sister's man, hanging in an iron chain up-bye this meenit—and jist because he didna put the irons on your precious John o' Gordon! Listen you, and you'll can hear him creak when the wind blaws!"

"Hanging? You mean . . . up on the parapet?"

"Jist that. Dangling ower the street." The other made an eloquent gesture with his index finger, round his neck and up. "For letting John Gordon o' Finletter escape. Man—only my second day it is as turnkey, and here's another Gordon in it!"

"Ummm." Patrick perceived the significance of that, with no rising of spirits. "So it was from here that Sir John broke out?"

"Aye then. And mark you—no other Gordon is going to do the like! My neck's to pay the price if he does!"

Hastily the prisoner changed his stance. "Mercy on us—who's talking about breaking out, at all! Or irons, either? It is my gillie, I want—my servant? See you. He has my gear, my baggage. A Highland gentleman must observe the decencies—even in Aberdeen Tolbooth! You will see that a message goes to my man. At the Provost's lodging . . ."

"No' me, Laird—even if you were Huntly's self! It's my orders you're to be held close, and no' to speak with a soul. In the Queen's name!"

"Damnation!" Patrick swore. "As God's my witness, the Queen knows nothing of this! I am her man—she gave me her hand to be kissing, not an hour back! This is the Bastard's work. . . ."

"Maybe, my mannie—but sae lang's it's the wark o' the lad that hangit Andra Duthie, I'm doing what I'm tell't!" And the little peep-door slammed shut.

Patrick Gordon bit back the majority of the cogent and relevant things that he had to say, with commendable restraint. So he was to be held *incommunicado*, was he? He would see about that!

Crossing to his solid wooden bench, the stone-vaulted cell's sole furnishing, he dragged and heaved and upended it, erecting it against the wall below the tiny barred window. Climbing thereon, he found his eyes on a level with the sill. The masonry was thick, and he was too low to gain any downward view, but he could see enough to confirm what his impression of the sun's position had suggested—that this window opened on to the front of the building, and therefore on to the street. The sounds of movement and talk came from outside, not

60

inside, the Tolbooth. He imagined that he was on the ground floor, too—there were unlikely to be stone-vaulted ceilings higher up. Which meant that he was probably standing only a few feet above the heads of the passers-by in Tolbooth Wynd. And there was no glass between them and himself, however much iron grilling.

So, accepting a splitting head as unfortunate but inevitable, Patrick commenced his oratorio, directed against the citizenry of Aberdeen in general, and those who might still retain a decent respect for their betters in particular. He lifted up his voice.

"Here is Gordon!" he shouted. "Locked up by the Bastard! Tell the Queen. Balruary in the Tolbooth. Bastard's work! Tell the Queen. Gordon of Balruary. Balruary . . ."

Thus he chanted through the open window—and went on chanting.

He had good lungs, at any rate, and could keep it up more or less indefinitely.

He had a good half-hour of this exercise, despite sundry wheeshtings and pleas and threats from the trap in the cell-door, before, husky and throbbing-headed, he was interrupted by the noisy arrival of the turnkeys and a party of men-at-arms. These pulled the up-ended bench from beneath him, brought him down, and ungently ran him out of his cell, along a flagged passage, across a larger prison wherein several miscellaneous malefactors were confined, cut-purses, debtors, wastrels, Catholics and the like, and into a tiny crypt of a place, dark and damp, where the only light came from a mere slit in the wet walling only a foot or so above floor level. Here he was thrown down, adjured to silence in no uncertain fashion, and left to the stench, the darkness, and his own thoughts.

And apart from an automatic and obligatory wrath at the man-handling of a Highland gentleman by Lowland riff-raff, Patrick's thoughts were reasonably contented despite the worsening of his immediate conditions. During his long and monotonous recital he had heard much stir, comment, and reaction from the street below him. He did not know his Aberdeen if even by now the whole tight town of four thousand folk was not buzzing with the talk that Gordon of Balruary was locked up in the Tolbooth. If the fact did not reach the ears of Black Ewan before the day was much older, he would be much surprised. And he had a lot of comfortable faith in Ewan. Also, he still was not in irons.

He had a look through the slit in the wall. It revealed little in the way of a prospect, but enough to suggest that it gave on to either a lane or a cobbled yard. Never having been around the back of the town's gaol, Patrick could recognise nothing. But movement materialised into a dog sniffing about —and where dogs could go, Ewan could go.

Searching for the driest and least foul corner of his kennel, the man sat down, and sought to school an impatient nature to wait philosophically upon events.

Out of philosophy, or an overdose of roast beef and a sleepless night, very shortly he snored.

It was a suitably rewarding and familiar sound which roused him, eventually, however inadequately rendered—the reedy and discordant whistling of 'The Cock o' the North', thin but unmistakable. Crouching down, the prisoner set his lips to the slit, and blowing his loudest, sent his own interpretation of the Gordon classic out into the evening.

In a matter of a few seconds, the faint light from the aperture was suddenly obscured, and Ewan's voice came through in a penetrating whisper. "Man—is that yourself? Here's me been lowing round and round this rickle of stones like Huntly's piper before meat! Are you hurt, at all?"

"Not me. But my throat is sore, see you. Lucky you were to have only to be whistling—and myself shouting out of that window like a stag in rut! You'll have to be getting me out of here, Ewannie."

"Yes, yes. That is so. *Dhia*—I will indeed. How?"

A thoughtful silence succeeded the whispering along that narrow channel in the masonry. "The Queen," Patrick declared, at length. "Only the Queen. You will have to see her, and tell her."

62

"And how is such as my own self to be reaching the Queen's ear, Patrick MacRuary?" the gillie demanded. "Never will I be getting near to her."

"M'mmm. *I* found it none so difficult! But . . . see you, ask for the Mistress Mary Mackintosh, the Captain of Clan Chattan's daughter. She is one of the Queen's ladies. She will help you, belike."

"Clan Chattan! Would you be beholden to that spawn of Satan? Mackintosh's daughter . . ."

"Hush, man—hush you! She maybe is not altogether to blame for her father. And she has a soft way with her."

"My grief! I'd have thought you'd have had enough of soft Mackintosh ways, Balruary, without . . ."

"Quiet! Away with you, dolt, and do as you are bid! I am to be out of here before morning. The Lord James put me in, in the Queen's name. Let the Queen take me out, in the Lord James's name! See you to it."

Black Ewan muttered something, presumably Heavenwards and pious since it failed to negotiate the narrow aperture to the cell. Then his shadow disappeared.

Patrick pursued the only course left open to a gentleman of spirit and breeding. He resumed his slumbers.

He was aroused, in time, but only to be presented with a bowl of cold and stodgy porridge. No light but only a draught now came from the slit in the wall, and he had no notion of the hour. If he waited, he would hear in due course the Tolbooth clock boom.

Long before it did so, he was asleep again, wise man. The town watch, as he went by with his German whistle and drummer, certainly did not penetrate to his dreams.

What did do so, waking him up with a start, was a hectoring voice beyond his door, crying: "Aside, dogs! Out of the way—in the Queen's name! Back, wretches—in the name of the Queen's Grace!" It was an authoritative voice indeed—but strangely familiar nevertheless.

Then Patrick's cell-door was thrown open, and, blinking in the rays of a couple of lanterns, he struggled to his feet. His

63

gaoler stood there within the doorway, carrying one lamp, and beside him four others—two men-at-arms, a fashionably-clad but ungainly figure who could be none other than the lute-player of the garden, Signor Rizzio, and a lady shrouded in voluminous travelling-gown and hood. And one of the men-at-arms, morion, breast-plate, pike and all, was Black Ewan Gordon.

Even as the prisoner stared at this unlikely company, backed by the peering faces of the Tolbooth's more normal denizens, the Italian turned, and taking a lantern, gestured to the other three men to retire. The men-at-arms stepped back, but the turnkey stood his ground, prepared to question the matter. Rizzio said something commanding in French, but without effect. It was the woman who acted positively. Raising an imperious hand, she pointed to the door silently—and looked not at the gaoler at all, but directly at the Italian. Spreading out his hands in prompt submission, that man put his lantern on the stone floor, and then bowing low, backed out of the doorway. Much impressed, obviously, the turnkey edged out with him. The door shut and the key turned, and Patrick and the lady were left alone.

"Madam . . . ?" he said, doubtfully, and stooped to pick up the lantern.

"Do not bend the knee to me a second time, sir," the soft Highland voice answered him, a little breathlessly once more.

"Ah—you, it is! I thought that there was something a morsel more substantial than her Grace under that cloak," the man declared, perhaps less than tactfully.

"Indeed, sir! I . . . I . . . as well for you that there is, perhaps, Master Gordon!" And Mary Mackintosh threw aside her cloak, to reveal a sword and a dirk hanging from a belt around her middle.

"Glory be—but that's the bonniest sight I've yet seen beneath a lassie's gown!" Patrick asserted, starting forward. "My heart's thanks, Mistress Mackintosh!"

"You are easily pleased then, sir!" she gave back, with true feminine contrariness, and a little stiffly for the circumstance. "I doubt but Anna of Dalnavert must have come to you wrongly equipped! I must tell her where she failed you. Naked steel is your fancy . . . and starveling women!" Head down-bent, she was seeking to unbuckle the heavy sword-belt as she spoke.

Grinning, he set down the lamp again, and his fingers superseded hers at the task. An arm encircling her, he had the belt caught before the weapons might clatter to the floor, and with a lamentable renunciation of opportunity, in a trice was buckling them around his own waist. "Another time, ma'am—another time, and I will discuss with you my fancy in women's shapes, Mary of Moy, in due detail! Now—shall we go?"

"Go . . . ? I . . . I would go gladly, sir—but I fear it is . . . less simple than that! There are six of my Lord of Morton's retainers in the guardroom at the outer door. We have come here by stealth—and I fear, must go by stealth."

"Stealth! Is the Queen's hand not in this?"

"Her hand, yes—but have you not seen how that hand is tied? Her Grace is much incensed. She would have you out of here with a flourish—and if the truth be known, I think, have those that put you here, in your stead! But she has not the wherewithal to do it. Her brother and the lords hold all the power in their own hands, and my mistress the name of Queen only. She has seen the Lord James, but he insists that your warding is necessary for the safety of the realm. The Council has ordained it he says, 'tis ever his answer to her. The Council! Her Grace has scarce a man to turn to, whom she may trust. . . ."

"She could turn to Huntly!" Patrick intervened.

"But could she trust him?" a true Mackintosh gave back quickly. "And perhaps Huntly's price is over high!" Then she shrugged. "But I know not. Huntly, anyway, is not here. And the Queen hath naught to send for your delivery but a silly maid and a posturing Italian!"

"And the key to my prison!" the man added, patting the sword at his hip. It was only a courtier's slender rapier, and no good substantial broadsword, but it would sing a welcome song nevertheless. "A Gordon will open most locks with a toy like this!"

"May be. But the lock opened, can you win through the door, with six men-at-arms blocking it?"

"Six! A score, mistress—a score!" Patrick assured. "Last night, on the Hill of Foudland . . . ! But that will keep. And there is my Ewan out-bye to account for three of them! And another with him . . . ?"

"My own gillie."

"Still—even a Mackintosh . . . ! Four, with the Italian. Better odds than is usual, i' faith!"

"I do not doubt your prowess, sir—but that there will be other help for the guard readily to hand. The Lord James is a cautious and thorough man. He leaves little to chance. If the outer door is held against us for even a little space, aid will reach them. The town is full of their kind. And, if I mistake not, Signor Davie, at least, has but little stomach for a fight."

Patrick nodded. "Very well, ma'am. I shall be circumspection itself and out of that door—and out of Aberdeen thereafter—like any whitrick."

"Yes. The horses are round in the vennel at the side, with one of Madam's French pages watching them. Then . . . the road we ride will be for *your* decision."

"We, mistress? The road *we* ride? You are not thinking to escort us, in Heaven's name?"

The girl drew herself up. "Sir—think you that I can go back to the Queen's company, after this? Think you that her Grace could spare me the wrath of the lords? This is supposed to be my own folly—the Queen's name comes not into it."

"She would have *you* purchase my freedom at your own cost!"

"Tush—the cost can be light enough, if you will but heed, sir. Her Highness has more on her mind than the well-being of a headstrong Gordon! She has her realm ever to think of. I know—I have watched her. This is the way that we planned it—the only way open. This is to be the deed of a foolish girl. I have not to return to her Court. I was to be leaving the Queen in a day of two, at Inverness, anyway. I have left her now, instead. Her Grace's command is that you are to see me safe to my father's castle of Moy, in her stead. That is the price of your freedom, sir!"

"By God His Grace!" Patrick Gordon declared and could think of nothing else to say.

She dropped her eyes demurely, now. "If it is too much to pay, too difficult a task . . . or too unpleasing, sir—then no doubt you could drop me just outside the town somewhere, I could find my own way. . . ."

"*Dhia!*" the man swore, abruptly. "At Moy I shall deliver you, never fear. And as soon as horseflesh can carry us!"

Prettily she nibbled her lip. "It is not haste so much that her Highness insists upon, sir—but rather that you should redeem her undertaking to my father to bring me to Moy safe, and—and sound!"

Noting that maidenly hesitation over the last word—and mistrusting every inflection of it—the man nodded briefly. "Brought to Moy safely you shall be—and as sound as you reached me!" he assured grimly. "Now—shall we make our move?" And he dropped hand to sword.

Promptly her tone of voice changed to the practical. "And how, think you, do we set about it?"

"Rap on this door, and have you call to be let out. And when the turnkey opens, this point at his throat!"

"And what if there be some of Morton's bravoes with him? What if he shouts? What if *they* shout? Will not the alarm be raised, and the outer door fast, before we can gain it?"

He shrugged away these finicking woman's doubts. " 'Tis a risk we have to take."

"We thought on a better way. A tumult might serve you well."

"A tumult? Methinks there may be sufficient tumult, i' faith!"

"Yes. But a tumult of the right sort—and in the right place. Here. Thus we conceived it. If you break out at the sword-point, the alarm will be raised belike, and the outer door manned and barred at once. But if the tumult sounds no threat to the guard and the door, then it may serve its purpose to confuse and yet leave the way free. . . ."

"And how, ma'am, may such a unique and satisfactory tumult be achieved, think you?"

She turned her face away from him and the lamp, a little. "Thus, perhaps," she said, small-voiced. "If a woman's cries for help against—against outrage, were to issue not overloud from this cell—what think you would be the result, sir?"

He stared at her for a moment, and then his hand slapped his tartan thigh vehemently, joyfully. "By glory, lassie—you have it! A woman's skirls for help—a woman that they think is the Queen—and they will be bursting in here to her aid. If the guard at the street door hear it, they will come running hither, rather than wait blocking the entrance."

"That is how we reckoned it, sir."

"On my soul, it is well conceived. Mackintosh or none, I congratulate you on your wit. . . ."

"The notion was her Grace's rather than mine. She sees many things as a man would. And, for sure, she could have the carrying out of it, with pleasure!"

"Ha! Do you misdoubt your ability to scream convincingly, mistress?" Patrick wondered. "Perhaps, with a little encouragement from myself . . . !"

"My thanks—but I shall manage without your aid!" the girl said shortly. "I only ask that you do not look at me as I do it! Indeed, the lantern would be the better put out. . . ."

"For shame! A more lifelike screaming I could win out of you, for sure, by some small initiative! In the interests of success, and the Queen's worthy planning . . . !"

"Enough, sir! We have talked a sufficiency. The gaoler will be waxing suspicious. It is arranged that, when the door is opened, the two gillies will come pushing in to further confuse the business. If you were behind the door . . . ? I shall be in the farthest corner. Now—if you are ready, will you dowse the lamp?"

"Assuredly. The vennel where the horses wait—it is to the right, is it not? You will be following behind me closely, to the door?"

"As close as I may, yes."

Patrick stooped, and blew out the lantern. In the consequent pitch blackness, the thin screak of his sword, drawn from its sheath, made the only sound.

He clearly heard her swallow, take a long breath, clear her throat, and then swallow again.

"Come, come," he encouraged, grinning into the dark. "Your virtue is at stake, ma'am!"

"I . . . I . . . will you hold your tongue, sir!" A pause. And then, lifting from a somewhat choking and uncertain start, rose a reedy cry, warbling and breathless despite all her respiration.

"Damnation!" the man lamented, "you sound like a lass being tickled in the hayloft, no more! I could do better for you than that!" And tiptoeing silently across the cobbled floor, he suddenly laid hands on her. And as his fingers slid over her curving person, lightly, only sketchily, but knowledgeably, her outcry opened up and developed and mounted satisfactorily to a full-throated authentic scream.

Even while delivering a swinging buffet, substantial and reasonably accurate, to the side of his head, she did not desist. Nor, altogether, did he.

There were raised voices and urgent steps outside, the lock clicked, and the door was thrown wide.

"Mercy on us—what's this? What's this?" the turnkey cried, in the doorway, holding his lantern high in one hand and a stout cudgel in the other. "Is the misbegotten scoundrel . . . ?"

That was as far as he got, before he was propelled willy-nilly into the cell by the urgent press of Signor Rizzio, the two gillies, and a third man-at-arms—presumably one of the guard, but co-operating as though briefed for the part. In they swept in loud-voiced anxiety for their lady's well-being.

Behind the door Patrick crouched, naked blade in hand. It was a small cell, and the inrush of men filled it. The light of the lamp, dipping and swaying in the gaoler's hand, cast enormous and contorted shadows on the in-curving walls and jumbled figures—but provided only meagre illumination and identification. For all that, the prisoner did not doubt that it was Black Ewan who put himself in front of him, screening

69

him, without abating his outcry—but leaving a space for a discreet man to slip past and out.

Patrick Gordon was that discreet man, and in infinitely less time than it takes to tell, he was out into the large common detention ward. There was no light here, save that which came out from his own cell, but it was enough to reveal several much-interested faces peering thither, all adding their considerable quota to the babel. But it was at the farther door that *he* looked, past these fellow-prisoners to the helmeted and corsleted man who stood with his back to it, halberd in hand.

Without a second's hesitation, Patrick sprang, his rapier flickering up. The guard, who would only see silhouettes and vague ones at that, probably did not notice the sword, and may have judged it no more than one of the town malefactors taking circumstances by the forelock. At all events, he merely grunted a contemptuous warning, and his halberd swung down and forward.

Patrick saw it coming, for such light as there was played on it, gleaming on hatchet-like blade and spear-point. Twisting to one side, he avoided its thrust with ease, and, inside its guard, his blade leapt up for the other's throat. Too late the sentry saw the rapier, and sought, first to swing over his halberd, a long and unwieldly weapon for close quarters. Realising this, he reached for his short hanger. But before his hand was more than on its hilt, his assailant was upon him, and he was defenceless.

The man's very helplessness was his saving. It went against the grain for such as Patrick Gordon to slit the windpipe of a helpless man, caught at a loss. But to merely wound would not serve the case; he might well thereafter use his lungs to alarm the door wards. In a split second these considerations flashed through the Gordon's mind, and as swiftly, he acted. Throwing up the rapier blade in a wide sweep that missed the other's face only by a fraction of an inch, he brought up the pommel in his clenched fist after it. As the slender steel lashed back over his own shoulder, the hilt smashed into the guard's jaw. And with a choking grunt he crumpled up, the halberd clattered to the floor, its owner slithering after it. Striding across him, Patrick flung open the heavy door, and out into the passage.

At the same moment, there was a yell in the cell behind him, swiftly smothered, and then the lamp went out. Patrick began to curse, since that abruptly-ending cry could not but be heard at the guardroom. But his imprecations went unfinished. Feet were pounding up the unlit passage towards him. By the faint glimmer of light, presumably from the guardroom doorway at its end, he gained a vague impression of hurrying figures. A further speedy decision was called for. The man took it and acted upon it in the same instant. He leapt backwards, further up the corridor beyond the door out of which he had just emerged. There was no light behind him, and none now coming out of cell or ward. The chances were that he would be quite invisible. He crouched, waiting.

With a clatter of armour and heavy boots, a man-at-arms thudded up, skidded on the stone slabs as, almost up to Patrick, he realised that he was passing the gaping doorway of the detention ward, managed to stem his rush, and turning, plunged through the opening. Immediately thereafter great was the fall of him, as he toppled headlong over his unconscious colleague. The pandemonium from within that pit of blackness was something that had to be heard to be believed.

Patrick had no time even to chuckle. A second runner on the heels of the first had heard the crash of his companion, and pulled up circumspectly at the doorway, to peer in, shouting his demands to know, in the name of an improbable deity, what was to do. Patrick heard the scrape of his hanger as it was tugged from its sheath.

Even as, receiving no reply, the fellow still leaned within the doorway, Patrick leapt. He could only dimly distinguish the man's outline. He had the dirk in his left hand now, as well as the rapier in the right. On the other's back he landed, reaching for the rear rim of his morion. Up and forward he tilted the helmet as its owner staggered beneath his weight. And punching with that left hand, he brought the dirk-haft crashing down on the uncovered nape of the man's neck. He and his victim fell together.

71

The Gordon was on his feet again, as though from a spring —and he was doing arithmetic the while. One in the cell with the gillies. One dealt with at the door. One in, and fallen over Number Two. And this one. Then, if Mary Mackintosh had counted aright, that left only two of her six.

Taking a chance, he raised his voice, to shout, "Ho! Guard! Help! Here—to me!" He hoped that he had made that sound as though it came from the gaoler. He had a good pair of lungs when he chose to use them—and needed them indeed against the current din.

He waited, but only for a moment. Speed was the essence of such a business as this, and time the commodity that he least could spare—though, up till now, the entire breakout had not occupied more than fifty brief seconds, however full. Running lightly, silently, on his rawhide brogues, he sped down the passage towards the street door.

There was a slight bend in that stone corridor, and even as he rounded it, two men came hurrying out of the open guard-room on the left. Such light as the scene boasted came from the room behind them. Beyond them, the door to the Tolbooth Wynd stood shut and barred.

Patrick hesitated for a moment in his running. They would see him—but, in the dim light, would they see who he was, note his tartan? Jerking his drawn rapier behind him lest it be observed, he succeeded in checking his career, and waved the men on with his left hand, dirk and all.

"Haste ye!" he yelled. "The Gordon! He has the lady held! Haste!"

The first man came on, pounding heavily. But the second seemed to smell a rat, shouted something, and halted. Then swinging round, he strode the dozen paces to the street door, turned, set his back against its timbers, and so stood, drawing his hanger. A man of his wits, unfortunately.

The Gordon spat out an oath. As the first man came thudding up, he thrust out his foot across the dark passage-way, and over it the runner tripped and fell heavily, with the clang of steel on stone. Patrick jumped on the small of his back, and heard the wind go out of him. Stooping, he

72

grasped the fellow's morion, raised it, head and all, and then crashed it down on the paving. If that did not concuss the consciousness inside, nothing would.

He rose to face the man who had turned back—this man, who despite all their fine planning and good work, could yet deny them their well-merited success. And this time there could be no surprise—he could see what had been done to his companion.

Patrick moved forward towards him slowly, grimly, now. The beam of light that flooded out from the guardroom between them, revealed each to the other. And as they closed, it revealed something else. The man facing him, as well as the short sword in his right hand, held a dag, a clumsy horse-pistol, in his left. He presumably was some sort of officer, the leader of the guard picket, undoubtedly, for these weapons were not in general use as yet. Patrick recognised a crisis.

With a sudden spring, he covered the few feet into the guardroom doorway. A foot or two inside, and he had a moment's grace. The other could not see him here, without coming forward from his stance at the outer door. In a flash, Patrick's glance took in the features of the empty room—and the lamp resting on the table in mid-floor. It was only a dozen feet away—but too far for him to risk leaping for; in the meantime this guard could also leap, and slam the door on him, and he would be trapped. There was but the one alternative. Sweeping his rapier under his left arm, in the same movement he tossed his dirk from that hand into his right, and in the back-swing hurled it, spinning, at the lantern. There was a crash, the lamp skidded along the table, toppled over, and smashed down on to the stone floor. There was abrupt darkness, blessed and complete.

No light nor reflection of light gleamed anywhere in that ground floor of Aberdeen's Tolbooth. Noise and shouting echoed from the inner fastnesses, but there was silence here beside the street door. Stretching his ears, Patrick could hear the other man's heavy breathing—he rather thought that he had moved a foot or two forward from the door. Himself, he sought to hold his breath, and edged on tiptoe nearer and nearer to the other's seeming position, his rapier back in his right hand again.

He heard his opponent stir, and reckoned him to be half a dozen paces off. Should he risk a lunge with his point? He would have to be very lucky—and he would be giving the fellow something to aim his pistol at. If only his plaid had been left to him, he would have chanced a throw with it, to seek to envelope the dag. But he had nothing but the rapier. . . .

Biting his lip, the Gordon made up his mind. Moving warily, silently, back again, his left hand tipping the wall behind him, he gained the open doorway of the guardroom once more. Backing through it, he spoke suddenly into the tense hush.

"I do not want to kill you, friend," he began. "You are the last of six, and . . ."

He got no further. The spark of flint, the blaze of powder, and the crash of the explosion, spoke louder than he. The splintering sound of woodwork as the ball buried itself in the door-jamb well to his right, was lost in the rolling echoes of the shot amongst all the corridors and cells of the darkened building.

Patrick swallowed the heart that had jumped unbidden into his mouth, and as the reverberations died away, endeavoured to maintain the same tone of voice as before. "As I say, I do not wish to kill you—but if I must, I shall. You have shot your bolt, and you cannot reload your toy in the darkness. I am Patrick Gordon of Balruary, and namely for swording in these parts. I am thinking that you are an intelligent man— the only one with wit to hold this door. A pity to die for your intelligence, when the witless ones are only stunned."

No word came from the other, though Patrick heard him gulp his saliva. He heard something else, too—movement coming along the corridor, groping movement in the darkness.

"Here are my friends," he went on—and hoped that it was the truth. "You have no chance, man. Yield that door, and no hurt shall come to you."

"Save a hanging from my Lord of Morton!" a husky voice answered him.

"Tcha! The night is dark, Scotland wide, and men of their wits scarce. Change your lords, man—Huntly will pay as well as the Douglas." Patrick, though he sought to maintain a cool and level voice, was counting the seconds, listening. Was that his own people creeping down the passage? And that pistol-shot must have been heard outside. There might be inquiry any moment. "Haste you, man. Your life or my steel?"

Even as he finished, there was an explosive curse from up the passage, and a stumble. The curse was in good Gaelic. That was Black Ewan falling over the last of the litter of recumbent Douglas retainers.

"Ewan Dubh!" his master yelled, in relief. "Was it sleeping you were at? I have the last rat cornered here, at the door. . . ."

The intelligent man thus miscalled drew a quivering breath. "I yield," he said, and again, "I yield." In token whereof there was a clang as he threw his sword down on to the floor. "God's mercy—I have no choice!"

"Wise, you are—as I said!" Patrick asserted. "That door? Have you the key?"

"It is in the lock." They could hear him turn round, and then the creak and clack as the lock turned over. "There are bars, too. . . ." His hands brushed the door timbers, groping. One bar dropped, and then after a pause, the other, and the heavy door swung open, revealing the blissful blue of the autumn night.

Patrick waited not an instant, but darted out into the wynd. Apart from a couple of drunken roisterers opposite, the street appeared to be deserted. "Come, you!" he shouted back to Ewan and the party behind him. He even had a word to spare for the late guardian of the door. "If you have the elements of sense in you, you will make north for Strathbogie, my friend." And then he was racing round to the right, for the vennel.

Four horses waited there, under the care of the same French page who had accompanied Patrick to the Blackfriars—and seldom can a youth have been more undisguisedly glad to see a comparative stranger. As he jabbered in urgent French, the Gordon grasped a fine bay horse's head, and turned to look whence he had come. Three figures were just rounding the corner of the building, at the run, the girl in the centre, her skirts kilted high. Signor Rizzio had already prudently disappeared into the night.

As Patrick hoisted the young woman on to her beast—and had to all but fight for the privilege with the jealously-scowling Mackintosh gillie—she gasped breathlessly:

"That noise . . . that shot? You are not hurt?"

"Do I look it?" He grinned, panting a little himself. "A pleasant exercise, that!"

"I cannot say . . . I found it so. . . ."

"Perhaps I had the advantage of you." He sprang up on to the bay's back.

"You did, sir—and took it!" she declared, with sudden spirit. "I have a good mind not to come with . . ."

"And disobey her Grace? Come, you—in the Queen's name!" And he slapped her horse's rump, and kicked his own mount into action.

VI

THE GORDON knew his Aberdeen—which was as well.
For though the town wall was far from intact, the gates
therein still were manned, and closed at night—for fear of
Gordons, Highlandmen, and other scourges—and after the
watch, with whistle and tuck of drum, had made his rounds
an hour after dark, it would have been difficult for any
unauthorised party of horsemen to leave the town. But the
ruins and deserted precincts of the former ecclesiastical city of
Old Aberdeen, to the north, formed the place's weakness.
Threading its empty streets and echoing causeways, the four
riders slipped through its broken wall behind the overgrown
pleasance of the Nunnery of St. Margaret, and so won out
into open country.

Patrick headed for the south bank of the Don. He was not
greatly fearful of pursuit, once they were out of the town,
especially by night. The country was much too unsettled for
any of the Protestant lords to hope that their minions would
achieve the capture of a Gordon save by a well-laid ambush.
But he led his party along at speed, nevertheless, partly to
improve their situation for the morrow, partly in reaction to
recent enforced inactivity—but mainly because that was the
fashion in which that man normally proceeded, anyway. He
kept his eye on the lady, at first, to satisfy himself that she
was well able to manage her mount—and thereafter would
consider any complaints as and when she made them.

The September night was not really dark, and they had fair
visibility. Patrick had no specific plan formulated, other than
to work up the Don valley, get back to Strathbogie with such
tidings as he had as quickly as possible, and then continue on
through the high hills to the west, to Moy of the Mackintoshes.
That was enough to be going on with—a decision as to their
best immediate route to Strathbogie could be deferred till

daylight. Meantime, there was no need to follow all the haughs and twists of the river all the way, and near Bucksburn they struck off due westwards for the high ground between the hills of Elrick and Tyrebagger, on a route that would bring them to Kintore and the Urie's confluence with Don, with a saving of many river miles.

As their steeds breasted the long slope up to Tyrebagger, their speed dropped to a walk, and Patrick found the girl by his side.

"Where are we?" she asked.

"Making up Donside, for Kintore. It lies eight miles over that line of hill in front," he told her. "What hour is it, think you?"

"I have scant notion. We left the Queen's lodging at the back of ten—and much has happened since then."

"But taking no deal of time," the man pointed out. "An hour, may be—no more, belike. We have five hours of darkness, then—enough to take us well out of the reach of the Lord James and his hirelings. You do not quail at so much horse work in the dark?"

"I should quail more considerably at certain other work of yours in the dark, sir!"

"Oh!" he said. "Ah . . . ummm." He scratched his unshaven chin, and glanced at her sidelong, doubtfully. "See you, ma'am—you need have no fear . . . on any score. I have given my word to bring you safe and sound to Moy Castle. That word shall be kept."

"At whatever cost to your . . . your inclinations, sir?" she added, with sheer feminine contrariness, and left him speechless.

Perhaps she relented—or, it may be, only shifted her woman's grip. "Moy is a long way off, I fear. I must do all I can to aid you in getting me there as quickly as may be . . . so that your resolution be not strained! I would not be more of a burden on you than I must."

"Have I said that you are a burden, mistress?" he demanded, stiffly. "So far, you have proved to be none."

"Thank you, sir."

He frowned. This was not the way that the talk should go—putting him in the wrong and not at his best appearance. "I would not have you think that I am ungrateful," he declared into the night, out of rather tight lips. "You served me very well, getting me out of yonder Tolbooth. You played a notable, an essential part, for a woman. . . ."

"I am overwhelmed, sir."

Abruptly he turned on her, all stiffness lost in sudden wrath. "*Dhia!* What's come over you, woman?" he cried. "Why carp you thus? Yesterday . . . no, it was but this morning i' faith, in the Queen's garden, you were a kindly decent creature, gentle and soft-spoken, using a man honestly . . . and a relief, upon my soul, from those pert ill-tongued Frenchified huzzies, Seton, Betoun, and Livingstone! But now you are as snippet and prickly and shrewish as the rest! What have I done to change you? You knew that I was a Gordon, from the start. I have done you no hurt . . . and you have done me this service at the Tolbooth! What in the name of Grace is wrong with you, woman?"

She had turned her face away from him, and for a moment, after his outburst, he actually thought that she was going to laugh at him—which would have been beyond all standing, 'fore Heaven! But when she spoke it was very small-voiced indeed, and keen-eyed as he was, he could trace no hint of mirth.

"I am deeply sorry, sir—grievously contrite," she murmured. "I had no notion that I was so shrewish . . . and, and prickly. Such behaviour is most unsuitable, I agree, towards one who holds me in the hollow of his Gordon hand! It shall be amended forthwith. I crave Balruary's pardon."

"M'mmm," he said, "well . . . I, er . . . granted, ma'am—granted."

There was a silence, then, and strangely enough, despite his victory, it was the man who exhibited all the signs of discomfort therein. Subconsciously perhaps, he urged his horse on to greater efforts.

The girl spoke, presently, and from a little way behind him, now. "We are in a great hurry, are we not?" she mentioned mildly. "You say that we are making for Kintore? Whither, thereafter? I do not know this Aberdeen country."

"We turn north, for Strathbogie," he told her. "Either by Urie, or by Leslie and Kennethmont."

"Strathbogie . . . !" she said, and there was no mistaking the hint of a quiver in her voice. "Must we travel by Strathbogie? Must *I* . . . ?"

"I have my commission to fulfil, to Huntly."

"Yes. But . . . I need not be with you, when you fulfil it. I have no desire to see the inside of Lord Huntly's walls! Lauchlan Mackintosh's daughter should seek otherwhere for shelter!"

He saw the point of that, of course, but shook his head nevertheless. "The Cock o' the North does not make war on helpless women," he asserted.

"Unlike his son, John of Findlater!"

That was a shrewd thrust—for Sir John, of course, even now had Ogilvy's lady, that he had made his own, locked up in one of Findlater Castle's vaults. "John Gordon is not his father," Patrick declared, hastily. "But, if it would please you better, I could be leaving you with the gillies in the hills above Strathbogie, and riding down to deliver my message to Huntly, and then returning to escort you to Moy?"

"And Huntly letting you!" she added, pointedly.

"Mary Mackintosh—I am Balruary, and no lackey of my Chief's, or any man! If I say that I shall return, return I shall." Brave words, but even as Patrick Gordon spoke them, his memory took him back to the very last words that Huntly had spoken to him. 'Patrick MacRuary, for your bonny mother's sake—come you not back to Huntly empty-handed!' Ominous words, and ominously spoken. He had not liked them as he heard them—and liked them still less now, with hands empty enough in all conscience. He was loyal to his Chief, of course . . . but, well—there were things about Huntly that scarcely pleased him.

All this set the man on a new train of thought, as they neared the summit of their climb. What *was* he going to tell Huntly? That the Queen was insulted by his proposals of

80

matrimony, that she would consider part of his message only—but that anyway, she had no power to do more than consider it, that she was little more than a prisoner of her brother and the Protestant lords? And tell him that the Lord James's answer had been to fling Huntly's messenger into prison, and name the sender a turkey-cock who would know his answer in due course? Fine tales to carry to the choleric Cock o' the North! What would be their reception—*his* reception? But what else could he say . . . ?

He turned to Mary Mackintosh again. "Know you the Queen's intentions—or, leastways, the Lord James's intentions?" he asked. "I took her a message from Huntly . . . and I gained no fair answer. . . ."

"Did you expect a fair answer to such a message?" the girl challenged. "I know a little of the style of your message—her Grace revealed it, in her distress about your imprisoning. If such are Gordon's methods, I think less hardly of the Lord James's offer to the Queen of aid, at the price of her marriage to a profligate younger son . . . !" Here was true indignation, and no designing woman's wiles.

"No. No—I do not mean that. Myself, I do not find the marriage proposal well-judged or, or seemly."

"I am glad to hear that, sir!"

"There were other proposals. Her Grace did not mention them?"

"No. It was only her hurt, I think, that drew this sore slight out of her. 'Tis not her habit to discuss affairs of state with such as myself. For the rest, all she told us was that her brother had said that they ride north tomorrow, for Inverness."

"Tomorrow! And by what route—did she say what route?"

"She did not, no. Save that the Lord James was set on being invested Earl of Moray at its chief message-place of Darnaway Castle, and that the sooner she granted him his wish the sooner she might have peace. . . ."

"Darnaway! They travel by Darnaway?" Patrick cried. "Here is the word I need. If they go by Darnaway, they go through the Laigh o' Moray, through the low country—despite Huntly's warning that the Laigh is risen against them."

"There is danger—for her Grace?"

"Danger for her brother, anyway, and his crew. But I warned him. The Queen also. I gave them both Huntly's message that the Laigh was risen. . . ."

"And who raised it, against the Queen's Grace, think you?"

"I do not know that," Patrick said—which was true, perhaps, though he had a shrewd idea. And that the young woman had likewise, had sounded clearly in her tone of voice. "Huntly offered to escort and convoy her through. But his offer is spurned. He must know of this, forthwith."

Mary Mackintosh said nothing.

In a minute or two they were over the summit of the Tyrebagger ascent, and facing the long drop towards Kintore and the river again. Before them the land sank away in vague deeply blue undulations to the impenetrable shadows of the wide strath, backed and enclosed by the distant black ramparts of the mountains that challenged the night sky to all infinity.

Skirting the sleeping village of Kintore heedfully, they approached the bridge over the Don below Inverurie. But here they were halted by an armed guard, and not waiting for closer investigation, Patrick wheeled his party around and plunged back on their tracks. The broad and swift-flowing Don made a formidable barrier, and its bridges might be held by any of a variety of factions. In the present circumstances, discretion was undoubtedly advisable.

Along the southern bank of the river, they continued to ride westwards. The next bridge was at Kenmay, some five miles further. This too, warily approached, proved to be guarded. There was not another until deep into the Forbes country—where a sensible Gordon would think twice of riding, day or night, without ample tail. There was a good ford at Pitfichie—but that was getting over-close to Forbes, and with its castle close by would probably be held. . . . But he recollected that there was a secondary ford, a couple of miles this side of Monymusk, passable only at certain seasons of the year. It had been a reasonably dry August, however. And no tower nor strength guarded it—only the farm-toun of

Nether Coullie. Thither they made their way. They found the haugh deserted, and the river running black, but, Patrick asserted, fine and low. If Mary Mackintosh doubted him, she did not voice her alarm. He put his bay to the water, and, as the level rose up to his brogues, was thankful that it was a tall saddle-horse that he rode and not his own short-legged garron. Letting the beast feel its own way across the dark flood, he shivered to the water's creeping halfway up his thighs. But it got no deeper. Reaching the far bank, he scouted about, and finding no sign of men, turned his mount's head, and waded back to the south shore.

"Mistress Mackintosh," he said, "are you for travelling wet or dry?"

"If dry is possible . . . ?" she began doubtfully, and then ended in a gasp, as, ranging his horse alongside hers, the man leant over, swept an arm around her waist, and lifted her bodily across on to his own beast before him, amidst a certain confusion of limbs and draperies. He gasped a little himself as he did so—for she was a well-made piece.

"Fine . . ." he said, and sought not to pant it. "Keep . . . your feet up," and with a less than expert hand strove to gather up and tuck in her skirts.

"Patrick Gordon!" she cried. "This is . . . unnecessary!" But she did not struggle nor wriggle, and though she pushed his fumbling hand away in no uncertain fashion, it was to complete his task of tucking-in.

"More seemly than hanging your skirts out to dry, on the other side!" he told her—and silenced her adequately.

She lay quietly within his arms as he put his mount to the water again, her legs stretched out straight. Behind, the gillies followed on, leading the girl's horse. Black Ewan said something apposite—but had to do his own chuckling. The Mackintosh appeared to be a dull stick.

Patrick did not rush that crossing—it would have been a pity to have splashed anyone. He found his passenger's small ear very close to his mouth, and wondered in an abstract fashion, what she would do were he to bite the lobe of it—a practice to which he was mildly partial. She swung that right hand of hers fairly fast, of course. Perhaps, on the whole, it scarcely would be worth it.

On the north bank the girl very promptly recovered her initiative, and had slipped from horse to ground before her escort was ready to transfer her.

"You are in a great hurry, to be sure," he grumbled. "Were you so ill-accommodated . . . ?"

"I had accommodated what I take to be the hilt of your rapier long enough, sir," she asserted, without turning her head.

Patrick ran a hand through his black hair—bare, for his fine feathered bonnet was gone, like his plaid—and missed his chance to her jealous gillie to aid the lady back on to her own steed.

Thereafter, unchallenged, they made good time up through largely wooded country below the eastern base of Bennachie, over the shoulder of hill above Pittodrie, and so down to the Urie at Oyne. They were moving almost due north now, keeping the river on their right, and Patrick was able to relax a little, both of speed and vigilance. They were nearing Gordon country, and the heather soon would be reaching out its kindly arms to them. Five or six more miles, and they would be back to the same Hill of Skares that the Gordons had circled less than thirty hours previously, astonishing as it seemed. And there they would rest a while.

The dawn was paling the stars in the eastern sky when the little party, weary now and silent, turned off the track and into the heather at last, within the jaws of the Urie's glen where it emerged from the Foudland Hills. Amongst a scattering of windblown pines, etched against the sky, they dismounted.

"Two-three hours' sleep will be the making of us," Patrick declared. He kept to himself the thought that some of them might well need that making before this new day was out.

Tethering the horses to a tree, they brushed the night's spiders'-webs from the heather, and sank down into its embrace. Patrick announced that a watch should be kept, and that he was the one to keep the first hour or so of it—after all, he had slept most recently of any there, had he not? To the young woman's doubts as to the need for watching now, he pointed out that they were only a few yards from one of the principal routes into Strathbogie, and it was known that, after Sir John Gordon's escape from Aberdeen, the Protestant lords had parties out to seek him and to try to chart his moments. Also, here, they were still on the edge of Forbes territory—and the Laird of Forbes was a known opportunist where Gordons were concerned. Moreover, the whole country was buzzing like a couped hive with armed men of one faction or another, or no faction other than warm self-interest, and it was a wise man who slept with one eye open when on the wrong side of a well-barred door.

Mary Mackintosh accepting that, showed a nice return to the gentle and seemly womanliness that first sight had given him, by expressing concern that he would be cold at his watching without a plaid, and offering in a tentative sort of fashion a corner of her own voluminous black riding-cloak. But the man, with the eyes of the two gillies upon him—plaidless themselves also, and still in their borrowed men-at-arms garb—declined. Another time, may be, he suggested foresightedly. He was not cold, and if he became so, he would be the less likely to fall asleep at his vigil. He would wake one of the other men in an hour or so.

The girl thereupon burrowed herself into the tall heather with the proficiency of one long at home therein, wrapping and covering herself entirely in her cloak so that only a strand or two of copper hair escaped, and the long sigh of her relaxation seemed to indicate a nature comfortably conformable to the exigencies of the prevailing situation. Donald Gorm, her Mackintosh gillie, settled himself at her side, maintaining a hand upon his dirk and a warning glare at Balruary the while—which even remained stamped upon his uppermost features long after his lower jaw had fallen open in stertorous snoring. Black Ewan threw away his helmet, curled up like a dog around a boss of outcropping stone, and slept immediately.

And out over the dark trough of the glen-floor Patrick, sitting with his back against another outcrop, watched the slow birth-pangs of the new day. From below, the sigh of the river drifted up to him: from hillsides far and near the curlews called in the extremity of their regret; a faint dawn wind breathed over the heather leagues as if to the slow respiration of the sleeping land; and at his feet the girl stirred beneath her cloak, muttered something smothered, sleepy, and strangely heart-warming, that brought a flicker of a smile to the watcher's dark face.

He yawned, and bent his mind to the consideration of how he was going to word his delivery to Huntly, knitting his brows to the effort. Knitted they remained, like Donald Gorm's. He shivered, and yawned again. Thus he would say . . . and thus! Cousin George, he would say . . . Cousin George—I . . . I . . . It was only the beginning of September, and not very cold— not cold enough, anyhow, to counter the inadequacy of four hours' sleep out of the last forty, at four-thirty in the morning. The man's stubbly chin sank upon his chest, and a lock of black hair fell forward over his knitted brow.

VII

PATRICK woke with a start, cramp in his neck and back, sun in his eyes and the sound of gruff laughter in his ears. Blinking, he peered, was grateful that the sun was suddenly blocked out—and then perceived that this was caused by a man standing over him, a large man wearing a ragged kilt. Moreover, something close by to the side still caught the gleam of the morning sun redly, rustily—and only a couple of blinks sufficed to establish it as a naked broadsword, scurvily burnished. He was for starting up, for due inquiry, when the point of the said ill-kept weapon transferred itself to the region of his Adam's-apple.

"You wear honest colours in ill company!" a voice accused.

"The company was the better before you joined it, then!" Patrick got out—the best that he could do at short notice, out of a daze of sleep.

"Keep you that tongue between your teeth—while you have it!" he was warned, and the sword-tip, however rusty, was sharp enough to draw a thin line of blood at his throat. "Your business in Glen Foudland?"

"More honest than yours, I warrant! I am Gordon of Balruary, on Huntly's business."

"With two Sassenach bravoes to your tail . . ."

"Speak them—and see if they are Sassenachs! You'll find them better men than what might be a poor sort of a Grant, if his tartan was clean enough to be recognisable!" Patrick was getting further into his stride.

"*Dhia!* For a man as good as dead, you talk loud. . . ." the other growled, but there was doubt in his voice, and in his look as he turned to consider the rest of the party.

Patrick followed his glance. Black Ewan still slept soundly, and at his head a tattered cateran crouched, cudgel in hand. Donald Gorm was sitting up, scowling and still silent, his arms

87

twisted behind him and a dirk at his throat. The girl was in process of waking and sitting up, alarm chasing sleep from wide eyes. Around them a dozen or so Highlandmen of the wilder sort stood, looking for trouble, Gordon colours amongst them.

Finding Mary Mackintosh's wondering and troubled gaze upon himself, Patrick spoke up again, with the force of his shame. "And your business, sirrah? Bold business, indeed, to interfere with a Gordon within a score of miles of Strath-bogie!"

The big stooping bearded man who stood over him, perhaps just a shade less ruffianly-looking than the rest, frowned his perplexity. "The woman . . . ?" he demanded. "Who is she?"

In that company, her name was best left unsaid. "My charge," Patrick asserted briefly.

Black Ewan was stirring, and to aid him the cudgel was prodded just below his breastplate. A full-throated if incoherent spate of Gaelic impiety followed, soundly substantiating his master's indication that this was no Sassenach. The leader of the band obviously noted the fact, and came to a decision.

"We shall see how loud you will be talking, presently," he said. "On your feet—and no foolishness, see you, or there will be no talking for you this side of hell's gates! Fetch them."

The late sleepers were hustled downhill towards the track, forthwith, Patrick finding the point of his own rapier between his shoulder-blades, Naturally, the thought of making a fight for it did not go unconsidered, but without weapons and out-numbered four to one, the thing would have been worse than futile. And he had his promise to Mary Mackintosh to fulfil.

In a string, they were led down through the heather. Behind, a man walked their four horses after them.

"Where do you take us?" Patrick demanded of the Grant who commanded, and received no answer.

He turned his head to the young woman being propelled along at his back. "I am sorry, Mary—for these oafs' man-ners as for my sleeping," he said. "I . . . I . . . well, I am sorry." And that was true. Never that he could recollect had he felt more humiliated—an infinitely worse state of affairs for any Gordon than merely to be captured and in danger of life or limb.

"I slept even better than you did, I think," the girl told him, out of her generosity. "Who would have looked for this sort of snake in Huntly's heather?"

"Quiet, you!" the Grant snarled. "Or the woman will skirl a different tune!"

Down the track they walked some way, till, below a little hillock, they came on the party's waiting garrons. Glancing back and up, Patrick perceived how the tree to which they had tethered their own mounts was visible from here against an immediate skyline. He cursed beneath his breath.

They were ordered to mount—though only the girl was given her own horse with its side-saddle, and well hemmed-in by their captors, they were urged up the track again for nearly a mile, and then down off it towards the river. They crossed splashing by a shallow ford, and then up through the brackens and birches about the northern skirts of the Hill of Tillymorgan, till a narrow hidden valley opened before them to the north, cleft in the broad flank of a green hill. And in the lap of it a shepherd's cot-house crouched amongst its fanks and folds, around which many men moved and horses grazed.

Down into this valley they rode, in the morning sunshine.

There were some cries at their approach, from the ragged company about the place, broken clansmen by their aspect, like their captors. The noise brought other men out of the house, of a somewhat better appearance, bonneted and plaided and bristling with arms. Two of these Patrick recognised at once— William Gordon in Delmore, and George Gordon in Tombae, natural sons of the laird of Strathavon and Cluny, notorious freebooters and uncomfortable neighbours of his own in Glen Livet, who had both been put to the horn a dozen times, and survived the process—mainly by the temper and agility of their own steel but partly, no doubt, because their old father was Huntly's uncle, a younger son of the third Earl.

So these were the hands into which they had fallen! Patrick was sighing his relief, when behind the others another man emerged—and seemed incongruous indeed to be issuing from the black hole of that turf-roofed hovel—a tall and handsome gallant, dressed in the colourful height of Lowland fashion, plumed cap, short cloak, slashed doublet and trunks, and long buckskin riding-boots over silken hose. Only the flared corselet of black steel picked out in gold hinted that he might be a man of action, and the tartan lining to his cloak that he was of the North. Patrick's sigh of relief altered to a whistle of astonishment.

But it was Mary Mackintosh who spoke. "The warrior on women!" she said, her voice uneven, husky. "Sir John of Findlater!" And strangely, "You . . . you will not fail me, Patrick Gordon?"

At her tone, he turned, surprised, to look at her, "No," he assured. "No—not again, *a graidh*. But, why?"

"I am afraid of that man," she said, and obviously meant it.

"Ho ho!" William Gordon, Delmore cried. "See what we have here—Balruary, and a woman to him!"

"A lady, say," Sir John spoke, sharply, behind him. And striding forward towards the approaching cavalcade, doffed his cap with a flourish. "Mistress Mackintosh—your servant. Well met, Patrick MacRuary!"

The girl inclined her red head slightly, but said nothing.

Patrick was less restrained. "Met, do you call it!" he cried. "Attacked and mishandled by your crew of cut-throat caterans, and dragged here under threat of death—d'you call that well met?"

"Tut, man—our meeting is well, whatever the cause. The times are ill regulated and travel uncertain—as I know to my cost, 'fore God! But if these cattle have offended a Gordon gentleman, or a fair lady, then you can have their heads for amends." And with a casual wave of his hand, he stepped over to assist Mary Mackintosh from her horse.

The girl darted a glance at Patrick, and he was struck by the fear and distress in her eyes—emotions which he certainly had not observed when she had been under threat of assault by their ruffianly captors. Actually, she shrank back from Findlater's outstretched arms.

All of which was very strange—for Sir John Gordon of Findlater was a personable man, and a handsomer was scarcely to be found in all broad Scotland. Taller even than Patrick, ruddy complexioned like all the Gordons, with a magnificent head of wavy amber hair and a trim pointed beard, his features were regular, strong, and pleasing. And his eyes were extraordinary, brilliant, almost glittering, humoursome and yet compelling. His bearing was noble, carelessly assured, with just a hint of the devil-may-care that no one would call a swagger. Certainly he was a man that women did not usually shrink from—and many had had the opportunity.

Patrick threw himself off his garron, and strode to the girl's side, and, almost as a child would, she put herself into his hands in preference to those of the other man. There was no coyness about her gesture. Behind Patrick, her own gillie pushed forward.

John Gordon smiled, and sketched an acquiescent bow. "You have your escort well in hand, ma'am," he observed. "I rejoice to see you in such good hands. My own are at your disposal, should an extra pair be required! Come—I have no seemly quarters to offer you, but such as there are, are yours to command." And he waved an arm towards the cot-house.

Around them, men fell back regardfully.

"Strange quarters for John o' Findlater!" Patrick commented, taking the young woman's arm, and moving housewards.

"Better than my last, Patrick MacRuary—better than Aberdeen Tolbooth, I can tell you. At least the lice are less active!" And he flung a comradely arm over Balruary's shoulder as they walked—and if the tips of his long fingers now and again brushed the arm of the girl at Patrick's other side, no one could have claimed it as other than accidental.

"They did not trouble *me*, but I was not long in your cell, see you."

"Eh . . . ? You? Do not tell me that you also have been decorating the town gaol, Patrick!" He leaned over, to peer, in laughing incredulity.

" 'Twas out of there that Mistress Mackintosh lifted me

91

not twelve hours back—with the aid of yonder rapier that your bullyrook has appropriated, these two gillies . . . and her Grace's wit."

"Soul of God—what's this? Mary Mackintosh, and a rapier! And the Queen . . . ? Here's a tale worth the hearing, I warrant. Mary—have I been mistaken in you?"

"No," the girl said, flatly.

"I wonder, I wonder. But I shall have the whole tale I swear. I won't be balked by your pretty modesty. But, first—have you eaten? Have you broken your fast? No. Then you shall eat such poor fare as we have to offer, and give us the tale the while. Unless"—John Gordon looked solicitous—"unless you wish your will worked on these cattle of Willie's, first? What is your mind, Patrick *mo caraid*? Can I beg of you not to have *all* their throats slit . . . for I'm plaguey short of men!"

"They did us little hurt . . . ?" That was Mary Mackintosh, to Patrick, urgent with quick compassion.

"Let them be," that man shrugged. "I am more eager for my breakfast than for teaching them manners. Let Willie Delmore give them the edge of his tongue—and rough enough it can be!"

"Willie—hear you that?" Sir John turned his head to the men behind him. "A lesson in manners to your spawn, there—but no throats cut, this time. See you to it."

So after the young woman had sought the dark and dubious privacy of the herd's house, and astonishingly emerged therefrom so considerably spruced and tidied as to be a changed woman, at least in her toilet, they ate in the sunshine on the grass before the house, and Patrick told a story that lost but little in the telling. And Sir John Gordon listened attentively—though he was no less attentive in serving his guests, in especial the lady, on whom he waited with a notable assiduity . . . and which kindled no apparent spark of answering warmth in her frigid self-containment. The circle of his shaggy lieutenants watched and listened and grinned—but at a respectful distance—and voiced no comment.

The telling outlasted the eating, and before it was ended, with Sir John standing close at her side, Mary Mackintosh's

92

toe was tap-tapping the grass, her lovely face set. Patrick, noting something of it, was perplexed—for never had he known Huntly's favourite son more gracious, more altogether amiable, and he could be otherwise.

The recital over, Sir John slapped his booted thigh. " 'Fore God—'tis the best jest I've heard this long while!" he laughed. "That smug hypocrite James Stewart beat at his own game! And by a couple of lassies!" he cried. "Mary Mackintosh— my salutations. Your wit and courage match your beauty, I vow!" And his hand fell upon her shoulder, and ran along it lightly, with just the hint of a caress. On the instant the girl was on her feet, trembling, her warm colour ebbed. "Unhand me, sir!" she cried. "I will not have it! I . . . I . . ." She turned swiftly away from him. "Patrick—will you fulfil your Queen's charge! Will you take me home to Moy—now? At once!"

Patrick rose, in some bewilderment. "Surely, surely—if that is your wish . . ."

John Gordon cut in. "Your pardon, Mistress Mary—I beg of you. You are overwrought—and small wonder. 'Tis not every night a lassie rapes the Tolbooth of Aberdeen at the sword-point! Nor suffers capture by such as Willie's caterans! What you need is a rest, my dear. . . ."

"A rest would serve you best, I think. . . ." Patrick agreed.

"No. I need no rest. I wish to be on my way, now—at once." Her voice was higher-pitched than usual, and brittle. "Patrick—you promised . . . !"

"I did, yes. We shall go on—right away."

"Thank you."

"I am afraid that will not be possible," Sir John's voice had changed too, and now was suddenly steely. "I cannot allow it. The country is too disturbed. You have already seen how it is, ma'am. I cannot take the responsibility of allowing you to run into further danger."

"Responsibility!" she took him up, sharply. "What responsibility is it of yours? God knows you have taken to yourself responsibilities enough—but *I* am none of them, John Gordon!"

"Myself it is that is responsible for Mistress Mackintosh's safety," Patrick declared. "She is in *my* care. . . ."

"And how have you discharged it, man, hitherto!" the other demanded lip curling. "Enough talk. In this country and in these circumstances, I am responsible. Mistress Mackintosh's well-being is too precious to entrust to the escort of three men at this pass—and I cannot afford to detach a guard. Besides, I ride north myself, before noon."

"To Strathbogie?" Patrick asked.

"To the north, at any rate—the direction Mistress Mackintosh must take, to Moy."

"But I have a message to deliver forthwith, to Huntly," Patrick pointed out. "It is urgent. From the Queen."

For a little Findlater considered him, those glittering eyes searching. "And that message is, Patrick . . . ?"

"For your father!"

"A-a-ah!" That was drawn out on the other's breath—and it was an icy breath. Momentarily that handsome face, thrust now near Patrick's own, was somehow no longer handsome. And then he smiled, and was immediately prepossessing again. "And am I not my father's right hand?" he wondered.

"It is your father's *ear* I am concerned with, John *mo caraid*." Patrick asserted steadily. "And, thanks to the Lord James, late I am already. You would not have me break trust with my Chief—and yours!"

Findlater shrugged. "As you will, Balruary. Go you, then—with your message. Alone and unencumbered, you may win through safely, I dare say."

Patrick did not need the sudden tight grip on his arm, to stiffen him. "Alone . . . ? I think not, Findlater," he rasped. "I have the Queen's charge, also, to deliver Mistress Mackintosh to her father's house."

"Then you will weigh up your duty to your Chief and to your Queen, Patrick MacRuary—and decide which is the heavier. Go, or stay—but *my* duty to Mistress Mary here is clear. She travels in safety—in my train!" And bowing deeply to the tight-lipped girl, John Gordon turned and left them standing.

94

Black-browed, Patrick glared after the elegant back, his lips moving, fortunately soundlessly.

"Oh—that man is a devil!' Mary Mackintosh whispered. "I hate him—have hated him from my first sight of him. So that is your Gordon—your choice for the Queen!"

The other's frown changed character a little. "He is not so bad as *that*, see you," he protested, but unhappily. "He is headstrong, and ill to cross. But there is no evil to him. . . ."

"A score of women could tell you otherwise!"

"Women, may be. But . . ."

"And women's opinions do not count! Is that the way of it?" She was quick.

"No, no. Not so. I meant but that, that . . ."

"To be sure, sir. I know just what you meant. And now, we are as good as captives again . . . and it is the woman who will suffer, I fear, whatever the worth of her opinion!"

"I think you need have no such fear," Patrick said slowly. "John Gordon, ill-judged though his methods be, is but seeking your safety."

"*You* may believe that—but I do not," the girl said tensely. "You do not know John Gordon, I think."

"I have known him since I was a laddie. He is the elder, but only by a year or two. We have played and hunted and fought together. I know John Gordon."

"But not as a woman knows him. In Edinburgh, he sought me out . . . amongst others! He . . . he . . . well, we need not go deeper into that. Some women he fascinates—at first. Others see him for what he is. These latter he pursues—and knows no mercy. Even the Queen was not safe from his . . . his hands." She drew a quivering breath at the word. "In Aberdeen he saw me only for a few minutes. But it was enough . . . !" She closed her lips tightly as though to prevent them revealing more, when they had already told too much.

The man eyed the tall green slopes that hemmed them in, sheep-strewn amidst the turning bracken, his discomfort evident in every line of him. "I am sorry," he said, almost gruffly. "I had no notion . . . at least, of the like of this."

There was silence between them for a space, and the bustle of a camp of armed men prevailed.

"What are we to do?" Mary Mackintosh asked, at length, helplessly.

Patrick put out a reassuring hand to her arm—and then hurriedly withdrew it, blinking. "Never fear," he asserted. "All will be well. You have my word, see you."

"The word of a Gordon, sir . . . !" She relented a little, even as she spoke. "*One* Gordon amongst . . . others!" she amended.

He shook his head, a trifle stiffly. "Perhaps you misjudge more than myself!" he protested. "And, not so long past it was Patrick you were naming me, and not sir!"

"That was for the benefit of . . . that man," she asserted. "So that he might think us closer. . . . I apologise for the liberty."

"Tcha!" Patrick snorted, and glared at surrounding men, hills and sky with equal disapproval.

Mary Mackintosh considered her fingers, and nibbled her lip.

They had something more to look at, in a minute or so. A party of horsemen, similar to that which had brought them in, arrived from the direction of Foudland, and even as they were being greeted, another cavalcade was to be descried coming over the skyline to the north-east and dipping down into the green valley, fully a score strong. These proved to be better clad and horsed low-country Gordons, under the sons of the lairds of Pitbar and Tarland. Interested, Patrick watched Sir John welcome them. He saw these young men, whom he knew after some fashion, glance in his direction—but neither they nor Findlater approached nearer.

Excusing himself to the girl, he got up and strolled over to the group of leaders—and was warily received, save by John Gordon himself, who smiled again genially.

"Here is the squire of dames," the latter greeted him.

Patrick nodded briefly to the others. "Findlater," he said directly, "I fail to understand your attitude. Why are you holding us?"

"Holding you, Patrick? I hold you not. You are as free as the air to blow where you list . . . though I put it to you that your likeliest part would be to bide with us, and take your vengeance on the Bastard and his jackals."

Patrick let that pass—while noting it. "I refer to my charge, from the Queen—the Mistress Mackintosh," he said, evenly.

The other raised distressed brows. "God's grace, my good Patrick—if you had an ounce of sense to you, you would perceive that Lauchlan Mor Mackintosh's daughter dare not travel through Gordon country without substantial escort—the thing is impossible, with the country in arms. Do you want a despoiled woman, or a corpse, to present at Moy Castle?"

"Who would know her to be the Mackintosh's daughter?"

"Red-headed beauties of her quality do not grow on every braeside! But enough of this, man—if you do not know your duty, I do."

Recognising the cold finality of that, Patrick shrugged. "Whither do you, do *we*, ride?"

"To the confounding of the Bastard. He takes the Queen north to Inverness shortly. Which route he will take remains to be seen. If he goes by the coast and the low country, my castle of Findlater will offer him seemly welcome. If he chooses the high road through the hills, by the Cabrach and others, my castle of Auchindoun will serve him equally handsomely. And I think not that he will take the middle route through Strathbogie and Keith!"

It was Patrick's turn to bite his lip. How much of what he had learned should he tell this son of Huntly's? Should he tell him anything? Had he the right to reveal to any but the man who had sent him, the findings of his mission? Was Findlater's proposed attack on the Queen's train such as he could support? Was it in accord with Huntly's design? Was it to the Queen's benefit . . . ? It could be called treason—and while the name meant little to him, how Mary Stewart fared therein meant a great deal. The grievous question-mark that had loomed before Patrick after that strange proposal of the Lord Gordon two nights earlier, and which he had pushed to the back of his mind, now grew prominent, demanding an answer, a decision. Where lay a man's duty, in this cauldron of conflicting loyalties? To whom and to what did he owe his first allegiance? To his clan? His Chief? His Queen? His country . . . ?

"Is it your father's plan, this attack on the Queen's train, or your own, Findlater?" he demanded, out of his perplexity.

"My father is growing an old man," the other shrugged. "I am his right hand, as I told you."

"Does he know what you propose to do?"

"Balruary—you forget yourself!" Sir John cried; "you presume too much. When I find myself in need of guidance from such as yourself, I shall ask for it! Come, gentlemen—we ride within the hour. I am trysted to meet with the Shaws at Mill of Lynebain before the day is much older. We have more to do than chaffer words."

Patrick found all backs turned upon him. Sighing, he returned to the girl's side. After one searching glance at his face, and an echo of his sigh, she had nothing to say to him.

Presently, after another small party had come in, their horses were brought to them, and Sir John came to assist Mary Mackintosh to mount. Though his aid was spurned and ignored, he persisted with the quiet smile of a man assured of his own power, Patrick the while being vocally in pursuit of his purloined rapier. It was noticeable that when the entire company of well over a hundred moved off, Balruary and the girl were enclosed within a tight circle of lairdlings and sprigs of very heathery Gordon, and separated effectively from Black Ewan and Donald Gorm.

As they rode out of that secret valley, at the tail of John of Findlater's magnificent black barbary, Mary spoke up clearly, distinctly. "Is this your vaunted Gordon power—this, this rabble?" she asked, with little of her suitable heart-catching mildness in evidence.

"Not so," Patrick assured, with corresponding clarity of diction. "This is only a scraping of birkies and younger sons and bogwallopers. Huntly has the clan assembled at Strathbogie—honest fighting-men by the thousand. This is no more than a rude clamjamfry."

Undoubtedly Sir John in front must have heard that, but not even a stiffening of his stylish back revealed the fact. At Patrick's flank there was a snarl from Willie Gordon, Delmore, and others of his kidney, and he was jostled on his horse. But without sign or gesture from Findlater, they went no further. And Balruary ignored them entirely.

Though supposedly their progress was to be northwards, it was almost due westwards that Sir John led his strung-out cavalcade, down into the glen of the Urie again, and up into the heather beyond. Over the west shoulder of the Hill of Skares they climbed, across the wide saddle between it and Hill of Foudland, and, keeping to high ground, headed along the Skirts of Foudland for Melshach Moss and the narrows of upper Bogie. The Mill of Lynebain that had been mentioned as a rendezvous lay a good fifteen rough miles to the west, in the upper valley of Deveron below the great mountains.

Nearby passed one of the difficult tortuous routes to the north through the outliers of the mighty land-mass of the Monadh Ruadh, the Red Mountains.

Over the purple and brown skyline of rolling heather moor to the north came a group of horsemen, riding hard as the terrain would allow. No more than half a dozen of them there were, but they brought the larger column to a prompt halt, nevertheless. Patrick was close enough behind Sir John to hear that man's muttered oath.

It was the banner that streamed above the second rider of the little troop that did it, undoubtedly. There were not many banners carried over the Gordon heather—and this one advanced with a confidence and authority notably disproportionate to the strength of its escort. Here came George, Lord Gordon, Sheriff of Inverness and Huntly's heir.

No man failed in some reaction to the tension that suddenly gripped that company drawn up there on the peat-pitted moorland.

The meeting of the two sons of the Cock o' the North held an underlying element of drama that none could mistake nor ignore—whatever the manner of their greeting. All men knew that they did not love each other—and that they both, after their individual fashion, loved Mary of Scotland. They were antipathetic and contrary in most respects—unlikely brothers. Where one was grave, thoughtful, slow of speech, the other was dashing, impetuous, and eloquent. To the elder's stiffness and cold-seeming the younger contrasted ease, assurance and élan. Where the Lord Gordon made few friends and no intimates, his brother was the born leader of men, the gay companion. One was a serious man who gloomed and brooded, the other a mirror of fashion, who laughed and lived and loved, and flourished exceedingly. Both were tall and well-made, but where one was merely dourly fine-featured, the other was wickedly handsome. And one was the heir of Gordon—but the other the apple of Huntly's eye.

As the newcomers came pounding up, then, out of a noticeably silent company John of Findlater abruptly waved demonstrative greeting.

"Welcome, brother!" he called heartily. "It does me good to see your sober face again, I vow—a surprise as it is. I jaloused you would be safely down amongst your Hamiltons in Clydesdale, by this!"

Perhaps a touchy man might have sensed a hint of a taunt in that—for the Lord Gordon's wife was daughter to the old Duke of Chatelherault, head of the House of Hamilton, and close to the throne. Also, George Gordon was known to be less of a warrior than his brother, than any of his brothers. Anyway, he spoke shortly.

"Yourself, I had heard that you were to be warded in Stirling Castle, by the Queen's command!"

"By the Bastard's command, you mean!" the other amended. "You would not have a son of our father pay heed to such, would you?"

"I would not have her Grace's authority flouted, by the Lord James . . . nor yet by yourself, John." That was stiffly and deliberately said. "Where do you travel with such array?" And his brows lifted to survey the company with seeming distaste.

"We go about . . . about my father's business!" Findlater announced irreverently.

"I take leave to doubt it. I have come straight from Strathbogie, where word was brought me that you were at large and assembling a tail in these hills. Our father knew nothing of it."

"It could be for his business and benefit, nevertheless, man—could it not? I hear that he assembles the clan at Strathbogie, himself. For a like purpose that I ride with these, I warrant!"

"But you are not riding to Strathbogie to join him!"

"In due course, brother, perhaps—in due course. Meantime, I have one or two ploys of my own to attend to—all for the good of the cause, I assure you."

"Whose cause?" Lord Gordon asked, flatly.

"Yours and mine, George. Gordon's cause. Huntly's cause. Scotland's cause. Would you doubt that?"

"I would, yes. In your own cause, I can well believe—and in none other's! In Huntly's name, I command that you repair to Strathbogie Castle forthwith!"

There was a shocked silence, with only the restless pawing of horses to break it. Just as the tension mounted to the insupportable, Sir John spoke, and softly. "I thank you—no, George. I cannot accept your word as Huntly's. Moreover, I think that I know my father's mind better than do you. We ride on."

A ripple of sound, as breaths were released, ran through the waiting ranks of horsemen. The Lord Gordon heard it, recognised its temper, and knew that with this lawless fringe of the clan he could avail nothing against his brother. He shifted his stance heavily.

"Is that Balruary I see at your back?" he demanded. "Huntly awaits him in Strathbogie—less than patiently!"

"Myself it is, Seorus Og—and unwillingly so," Patrick began. "I am . . ."

Findlater interrupted him. "Balruary prefers to ride with us rather than to hasten to Strathbogie . . . and I don't know that I can find it in me to blame him overmuch!" That was added with a smile and a faint backward jerk of the head in the direction of Mary Mackintosh. "I have no doubt that you will understand the situation, George?"

101

"Not so. Findlater it is that holds my charge, the Queen's charge to me—Mistress Mackintosh. . . ."

"Silence! In God's name—will you bicker and bandy words with Huntly's sons!" Sir John cried, in a noble fury. "Keep your tongue between your teeth, Balruary, when your betters speak!" Plain talking, indeed.

A menacing growl of approval rose from a hundred throats. Patrick was realist enough, and clansman enough, to do as he was thus forcefully bid; the authority of the clan must be upheld.

No doubt the Lord Gordon acknowledged a similar pre-occupation, for he did not pursue the matter, though he looked searchingly from Patrick and the girl to his brother. "Then you choose to go your own way, John—against the command that I have put on you?" he asked, heavily.

"I prefer my own interpretation of our father's wishes."

"Does that include an attack upon her Grace's person, by any chance?"

"Her person—no, only on her Grace's gaolers and their jackals."

"With this . . . this riff-raff?"

"This riff-raff holds harder smiters than most of your low-country levies, George—and this is just a beginning. We ride to meet Farquhar Shaw and his tail, from Strathaven."

"That freebooter! Nice allies for the House of Gordon!"

"But sharp blades all, man—and practised! I'd liefer lead such than all the hirelings of the Protestant lords—God scourge them! And a parcel of Ballindalloch Grants will be awaiting me in the Cabrach."

"Would you, Huntly's son, lead half the vagabonds and broken men of the North?" the elder brother charged.

"I would indeed—so long as they aid me rid the North of worse men than they!"

The Lord Gordon sighed. "I cannot commend your judgment, nor your taste . . . nor yet your loyalty," he said slowly.

"I do not ask you to, brother. All these are my own! All I ask is that you no longer delay our passage. I have a tryst with Farquhar Shaw." Sir John smiled brilliantly. "And you would not deny me opportunity to teach a lesson in good manners to such as he?"

The other stared at the reins in his hands. "I keep that tryst with you then, John, I think," he said.

Findlater turned his horse's head away. "As you will," he shrugged, and dug in his spurs. As the augmented cohort moved off, Patrick found the Lord Gordon riding at his side, his cold eye warning back the presumptuous who might press too close. Gravely he doffed his bonnet to Mary Mackintosh.

At his back, his standard-bearer and four kilted stalwarts formed up, looking notably respectable in this company.

VIII

FOR a space, John of Findlater led the way at a pace that precluded any further discussion or comment, heading southwards into the welter of brown hills that were the outposts of the mighty Monadh Ruadh. The steeply lifting heather brought them at length to a walk. They made a considerably less compact party now, naturally.

The Lord Gordon kept close to Patrick, however, with his escort near at hand—and it was noticeable that, dispersed as pace and terrain might dictate, there was always an unbroken ring of riders around this central group. They could hardly fail to perceive the fact.

George Gordon, looking about him, made no comment. Instead, he glanced along past Patrick. "I do not know the lady, I think—but did I hear the name of Mackintosh?" he asked.

"Lauchlan Mor's daughter—the Captain of Clan Chattan," he was told. "And one of the Queen's ladies."

"Ah!—Ma'am, you have a namely father."

"And you, sir, a scoundrelly brother!" The girl's first remark for some time evinced no great softening of attitude.

Lord Gordon saying nothing to that, Patrick hastily explained that the Queen had charged him with the task, the privilege, of delivering Mistress Mackintosh home to Moy. This he had been doing when John's caterans fell upon them. But now the same John would not let them go on, save under his own guardianship, under the pretext that she would be dangered.

"Dangered!" Mary cried. "When, Heaven knows, the greatest danger I run is from himself! The man is a satyr!"

Her two companions kept their regard on the skyline ever rising before them.

"Mistress Mackintosh lifted me out of Aberdeen Tolbooth—

with the Queen's privy connivance. The Lord James had me thrown therein." Patrick went on, in somewhat stilted fashion, when the other man made no comment. "She could no longer remain at Court—the lords would have paid her in but crooked coin. . . ."

"Mary—the Queen? She suffers no hurt?" the young Chief interrupted. "Her brother will work no hurt on her, out of this?" It was not difficult to perceive where the Lord Gordon's concern lay.

Patrick shrugged. "I cannot say. It was to look like the act of Mistress Mackintosh alone."

"James Stewart has the nose of a staghound—he will sniff it out! Her Grace should not involve herself in difficulties thus, over small matters—there are large enough thronging her, as God's my witness! Will she never learn . . . ?"

Nettled, Patrick frowned. "Do you call it a small matter for Huntly's envoy to be thrown into the Tolbooth, the common gaol, when the Queen just bid him God-speed?"

"Tush man—in the affairs of the realm, that is a mere flea-bite, a trifle, not to be measured against the dire troubles that shake the State." George Gordon dismissed any such incident with a stiff wave of his hand. "These things are of no import. Individuals such as yourself, Patrick MacRuary, or such as myself either, count for nothing in this crutch of affairs." The man's heavy deliberate voice was as near to passionate as the other had ever heard it. "The throne itself is in direst danger, and with it our whole land. Elizabeth spins her spider's-web of gold in every corner of the kingdom, jerking her puppets to dance to her treacherous tune. . . ."

"And her nuncio, Sir Nevil Cleavely, sits in your father's hall!"

"I know it—and grieve for it. But that is open, and known of men—and Huntly is a fly old in the ways of spiders. Whereas James Stewart and Morton and Lethington and the rest take English gold, privily. Elizabeth, a bastard herself before God and His Church, would see no ill in Scotland's Bastard on his sister's throne . . . for a little . . . and in *her* purse! Cecil sees Scotland a vassal, and his Gloriana on a double-throne—the Protestant Queen! And the Protestant lords will play her game . . . if paid high enough."

The younger man shook an unhappy head. "Here is damnable treachery—beyond belief. Though there is little that I would disbelieve of James Stewart. But . . . how does all this concern us? Where come we into it?"

"Have you no wits, man? Embroil the Queen in any sort of armed clash, and Mary Stewart will be the first to fall! The Bastard will see to that—it is what he works and plots for. To attack her Grace's train now, will be to play into James Stewart's hands . . . and sign his sister's death-warrant!"

"*Dhia!* They would not dare . . . ?"

"They would dare more than that. When the prize glitters thus bright, what is a young woman's life to stand in their way? It has to be done with a semblance of decency, with a clash of arms, and Mary ever impetuous. And if the blame can be laid at the door of the House of Gordon—how excellently convenient!"

"I cannot believe it!" That was Mary Mackintosh, staring over at the speaker. "Even the Lord James would not be so monstrous."

"Think you so, ma'am? Know you not that the same man sought to bribe the bishops to swear that they had witnessed the secret marriage of King Jamie to the Lady Margaret Erskine, his mother, *before* the union with Mary of Guise—thus making our Queen a bastard and himself legitimate and the true king? And when that ploy failed, he concocted a new one, traducing further his own mother by having it said that she had lied about his birth, that his father was not the King but his natural brother, James Earl of Moray, and that therefore Mary was not his sister—all so that he could wed her, and thus gain the Crown Matrimonial! That is James Stewart for you!"

Shocked into silence, the girl shook her head, as from away ahead and above, a voice came down to them, hailing:

"Can I urge you to ride less slow, brother? We have still a long way to go."

The Lord Gordon gave no sign that he had heard.

106

"He is ill-pleased that we should be talking, I think," Patrick mentioned. "Can you not tell him what you have told us, Seorus Og—dissuade him from his intentions against the Queen's train?"

"That is why I am here—why I ride with him thus. But first I would hear from *you*. What is your word from the Queen to Huntly?"

The younger man looked troubled. "That I have refused to tell to your brother—and for the same reason I may not tell you, Seorus Og. I am the Chief's envoy in this. . . ."

"Think you I know not my father's message, man? I hope . . . I hope 'fore God that the Queen would have none of his offers?"

Patrick bit his lip. "Huntly is my Chief . . ." he began, doggedly.

"God's grace—are you still in this pother of loyalties! Have you not learned yet to judge between right and wrong, between your Queen and all others soever—Chief or none!"

"Thrice, in my hearing, he swore his true service to the Queen's Grace," Mary Mackintosh asserted, from Patrick's other side.

"Yes. But . . . see you, I would do no disservice to the Queen. I . . . I greatly admire her. But the clan must be served, too. . . ."

"Think you *I* forget the clan?" the young Chief charged him. "I seek to save it from being crushed by the Bastard . . . and those who would gladly join him in the work. And many there are, would bring Gordon low if they could." And he glanced sidelong at the girl. But only for a moment. "Tell me—does the Queen come to Strathbogie?"

"No," Patrick said, and sighed—his decision taken at last. "No—the Lord James takes her north today . . . and they travel by Darnaway and the Laigh."

"Ha!" the other cried, and then his lips pursed for a moment. "Darnaway! That means the Earldom for him!" For a space they rode unspeaking. Then he asked. "Does John know of this?"

"No. Else would he ride thus into the hills? Best that he does not know. Though he will learn, soon enough."

"Yes. You are right. Today, you say? She will be on her way now, then. You do not know where she purposes to lodge, this night?"

"No. I do not think the Queen purposes anything in it. It is her brother that makes the decisions."

"Yes, yes. But if we but knew . . ."

They had at last reached the summit of the saddle, and the great spread of rolling watershed lay before them backed by the towering mountains. John Gordon was waiting for them, with ill-concealed impatience.

"We must make better speed than this," he asserted, shortly. "If you would ride with me, George—and you, Balruary— you must stir up your beasts. I have seen Mistress Mary hawking at Falkland, and know that she can ride passing well." He raised his brows, glancing significantly at Willie Gordon and his brother. "We shall keep together!"

Thereafter, the trio found themselves hemmed in closely together with Lord Gordon's little escort, the shaggy mounts of the caterans almost jostling their own. There was little opportunity for sustained talk, very definitely.

There was nothing to prevent them thinking, however, and Patrick for one did not fail to do so. Actually, he had taken his all-important decision beforehand, but now he had time to acknowledge it to himself, and to consider its implications. He had come to the conclusion that George Gordon probably had the rights of it; a man's first loyalty was to his Queen and his country, with his clan but second . . . more especially when that Queen was the lovely, gallant, and unfortunate Mary Stewart. But did service to Queen Mary necessarily conflict with service to his clan? George Gordon did not seem to think so. Was not the young Chief's policy better for Gordon than was his father's? Did he not display more chiefly, more praiseworthy and responsible qualities in this business than did Huntly himself? Could a good Gordon not better serve his clan by supporting the Lord Gordon, in his efforts to save the Queen, to save Scotland, and therefore to save Clan Gordon itself? Patrick reckoned that he might.

But having picked their way across the watershed's sodden

108

hags and streams innumerable, and thereafter started to pound down the long slope towards the Deveron valley, the next in that great system of north-south rivers, against the grain of which they travelled, a different kind of thought began to preoccupy the man's mind, diverting his consideration from the abstract problem of loyalties to the more immediate question of topography. Down there the land lay under spreading woodland of birch and pine, a wide coverlet of trees that happed the valley floor and reached far up the further hill-slopes. Though it stretched away to south and west of their route to Lynebain, an outlier of it all reached over to this side of the strath, and through its constriction they must pass. Down towards the half-mile black and gold belt of it they were now heading.

Patrick urged his mount over, till his knee was touching George Gordon's. "Look," he jerked, as low-voiced as he might. "Here is our opportunity. A break for it, in yonder trees. Will you aid us?"

The other glanced from the land to the man at his side, keenly. "Aid you to what, Patrick?"

"To do my duty to the Queen. To get Mary Mackintosh out of Findlater's grasp. To take her to Moy."

The Lord Gordon, with another glance over the landscape, nodded briefly. "I am not concerned for your Mary Mackintosh—'tis Mary of Scotland I serve. I will aid your Mary, if you will aid mine."

"Yes," Patrick agreed. "I am the Queen's man, too . . . as well as Gordon's."

Quickly his companion scanned his face. "Good. Then here is what you must do—once free of this coil. Rouse the hill clans, in my name—such as you can reach quickly. Grants, Shaws, Frasers—yes, and Clan Chattan too; Mackintoshes and Macphersons. Bring them down to Inverness, in the name of George Gordon, Sheriff of Inverness. See—take my ring. 'Tis known."

"I have Huntly's own ring, yet. How shall I return it to your father?"

"I shall do that for you. Give it to me, in exchange. I shall do what I can with my father, and with the low country. In a sennight—no, in ten days, I shall be awaiting you, outside Inverness. At Fraser of Dalchoin's house. You have it? In ten days, at Dalchoin . . . with as many Highlandmen as you can raise?"

"I have it, yes. What are they for, these men, Seorus Og?"

"To save the Crown of Scotland," he answered simply, but with the proud finality that he no more lacked than did his father and brother.

With that Patrick had to be content. He nodded. "I will do what I can. But . . . my message for Huntly?"

"I will carry it—with the ring."

A stretch of bog forced them apart a little, and the first of the trees were near when they could speak together again. Patrick held out Huntly's ring.

"Not a deal to tell," he panted. "The Queen will have none of your brother, as husband. She is angered at the notion."

The other muttered something to himself.

"But she is not against Gordon. She wills us no ill. But she is sore held by her brother. She will consider the rest—but has but little power to act. And the Lord James's answer, you know."

"Aye. I will tell my father that—and of your . . . difficulties. I hope . . . I pray that he may heed me—that I can save himself, and Gordon, from his pride and from my brother's folly. Now—what is your plan?"

"This. The track through this wood is narrow. They cannot keep us surrounded. Two abreast in places—no more. You and your people in front and behind us—separating us from these others. We break away, into the trees. You hold back pursuit for a little. Will you do that?"

"Yes. Good. You are well horsed. Mistress Mackintosh, too. You can outpace all but John himself, once across Deveron. Tell her. I'll give the word to my people."

So, with the outposts of the dark twisted Scots pines already past, Patrick dropped back a little to the girl's side, while George Gordon beckoned up his standard-bearer.

"We plan an escape. In those trees," he told her.

"Yes. I heard a word, here and there."

"You will take the hazard?"

"I will hazard anything, to escape John Gordon!"

"Yes. Be ready then to plunge into the trees when I give word. There is a narrow place I know of—a burn. Cover your face with your cloak. The branches . . ."

Already the track was narrowing. Findlater's horsemen on either side of them were being pressed in, forced into file. The column lengthened, and its pace dropped. More and more riders fell into position between Sir John at the head of the line, and his prisoners. Looking about him, Patrick could see no sign of Black Ewan and the Mackintosh gillie.

George Gordon turned, and nodded his head. The standard-bearer allowed himself to be passed, so that now the prisoners were separated from immediate contact with Findlater's men.

The woodland on either side was not really dense in the growth of its trees; it was the russet-turning junipers that formed a maze that would swallow up the wayfarer in a few green yards. Watching its every stretch and glade, Patrick sought to recollect. He had hunted through here with Gordon of Lesmurdie. . . .

The track they followed, twisting suddenly around a thrusting birch knoll, immediately they were at an abrupt little slope with a burn at its foot, the track rising again beyond and swinging away out of sight in broken ground.

They had come upon his selected spot more quickly than Patrick had anticipated. He gestured to the group behind, and then shouted a word to Lord Gordon in front, already splashing across the burn.

To the girl he jerked. "Now! Follow me!"

As his own horse's hooves raised fountains in the water, he slewed the brute's head round to the left, and kicked it into livelier speed, plunging on up the narrow stream. Behind him he heard Mary doing likewise, and still further back a commotion broke out—shouts and the scrape and slither of hooves. Ahead, George Gordon pounded on up the further slope, after the van. Patrick wasted no more attention on what was going on elsewhere. The burn made but poor going, its bed alternating rough stones with pockets of mud. The first passable

111

opening out of it, through the prickly screen of the junipers, he took. Mary Mackintosh, her face set, was just at his back, putting her beast to the little bank. She waved him on.

"Watch your face in these bushes," he cried. "Too bonny it is, to spoil!"

He won a fleeting smile for that, as he turned to face the thickets.

The next ten minutes or so were not pleasant. Once off the track, that woodland was a nightmare for horses and riders. It was not only the junipers, though their bristling branches were like a legion of scorpions; the lowermost boughs of pines and birches were a constant menace, and if less all-prevailing were the more dangerous; the ground too was little more than a succession of pitfalls—fallen trees, exposed roots, ant-hills, rabbit-holes, and bog-filled hollows. Anything more than a walking pace would have been disastrous, indeed impossible. The horses had to be left to pick their own unwilling way; garrons would have been better here, with their sure broad feet. Bent low, an arm across his already scratched and bleeding face, Patrick ploughed on.

At least, it would be as bad for the pursuit—they had that consolation. Whether there was indeed any pursuit, as yet, they could not tell. With Sir John Gordon so far ahead of the scene of trouble, delay could be hoped for. . . .

Anyway, Patrick soon had given up concerning himself with what might be going on behind—to keep moving forward occupying all his capacities. Very soon he was dismounted—though he urged the young woman to remain in the saddle as long as possible, thinking of her wide and flowing skirts.

Poor Mary was having a rough time of it—though she nowise held her companion back. And she made no complaint.

They found deer-paths, which were a slight easement to their going, but they were erratic and wandersome. Now and again an aisle or glade opened in approximately the right direction. But by and large, they had to battle their way. Slow weary work.

They found a burn presently, which though it swung away

112

further to the right than Patrick would have wished, did better for them than they had reason to expect, for alongside it a well-defined deer-path ran, providing easier going than they had found hitherto. Sooner than they had anticipated the trees thinned before them, and their stream led them out into green haughland, with the river—the Deveron—coiling perhaps four hundred yards ahead. Cattle dotted that level meadow—moving cattle, moving towards them from the northwards. Even as the girl began to ask if they were safe, to disbelieve that they could be free of Findlater so readily, her companion, nodding agreement, perceived the significance of those drifting cattle. Urging horse forward, he peered round a spur of the trees, up-haugh. Yes—up there, the stirks were moving faster, bunching, tails in the air. And behind them, at no great distance, came mounted men. Findlater presumably knew the wood too, and had sent a party to stop the gap.

Patrick brought his open hand down hard on his mount's rump.

Down across the greensward they thundered. The horsemen were something under half a mile away, and the river half that. But the chase could ride diagonally to their own course—cut a corner. The man clung to the burnside. He did not remember how fordable was the Deveron up here, though in these upper reaches it ought not to be a serious barrier, save in spate. But if there was anywhere that shallows might be looked for, it was just below the inflow of a tributary, where wrack and silt ever tended to form a natural bar. They could but hope. . . .

The grassland sank to the river with only a low bank—though at the other side the ground rose steeply with trees almost to the water's edge. As the fugitives pounded up it was to find a floor of green-brown pebbles beneath the amber peat-stained water, shelving out of sight at the far side. Just below the confluence of the burn, this pebble strand seemed to reach out farther—but how far could not be descried. Reining up, Patrick cast his urgent glance upstream and down. "Go on—oh, go on!" the girl cried, coming up. She even passed him, heading her beast right into the water. "We cannot wait."

113

The man caught a glimpse, over his shoulder, of the horse-men, perhaps a dozen strong, no more than three hundred yards away, having sliced off a considerable angle. He found himself actually following the girl across, in her shower of spray.

Deveron was roughly thirty yards wide at this point, and they were more than halfway over before the horses began to go deeper than their knees. But thereafter the bed dropped sharply. A few yards more, and Mary's horse stopped, trem-bling, with the water up to its belly, and still eight or nine yards to cover to the steep bank beyond. Patrick, coming up on her right, and lashing his bay on cried:

"No good. Could not climb out there. Further down." And he pointed to where, about twenty-five yards downstream the opposite bank obviously shelved at a lesser angle. "Swim for it."

Under his flailing hand the bay plunged on—and he knew the stoun of cold water as the river-bed dropped away and the flood surged up round his waist. But head up, neck outstretched, his steed was swimming gamely, swinging more and more downstream.

Patrick glanced round. Mary Mackintosh was beating her mount with small clenched fists, and even as he looked, it reluctantly followed the bay's lead. He saw the girl's cloak and skirts billow up and out on the water, and the physical shock reflect on her face as the chill struck through her. But her resolution was equally discernable thereon.

"Up the Mackintoshes!" he called, encouragingly.

Facing front again, he steered his beast for the shelving bank where the red earth offered a possible outlet. The pursuit was close at hand now, shouting. Without any close inspec-tion, he gained the impression that Sir John Gordon was not amongst them—and found no fault with that.

With a flood of relief he felt the brute under him strike solid ground, scramble, slither, and then secure a grip.

As the bay scrambled out, Patrick, turning to a cry, checked it violently. The girl's horse was not answering her left-hand drag on its reins. It was even veering away out towards mid-channel, tug as Mary would. In a moment she would be swept past.

The man acted. Flinging himself over, he bent to make a grab at the reins. He failed to reach them; they were too low for him. Even as he missed them, he recognised all that now remained. Convulsively gripping his saddle with his knees, almost in the same movement he jerked himself upright again, reached over at farthest stretch, and grasped the young woman around her middle, his right hand sinking into her armpit. And exerting all his strength, he lifted her off her horse, for the second time in twenty-four hours, and to him. Part in the water, part on his bay horse, clinging to man and beast, Mary remained suspended while her own mount swept on downstream.

Hoisting her somehow, anyhow, up before him, Patrick kicked his steed once more into motion. Trembling, snorting, and cascading water, it climbed out on to dry land, a noble brute.

Merciless, and without backward glance, Patrick put the creature slantwise to the hillside.

Mary Mackintosh, who might have been forgiven some distraction, maintained her wits about her, and even as she improved on her precarious position in front of the man and sought some rearrangement of her soaking draperies, was peering round and downhill, to observe the pursuit the while.

"He is not there," she panted—and there was no need to ask of whom she spoke. "They are crossing, already—the first are in the water."

"Any saddle-horses—or all garrons?" he demanded.

"Garrons, I think—all of them."

"Good. We still have a chance, then. This is a good beast."

Beyond the first crest of the rise, the ground dipped a little, in birches and bracken, and then lifted again in a great braeface. And threading the dip, a broad track ran—the Cabrach-Glass road. It required only a moment for Patrick to decide on their course. For a few precious moments they would be out of sight. The road would give the advantage to their bay's long legs, rough hill to the pursuit's garrons. The road for them meantime, then—and southwards, since northwards they would be expected to head; also, only three miles north lay Mill of Lynebain, where Findlater was trysted to meet Farquhar Shaw and his ruffians.

Left-handed then, he pulled, and swishing down through the brackens, reached the hard-beaten track. As the beast stretched its legs into a full gallop, the man grinned into the red blown hair that covered his face. This was better—the excellent sensation of power and movement. "Brave brute!" he cried. "We'll show them our heels, now. Once round this bend . . . they will not see us." He had to splutter out sundry strands of hair to enunciate that.

The owner of the inconvenient tresses clung to him frankly, keeping her awkward and uncomfortable seat with difficulty. But after a few bouncing yards of it, at this pace, her grip on the man suddenly tightened. With a convulsive heave, within his arms, she jerked and kicked aside her sodden cloying skirts, threw up her left leg right over the horse's arching neck and streaming mane, to land astride its withers, facing full front. An agile and effective performance.

Patrick was not so much preoccupied with flight as to fail to note and appreciate the revelation of a deal of long and shapely limb, as well as the efficacy of the move.

"That is better," she asserted, making the necessary attempt to pull and smooth down her skirts on either side—without much success.

"Much," he agreed earnestly, and took a good manly grip of her.

That was a winding road, inevitably, following the contours of the timbered hillside. The first sizeable bend was no more than a hundred yards from where they joined it, and as they thudded round the man looked over his shoulder. There was no sign of riders as yet. That meant the chase would be at a loss when they surmounted the slope—until they traced new hoof-marks on the sand of the road, they would not know which way their quarry had gone, left, right or straight on up. That ought to give them vital extra seconds.

How long it took the pursuit to discover their line of flight, the fugitives never knew. For the drove road continued to turn and twist through hanging woods, with no field of view, back nor front—and for that extent at least, they continued to have the hillside to themselves. And the bay kept up a gallant pace.

At the summit of something of a shoulder they looked back, and saw only the woods. Thankfully, they headed into the valley beyond.

IX

"IF I was your own self I would have off half the clothes you've got about you," Patrick Gordon observed judiciously. He avoided her eye, however, as he said it, and concentrated on his task of seeking to wring out the last drops of Deveron from her heavy travelling cloak. "I would so."

"Would you, indeed!"

"I would. The lower, er, reaches, anyhow. They are no good to you, at all. They are wet. They are muddy. They drag in the heather. They catch on bushes. They must be a weight to carry."

"Am I complaining, sir?"

"Not by word. But you are looking weary and pale. Peaked is the word, I think. It becomes you ill. . . ."

"Then you need not look at me!"

"That is so. But that will not make the heather any kinder to all your skirts. By the time that you get to Moy, I warrant you'll be worth the looking at! You'll be in tatters, i' faith, from the middle down!"

This exalting of the issue to the serious plane of appearance and visual impression, had its effect. Mary's brow furrowed—but more thoughtfully. "Nonsense," she said, but without conviction. "How long is it going to take us to reach Moy?"

He shrugged. "It is thirty or forty miles from here to Moy, as the eagle flies—over the roof of Scotland. But we are no eagles. And if I know John Gordon, all the strath of Spey that lies between will be raised against us. If we can make Moy in twice forty miles, myself I shall be pleasantly surprised. And that over some of the roughest country in the kingdom."

Mary Mackintosh was hill-woman enough to know what that meant. She did not argue any more, but inclined her head calmly, deliberately meeting his eye. "You will wait here then—while I go behind yonder boulder," she said. "And not a move out of you, Patrick Gordon!"

"Just so, indeed," he agreed, grinning. "What if we are beset?"

"Then you will fight like a lion for my honour—at a respectable distance, sir! And forget that you are a Gordon!" That last she threw back scurrilously, as she made for the cover of a large granite outcrop, her gown and petticoats upheld above the knee-high heather.

They were in a hollow, high on the broad purple breast of Corriehabbie, the highest of the Glen Fiddich hills, and nothing more earthbound than one of Patrick's eagles was likely to beset them there, indeed. Below them the land sank away in vast heather waves and folds to the tree-level and the scattered woods of lower Glen Fiddich, glooming in lilac shadow where the sinking sun could not reach. Of man and his small affairs, only the one sign was traceable in all that far-flung panorama—the shieling above the glen-floor where the fugitives had recently obtained from a no doubt wondering Farquharson herdsman and his two sons a supply of oatmeal and half a haunch of cold venison, the tartan of a Gordon laird providing sufficient warranty, and Highland manners debarring unseemly questions.

They had travelled far and fairly fast that sun-filled afternoon, though for the last hour they had been leading the horse, in pity. Now, near the two-thousand-foot level, they could relax pace and vigilance to some extent. John Gordon, however angry, was unlikely to be able to detach sufficient men to comb these fastnesses for them. And they had seen no horsemen since Deveron.

That was all right for the time being. But as sure as night followed day, Findlater would not lie down under this affront to his pride. Every inhabited glen presently would be alerted to watch for them—and with the manpower of the clan and its septs so largely assembled at Strathbogie Castle, a freer hand would be offered to the caterans and broken men that he was using, especially when acting in the name of Huntly's favourite son. It behoved them, then, to press on before the glens were effectively raised against them.

But the horse was all but foundered, and the girl was

showing her fatigue. A balance must be struck. If Patrick had been a little less leaden-eyed and weary himself, he might have been able to see where to strike it, more clearly.

Not that there was anything somnolent or heavy-eyed about his reaction to the sight of Mary Mackintosh, when she emerged from behind her rock. Where a slightly drooping and bedraggled court lady had disappeared, a lissom shapely daughter of the heather replaced her. Gone—or at least, over a bare arm, were the fine stuff gown of olive green, and certain of the multiple petticoats that fashion demanded, also a pair of silken hose, sadly torn and stained. In place of them all she wore simply her shift, sleeveless, low-necked and clinging frankly to her well-turned body, and her outer petticoat of saffron linen, hitched up to knee-height and tied round the waist, while draped over her white shoulders to form a very inadequate plaid was what apparently was another petticoat torn down the middle. To even formally mask a prominent and entirely delectable bosom, this latter would have to be kept continuously held in place, as now. Her red hair was gathered up and tied in an improvised snood, and her legs and arms were bare. Fortunately her shoes were of good stout tanned leather, for travelling. The general impression was effective, practical, and arresting. Mary Mackintosh, in her attempts to meet the claims of hard circumstance had not had entirely to outrage all claims of the eye. Eye-catching she was, indeed.

The man's breath caught, as well as his eye. "God is good!" he observed, somewhat thickly, but with conviction. "I . . . ah . . . umm."

"Don't mutter! And don't stare," she said. "There is nothing to stare at." Which, all things considered, might have been contested—especially when she had taken all of five minutes, in practical feminine fashion, to assure herself that whatever must be exposed, was so to the best advantage.

"No," he agreed, vaguely. "That is, yes. Quite. At least, you are less pale!"

She had the grace to flush still further at that.

He took the bundle of mud-stained finery from her, for

120

the horse to carry. Then he peeled off his own green tartan doublet. "This will help, when it gets colder," he suggested.

"And you?"

"I shall wear your heavy cloak."

"Thank you, Patrick," she said, then, in a more normal voice, and let him help her into the doublet—the same that she had mended in the Provost's garden. It fitted her none so ill, its excess at the back and shoulders compensating for its dearth at the front.

With the graceful peak of Corriehabbie towering on the left and picked out in the golden glory of the dying sun, they resumed their climb.

Through all the shadowy hills, over ridge after ridge they went, and in time even the last warm glow of the sunset was lost to them, and they walked on in the grey half-light, stumbling, weary. For a long while they had been silent, the man working out their further course across a hostile land, the girl thinking her own thoughts. But when presently, Patrick began to note his companion's increasing exhaustion, he found his tongue again. He told her that he would have wished to take her to his own Balruary, that was only six or seven miles further, where his mother would comfort her. But that would be dangerous—Balruary would be the very place where Findlater would look for them. A pity, for he would like her to meet his lady mother.

Mary's heavy eyes lightened with some interest. "Ah, yes— your mother. Have I not heard tell of your mother, Patrick? Is she not a great beauty? Anna Mackintosh, of Dalnavert, said . . ."

"She was, maybe—when she was younger. My father thought it—and so did Huntly. He would have wed her, I have heard— but she chose my father. My grandsire was an angry man— a heather laird like himself for good-son when she might have had the Cock o' the North! Huntly has a fondness for her still, I think. She is dark and tiny. . . ." Sidelong, he glanced at his companion. "Myself, now—I prefer a more strapping wench, with, shall we say, reddish hair . . . and freckles!"

121

"Like Anna of Dalnavert!" she flashed back at him, fatigue or none.

"Damn Anna of Dalnavert!" he said, unchivalrously.

"Shame, sir! She is an excellent soul . . . if something weepy!"

"Weepy," the man nodded. "Just that. . . ."

They halted, at last, where Patrick conceived them to be safe, just within the first of the wind-swept pines above Glen Livet, where a burn sang its endless refrain to the sough of the air and the thin creak of boughs. A little dip amongst the heather and blaeberries offered them couch. The man watered and tethered the horse, and, since to light a fire was too risky, made a paste of oatmeal and cold water in a corner of one of Mary's useful petticoats, and sliced off some chunks of their cold venison. Coming back to her with these offerings, he found her crouched in a sort of stupor, from which he had to arouse her and force her to eat. She shivered once or twice as she toyed with the food, in great shudders that seemed to rack her whole body. Concerned, the man took off the cloak from his shoulders to drape it around her. But she would have none of it, pushing it back at him, and declaring that it was *his* cloak now, in fair exchange for his doublet. When he persisted, her objections even grew broken, almost tearful. Heedfully, he let the cloak lie between them on the heather, but decreed that she must eat. He all but fed her with his own hands. That she had taxed her strength and endurance to breaking-point was only too evident. A little alarmed, the man blamed himself for not having called a halt earlier.

He took a final look round, saw that the horse was secure, made his brief toilet, and giving his companion opportunity to see to hers, gazed out over the pit of the glen, out of which one or two lights were gleaming faintly. When he got back to the hollow, it was to discover the girl slumped over where she had been crouching, fast asleep in the heather. He noted the recurrent twitching tremor that ran through her every ten seconds or so. Frowning he considered her, biting his lip. Then suddenly he picked up the discarded cloak, slung it round him again, and seated himself beside her, his back against the little bank. Leaning over, and raising her limp body gently in his arms, he drew her back to him, across his thighs. She mumbled something incoherent, but did not really awake, and certainly offered no sort of resistance. Her head sunk against his shoulder, her weight a-lean on him, he pulled the cloak about them both, tucking in its folds around her bare scratched legs. Easing himself back into the equally kind embrace of the heather, Patrick held her close.

"Better?" he asked.

There was no reply. But after a minute or two she uttered a small soft grunt of such sheer animal content as to bring a smile to the man's dark face. As each tremor shook her, he held her the tighter. But soon the spasms lessened in frequency and intensity. A grateful pleasant warmth was generating between them. He could feel her breathing deepening, the heart under the firm breast that he cupped in his left hand thudding steadily.

His chin resting on her head, he stared up at the single star that winked down at him through the tufted pine branches.

He did not wish to sleep, now—though he was afraid that he was going to, any minute. Much better, much more satisfying and delightful, just to remain thus. Or—not exactly satisfying, perhaps! Full satisfaction would entail still further development. He stirred a little. But, for a weary man . . . ! Yawning, he nodded at their watching star. "See that I keep awake," he said aloud.

He began to count her heartbeats. How they went on. Suppose they did not! Suppose they were to stop, under his hand? Could they indeed keep up this endless thudding? Never miss a beat! Suppose . . . suppose . . . ?

Patrick Gordon slept, his face amongst her hair.

Many times that night he came near to the verge of wakefulness, was dimly aware of stirring, of discomfort, of cramped limbs, of searching fingers of cold. But only once did he really wake up, and that by degrees, gradually. It was very dark now, with no star to be seen, and the wind had risen with the night empty and inimical around them. Around *him* . . . Empty! It was the feeling of emptiness that fully wakened him.

123

His arms, cramped and stiff, were empty. The girl was not there. She had gone. He had not just been dreaming? She *had* been there, in his arms? Slowly, painfully, he turned a stiff and aching neck. Cramp. No—she was gone.

The man was beginning to force his sleep-drugged senses and will to do something about this, to cope with this dire problem, when he sensed movement, heard the swish of steps in the heather, coming close. And then, she was there at his back. She was standing above him, stooping—and, Glory be, inserting herself back inside the cloak, on his lap, within the circle of his arms. In she snuggled, bending her legs under her, and tucking in that cloak around them again. With a long sigh she laid her cheek against his chest once more, bare where his shirt's neck gaped open. Her breath was warm in little puffs against his skin. His grip tightened upon her. He found no words to express his feelings.

His bemused brain was still seeking to think up something apt and appropriate and adequate, when he realised that she was asleep again. Or making a very good imitation of it.

He sighed, but without real complaint. Her thigh was soft and smooth, smooth as velvet—no, satin? No, not satin, either. It was important to decide what it was as smooth as . . . but he just could not think of it. Not at the moment. A shame. A shame that it should be so scratched, thus. A shame that he must be so damnably sleepy. A shame altogether. He could have wept. . . .

He did not weep. Presently, he snored a little instead.

The grey light of dawn was already seeping through the dark pines when Patrick wakened again, this time not by degrees. The young woman was standing beside him, once more, and shaking his shoulder.

"Wake up!" she was saying. "Wake up. It is getting light. We are late."

This was so obviously true that the man required no further rousing. For all that, he made a slow business of getting on to his feet, so cold and cramped and stiff was he, in every bone.

Stretching himself gingerly, he looked about him, greyly. A

chill wind, a smirr of rain, mist caught in the tree-tops, and the barbarous hour, combined to paint a very different picture for him from that of his last conscious impression. Mary too, though she looked surprisingly, almost offensively fresh and tidy, was subdued, not meeting his eye. A silent, somewhat preoccupied pair, they decided to eat their unappetising breakfast as they went, and unloosing the horse, set off on either side of it, downhill, with a minimum of delay.

It was that sort of morning.

Down at the valley-floor, they mounted, the girl first, and making perhaps an unnecessary pother about the brevity of her skirt. Patrick of course, knew this area of Glen Livet like the palm of his hand, and so was able to avoid the dotted crofts and cot-houses, where the first columns of smoke from newly refuelled peat fires were beginning to lift, and by devious ways cross over into the parallel valley of the Avon. This was a deeper and more powerful river than the Livet, and a fording place had to be picked with care, but they crossed unnoticed and only slightly splashed, and faced the long lift of the Cromdale hills, whose rounded summits still lay lost within nightcaps of cloud.

The cloud lifted before them, however, as they climbed, and by the time that they were a mile or so up, a watery and stripling sun was pouring its level beams over the heather, casting long grotesque shadows, and glistening on the myriad spiders'-webs.

Patrick greeted its dazzle with approval, now that they were safely past the haunts of men, relaxing his grim morning sourness. "That is us, then—we are out of it," he declared, to his equally silent passenger. "Only these wild hills of Cromdale ahead. Till Spey."

She nodded.

"Did you sleep well, at all?" he asked, courteously.

"Thank you, yes." That was short.

"I thought it. You seemed fairly comfortable. And warm." At her continued silence, he shrugged. "A pity that you snore."

In front of him she jerked erect. "That . . . that is a lie, I vow, Patrick Gordon! I do not snore. I have five sisters—they

125

would soon have told me if I snored. You . . . you are insupportable!"

"Perhaps it is only when you bury your nose in somebody's chest?" he suggested helpfully. "You will not do that with your sisters. You would suffocate, belike. . . ."

"Oh!" she exclaimed, wriggling within his arms. "Let me down, off this horse! This instant."

"Not so," he said, grinning over her red head. "I have the Queen's command to take you to Moy—you recollect? Safe and sound. I intend to do so—as soon as may be. Sit you still."

Bolt upright she sat, stiff as any poker, though she was at some pains to keep her kilt-like petticoat over pink knees. But she did sit still.

The man whistled 'Cock o' the North' into her blown hair, and felt entirely masculine, effective, and satisfactory.

He was a good whistler, with a fairly extensive repertoire. By the time that he had given her 'Gillechattan's Wedding', he felt that he could hardly do more. Moreover, the hill was levelling out to high moss and watershed, where the peat-pitted going was likely to take up most of his attention.

Perhaps she was not entirely unappreciative, for presently, as their steed was negotiating a particularly involved system of tussocky grass and quaking peat-hag, she spoke carefully and not at all impetuously.

"I would not wish you to think that I am ungrateful for—for what you are doing, Patrick. Even for last night. I . . . you were kind. But it was unsuitable. Unseemly. I was tired. Not myself." She nodded her copper head, with her decision. "It must not—it *shall* not happen again."

"No?"

"No. Such measures are not proper. I have my reputation to consider."

"Reputation! On my soul, you have more than that to consider, woman! Your safety. Your health. Your comfort. And how will your reputation suffer more by being warm at night, than by merely being alone with me on this journey? Nobody is to know, save our own selves, see you. If tongues

126

must wag, they will do so, however you pass the night." He smiled. "Myself, I'd say that reputations should be dispensed with above tree-level! Do Mackintosh girls never go shieling?"

"Of course," she said. "But that is different. And I am Clan Chattan's daughter!"

"Poor lassie!"

"Tonight, we shall make . . . other arrangements, nevertheless."

"And you win your death of cold!"

She ignored that. "Where do you expect us to be, by night? How far on, think you?"

"It depends on where we decide to cross Spey. As you will know, likely, Gordon's word runs well up the strath. But it is Grant country, and the Laird of Grant himself loves not Huntly—whatever way his lower country branches may act. We might venture a call at Castle Grant. I have to speak with John the Gentle anyway, on the Lord George's behalf. If we . . ."

"No," the girl declared, firmly. "Not Castle Grant. The Laird of Grant loves not my father, either. We must not go there. Nor to any Grant house."

"I feared as much." Patrick accepted and understood only too well the situation. He had been brought up in it—the situation where clan chiefs were in a state of chronic rivalry, animosity, or outright feud with most of their neighbours, and where members of the household of one would not pass through the territories of another, much less enter his house, without the insurance of a suitably strong escort. This was normal at any time in Highland Scotland, and the more so in these days when dynastic and religious differences imposed their added stresses. "Yet I have to see Gentle John," he pointed out.

"Then see him *after* you have brought me to Moy. It is not so far to return. Our houses are only a day's journey apart—as we know to our cost! You can come back to Castle Grant. Have you not Cluny Macpherson to see, also?"

He nodded. "Very well. If Clan Chattan's daughter must avoid Grants, as well as Gordons, then we should cross

127

Strathspey at its narrowest, and by darkness if possible. But the river remains. All the ferrymen will be Grants. And they will not ply their boats by night."

"Is there nowhere where we may ford it? Or even swim?"

"Spey is not Deveron! It is wide and swift and deep. Though I do not know Strathspey as I know the country that we have passed, I fear that there is nowhere that we may cross its river, save by ferry."

"What are we to do, then? How shall we win over . . . ?"

The man had halted the bay—or rather, had accepted the beast's own halting. He dismounted. "It is more necessary that we win across this moss, meantime!" he declared, and helped her down. "But we shall master both of them yet, never fear."

For the next half-hour, then, they devoted themselves to a different problem, hopping and jumping and plowtering and floundering their circuitous way through as evil a specimen of peat-moss as either of them had ever experienced. Bogged time and again, all but marooned as frequently, forced to retrace their erratic steps with depressing regularity, they worked their way somehow across its black and emerald treachery, forcing their unhappy steed to follow them—its weight a large part of their problem. From island to tussock to crumbling peat-bank they leapt and plunged and balanced, helping and hindering each other, guiding, pulling, and apostrophising the horse, and anathematising Cromdale and everything about it whatsoever—which was hardly fair. Why it was so shunned of man was now only too evident.

By the time that they had won out of its wide maw, panting and breathless, all stiffness had gone from them, physical and conversational chill was a thing of the past, and restraint dissolved in honest sweat. But more than that resulted. The answer to the larger of their problems stared at least Patrick Gordon in the face. Pointing in a thoroughly natural if deplorably unmannerly fashion, at the young woman, he hooted his mirth. "Good grief!" he gasped, "Like that, you could walk through every clachan in Strathspey, and never be guessed as Clan Chattan's daughter!"

And that was probably true. In her bounding and scrambling, the girl's hair had worked loose from its fillet, and now hung in glorious disarray, smeared, like her flushed face, with streaks of the glutinous black peat-broth where a hurried hand had sought to restrain it. She had dispensed with the man's doublet, for ease and coolth, and had hitched her kirtle still higher out of harm's way, and, to save her shoes from being sucked away, carried them in her hand. Her legs were stained black to the knee, and her arms to the elbow. And despite— or because of—it all, her vivid eager womanhood hit the eye and the consciousness—at least, Patrick's eye and consciousness—as never before, with its pulsing elemental excellence, its glowing and shapely vitality. "You . . . you . . ." He was lost for words, and more than words.

Mary, though she did not point, was laughing too. "Look— look at yourself!" she requested, impracticably. "Was ever such a bog-bogle made out of a Gordon gentleman!"

He did not even waste a glance at his own mud-smeared dishevelment. Why should he? "I' faith—if it was not that I'd sworn to deliver you safe and sound to Moy, I'd . . . I'd . . ." He swallowed, and shook his head. "Mercy on us!"

For a moment her glance met his, bright-eyed, unveiled, candid. Then she had the mercy on him that he asked for— but did not want—and turned away. "Come," she said briefly, firmly. "Time that we were nearer to Moy. Come." And, stooping to slip on her shoes again, set off at a stout pace over the solid ground that now lifted towards the spine of the range.

At her back the man took the horse's bridle, and followed on. "*Dhia*—in such a state we could travel the breadth of the Highlands unquestioned—keeping that doublet out of sight. Down to the Spey with us, then and across at the first boat."

Perhaps they had been over-fearful, for they crossed the lowlands of wide Strathspey not only without challenge but with many a casual greeting—for it was a populous country this—and were ferried over the great river with no more questions asked than any young man escorting a personable

129

and distinctly tousled young woman might have expected. By afternoon they were high in the lonely hills to the north, that cradled Lochindorb, and before the sun was down had reached boisterous Findhorn, the fastest of all Scotland's rivers. Splashing across its bleached shallows, they turned west along the drove road on its north bank, and settled into a steady if less than eager jog-trot as the excellent and patient bay proceeded to eat up the monotonous miles. For that was all that lay between them and Moy, now—just the long and featureless miles of the upper glen of Findhorn.

Soon both man and girl slept in the saddle, her cheek jogging between his shoulder-blades, her arms around his waist.

Some unspecifiable time later, with the sunset working its miracle over the uplands, Mary Mackintosh awoke, evidently and quite unsuitably refreshed and revived, her disapproval of the afternoon seemingly forgotten. The man's admittedly somewhat owlish state and monosyllabic reactions provided her with much innocent amusement. Such is woman.

Further contrariness evidenced itself presently when, a house coming into view ahead, Patrick suggested a call for food—possibly even to borrow a garron to relieve the horse; after all, these would be Mackintoshes, presumably?

But the girl decided otherwise. She was not for entering any Mackintosh house—any more than she had been for entering a Grant or a Gordon one, previously. She was not going to be recognised—not in these circumstances. She was known, and respected, it seemed, in all this country—and intended to remain that way. She even hid her face, and sought to cover up her red hair, as they passed near the place.

Her companion was not sure whether it was her appearance, her situation, or the company that she was in, that she was so ashamed of.

Once safely out of sight of that house, she called on him to halt, and dismounting, demanded the bundle of her clothing. "Patrick Gordon," she announced, "you are very surly—in need of a sleep, I think. Go you around that bend in front, and shut your eyes. I shall wake you when I am ready for you."

"Indeed!" he said aggrievedly, and glowered at her.

"Yes. Off with you." And she shooed him away like a refractory barndoor fowl. And then, on second thoughts, she called him back, and tossed his tartan doublet to him from the bundle. "Perhaps, before you sink into slumber, you had better clean your*self* up," she suggested. "We are getting into respectable country, now! But . . . go well round that bend in the river." She was very much Clan Chattan's daughter, again.

The man went off, muttering.

Tired as he was, he did not go more than a yard or so around that bend ahead—far enough it was at a hundred-and-fifty yards or so. And there he left the horse to graze, and doffing his shirt and rolling up the legs of his trews, moved down to the waterside to make his ablutions. At the edge he considered. It was not much of a bend that the river took. If he was to wade out a bit, and do his washing in mid-stream, she could not complain, could she? Wasn't the water cleanest there? And him not contravening any instructions so high-handedly given! Well, then.

Out into mid-Findhorn he waded, finding the stones distinctly uncomfortable underfoot, and intent on finding exactly the best place for a man to wash a great deal of peat-mud from his person. He found an excellent spot—and it so happened that when he glanced downstream, it was to perceive round the curve of the bank, a white figure splashing about in rather deeper water beyond. He was lost in admiration for the thoroughness of her lavation. Busily he went to work to give himself a suitably meticulous scrubbing—according to orders. A pity to be outdone in cleanliness.

The fortunate part of it was, how little the man suffered from leaden eyelids and general lassitude, by the time that he waded back to the bank. The tonic effects of cold water, no doubt!

When, presently, she rejoined him, Mary Mackintosh was once again one of the Queen's ladies, gracious, assured, and just a little remote, gowned, cloaked, with even her hair disciplined. Patrick marvelled anew at woman's ability to preen and furbish herself in unlikely circumstances—though, all

131

things considered, he preferred her as she had been. At least, he noted as he aided her to mount, she had not returned to her tattered hosiery.

Whether or not she had observed him at his search for cleanliness in mid-stream, she did not say. Her only remark was the formal comment that he seemed to have found something better to do than to snatch the wink of sleep that she had advised.

He took that to refer to his own improved appearance, not unnaturally.

They rode on into the deepening shadows.

The land of the Monadh Liath, the Grey Mountains, was grey indeed, stark and colourless under the veil of early night, when at long last the travellers reached the dull pewter mirror of Loch Moy within the guardian circle of its brooding hills. A great barking of dogs greeted them, and then men emerged from the doors of the many houses that fringed the loch-shore. Mary's clear voice uplifted to call reassurance to all, to be drowned by a roar from a great giant of a man who came long-strided from the house nearest to the stone jetty that thrust out into the water.

"*Mairi, mo bhain-tighearn*—by God's grace, is it yourself! Mary of Moy, my little red calf, my trout, my dove! Where, in the name of all the blessed saints, have you been? We have been in the crutch of sorrow. . . ."

"Hush you, Angus the Boat—you are like a bull bellowing!" the girl cried. "Finely comfortable you've been in your sorrow, I swear, and your mouth still full!"

Somebody appeared with a flaming torch of bog-pine, which Angus the Boat promptly grabbed and held high. "Och, hear you that—and us scarce able to swallow our meat for thinking of you and you lost to us! Those Gordon scoundrels . . ."

"How did you know . . . ? Why did you think me lost? Why did you worry? I was not expecting to be home for days yet. What do you know about the Gordons . . . ?"

The big man did not have to answer all that. Out from a further house two men came running, rubbing the sleep from their eyes, Black Ewan Gordon and Donald Gorm Mackintosh, to throw themselves like ill-trained, jealous and affectionate hounds upon the riders—at least, on such parts of them as they could reach. Loud-tongued incoherences filled the night.

When order and intelligence could be won from the welter of words and emotion, it transpired that the two gillies had arrived at Moy that same afternoon, bringing with them anxiety, despondency, and some shame. At the upheaval in the wood at Deveronside, when their principals had made their dash for freedom, their two attendants, well to the rear, had found a good-going fight in progress, and no interest or attention being paid to themselves. Ewan had been for joining in, apparently, on principle, but Donald had wisely persuaded him otherwise, and they had slipped into the thickets themselves, unheeded, there to lie low until the storm was past. Then they had made their way through the wood northwards—for in that direction lay Moy—and in due course reached the Deveron, found the area deserted, and crossed in comfort. In fact, comfort seemed to have been the keynote of their entirely uneventful journey hither, travelling north and up Findhorn. They had been looking out for master and mistress all the time, they asserted, making discreet inquiries and finding no trace. Where had they got to, at all?

Tomorrow, the monumental Angus the Boat announced terribly, they had been going to comb the land for them—and incidentally wipe the deplorable Clan Gordon off the fair face of Scotland.

Perceiving complications and fatiguing reactions to this line of conversation, Mary Mackintosh firmly called a halt, declared that she was very tired, and that they would hear and tell all tomorrow. Angus the Boat was to pull her and her guest across to the castle forthwith.

And so, the gallant bay left in good hands, and the two gillies in urgent attendance, the wanderers were rowed across the quarter-mile of darkling water to the island where the tall battlements of Mackintosh's castle loomed blackly. And before a hundred yards were covered, Angus's vast lungs were proclaiming the news before them, to echo back from every enclosing hillside, that Mary of Moy was home again.

X

PATRICK GORDON found the castle of Moy very much to his taste, and would gladly have rested and relaxed in its pleasant precincts after his surely adequate exertions. But he had his mission for the Lord Gordon to fulfil, and only a week to do it in. It was hard on a man, in the circumstances.

For the circumstances were very propitious. Despite its grim exterior, Moy Castle was a felicitous friendly place, sternly masculine without, warmly feminine within. Entirely feminine, at the moment—a house of women, young women. Lauchlan Mor, Chief of Mackintosh and Captain of the Clan Chattan federation, had begotten a fine family of seven sons and six daughters on Agnes, daughter of Mackenzie of Kintail, and while the sons were all meantime gone into Lochaber to assist their father in carrying out the Queen's commission of fire and sword against the execrable Camerons, the daughters remained and reigned supreme on Loch Moy, their mother having departed to a more restful and less exacting bliss above.

Patrick's arrival was accepted as a gift from whatever gods look after spirited young women, and his reception into the gay and chattersome throng next to overwhelming. He was a hero—but a hero not to be adulated so much as exploited. Much was expected, demanded, of him. The fact that the only man about the house was Anna of Dalnavert's old Uncle Aeneas, the Chief's Seneschal, only added piquancy to the situation. The guest found himself actually receiving a marked degree of protection from Mary—and needing all of it. As eldest daughter, no doubt she felt that such was her duty.

Mary's attitude towards the man, indeed, had undergone a subtle but noteworthy change, from the moment of their arrival at Moy. She was consistently and infallibly kind. She indulged in no more tantrums—and no more displays of

134

tomboyishness. She was not diffident any more, but on the other hand she was far from forward, carrying about with her an air of graciousness, unassuming authority and incontrovertible serenity, that much impressed Patrick however much it seemed to infuriate her sisters. Given a little time, the Gordon felt that he could have this situation suitably in hand, and productive of considerable satisfaction.

But he could nowise allow himself that time. If he was going to serve Lord Gordon's, and the Queen's, cause, his own must wait. If he was going to see the Laird of Grant, Cluny Macpherson, Shaw of Rothiemurchus, and possibly some of the lesser Badenoch chieftains, he would need every hour of his time. He had given his word to Seorus Og; moreover, he had sworn to Mary Stewart, in that garden, that he would make amends for the pain that he had caused her. His duty, then, was not in doubt.

Accordingly, and regretfully, he allowed himself only the one complete day at Moy, and amid the protests of three at least of Mackintosh's daughters took his leave of that hospitable household first thing on the second morning. Mary, unlike her sisters, made no attempt to delay him. He noted the fact.

It might be said, indeed, that she sped him on his way. She found a bonnet for him, and one of her father's own eagle's feathers to grace it; also a Mackintosh plaid for his shoulder, and a philamore or great kilt of the same tartan for Black Ewan. And because all the Badenoch clans save the Grants were in the Clan Chattan federation, she provided two stalwart Mackintosh gillies, one of them Angus the Boat who was well known to all connected with Moy, as guides and warranty. Fresh garrons too, she lent, and even a token to reinforce the Lord Gordon's ring.

The entire magpie throng came across the loch and through the trees to the drove road to see them off, Mary the least effusive of them. Amidst the sustained barrage of farewell, advice, invocation, and raillery, she held back, a little aloof. It was only when Patrick, mounted, sought her out with his eyes, that she came forward.

135

"God speed," she said quietly. "Thank you for the good care you took of me. I do not forget that you made an enemy of John Gordon, for my sake."

He shook his head. "I would make an enemy of any man, for the same sake," he asserted. And he did not say it gallantly, as he was apt to say such things. Nor did he smile his Gordon smile.

She inclined her head slightly in acceptance of that, saying nothing.

"I wish . . ." he began, and stopped. "I wish . . . oh, many things."

"Yes. Do not we all!"

"I shall come to Moy again, one day."

"And be welcome."

"Yes. My thanks." There was much more to be said, surely —but no words for saying it. He whipped off his borrowed bonnet, made an inclusive bow to all the girls, and dug heels into his garron.

They rode south, to the high skirling of young voices.

Patrick Gordon's mission to the Spey and Badenoch chiefs was only partially successful. The Lord Gordon was respected of them all and had call on their allegiance, but jealousies, suspicions of his father and the power of Gordon, doubts as to the Bastard's reactions, and the ever-present danger from local feuding clans, tended to hold their hands. Gentle John, twelfth of Grant, and a perfervid Reformer, promised a hundred men, when he could have sent five times that. Shaw of Rothiemurchus grudgingly agreed to fifty. Cattenach, at Glen Tromie, found only a dozen—but then he was a small man in lands, although head of an ancient line. As for Cluny Macpherson, that wily fox could have provided more than Grant, but he would make no promise at all, and had it not been for a fortuitous meeting with his fiery young cadet, Macpherson of Glentruim, who gave personal assurance that he would bring as many of the clan north as he could screw out of his Chief, Patrick would have had to admit complete failure where he had hoped for most.

136

Turning north again, by the Corrieyairack Pass, he came to Loch Ness-side, Fraser country, where Farraline, distantly related to Gordon, raised almost a hundred. There were many lesser men, of course, small chieftains and lairds, but Patrick had no time to solicit their more modest aid. As it was, there was no time to be lost. Travel over such inaccessible and mountainous country was not speedy. And the weather had been atrocious—the same weather that Randolph, Elizabeth's ambassador to Mary's Court, was bewailing in his dispatches to Cecil as being "extreme foul and cold". On the sixth day after leaving Moy, Patrick rode up the Great Glen of Scotland, at Fraser of Farraline's side, towards Inverness, as a watery sun rose over the drenched and sodden world of the mountains.

It was good to have finished the task. It was good to see the sun again, and colour in the land, and everywhere the gleam and sparkle of water. It was good so to ride, in warlike array, in the brave company of armed men. Here was no furtive skulking, no hurried heedful wayfaring through doubtful territories, no tactful forbearance and humble-pie-eating. This was more like a Gordon's progress . . . even behind Farraline's pipers, playing Fraser airs. Patrick whistled with the best.

They took the day to their march, and it was evening before they drew on to the long lift of Drummossie Moor. Away on their left the smoke of Inverness and the tower of its castle rose above the plain. Through birken knowes and grassy hummocks they came in the gloaming to the pleasant secret place of Dalchoin in the skirts of the Moor, and saw the blue pillars of half a hundred cooking-fires ascending into the still evening air, and heard the stir and hum of men, many men. Farraline ordered his pipers forward to play their damnedest.

Thus heralded, they came, and, duly warned, a small company rode out from the thronged levels about the house, to meet them. In the forefront rode the Lord Gordon, clad in half-armour. And prominent amongst the gentlemen at his back, a young woman, plaided, booted, and bare-headed. She had noticeably red hair, even in the gloaming.

137

"*Dhia!* It is not the Queen's self, is it?" the Fraser demanded.

"No." Patrick shook his head, but kept his eyes to the front. "No. I made that mistake, one time, my own self!" And suddenly he laughed, spontaneously, involuntarily, and raised hand and voice.

But his shout was quite overborne and lost in the vast bellow from Angus the Boat behind him. "My pigeon! My fawn of the woods! Mary of my heart—God is good!"

The Lord Gordon, sober man, stared, as well he might.

Just in time, Patrick recollected himself, and the requirements of the situation, and addressed himself to the Heir of Gordon. "Greetings, Seorus Og. I see you in good company—and unexpected!"

Lord Gordon nodded. "The company is the better for your coming, and those you bring with you, Balruary. You have done well."

"I have done what I could." Patrick was looking at the girl. "The Gordon cause would seem to prosper?"

"The Queen's cause," Mary Mackintosh amended.

"Ah, of course. I beg your pardon."

"The Queen's cause, yes," George Gordon agreed, gravely. "What of Cluny? I see no Macphersons here . . . ?"

"Cluny is well content with Cluny Castle, I think. I fear you may count of little from there—though Glentruim has promised to bring as many as he may."

"I was afraid of that." As Lord Gordon turned to greet Fraser of Farraline, Patrick ranged his garron alongside the young woman's horse. "So Moy could not hold its Mary?" he observed. "You have not had your bellyful of traipsing the heather?"

She shrugged. "With my father and brothers gone, I could not allow Mackintosh to fail the Queen in her need!" she asserted, almost defensively. "I scraped Moy and Daviot for what was left behind for the harvesting, and came down this morning with forty men. Having given you our token to rouse others in Clan Chattan, could I do less?"

"And what did all your sisters say?"

138

Mary actually flushed at the vivid recollection of what those sisters had said. "I do not let my sisters rule my actions, Master Gordon!" And then, as he grinned, she smiled likewise, ruefully. "Though indeed, every hour I am looking to see the troop of them come riding over the lip of Drummossie Moor!" She turned to him. "And you, Patrick—how has it gone with you? The rain—I was thinking of you, day after day. . . ."

"Then the weather served me well!" he declared, with a bow.

They rode side by side, through the thronging clansmen, towards Dalchoin House.

There seemed to be a lot of men in that hollow below the vast moor—but the Lord Gordon saw them as few indeed. The Laird of Grant had kept his promise and sent five score. Alan Shaw had produced only a grudging thirty from Rothiemurchus, and though the Cattanach had been rather better than his word, his devoted fifteen did not make a deal of difference. As yet there were no Macphersons. George Gordon himself, apparently, had spent most of his time trying to convince his father of the need to support his action, for Gordon's sake as much as the Queen's, and failing that, at least not to support his brother—but with indifferent success, evidently. In the remaining short period at his disposal he had managed to collect only a few more than a hundred mixed Munroes, Roses, and Brodies from the Laigh—where he was less than popular and his known preference for the men from the hills a liability; only his office of Sheriff of Inverness had obtained him these. His total force, therefore, with the Frasers, was only slightly over four hundred men. He saw it as distinctly inadequate to alter the course of history.

Whilst the newcomers partook of Dalchoin's hospitality in the much overcrowded and modest laird's-house, the situation was further explained to them as the Lord Gordon took council of his leaders. The Queen had arrived in Inverness that very day, the eleventh of September, from Darnaway, with perhaps a thousand men in her train—or, at least, in the train of her half-brother, newly created Earl of Moray. The Lord James had ridden up to the loyal castle on its hill above the river Ness, found it barred and held, and demanded admittance and shelter in the Queen's name. He had been refused. Captain Alastair Gordon, constable of the castle, declared that he had orders from the Earl of Huntly, Lieutenant of the North, to open to none but himself. Moray's ire had required no telling, and it was said that her Grace also was much incensed. The Lord Gordon's spies in the town, less than an hour's ride away, kept him well informed. Huntly himself was on the march—and last night had been at Kinloss, on Findhorn Bay, only thirty miles or so away, where Mary Stewart herself had slept but three nights before. He had a host with him that rumour put as high as three thousand men. And John of Findlater was said to be advancing on Inverness from further inland and still closer at hand, with a cut-throat array of broken men and young blades, variously numbered from three hundred to a thousand. The Laigh of Moray itself was flocking to arms—to join which side, only circumstances would reveal. This was the powder magazine that awaited its spark that September night.

George Gordon had done more than merely to wait at Dalchoin. He had immediately sent word, as Hereditary Keeper of Inverness Castle, by his own channels, to Captain Gordon to ignore Huntly's order and to open up the castle to the Queen forthwith. He had sent a messenger to her Grace apologising for the affront and assuring her of his own loyal duty. He had dispatched a courier to his father at Kinloss, urging him to return to Strathbogie, and to leave himself, as Sheriff, to handle this affair. And he had arranged for scouts to find and keep him informed on the whereabouts and movements of his brother John.

But knowing his family, and the stresses and strains that had led up to this crisis, George Gordon was unhappily aware of his own comparative impotence, with four hundred men and the best will in the world, to affect the course of events and to restrain the forces so precariously leashed. Given time, he might be able to save the situation—muster the more remote hill clans, the Chisholms, the Lovat Frasers, the Mackenzies, even the Clan Ranald and the Glengarry MacDonalds. But time was the commodity that he was unlikely to be given—not with James Stewart, Huntly, and John Gordon involved. What he could do in the present circumstances was the problem, then, before the council. The decision reached was not dramatic, but the only one practicable; to seek to act both as buffer and a mediator, and even as a threat, between all sides, in an effort to prevent any all-out clash—an unenviable task likely to earn them the gratitude of none, but which might conceivably hold an uneasy balance and provide time for mustering of the hill clans, and, equally, for cooler thinking in some quarters.

Patrick contributed but little to the conference. He was a very minor character in this drama now, with no tail of broad swords to back the weight of his youthful counsel, no real experience either of warfare or of the affairs of state. He was now merely one of the Lord Gordon's gentlemen, content that his young Chief should speak for him. Moreover, his thoughts were apt to wander towards that other part of the establishment where the lady of the house and her daughters superintended the victualling of four hundred hungry men. Thither Mary Mackintosh had disappeared, council tables being no places for young women.

It was late before Patrick was able to withdraw himself, and find his way into the domestic quarters. He found the women-folk on the point of retiring to bed, and Mary, strangely enough, in what he considered to be an unsuitable and somewhat tart frame of mind. She gave the impression almost that she thought that a great deal of unnecessary talk had been going on in the house, while they had been devotedly working, and that Patrick was largely responsible in some way. She even went so far as to hint that more whisky had been drunk than was seemly, and that men altogether were a fairly feckless and pitiful lot. Whereupon, not allowing him a chance to mouth more than a few protesting incoherences, she swept upstairs, to bed down with the two Fraser daughters.

Which, considering that he had come as quickly as he could, and had actually sought her out in order to tell her something important, very important—even to a daughter of the Captain of Clan Chattan—was quite deplorable. It just confirmed what he had always previously asserted—and tended to forget awhile —that women were essentially unreliable, unfair, and superficial. They lacked balance, vision, and even elementary loyalty. Who would have thought that the same blushing gentle creature of the Queen's garden would at heart be an ill-natured termagent like this—a scold, a vixen, and a shrew? As well that he had not had a chance to say what had been in his mind to say—a blessed escape.

Thus doubtfully consoled he found his way back whence he had come, wondering objectively whether any of that whisky might have survived the onslaught of his drouthy companions. This further consolation he was denied, unfortunately. He had a good mind to go seek a warm and kindly couch and some co-operation amongst the cot-houses of Dalchoin's folk— though admittedly the competition that night would be keen, keen, and him a latecomer.

A disgruntled man, he curled up on the floor of their supper-room, wrapped in his plaid alongside Shaw of Coylum, who slept loudly with his mouth open. In the morning he would show her. . . .

But in the morning, Mary Mackintosh was exceedingly bright and cheerful, and difficult to show anything to. She appeared to have arisen at an unconscionably early hour, along with the other women, and was bustling about amongst the sleepers' feet in a provocative and thoughtless fashion, even singing, opening windows, and the like. Probably this accounted for the headache from which Patrick was to suffer until the forenoon's events finally banished it.

He was seeking opportunity, later, to hint at what she had missed and therefore irretrievably lost the previous night, the sad but inevitable fate of viragoes, and the general incompatibility of women with serious military operations, when Mary further confounded him by assuring him that she was going home to Moy, probably that very day. Apparently she had not meant to do anything so unladylike as to come campaigning with them, but had only brought her Mackin-

142

toshes down in the absence of any of her male relatives, and now was merely waiting for Donald MacQueen, Younger of Corriebrough, to appear with some of his people when she would hand over her men into his command. Master Patrick did not think that she was one of those Amazon women, did he?

This information somehow altered the entire picture of the expedition, for Patrick Gordon. And he conceived an instinctive dislike for young Donald of Corriebrough. All this before breakfast was adequately digested.

But ere long he had other matters to consider. A messenger arrived hot-foot from Inverness with dire word for them. Captain Alastair Gordon had opened up the castle to the Queen's forces, in response to his young Chief's command— and now he and his entire garrison were hanging in chains from his own gate-house. And one other hung there with them—Lord Gordon's own courier to the Queen. The Lord James had sworn so to treat all Gordons soever.

"As the great God is my witness—here is villainy!" the Lord Gordon cried. "When Huntly hears of this, there will be no holding him! Fools! Fools and knaves! This is ill done . . . for Scotland's sake. And Alastair—he was my good friend and servant. By so ordering him, I have caused his death, and these others with him! Mother of Heaven—have mercy upon me!"

In the storm of anger and hatred that shook the Gordon's company, cursing James Stewart and all his works, it was noticeable that only the young Chief himself called not for vengeance and the sword, but for sorrow and heed for the desperate plight of poor riven Scotland. But when the name of the Queen herself came in for blame and resentment, he threw off his sorrow like a cloak, and stood up, the sober quiet man quite transfigured for the moment.

"Silence!" he thundered, his father's son for all to see. "The man shall lose his tongue who miscalls the Queen's Grace! Mary Stewart is guiltless of this evil, as of others. She is helpless in that devil's hands—Scotland's fair Crown trampled in the mire! She must be saved—or honest men can no more face their God! Let children and fools talk of vengeance in this

143

hour of our land's travail. It is to save the Crown, and save Scotland that we are bound—for that cause I will give life and honour and father and kindred and clan! Not for empty vengeance!"

No man met his eye nor questioned his word. George Gordon perhaps was a man born out of due time. Patrick's last doubts as to where his loyalty lay, vanished quite.

But as the Lord Gordon wrestled with this worsened problem, word of another sort reached them, from Kinloss. Huntly had turned back—not of his son's urging, but on account of divisions in the clan. Its fatal dichotomy had found him out—and not as he might have expected. It was the Lowland Gordons, the fat Laigh lairds, that were failing him, deserting his standard—he that had turned Lowland lord himself in place of Highland chief. His Highland clansmen still loyally supported him, such as formed part of his array— but they had made up the lesser proportion of his present host, their chieftains looking rather to his elder son for leadership. The rest, the plainsmen, were melting away. They had prudently decided amongst themselves not to treasonably take up arms against the Queen—or against the new and potent Earl of Moray. Attacks on their neighbours, and campaigns against rival clans, was one thing; armed challenge to the forces of the Crown such as Huntly seemed bent on, was something altogether otherwise. The Gordon legions were shrinking fast.

But even previously, the messenger reported, Huntly's army had been grossly overestimated. He had brought only eight or nine hundred men north with him; now, with barely half that number of Highlandmen, whom he was only with difficulty restraining from falling upon their deserting low-country namesakes, he was falling back on the mountains, there to rally his neglected hillmen.

This rift, this duality, in the Clan Gordon was no new thing of course, nor attributable merely to the differing conditions of living of the hillmen and the plainsmen. The division went much deeper than that, down into racial origins and language and tradition. The fact of the matter was that Gordon was

144

not a clan at all, in the accepted sense, nor truly Highland. The Gordon lairds had come north from Berwickshire in the fourteenth century, to Donside and Strathbogie, and by nimble wits, ready steel, and judicious marriages, had attained for themselves vast lands and ever-increasing power. And the less acquisitive and less ruthless peoples who had come under their sway, as time went on and according to Highland custom, had assumed the patronymic of Gordon, and gradually the superficial appearance of a clan had evolved. But, while taking the name, there never had been any real amalgam of the three distinct constituents—the ruling house and its innumerable cadet branches, the low-country Doric-speaking population, and the purely Celtic and Gaelic-speaking hillmen. Astute leadership and an ever-alert awareness both of the advantages and the weaknesses of this racial mosaic, had enabled successive Chiefs of Gordon and Earls of Huntly to hold together and balance, to weld and wield, this mighty manpower. Today that balance was disregarded and upset and the Gordon empire in danger of falling apart.

To the company at Dalchoin, then, the situation was again transformed. There was a breathing-space from that quarter, at least. And it behoved the Lord Gordon to take swift advantage of it. For the space would be a brief one. Undoubtedly his father had not yet heard of the hanging Gordons of Inverness. And once the Cock o' the North bestrode the glens again, in proud fury, donned his despised tartans and eagles' feathers and became the Highland Chief once more, the hillmen would flock to his banner joyfully, whatever the cause. And Gordon was still the greatest clan in the north-east. Forgetting the low country, Huntly could raise three thousand broadswords in a week.

His son made up his mind now, with commendable speed. His own messengers, many of them, must go out at once, with all haste, to the Gordon chieftains in the glens, urging them, as they trusted and believed in him, to wait for his word. Rally to his father's summons by all means—he could nowise stop that anyhow—but hold back from action until he himself had come to them, to the gathering of the clan. Come he would. If his devotion to their kind and cause meant anything to them; if his unpopularity with his family and the Lowland lairds had earned him their trust, let them hold their hands until he came. Thus Seorus Og Gordon of Gordon.

Other action he decided upon, also. Representations must be made privily to the Queen immediately, informing, advising, petitioning, warning her. She need not be quite so helpless in her brother's hands as she was. And since he was for sending no more of his people to their deaths, he, George Gordon, would go himself to Inverness. It was his duty—and even the Lord James surely would not dare assault the Heir of Gordon.

But there he met the unanimous and violent opposition of each and all of his supporters. On no account would they agree to his going. The Bastard would no more respect him than any other Gordon. He had publicly sworn to hang all of the name. He would seize Huntly's heir with glee. And even if he did not hang him, he would lock him away in prison, as he had Sir John and Balruary. And then who would save Clan Gordon? Who would save the young Queen? Who would keep the hillmen in leash?

George Gordon bowed to their clamant opposition. Who else would serve the case, then? Who else dare he send to the Queen?

Two voices spoke up in simultaneous response. "I will go!" each declared. Mary Mackintosh and Patrick Gordon.

Patrick had the stronger lungs, and his voice prevailed. "I will go—secretly. I will enter Inverness like any cateran from the hills, and find my way into the Queen's presence. Her Grace will heed me—as she did before. I shall be your courier, Seorus Og."

"No!" Mary cried. "What hope has any cateran from the hills of gaining the Queen's presence? *I* shall go, openly— Mackintosh's daughter, with a score of gillies in my train, come to pay my respects to her Grace. . . ."

"Think you the Lord James will have forgotten Aberdeen Tolbooth?" Patrick demanded.

"No—I fear not. But Inverness is not Aberdeen. This is *my* country. My father names Inverness his Capital! The daughter of Clan Chattan, with armed men at her tail, is vastly otherwise from the single helpless girl of Aberdeen. The Lord James will think twice before assailing me. And he will not hang a woman! Anyhow—no one else here is advantaged thus. Myself, it must be."

"Mistress Mackintosh speaks good sense," George Gordon agreed slowly. "She alone of us is like to go unscathed."

"I warrant *I* would go unscathed," Patrick asserted strongly. "Give me dirk and broadsword, and Black Ewan at my back, and I will find my way into the Queen's presence and out again. It will not be myself that suffers scathe!"

"Have *you* forgotten Aberdeen Tolbooth, now?" the girl challenged. "You had better have me nigh to lift you out again!"

He blinked. "That time I trusted the Bastard, and the Queen's power," he gave back. "This time I shall trust only my wits and my right hand."

"The pity for you . . ."

"The lady has the rights of it, I think," the Lord Gordon intervened decisively. "She had better be nigh to aid you. You shall both go. You can go, Patrick, in Mistress Mackintosh's tail, as one of her gillies." The hint of a smile played about that stern mouth. "The role will suit you well! Between you, you must gain the Queen's ear. She has more power than she thinks, if she does but use it skilfully."

Patrick and the girl glanced at each other, the former doubtfully, the latter with her own woman's smile. "When do we go?" she asked.

"This very day. There is no time to lose. The word is that the royal train is already preparing to move back into the Laigh, to return to Aberdeen. The Lord James feels less than secure in Inverness. The Queen, it is said, is incensed against my father, who is represented as in open rebellion, and goes to teach him a lesson. I fear that she may go to her death. She talks of leading the van, demanding buckler and breastplate and broadsword! She is valiant—but 'tis what her brother seeks for her. An armed clash . . . and no heir to the throne of Scotland! She must be warned."

"She *shall* be warned," Patrick assured. "If we could but lift her out of the Bastard's clutches . . ."

"He keeps her close as any prisoner—with a thousand men to watch her. And she is proud, proud. She is the Queen, she will not flee. . . ."

The eldrich skirl of clashing pipe-music heralded the arrival of a further contingent of Clan Chattan—or rather, two contingents, for they kept noticeably apart—Glentruim with some eighty Macphersons from Cluny, and the MacQueen's son with thirty of his folk from Findhorn. And already the two young leaders were on less than speaking terms; the Macpherson claimed that as representing Cluny, the second man in Clan Chattan federation, he should have command of the entire party; the MacQueen, as a Chief's son, even if a small one, as against a mere laird, resisting strongly.

Mary Mackintosh, as her father's daughter, was called upon to resolve this very typical Highland problem of precedence and command, and she did so with such kindly smiles and fluttering of eyelids towards both fire-eaters, that she was able to appoint Angus the Boat as her lieutenant over both of them—after all, he was a warrior of experience, a Mackintosh, and her own cousin at only eight removes.

When this business was amicably settled, Patrick withdrew to don borrowed Mackintosh kilt and plaid. He changed his already somewhat tattered shirt for a considerably worse one, of once-saffron homespun and tickly in the extreme. With a sigh he extracted the feather from his bonnet, and equipped himself with circular leathern targe, heavy broadsword, and dirk. Rawhide brogans he tied on, and thus accoutred, with bare legs, and largely bare chest and arms, he rolled up his own clothes in a bundle, and went in search of Mary Mackintosh. He made as ruffianly competent a figure as any to be seen, and did no injustice to any kilt or tartan.

The young woman was with Lord Gordon and his lieutenants, and sitting down to the midday meal, when Patrick made his unsuitable entry. There was no lack of comment. But ignoring the others, as was fitting, he presented himself directly to the girl.

"Your servant and clansman, Mary of Moy!" he intoned.

She looked him up and down calmly. "You will require to behave yourself in my tail, and in those colours, sirrah!" she said. "We have our standards in Clan Chattan—and our methods of enforcing them!"

Patrick lifted his glance over her head, to the young Chief, who raised one eyebrow but held his peace.

Mary's tone of voice relented by a shade. "You have a fair leg for a kilt, I will say. But is it my fancy, or do you smell somewhat?" And before the man could make response, she had turned away. "My Lord of Gordon—this once might I crave your indulgence for him to sit down to meat with us?"

While they ate, George Gordon gave his messengers their instructions. They must acquaint the Queen of the full perils of her position. They must inform her of the involved Gordon situation. They must endeavour to restrain her from adventuring herself into any circumstance of which her brother could take advantage. They must urge her to take to herself a husband, with as great haste as decency would permit.

At this last, it was not only Patrick who looked up askance. But the speaker shook an impatient head. Let there be no misunderstanding, he charged. This exhortation had no reference to the House of Gordon. If the Queen, and Scotland with her, was to enjoy any peace and security from the evil ambitions of her brother, she must marry and get herself with child as speedily as God would let her. An heir to the throne there must be, or Elizabeth and the Lord James would achieve their ends. He, George Gordon, found it hateful that her Grace should have to wed thus—and the man's expression and voice confirmed that he spoke no lie—but her life and the continued independence of her realm more than probably depended upon it. Let them leave her in no doubts of that— Elizabeth Tudor, her good cousin, meant to have Scotland, and would stop at nothing. Tell Mary Stewart not to trust Lethington, the Secretary—he was in English pay. Nor Morton, the Douglas—he likewise was a pensioner. Ruthven might not be bought—but he was a blackguard and a boor. Some few others of the Lords of the Congregation might pass for honest—but if so they were apt to be fools, and the creatures of men who were neither. Let her trust none of them."

"God help the Queen's Grace!" Mary Mackintosh breathed.

Lord Gordon said Amen to that. But she could trust *him*, and many another whom he could name. And given time, he could rally half the Highlands to her standard. Let her not despair; there were leal men everywhere—save close around her person and in the rule of her kingdom! Let them comfort and uphold her, as well as warn her. For she had a great spirit. And let them stay by her so long as they might—even to Aberdeen, if ever she got there. . . .

Here Patrick made protest. A message he had thought to deliver—not to attach himself to women's petticoat-tails . . . even the Queen's! He could serve Mary Stewart better in the field surely, than trailing along after her Court . . . ?

The Lord Gordon thought otherwise, and said so. One broadsword more or less—even one so valiantly wielded as would be Balruary's—could make little difference. But someone who could reach the Queen's ear, who could counter the lies of her brother, who could act as link between her Grace and those who would fight for her cause—such a one would be precious beyond price. Let there be no more talk to it.

When the Lord Gordon spoke thus, talk died.

XI

BEHIND four pairs of pipers blowing lustily, Mary of Moy rode into Inverness at the head of forty Mackintosh fighting-men late that afternoon. She made an eye-catching entry, and knew it—and there were many eyes to be caught.

Inverness was a singularly different place from Aberdeen. Though both stood at the mouths of great rivers, at sea-level, one was as distinctly a Highland town as the other was Lowland. Inverness indeed was scarcely a town at all, the Highlander being suspicious of towns ever, but rather a vast and sprawling scatter of cot-houses and cabins and tanneries and mills without enclosing walls and gates and with little in the way of definite streets. Cattle wandered at will and in astonishing numbers, as did domestic poultry, nibbling where they might. Churches and religious houses were sited amongst byres and midden-heaps, duck-ponds islanded maltings; lairds' town-houses rose out of the huddle of their dependents' shacks, just as the royal castle on its hill above the river rose out of the midst of all. Inverness in the sixteenth century of our Lord was rather a dozen Highland townships loosely linked together than any city in its own right. Here a different set of values prevailed from those of any tight and huddled Lowland town. Here the eagles' feathers of chieftainship counted for more than the fat purses of merchant burgesses, clan slogans spoke louder than the voices of guilds and corporations; money-making yielded pride of place to parade and argument and imaginative competition, business to laughter and tears. Here the Old Religion flourished yet, with almost every day a Saint's Day, and labour a degradation to be avoided at all costs, or decently left to women.

In such conditions the Lords of the Congregation and their hirelings were considerably less at home than in the streets

151

and wynds of couthie stone-walled towns. Though they asserted their authority, of course, ducked all the priests that they could lay reformed hands on, accidentally drowning three of them, and generally showed their contempt for slovenly Highland habits and the lack of amenities and backwardness of the place—nevertheless they made no such impact on outspread Inverness as they had done in Aberdeen.

So, as the Mackintosh contingent made its devious way between cattle and peat-stacks and drying-nets and houses, it did not have to beat a way for itself by the flat of the sword nor counter the obstruction of graceless men-at-arms. Watchers there were in plenty, and the lords' retainers very evident amongst them, of course, but here they did not dominate. Also, undoubtedly, the compact and confident Clan Chattan company was not the sort of body idly to hold up.

Uninterfered with, then, they came by the Gallows Moor to the rising ground crowned by the castle, and there they found the Lowland host camped in close array. The impression of wary readiness was very evident—and in marked contrast to the arrogant ease and indiscipline that had prevailed within Aberdeen's guardian walls. Here was the aspect of an army in enemy territory, much aware of it, and unsure of itself. Directly towards the thick of the press Mary Mackintosh pointed her pipers, heading for the gate-house above which a row of dangling corpses swung and twirled in the breeze. Over them the royal standard flapped, the ramping lion replacing the three boars' heads of Gordon.

Armed men made involuntary passage for the tartaned newcomers—and there were no taunts and jibes anent bareshanked heathen and red-kneed bog-wallopers. Questions there may have been—but if so they were drowned in the pipers' zestful rendering of 'The March of Moy'. With their lords and leaders within the castle, they would have been bold mercenaries to seek to offer interference to that positively bristling cavalcade—or to the level-eyed chin-high young woman who led it.

Within the gate-house archway, however, a solid phalanx of pikemen was drawn up awaiting their loudly heralded approach, commanded by an officer in full armour. Mary signed for the pipers to cease from blowing. Before the officer could challenge them above the expiring groans of the instruments, a Mackintosh voice rang out.

"Mary of Moy, Clan Chattan's daughter, to pay her duty to Mary of Scotland the Queen's Grace!"

The acting constable raised doubtful brows under his plumed morion, but the girl suddenly appeared to notice him, and transformed her lofty and authoritative mien by turning her sweetest smile full upon him. A youngish man, and not unimpressionable, he bowed.

"William Douglas of Cavers, ma'am, at your service." And he waved the pikemen back.

"Greetings, Master Douglas. I prithee conduct me to her Grace." And without waiting for the other to protest that he was no page, she nodded anew to her musicians, and urged forward her horse.

Very promptly her lead was taken up, and the detachment surged onwards within the castle walls, Douglas of Cavers having almost to run on after her, to the clanking hurt of his dignity. Patrick Gordon, at her horse's heels, marvelled and should have taken warning.

The great donjon keep of the castle occupied the crest of the rocky hillock, and there still was a climb within the walls to reach it. But despite the gradient, the pipers maintained their full blast, and within that enclosed space made a considerable impression. Not a window nor door of the extensive range of buildings remained unfilled, before the Mackintoshes and the clangorous and perspiring constable had reached the great doorway.

The satisfactory winding-up of the music, the drawing up and dismounting, and the panting gyrations of the flustered Douglas, occupied some time and created no little to-do. Patrick, pushing aside the jealous Donald Gorm, handed Mary Mackintosh down from her saddle, and exchanged a whispered word or two the while.

"Good," he declared, "you have them by the ears! You fare finely. Keep it up, Mary of Moy."

She shook a hurried head. "I am afraid Patrick! I could . . . scream. The Lord James . . . ?"

He squeezed her arm, suddenly aware of a great tenderness towards her. "Hush, you," he chided. "You are Clan Chattan's daughter . . . and a Gordon's wife-to-be! You shall not scream."

She turned to stare at him, eyes wide, and widening. He felt her tremble, now—whether her fear had been making her tremble before or not. Her lips parted, but she did not speak.

He nodded, and the surprise that he knew in his own words did not show in his smiling eyes. The compulsion that he must say it, and say it there and then, was not to be withstood. "We will wed, yourself and myself. Our children will be . . . magnificent, will they not."

Still she gazed at him, speechless, with a welter of emotions in her eyes—emotions that it would have taken an even bolder man than Patrick Gordon to interpret. And then a cool and carefully modulated voice spoke behind her, and slowly, almost bemusedly she turned round.

"Mistress Mackintosh again, I see! This is a surprise, upon my soul! You . . . honour us!" Mr. Secretary Lethington, elegant as ever and fingering his trim pointed beard, stood within the crowded doorway. "My Lord of Moray awaits you."

All within ear-shot must have heard the catch in the girl's breathing, but there was no catch in her voice as she answered him. "I am honoured by my Lord's interest—but 'tis not him that I have come to see. I desire audience with the Queen."

Lethington's long upper lip seemed to grow suddenly longer, synchronising with the gasp that rose from the thronging watchers. "My Lord, I think, will see you first, ma'am, nevertheless," he said coldly.

"I will speak with him only if that is her Grace's direct command," Mary Mackintosh said, and if there was a tremor behind her words, it might have indicated only the imperious complement of her high-held head. "Inform the Queen, I prithee, sir, that Clan Chattan craves privy audience!"

"You are passing bold, ma'am . . ." the Secretary of State

154

began, and stopped. Patrick Gordon, from amongst the tight ranks of the Mackintoshes, growled, deep in his throat, and immediately the growl was taken up by every clansman there, in a hoarse and menacing snarl that grew and maintained, to ebb but slowly. William Maitland of Lethington took an involuntary step backwards, and swallowed; if there was one thing that a cultured and civilised gentleman such as himself should abhor, it was any close contact with violent and boorish savages and any hint of their rude methods. He turned, and said a brief word to his esquire, Michael Erskine, at his shoulder, who slipped away within.

There was a pause, distinct and significant, and the clans-men moved up almost imperceptibly closer around their mistress. She spoke up. "He goes to inform her Grace, sir?"

The Secretary inclined his head, but said nothing.

Mary tapped the toe of her shoe lightly on the outcropping rock on the castle hill. The tension could be felt by all.

There was a stir from inside the building. Heads turned, and the throng in the entrance pressed back, to offer respectful passage. Three men stalked therein: James Stewart, Earl of Moray, the red Earl of Morton, and the esquire Erskine.

There was no sound other than Morton's heavy wheezing and the tap-tap of the young woman's shoe.

James Stewart, dressed all in soberest black, after the briefest darting glance at the scene, considered the flagstones at his feet as though with extreme distaste. Pale, cold, self-conscious, a picture of patent unease and a source of unease to all present, he stood silent, seeming to wait. Patrick Gordon, from the crowd of clansmen, wondered anew that this should be the man who had Scotland by the ears.

Lethington, bowing obsequiously, began to speak quickly, quietly, but Morton abruptly interrupted with his spluttering bellow. "Pest! What's this, ha? Damme—a bitch yapping at our door? A wheen redshanks at her backside! What's this, Mr. Secretary, in God's name? Perdition take my soul—would you summon us for the like o' this?"

"My Lord—the lady is . . ."

"A bitch, I said! A Hielant bitch. We ken her fine—and

155

what to do with her! I've broken plenty like her, to bark another tune! Fetch her ben, man, and . . ."

The Lord James raised his white hand almost as though to pronounce the Benediction—and astonishingly, the noisy Douglas gobbled into silence. "My Lord, my good Lord—a moment, pray," he said, in his flat colourless voice. "Mistress Mackintosh has some questions to answer us indeed—but not here. We do not shout the realm's business to the rabble thus. Her Grace must be more privily served than this. Almighty God in His Providence will guide us the more surely in our chalmers, on our knees. . . ."

"Certes—in our chalmers!" Morton chuckled. "I' faith, you hae the rights o't. The chalmer's the place for the likes o' her. But knees, man—knees! *Her* knees, I grant ye. Or, better, her . . ."

Patrick Gordon's angry rumble burst from his lips, tightly as he was holding them. As well for him that the Mackintosh ranks were so instant in following his lead, for the sound drew all eyes, even a swift and furtive-seeming glance from the new Earl of Moray.

Through the noise Mary Mackintosh's clear young voice lifted, to draw attention back to herself—as a woman will, not always so disinterestedly as this. "Master Maitland—I bade you inform her Grace!"

Lethington looked at the Lord James, brows raised, and that careful man addressed the dog-toothed moulding of the doorway sourly.

"Mr. Secretary—you will convey Mistress Mackintosh to our chalmer . . ."

"No!" the girl cried. "You will not! The Queen I will see—and none else. That is why I am here—and that only."

"Her Grace is not to be importuned by ill-mannered huzzies!" Lethington declared frowning, his habitual suavity upset.

"God's death—truce to words!" Morton roared. "Hae the jaud in, man." And his great red hand dropped to his sword.

Mary took a step back in the same moment that her escort, in unison, took a step forward.

156

James Stewart permitted himself to look even more pained than was his usual. "Mistress Mackintosh, you will come with me—there to await her Grace's pleasure," he said levelly.

"I shall await her Grace's pleasure here, my Lord."

"God give me patience with headstrong and stiff-necked women!" the Earl prayed, eyes Heavenwards. They swivelled thereafter, however, in the direction of the constable, Douglas of Cavers, one thin eyebrow raised. "To your duty, man," he mentioned—and insignificantly as it was spoken, more than the constable recognised the significance of that.

There was a seething amongst the Highlanders, a glancing back towards the gate-house, hands on broadsword hilts.

Then, as the answering stir elsewhere resulted, suddenly it was galvanised, at least about the keep's entrance. Men pressed back on every side. The impulse was communicated even to the authoritative group within the doorway, James Stewart himself turning, frowning, and then stepping reluctantly back also. A subdued murmur arose.

"The Queen! The Queen! Her Grace! 'Tis the Queen's Grace!"

And down between the ranks of stern men, Mary of Scotland came. She came running, entirely a girlish figure, far from consciously the Queen, one hand outstretched before her, the other holding up her full skirt and farthingale above twinkling toes, her lips parted in a brilliant smile.

"Mackintosh! Mackintosh, *ma chérie*! Welcome, a hundred times! God is good—'tis a joy to see your face, I vow!"

Mary Mackintosh attempted some sort of curtsy, but the Queen was impetuously upon her ere she had but started, and in a moment the two red heads were side by side and touching, as the girls embraced.

Men stared, blinking.

Mary Stewart laughed happily, as she hugged the other. "My bashful timid Mackintosh! My blushing Hielant rose! I saw you from the topmost window yonder, coming with your glorious hairy warriors! I'd know that copper prow from any height, I'd warrant! Heigh-ho—'tis good to see you again, Mackintosh." And she stood back, holding the older girl at

157

arm's length, the better to look her up and down, apparently oblivious of the silent watching masculine throng.

" 'Tis a joy for me also, your Grace," Mary Mackintosh assured, her voice a-tremble now for all to hear. "God . . . God keep your Highness!"

"Ah, God—He turns an eye on me, now and again, I verily believe! And when He is otherwise occupied, my good brother here acts exceeding conscientious as His deputy, I vow!" And there she was Queen again, conscious monarch and conscious woman, sweeping round with an elaborate wave of be-ringed hand towards the Lord James. "My Lord—I think you will recollect kindly our good friend and companion Mary Of Mackintosh?"

Stiffly, almost imperceptibly, Moray inclined his head, the corners of his thin mouth turned down in a sickle.

"My Lord of Moray is delighted to see you back with us, I am assured—as are we all!" the Queen asserted gaily. "You are well, girl—marry, you look as though . . . as though your activities have agreed with you! And how is . . . *you* know who?"

The Highland girl flushed, and her glance flickered—though not in the direction of the discreetly inconspicuous Patrick Gordon—a flicker that by no means escaped the keen eye of the other young woman. "Well, I believe, your Grace," she said, small-voiced.

Mary Stewart clapped her hands, delightedly. "Excellent. I would swear that you are to be congratulated—no?"

Quickly, too quickly perhaps, Mary Mackintosh countered that. "On being admitted to your Grace's presence again—yes. And in being permitted to bring this token of Clan Chattan's strength to your royal support, Madam!"

"Ah." The Queen smiled, and then turned to look over the serried rows of clansmen, still smiling. "I see. That is well said, Mackintosh. They are very fierce, are they not? I . . ." Mary Stewart's voice faltered for a moment, as the royal eyes, slipping with frank womanly admiration over all that stalwart manhood, momentarily met Patrick Gordon's gaze, and held. But only for an instant. "I commend your wisdom, *chérie* . . .

and only hope that you can keep them in order. Promise us that, and we shall feel the safer for their presence!" And she turned back to the girl.

"Yes, your Grace. And I have brought you messages of support and loyalty from others . . . for your privy ear, Madam."

"Surely. Surely. Come with me, Mackintosh. My privy ear tingles already. Come."

"My . . . my clansmen, your Highness! May they be comfortably disposed, and—and treated well. They are my trust. . . ."

"And mine, girl—mine, now also. They shall be my bodyguard, I vow. How excellent, is it not, brother, that here in the North I should have a Highland bodyguard? I . . ."

"Your Grace has a thousand men for bodyguard—you are in *my* keeping," Moray asserted flatly.

"Keeping, sir! Keeping? I am Scotland, and in no man's keeping! Rather, you are in mine—and God's! All of you! Is that not so, sir?"

Her brother cleared his throat and bowed in silence, and as her eyes swept round all assembled there, each man bowed in his turn.

"Yes," she said, head high. "I am glad to remind you of it—of your Queen's love . . . and keeping, my Lords!" And in a different voice; "Constable—who is constable? Ah, Master Douglas—see you to it. See that my bodyguard of good Clan Chattan is well served, with every respect and comfort. I shall require it of you, sir. They bide within the walls at my near command. You understand?"

"It shall be as your Grace commands."

"It shall indeed. Come, Mackintosh." And the Queen linked an arm through that of the other girl.

As they moved amidst the bowed heads of men, towards the smiles of the other three waiting Maries within, Mary of Moy turned her head for a moment. "Donald Gorm!" she called, over her shoulder.

And in the pack of clansmen, dour Donald Gorm Mackintosh turned and grinned gleefully, almost leered in Patrick Gordon's face, and hurried to follow his mistress.

159

*　　　　*　　　　*

Though the quarters that Douglas of Cavers eventually found for the comfortable and respectful disposal of the Mackintosh clansmen were far from palatial, being in fact only the cobble-floored meal-store in the base of the donjon-tower itself—still, no doubt he did his best to carry out the royal commands; for Inverness Castle, those September days of 1562, was undoubtedly more crowded than ever before or since in its history, and the greater portion even of the gentry had to lodge without its walls. Indeed, it soon transpired that, save for a few of the personal attendants of the Queen's household and of the great lords, the Mackintoshes were the only group of fighting-men installed actually inside the main keep. What the Lord James thought of this arrangement was not to be known—unless he saw some advantage in having them at least close under his eye.

At any rate, there they were ensconced, and if the amenities were no degree better than those of the Aberdeen Tolbooth, Highlandmen used to bedding down in open heather in all weathers found them fair enough, and certainly made no complaint. As well that they had brought their own marching rations with them, however, for that meal-store was already empty of meal, and the royal army was notably short of meat—the Lord James being sufficiently aware of their exposed position not to unnecessarily antagonise Inverness and the clans by wholesale requisitioning of their cattle, as had been done further south; the Queen was paying for every bullock eaten—and the royal treasury was almost as empty as the meal-store.

It was after a late and somewhat frugal supper, then, with the clansmen in their unlighted cellar curling themselves up in their plaids on the knobbly floor—such of them as were not detailed to mount wary guard—that Donald Gorm Mackintosh, secret, consequential, and as full of importance as an egg of meat, appeared amongst them, to beckon Partick Gordon in a superior manner to follow him.

By a vaulted passage, past the kitchens, he led, and up a narrow turnpike stair within the thickness of the walling, past the first main floor and its entresol, past the second, to open

160

a door on to the third, which gave access to another passage, lit this time by a slender window through which the wan light of the gloaming filtered. Beneath the second door along it a bar of light gleamed yellowly. At this, Donald Gorm, with what could only be described as a conspiratorial flourish, knocked.

There was a rustle of skirts, and a young woman opened to them. It was Mary Livingstone, the pert piece whom last Patrick had left at the Provost's table at the Blackfriars of Aberdeen.

"Welcome to my bedchamber, Master Gordon!" she said. "Though as God's my witness, you are such a wild man become that I misdoubt if I shall let you in!"

Patrick had no answer ready for that. Stepping inside, he perceived that it was indeed a bedchamber, and no large one at that. Within the window embrasure stood Mary Mackintosh, and on the bed sat the Queen of Scots.

She held out her hand to him, and the man strode forward to drop on one knee and kiss her fingers. "My true Gordon!" she smiled. "Or . . . Mary's Gordon, at any rate!"

"Yours, Madam—to my dying breath."

"La—who talks of dying, sir! Lusty-seeming as you are, you could do better for a woman than die for her—eh, Mackintosh? Stand back, Patrick Gordon, and let me look at you."

"Your Grace it is that is worth the looking at," he spoke up then.

"That is more like it, *mon brave!*"

"I'd say the kilt becomes him better than the trews, think you not?" Mary Livingstone suggested judiciously. "I vow he makes an ornamental savage. So brutally hairy a chest!"

"Hush, Livingstone—I have eyes of my own! And he was admiring *me*—which is as a breath of life to me, this-a-day, *le bon Dieu* knows. Pray proceed, Master Patrick."

But the man had his tongue between his teeth now. "Your Grace looks very . . . well," he said stiffly.

"Well?" The Queen sighed, shrugged, and spread eloquent hands. "Alas—is that all? The moment is gone—*pouf!* 'Tis

161

ever the way. To look well is the privilege of every bouncing kitchen-wench and dairymaid!" She turned to Mary Mackintosh, who thus far had said no word. "Mackintosh—is he ever thus with you? You have him better in hand, I wager?"

The Highland girl considered her toes. "I would not say that I had him in hand, your Grace," she said, level-voiced. "The Gordons make but chancy handling!"

"Ah, yes. You have the rights of it. The Gordons—they act like our masters, not our servants! As well that we recognise the fact, and act accordingly." Mary Stewart turned to Patrick, the banter gone out of her lovely voice. "Master Gordon—Mistress Mackintosh has been telling us something of what George, Lord Gordon, would have us believe. With his father and brother in revolt against us, and himself with an armed force on our royal flank, the Lord Gordon's voice sounds more than a little suspect! But believing you to be leal and honest, I am prepared to hear what you have to say on his behalf."

"I thank your Grace. I am your Grace's true man—as I swear 'fore God is George Gordon. He loves you, Madam. . . ."

"So does his brother John—so warmly that he would climb into my bed! But he draws the sword against me, nevertheless, and holds the castles of Findlater and Auchindoun against me. And I have oft-times listened to my Lord of Huntly's protestations of love—but his army challenges mine and he makes threats against my person."

Patrick shook his head. "Not against you, Ma'am—neither of them. Huntly would serve you—but will not serve your brother! John of Findlater is headstrong and foolish—but in his fashion he loves you too, I believe. . . ."

"As the eagle loves the dove, Gordon! And Mary of Scotland is no dove!"

"I believe it, your Grace. But do not mistake—their arming, father and son, is against the Lord James and his friends, not against your Highness. It ill becomes me to miscall your brother to your face . . . but he has set himself against all that Gordon stands for, and uses the royal power to work his will. You cannot expect Gordon to abide that."

The Queen sighed. "Mayhap not—but it seems that *I* must abide it. I have no choice. And so long as there is this Gordon power in the land, there is like to be no peace for my realm . . . nor for me!"

"Think you, Ma'am, that there will be peace for you, when Gordon is struck down? See you not that Gordon alone can act as counter to your brother? Can you not see . . . ?"

"Oh, man, man—how easy for you to talk, by God His Grace! Think you that I see not all this, and a deal more? But I am thronged, bound, held fast. In small things only am I the Queen—in large, the Council acts. And the Council is my brother. Think you, if I could rule in my Scotland, I would not do so? Think you that if I had men of my own, even a few men, I might not sing another tune? Think you that if my nobles cared one tithe for their Queen and the country that they care for their own advantage and their own feuds, I should stand by and watch them snarling over the body of my bleeding realm? I may only watch and wait, nibble here and gnaw there, like any mouse—seek to set one rogue against another, Mary Mother pity me!" The Queen had risen from the bed, eyes blazing, her small fists clenched, shaken by the tumult of her passion. And then, before their abashed regard, she controlled herself, with a great and visible effort. "You will forgive me—there was speaking a foolish and helpless girl. I must be other than that—and will be, God willing."

Patrick swallowed. "Your Grace . . . I, I . . . there are many who would aid you in that, I swear. That is what I am here to tell you. . . ."

"Then I must believe it, sir. But I cannot yet accept Huntly and Sir John Gordon as wholly concerned to aid me to be Queen indeed!"

"Then, Ma'am—at least accept Seorus Og . . . *George* Gordon. He is different from his father and brother—from any other that I know. He is a strange man—but you can trust him, I am assured. He has said that your Grace must be saved from your brother, or honest men may no more face their God. He said, to save the Crown and save Scotland, he would give life and honour and father and kindred and

163

clan! That is George Gordon. And that is my message. Trust Gordon."

There was silence within that small stone-walled room for a little, as Mary Stewart stared at the man, stared through him, as though to see to the heart of that other man beyond, the look of the girl who wished to believe struggling with the disbelief and cynicism of the woman who had found all men, or almost all, to be base—an ill look to see in those beautiful hazel-green nineteen-year-old eyes. Then, with the sigh of only compromise—for she was one who would have preferred her heart to rule her head—she sat down on the bed again. "At least we shall hear George Gordon's message . . . and judge of its worth after," she said. "Proceed, Master Patrick."

"This is what he says then, Ma'am. He believes that you are in grave danger. He has it that the Lord James actually seeks to encompass your Grace's death!"

"Go on, my friend," she said, evenly.

"Yes. He would do it, not openly, but by a stratagem, through a trick, so that he may mount your throne thereafter. He is in Elizabeth Tudor's pay—as are Lethington, Morton, and the rest . . . all traitors. Elizabeth and Cecil will have your kingdom, Ma'am, by fair means or foul, and the Lord James on the throne will serve them well, bastard or none. The Lord Gordon says, venture not your person in any foray or clash of arms—or you will be the first to fall. Keep yourself surrounded by your ladies and the few that you can trust, day and night. Do not sanction any fighting, if it is in your power to stop it. . . ."

"That would be convenient for Gordon, I agree!"

"Madam—believe me, you do George Gordon injustice. 'Tis yourself and the Crown that he is concerned for, not himself nor his family. Nor yet, in the first place even the clan. He has gathered this Highland force solely to be keeping it between you and his father and brother. He will seek to use it as a curtain, a bulwark. He is trying to persuade Huntly to return to Strathbogie—indeed his father has already turned back from Kinloss. He is seeking to rally the Gordons of the glens, the Highland part of the clan, to his own standard—

164

and he has much influence with them. He is your friend and servant, Ma'am."

"I would that I might believe it. But, even so—will the Clan Gordon not obey its Chief, Huntly?"

"Yes, and no. The clan is divided, Highland and Lowland. Huntly has neglected and failed the Highlanders—they respect more Seorus Og. But . . . it is important that Huntly should not be attacked, or they may rally to the aid of their Chief. And they are numbered by the thousand."

"If I was not trusting you as my leal servant, Master Gordon—I vow that could sound like a threat, a dagger at my throat!"

Patrick bit his lip. "That it is not, your Grace. I confess it could sound that way—but 'tis only the true facts of the business which must be faced. You must see that." He appealed to Mary Mackintosh, who stood silent, watchful. "*You* are no Gordon—you do not love Huntly nor his sons, Huntly who killed your grandfather! But you believe that George Gordon speaks truth, do you not?"

The other girl nodded. "I do, yes. I have told her Grace that I believe him to be honest, and his counsel good."

"Yes, yes—but methinks even you might have become prejudiced towards Gordon a little, my Mackintosh! But you may be right—who knows? Ah, me—who would have the guiding of the ship of State in such a storm? And the rudder wrenched from my hands by others, who steer for their own ends! And there is the rub—what matters it whether I believe George Gordon or no? I can do nothing, nothing. The Council will do what my brother deems fit."

"Seorus Og says that you have more power than perhaps you think, Madam. He says, do not weary of thwarting the Lord James—for there are many in Scotland who hate him. Even seek to play his own creatures against him—Ruthven and Lindsay and Argyll. Even Morton and Lethington. By capricious royal favour, George Gordon says, you can set them against each other, and encourage those who hate them all."

"I have not failed to consider that, either," the Queen declared wearily. "But the Kirk is solid against me. The Kirk binds them all. Every road I turn, I find the Kirk glowering at me. Every move I make is said to be for the restoring of the Old Faith. That is my brother's trump card. The Kirk at his back, and hell's fire for all whom I favour!" She sighed, and then straightened up. "Still—I shall do what I may, the Saints aiding me. Not only for Gordon's sake. I will hold back, where I may, from all blood-letting. You may tell George Gordon that I shall not lightly dismiss his message. And I thank you for your stout bearing of it—would I were as well served as he is! But . . . I think the greatest service you have done me is the bringing of these two-score Highlanders to my side. With even two-score that I may trust, I can speak with a firmer voice. Bless you, Mackintosh *ma chérie*—you will stay by me?"

"Until you send me away, your Grace."

"And what if Gordon calls?"

"Gordon must call in vain, Madam."

"Ah." Sidelong the Queen smiled at the man. "You hear that, Master Patrick?"

"I do, Ma'am. And I can think of one Gordon who will not have far to call!"

"Well said, Gordon! Methinks I shall have to be speaking a word in my good Father Roche's ear! Ah—but you are of the Kirk, are you not? A Protestant?"

"In a sort of a way, yes. But . . . i' faith, I'd sooner be wed by a priest than not at all!"

Mary Stewart clapped delighted hands, but Mary Mackintosh, flushing, stamped an indignant foot. "Two it takes to a wedding, I'd remind you, sir!" she cried. "When I am married it will be because I decided it—no one other! And while we touch the subject of marriage, I'd have you recollect that you have not mentioned one important part of Lord Gordon's message!"

"I'mmm. Ah . . . ummm." Patrick Gordon coughed, looked at his brogues, and ran a hand over his chin. "Yes—that is so. I had clean forgot. I . . . he says that your Grace should take to yourself a husband just as soon as it may be, and . . ."

"Mother of Heaven—he also! So that is it, after all—another of them! I might have known . . ."

"No, no—you have it wrong, I swear. 'Tis not himself—he names no names. It is just the policy that he urges. For your own sake, for the Throne's sake, for Scotland's sake—and to confound your brother and the English Queen. A husband to stand between you and the lords, and an heir to your throne, Ma'am. A child, the realm needs. He urges that you gain both, and as speedily as God wills."

Mary of Scotland laughed mirthlessly. "I see. *Pardieu*—the Lord Gordon is thoughtful for my comfort! And unselfish in his love for me . . . though, no doubt, he would not deny that a Gordon husband would be the wisest choice! There are others, of course, seek the same couch. *Dieu de Dieu!* Who is it to be—the Prince of Spain, or the Duke of Austria? Dudley whom Cousin Elizabeth is prepared to spare me, or the Lennox cub, Darnley? The gibbering Arran . . . or Master John Knox himself? All would wed Scotland, I hear—and have me in the by-going. Ha—and the Kings of Sweden and Denmark are added to the list, they tell me. Would the Lord Gordon prefer one of them to father this needful child?" Mary Stewart was on her feet again, and very much the Queen. "We have had ample food for thought for one night, I vow. I thank you both. Now, I am a-wearied. Goodnight to you, Master Patrick. Ladies—attend me to my chalmer."

As the two other girls curtsied low, Patrick strode to the door, and opened it bowing. "Your Grace will forgive if once again I have grieved you . . . ?" he asked.

"Fie, man—such as you will be grieving women so long as you draw breath," she declared, as she swept past him. "Note you that, Mackintosh! 'Tis our lot—red-heads or none."

The man's eyes met those of Mary of Moy, as she followed the Queen. And he was surprised to find them smiling.

XII

O N the morrow, in mid-forenoon of the fifteenth day of
September, in a chill smirr of rain out of the north-west,
the royal train left Inverness for the south, travelling as it had
come by the low country route through green Moray—and
without a doubt, Inverness was glad to see it go. Advance-
guards of men-at-arms rode well in front, companies protected
their flanks, the Earls of Argyll and Cassillis led the van, and
the Lords Ruthven and Lindsay the rear. Morton commanded
the main body, under the Lord James, and early came into
collision with his monarch, by whose express desire the forty
Mackintosh clansmen marched in close order around her
person and her ladies. The Douglas did not like it—and said
so, in typical fashion. The Queen was firm, imperious indeed,
and her heedful brother spoke a word in his blustering colleague's hairy ear, and even produced a dull glimmer of a
smile.

They were hardly out of the sprawl of Inverness before
Morton gave the order to increase pace to a fast trot. The
Highlandmen were the unhorsed element of the array. And so
the kilted throng commenced to run, inevitably, and kept on
running, with the long loping stride of hillmen, around the
ladies. The Queen, after an initial frown of vexation, glancing
around and noting the runners' cheerful grins, and Patrick
Gordon and Donald Gorm already each with a hand gripping
Mary Mackintosh's saddlery, beckoned up two more of the
clansmen to do likewise at her own side. Her ladies and
attendants all promptly followed suit, and none of the Highlanders was left without the support that a horse could give.
Thus they ran through the chill misty forenoon, along the
road to Nairn.

It was not such an ordeal to maintain as it might sound, of
course. The clansmen were wiry, lightly-clad, nimble on their

168

feet, and well used to this mode of progress. Moreover, the roads of the time were such that even around her Capital the Queen of Scots could find no profit in owning a carriage; here in the North, and after the recent heavy rains, they were kinder on quick-eyed leaping men on foot than on heavy-laden horses. Shout and curse as he would, Morton could not keep up his fast trot, nor frequently any trot at all. The Queen's new bodyguard was able to retain ample breath for apt comment.

After midday, the array halted for food and rest, near Culloden, with a mere seven miles covered—miserable progress, by the Highlanders' standards. The Queen herself saw to it that her surly Master of the Household, James Ogilvie of Cardell, supplied her Mackintoshes with their fair share of what was available. Patrick was at pains to keep his face turned away from Ogilvie and from such others as might conceivably recognise him—though who was like to look for a Gordon laird amongst rough Mackintosh caterans?

The dreary wet afternoon took them through featureless level country along the fringe of Culloden Moor towards Croy. The Queen was gay now as only she could be, enlivening all who were near her, rallying even her sombre brother and his boorish lords—to their infinite unease. Even Randolph, the disapproving English ambassador, was forced to comment on her spirits in his so regular and conscientious despatches. 'In all these garboils I assure you I never saw her merrier, never dismayed, nor never thought that so much be in her that I find.' Patrick Gordon marvelled anew at that spirit. It was the only sun that shone for them that day.

They made an early halt at Kilravock Castle, little more than a dozen miles from Inverness, where the Chief of Clan Rose provided them with the hospitality which he had prudently prepared for the Earl of Huntly the day before. And here the Lord James's scouts came in with word that the Lord Gordon's army was moving parallel with their route, no more than five miles inland, a host of Highlanders estimated at at least a thousand, working down the valley of the Nairn, with outriders watching them from up on Culloden Moor itself. Moreover, his brother, Sir John Gordon, with another horde

169

of rebels, was said to be on higher ground still, up in the Cawdor woods and moving north-east. Both armies might well join somewhere about Kildrummie Castle, to contest the royal train's passage of the Nairn River thereabouts. Of Huntly himself there was no word, but the worst was feared. The Queen's Council deliberated on these reports for much of the evening, and urgent demands for loyal Moray to rally to the aid of its Earl and Queen were dispatched from the Rose's castle. The Queen herself of course, was not consulted anent such warlike man's business, though she sent word by the Secretary of State that she believed the Lord Gordon to have no designs against her royal progress—indeed, that he was guarding her flank—and that his brother John's threat was vastly exaggerated. If the Council considered this point of view, it was not reflected in its decision. The royal train was put in readiness for instant attack. Patrick Gordon had no opportunity for private speech either with Mary Mackintosh or with the Queen. His position as a humble clansman had its drawbacks as well as its advantages.

This was further brought home to him when, curled up asleep in his plaid in the open that night, he was roused by one of MacQueen of Corrybrough's gillies with a message from George Gordon. It was to the effect that he had learned that his brother John was intending to make a raid on Darnaway Castle, the seat of the earldom of Moray, as a gesture of defiance, and that it would be best for all concerned if the royal army could get there first—in which case there would be no raid, for John of Findlater had a mere three hundred men. But the Queen's force would have to move fast—much faster than it had moved hitherto—for his brother's caterans were no sluggards. He, George Gordon, would do what he could to delay and dissuade Sir John—for such a raid on Darnaway would only increase bitterness, and possibly touch off the spark that would explode the entire North.

Patrick sought to deliver this information forthwith to Mary Mackintosh for the Queen's ear, but quite failed to gain admission to Kilravock Castle, or even to get one of the contemptuous sentries to proceed with a message. Only abuse and threats he received. Some link of communication would have to be arranged for the future, obviously.

Consequently, it was morning before he was able to get the tidings to the Queen's ear, and before her suspicious Council could consider the matter. The Lord James saw it all as a trap—to get him to divide up his forces, one part to go off on a wild-goose-chase to Darnaway, the other to be fallen upon and annihilated by the combined armies of Gordon. But the man's cupidity and fear for his new-won possessions pulled the other way, and he compromised, and the Council with him, by deciding that while there would be no dangerous splitting of forces, the whole train should make hot-foot for Darnaway forthwith—and short shrift for any who dawdled!

So that day was spent still more energetically, especially by the running Highlanders. It was only a dozen miles to Darnaway as the crows flew, but nearer twenty as the royal army had to move, with sizeable rivers to ford. The Lord James set an urgent pace, and many were the complaints from folk unused to such cantrips—but none came from the Queen and her young ladies, and certainly none from the loping Mackintoshes. They were through the town of Nairn and across its river beyond, before the lords recollected that they had expected to be ambushed there.

Darnaway, amidst its vast woods, was reached in mid-afternoon, and without any glimpse of the enemy. But these forests could be full of hidden men. Scouting parties were sent out in all directions, but no actual contact with the Gordons was reported, though the country buzzed with rumours of their presence.

James Stewart, Earl of Moray, was in a state of extreme agitation, irritation, and indecision. He gave orders to one effect one minute, and countermanded them the next. Which was not like him, that coldly calculating monument of shifty-eyed piety. He seemed almost to fluctuate between fear that there would be an attack on his castle, and fear that there would not. Instead of being thankful that they had arrived at Darnaway in time he indicated resentment that they had been brought there for nothing. Indeed, he was hardly installed within its walls before he began, not consolidating a defence, but arranging for the moving of some substantial portion of his force back down to Brodie Castle, three miles to the north, to be summoned hither again if need be. It was whispered that the new Earl of Moray's trouble was that the expense of keeping and providing for the royal train would fall on himself so long as they were at Darnaway; he had already had an unavoidable dose of this on the way north, when he had been infefted in the property, and certainly had not intended to touch his own land again on the return journey; such inflictions fell much more suitably upon others, especially those of doubtful affection towards himself—such as the Brodie. It was a trying situation for a careful man—the choice between possible sacking and despoilment by ravaging Gordons, and the piecemeal locust-like eating up of his hard-won substance by the innumerable minions of the Protestant lords.

Consequently, the royal array did not linger at Darnaway. After an uneventful night, they were off at an almost indecently early hour in the morning, heading for Spynie Palace, where Bishop Patrick Hepburn, the deplorable Earl of Bothwell's reprobate old uncle, was certainly overdue for a process of displenishing. Needless to say, the Lord James managed to spare a substantial and well-armed force of two hundred men to stay behind and reinforce the permanent garrison of his castle. A provident man could do neither more nor less.

It was while proceeding down Findhorn-side thereafter, and necessarily much strung-out along the winding and narrow track through the Forest of Darnaway, that Mary Mackintosh chose to dismount and walk amongst her clansmen for a little way. The upshot of this exercise was that, at a bend of the rushing river, where the woodland was conveniently thick, Patrick Gordon slipped quietly and swiftly into the junipers and away, Black Ewan at his heels. He bore the Queen's urgent words to Lord Gordon.

Patrick found no difficulty in fulfilling his latest errand—in fact, it was absurdly easy. The two men merely worked their

172

way discreetly up the Findhorn, southwards, for two or three hours through the unending forest, till, as they were fording a brawling tributary of the larger river, a picket of Frasers rose up from the bushes before them, broadswords drawn. Fortunately they were of Farraline's people, and recognised Black Ewan, even if they were a little suspicious of Patrick in his borrowed plumes. They acted as escort for another mile perhaps, to deliver the travellers into one of the few wide haughs of the headlong Findhorn, at Coulmony, where the Highland host was concentrated, awaiting the reports of its scouts.

The Lord Gordon received his now blackly-bearded and desperate-seeming fellow clansman, with his own quiet and undemonstrative brand of satisfaction, as one who would give him first-hand information as to the royal army's movements. But this modified satisfaction faded perceptibly as Patrick expounded the Queen's message.

"Her Grace is now prepared to accept your goodwill and good faith, Seorus Og, and to think a piece more kindly of Clan Gordon—or some of it! But that is personal to herself. Before she can prevail in any way on others about her, on the lords and the Court and the Council, she must have a sign, see you—a demonstration, that the clan is not wilfully defying her royal authority. Without that, she says, she is helpless to turn away the doom that the Bastard has pronounced on all our House! She accepts your word that her policy is to seek to divide her brother's jackals, and recognises that not a few of her nobles have their own fears that if Gordon goes down, the Lord James will be so strong in Scotland that all shall be his servants. But her Grace can do nothing, she says, so long as Gordon publicly flouts her royal command."

"Which command is that one, Patrick?" the other asked.

"Her Privy Council's order that Sir John Gordon of Findlater yield himself to ward within Stirling Castle forthwith, to await trial for assaulting the Ogilvies in the High Street of Edinburgh."

"That tuilzie! Is Gordon's fate, and Scotland's, to depend on a flea-bite such as that?"

Patrick shrugged. "So long as the order is spurned, and Sir John roams the country in arms, the Queen says, she cannot smile on Gordon. And so long has her brother all the excuse that he needs to seek to crush our clan."

George Gordon paced a few slow steps to and fro on the cattle-cropped grass of Coulmony haugh, his brows knit. "And would Mary Stewart expect me to urge my brother to give himself up to the Bastard's own uncle at Stirling."

"I' faith, she expects more than that! She requires you to prevail on Sir John to deliver up to the Crown his castles of Findlater and Auchindoun, as a gesture of submission to royal authority, and to state that he will then betake himself to ward at Stirling!"

The other's eyebrows rose, but he said no word.

"Her Grace says that she would contrive to have Auchindoun restored to him, in time, and that so long as he *said* that he would submit himself at Stirling, and set out therefore, she cared not greatly if ever he reached it! But Findlater Castle must go back to the Ogilvies—on that she is decided."

"Is that all?"

"Save only that your father must keep himself at Strathbogie, send his clansmen back to their homes, and declare publicly that he never sought nor thought to have the Crown Matrimonial for any of his sons! She says this is the price that Gordon must pay for her good offices. Give her this and she believes that she can confound her brother's design to bring down our House in ruin."

"But . . . man, think you that she knows what she asks?" the other demanded. "That she is dealing with Gordons, not with low-country lackeys?"

"I think that she knows—but no less will serve. And, Seorus Og—the price could be higher . . . for the survival of Gordon as a power in the land!"

"I know it. But I know my brother and father also!" George Gordon shook his head. "Well—I can but try. I shall do what I may. My brother lies little more than three miles away, at Ardclach—or did, this morning. But I fear that I shall achieve little with him. John is scarce like to see himself as burnt-offering for Clan Gordon, in name or in fact. With my father there might be more hope—but he is less like to heed my counsel than that of any man of his name. I fear the breach between us is complete. He names me traitor, I hear."

"Then he is the less to be honoured, Seorus Og! Myself, I look to you as true representer and leader of the clan."

"Yet my father is Chief . . . and it is to my grief that I must seek to counter him. But such is my lot, and I may not abandon my convictions and retain my own respect." The Lord Gordon sighed, and then looked up. "See you, Patrick, *you* would serve best to carry this word to my father."

"Me! On my soul—no! He would devour me, just! If he names *you* traitor, what will he name me . . . ?"

"Not so. Your position is quite otherwise. Why should he think ill of you? He spoke no ill of you when I handed him his ring from you, and told him of your situation. You have not done him any hurt—and even though he takes John's part, you did *him* no injury by escaping from his unwarranted ward."

"But . . . could you not send some other? I see Gordon tartan about you, now. Is that not Abergeldie, there? And Tillyangus . . . ?"

"Man, Patrick—think you any Gordon laird known to have brought men to my standard would dare to put himself in my father's hand, just yet? Your situation is otherwise. Balruary has produced no men for me. You are a messenger, accredited—an envoy. To send other than a Gordon, on Gordon business, he would take as an insult. I cannot go myself. 'Tis yourself or none, Patrick."

"My place is at the Queen's side, is it not . . . ?"

"Later, yes. But now, if this is the Queen's word, then this is the way that you can serve her, and Gordon, best. With his Laigh folk deserting him, he may listen to you. And if you can convince him, then he may be able to prevail with my brother—and he is the only man under God who can. Even he might act for him, if John will not bend. The Queen could do more with Huntly's word than with John of Findlater's, I dare say?"

175

"I know not." Patrick sighed, and shrugged. "The Chief—where is he, then?"

George Gordon shook his head. "I have no sure word. I am not in touch with him. He has been moving south through the Braemoray glens, sending out messengers to the chieftains as he goes. Some say that he is moving seawards again, down Spey, to cut off the Bastard from the south, and challenge him at the crossing of the river. But I think not. I think that he is making for Strathbogie, and will call the hill clans to him there. It is the thing that he would do. But, whatever the way of it, Patrick, the Cock o' the North ought not to take a deal of following!"

"No. That may be. But I cannot thank you for this task that you are laying upon me, Seorus Og."

"I do not ask your thanks, Balruary—only your service as a true Gordon and a true Queen's man," the Lord Gordon declared, not coldly but with that simple and direct singleness of mind that was the man himself.

And Patrick Gordon bowed his head to that in entire acceptance. He gave the other such information as he sought with regard to the Queen's situation, her attitude, and the proposed itinerary of the royal progress, so far as he knew it, intimating that she expected to reach Aberdeen again in five or six days' time. There, the talk went, the Lord James would gather his forces for the decisive blow at Huntly . . . if the Queen could not prevail otherwise.

An hour later, mounted on sturdy garrons, and with Gordon plaids superimposed on their Mackintosh tartans, Patrick and Ewan Dubh set out south-eastwards on their new mission.

XIII

GEORGE GORDON had spoken truly. It was no difficult task to follow the Cock o' the North's trail. He left his mark—though ravished glens, spoiled townships, and a burned kirk of the Reformed persuasion, tended to produce angry men in his tracks, whom the two travellers were concerned to avoid. By Braemoray, Spey, and Livet, they went, and were able to spend one comfortable night in their own Balruary, where Patrick's gentle patient mother opened warm accepting arms to him, swallowing back a crystal tear and no doubt a flood of questions and entreaties likewise. What she wanted to know she would learn by other means—and did, as much from what her son did not tell as from what he did. In exchange, he learned that Huntly himself had been at Balruary only the day before—and whatever he had come for it had not been to complain about the ongoings of its young laird, apparently. Huntly was faithful, after his fashion. He had left with ten of Balruary's young men to swell his tail, and requesting more to follow. As placatory offering, Patrick scraped the barrel, and ordered another ten men to ride with him to Strathbogie on the morrow. He sought his own bed late, with his secrets, he imagined, also his own—as many a man had done before him.

It was with some surprise, therefore, that still unshaven but clad in his second-best clothes and a Gordon gentleman again, he was bidden farewell in the sunny morning with the smiling request that he would let his mother know in good time when he would be requiring her best bedroom for Balruary's new mistress.

Superficially, Strathbogie Castle appeared to the travellers very much as it had done that other early evening three eventful weeks before. It still rose proudly red above the blue haze of the cooking-fires that dotted its surrounding haughs. The

177

concourse of armed men still invested it, and the vast herds of cattle and horses were penned conveniently nearby. The great courtyard still seethed with the gentry of the name. But Patrick's reception was different—just as the entire atmosphere of the place was somehow different. He was greeted warmly, boisterously even, by men who knew him and saw in him a fellow in the clasp of danger, reinforcement to bolster their cause. And all that throng wore the tartan, ragged kilts, stained plaids, or well-cut doublets and trews. Eagle's feathers, single and occasionally double, flaunted in the courtyard. Morions, breastplates, trunks and hose, and buckskins, had gone. This was a Highland host only—and an uneasy one.

No elegant esquire conceded his admittance to the castle proper, but a lusty Glenlivet cousin of his own, Gordon of Clashmore. And there were noticeably fewer folk cluttering the chambers and corridors of that vast pile. Glendoig, the Seneschal, admittedly met him as before at the first-floor landing, and with no warmer welcome than heretofore, but he was a subdued man and proffered neither advice nor comment.

On this occasion Patrick was shown, not into the great hall of the castle, but into a smaller chamber on the next floor, where he found Huntly crouched over a roaring fire, in the company of his stern-featured Countess and coldly-beautiful daughter, the Lady Jean, fated to be the wife of Bothwell. At the newcomer's arrival, both ladies rose and left the chamber— to Patrick's relief rather than resentment, for he found each of them difficult.

Huntly turned his head to eye his visitor, his hands still outstretched to the blaze—an old man's posture. Indeed, he seemed to have aged indefinably, since Patrick's last sight of him—despite the brave panoply of tartan in which he was now wholly garbed, the flashing brooches, and jewelled buttons and buckles and dirks, all agleam in the firelight, and the bonnet with its three tall chiefly feathers that crowned his grizzled head. In fact, those proud feathers, pointing up almost into the open chimney as their wearer huddled forward to the warmth, were so utterly incongruous as to draw from the younger man a feeling akin to pity for his awesome Chief, for the first time in his life—uncalled-for and somewhat previous as the emotion was, no doubt. His own bonnet doffed, he stood just inside the room.

"Balruary, at Huntly's command, cousin," he enunciated, bowing.

"Aye. Oh, aye," the thick voice croaked. "Patrick Mac-Ruary." He blew his nose between finger and thumb, into the fireplace, with less than complete success; evidently the Cock o' the North was suffering from a dose of cold. "A wee thing late, are you no', Patrick?"

"Yes. I have been delayed, sir, and more delayed. A long story, Huntly . . ."

"Aye, aye. Well, don't stand back there, man, to tell it. For once, I've a stiff neck, see you—and I'm no' raxing it on *you*. If there's any necks raxed at Strathbogie this night, it'll no' be Huntly's!" That sounded more like the familiar Cock o' the North. "Come closer, man, where I can see you. Ye'll no' deny me a sight o' ye, after all these weeks I've waited on ye, Patrick?"

The younger man moved forward, and perhaps his tongue just moistened his lips as he went, his pity for the other no longer distressing him. "I have been following you, Cousin George, across Moray. I left the Queen's side only two days since, with her messages."

"Is that so, boy?" Huntly looked him up and down, and rheumy or not, Patrick sensed no lack of acuteness in those small eyes. "So ye've grown a bit hair to your neck, I see, Patrick; think ye maybe ye'll cushion the rasp o' rope, lad?"

The other swallowed. "No Gordon gentleman looks for rope to his neck, sir! I did but seek . . ."

"Ye've come from my son, George Gordon?" the older man interjected harshly, swift as the thrust of a dagger.

Patrick's hesitation was only momentary. "I have come from the Queen's Grace. But I saw the Lord Gordon on my way here."

"Why?" That was a bark.

"Because the Queen sent a message to him also. Some of

179

his men intercepted me, and took me to him. He . . . allowed me to proceed. Her Grace sent a message, too, for John of Findlater—but him I did not see . . . this time!"

"Ha! I jalouse not! Ye'd be over-careful for that neck again, Patrick? So ye bring me but a secondhand message from Mary Stewart, eh? And the honour o' your belated presence!"

"And ten more men for your tail, from Balruary, Huntly—making a score in all!"

"Aye. Uh-huh. Oh, aye. So you've been home, as well! Man, it's fine to be young, and jig about the countryside seeing your friends and passing the time and sleeping with the pick o' the lassies. Myself, I'm getting ower ould bones for it, I fear. . . ."

"Sir—I came hot-foot . . ."

"Hot-*foot*, eh? Oh, ye're the hot one, Patrick. Have ye got the dastard Lauchlan Mackintosh's wench with ye, this time?"

Patrick stiffened. "I left Mistress Mackintosh with the Queen, at Darnaway, two days agone. . . ."

"Darnaway! God's blood!" The thick voice rose in the three words almost to a scream. "Name ye that thrice-damned place wi' me? May it sink into the boiling abyss of hell, and the Bastard James Stewart with it! Let the name of it never defile my ears . . . !" The three eagle's feathers quivered to the intensity of the violence that surged below them.

And for a little there was silence in that shadowy chamber, save for the crackle and spurt of the log fire.

"Well, man—speak! Are ye dumb? Out with it," the Chief all but snarled, presently. "What in the name of all suffering saints is the lassie's message for Gordon?"

Patrick drew a deep breath. "It is the message of a Queen, sir, and no bit lassie. . . ." he warned.

"Perdition—preach Huntly no sermons, ye unnatural spawn o' Calvin!" the older man rapped. "The message?"

The other addressed the fire. "Her Grace is aware of her brother's design to bring Gordon low, and would counter it if she were able. But she has no direct power. Before she can prevail in any way against the Bastard, she needs aid from Gordon—not armed aid, which will only unite the Protestant lords, but aid nevertheless. She must have a sign, cousin, that our clan is not wilfully defying her royal authority."

"Words, man—words! Come to the bit. What seeks she of me?"

"Three things. That John of Findlater agrees to yield himself to ward in Stirling Castle forthwith, as commanded by the Privy Council four months ago. That he delivers up to the Crown his castles of Findlater and Auchindoun. And that you, sir, bide here at Strathbogie, disband your clansmen, and make pronouncement that you never sought to marry son of yours to the Crown. Do this, her Grace says, and she will seek to turn from you the weight of the Bastard's ire."

Slowly, almost reluctantly, Patrick Gordon turned his gaze from the leaping flames to his Chief. The older man appeared to be taking it more quietly than might have been expected. He sat still in his chair, wordless, And then, Patrick's eyes widened. Huntly indeed was still sitting, but not in the same posture. Instead of crouching forward he was leaning back. But not relaxedly. His back was straightening, and jerkily. Patrick suddenly realised that all the older man's limbs were stiffening, as a puppet's might, and twitching in the process. The light was not good, but there could be no doubt that he was changing colour; always plethoric and florid, Huntly now seemed almost black in the face, his eyes staring. Even as Patrick peered in alarm, the other's breathing grew stertorous, short and getting shorter. The gross body was almost rigid now, half off its chair.

Appalled, the younger man strode for the door, to throw it wide and shout for help. "Ho! To me! Hasten—the Chief is stricken! Come—come quickly!" And thinking of the inner door through which the ladies had disappeared, he ran thither, still calling.

Before he could reach it, the door was flung open and the Countess swept past him, to fall on her knees at her lord's chair, busy hands freeing his thick neck, her wailing as ill a sound as Huntly's choking breathing. Pounding footsteps heralded running men from all quarters, shouts ringing out for the Apothecary, the Seneschal, the guard. Patrick, pushed aside and jostled, found the chill and proud Lady Jean Gordon looking down on it all with dispassionate calm, as she stood nearby.

"Is he . . . ? Will he . . . ? *Dhia*—what is it?" he faltered.

"Overmuch blood," the girl said coolly. "Bad blood. Gordon blood." That was all.

Shocked, Patrick stared from her to her palsied father. And in all the turmoil and confusion, he became aware that things were not entirely as they seemed, that Huntly was not unconscious, that indeed his eyes were seeing, and trained on himself—and their expression less than benevolent. Amidst the coming and going, the passing to and fro between them, the lifting and propping, the exclamation and clamour, that glance remained steady with a fixed intensity, on Patrick Gordon. The recipient all but shuddered.

A litter had been brought from somewhere, and the heavy prostrate Earl transferred thereto, before the blue-black lips began painfully to twitch, to move deliberately. And before they moved to any effect, the bearers had him all but through the open doorway. Then, blurred, indistinct, but unmistakable nevertheless, came words.

"Stop . . . ! Wait . . . ! Back . . . I say."

Men halted, stared, and hesitated.

A single finger stirred from the litter, to point feebly but with entire authority back towards the fireside. The Countess spoke.

"Place my Lord where he wills—beside his chair."

Back the bearers moved, doubtfully, to set the litter down near the fire again. The heavy breathing, harsh and laboured, dominated the chamber. One hand rose a little way gradually, trembling, and that stubby finer pointed—to the door. The lips framed the word, carefully.

"Be . . . gone!" Huntly ordered.

Men glanced at each other, shuffled, and went, the eyes of the prone man rounding them up, slowly, deliberately, as a dog sees sheep into their pen. No man sought to withstand them.

"Bal . . . ruary. Glen . . . doig." Still painfully, but with a little more strength, the words were enunciated.

The two men named, halted and waited.

Once again eyes and finger worked round, to the women. "Go. . . ."

The Countess took a step towards her husband, but that glance and pointing hand did not waver, and with a sigh she turned to follow the Lady Jean, who had moved for the inner doorway without change of expression or bearing. Both doors closed, leaving the three men alone in the firelit chamber.

For what seemed to Patrick an interminable time, there was silence while Huntly stared at or through him, presumably gathering his strength. At length words came.

"The Stewarts—would fell—Gordon. If Gordon—falls— Mary Stewart—will fall. I see—her blood—and her brother's." There was a long pause. "I see—Scotland's ruin. The North— desolate. But—Gordon—will—survive. Cock o'—the North! I see it. Gordon holds—its own. When Stewart is—gone— Gordon stands. I fight. You hear?" The bloodshot eyes moved from one to the other of his hearers.

"I hear, Huntly," Glendoig muttered. Patrick nodded, unspeaking.

"Aye." That came out on a quivering sigh. "Balruary gave— his message—right well. Messenger—of fate—Balruary! Like his—father. He deserves of—our best, Glendoig. See you to it. Our best—you understand, Glendoig? In—Donald's Tower. Every respect—and comfort. See to it, Glendoig. Donald's Tower . . ."

"It shall be as you say, my Lord."

"Every attention. An honoured guest—in my house." Huntly panted. "Now—the Apothecary—to bleed me. And the women—my wife . . ."

"At once, my Lord."

"Huntly—I regret it if my tidings have, have . . . wounded you. On my soul, deeply I regret it . . ." Patrick began. But the upraised hand from the litter checked him imperiously.

"Go," the voice croaked.

The Seneschal touched his plaided shoulder, and shaking his head and bowing it in one, the younger man turned to the door. One glance back, he gave, and found those red-rimmed eyes still fixed upon him inscrutably, before Glendoig had him out into the passage.

There a huddle of men stood waiting, whispering. To them the Seneschal spoke curtly, commandingly. "Take Balruary to Donald's Tower. He is to have all respect . . . and the key turned on him!" And swinging on his heel, he stalked stiffly away.

Half a dozen pairs of hands grasped with all respect at Patrick's person, and he found himself being practically propelled along stone corridors, part-hauled, part-pushed up a narrow turnpike stair, and along a further passage. Practically unresisting, he went—for in Strathbogie Castle resistance would be unseemly as it was useless. Up still another turret stair, lit by deep arrow-slits through which cold air blew, he was urged, to be brought up short by a stout oaken door. When this was thrust open it was to reveal a tiny circular chamber, little more than a cell, and obviously within a small tower, furnished after a fashion. Therein he was projected, left, and the door slammed on him, the ominous creak of the lock following.

Patrick Gordon was Huntly's guest, without a doubt, for better or for worse.

XIV

AND so commenced a strange, unreal, and distracting
period in Patrick Gordon's somewhat chequered career,
a period of contradictions, of contrasting conditions, of physical calm and mental turmoil, that was something new to his
experience and at times almost beyond his bearing.

The full recognition and acknowledgement of his situation
did not dawn on the man at once, of course; he took days to
appreciate the true position, days in which he waited in varying
states of mind, for Huntly to act, to make pronouncement in
answer to his repeated representations, or possibly, to die.
But Huntly did none of these things—whatever else he may
have been doing. And the prisoner in Donald's Tower began
to realise that that was what he was, and was likely to remain.

For prisoner he was most certainly, despite the continued
and infuriating maintenance of the absurd fiction that he was
his Chief's honoured guest, and all the comforts and attentions
that went with the masquerade. An eagle with its wings clipped
and caged in an eyrie with the world before it.

Therein lay the refinement of Patrick's treatment. Donald's
Tower was perched right up at battlement-level, an angle-turret
projected on corbelling, to balance architecturally the cap-
house that covered the main stair-head of the keep—a self-
contained roost amongst the chimneys of Strathbogie accessible
only by the narrow corkscrew stairway, with its own entirely
isolated stretch of parapet-walk, and views over scores of
square miles of the Gordon domains. Here, in all space, an
energetic and impatient young man was penned in a cylinder
of eight feet diameter, with one window giving on to the twenty
feet of parapet-walk and the other opening only to the rushing
Deveron over a hundred feet below. Here, fed on the fat of
the land, with Huntly's own piper to play outside his door
night and morning, with his own fire to warm him, his own

rain-barrel to wash from and his own garde-robe for sanitation, Patrick fretted and fumed and paced, while history was made in the North and dies were cast.

At first, he took it all with a show of patience, assuming a short duration to this outrageous treatment. Glendoig, who had never liked him, would be responsible. Huntly, when he came to himself, would see that this farce could not go on; even if he were minded to show displeasure, he could show it more suitably than this. But as day succeeded day, and messages were delivered by smiling and so very respectful servitors, ostensibly from Huntly's self, such as any thoughtful host might send to an esteemed guest unfortunately laid aside with some virulently infectious disease, Patrick's forbearance and hope ebbed, both. Was Patrick MacRuary perfectly comfortable? Was Strathbogie's poor victuals to his taste? Would he prefer his venison soaked in claret? He would forgive an old, done, and sick man from climbing up to his fine viewpoint, just yet? And so on, *ad nauseam*. The thing became beyond all suffering when, from his so-excellent look-out Patrick was able to discern Huntly himself moving about amongst the clansmen camped in the great haugh below, and even riding afield. The Earl had made a better recovery than had seemed likely—or than his cadet was prepared just then to rejoice over.

Beyond suffering or not, however, Patrick must needs suffer it. He sent messages of course, requests to see his Chief, demands indeed. But to no effect. He did not even see Glendoig. Apart from the servitors—who always visited him in pairs, however deferential, with a third blocking the stairway—the only person with whom he ever exchanged direct converse was Daffing Davie Gordon, a familiar of Huntly's, that rumour called a bastard brother, hunchbacked and not quite balanced in his faculties. Davie had the run of the castle, and soon nosed Patrick out; but he was by no means witless, and knew very well the consequences of offending the Earl. He offered no feasible avenue of escape, however willing he was to chatter, and even to carry messages downstairs.

Escape, needless to say, was not long in becoming a major

preoccupation, however unseemly in the circumstances. But if Patrick was a seasoned escaper, Huntly was a still more seasoned gaoler, with Donald's Tower built to his orders. There was no direct means of egress open; the stairway was narrow and well-guarded—and Patrick, as was obligatory, had carried no weapons into the private chamber of his Chief. Reason, cajolery, or bribery, were equally unavailing with Huntly's well-schooled and disciplined minions. The parapet-walk gave access to nothing save sheer walling and a tall chimney stack. The idea of an improvised rope, made from bedding, failed in the face of a hundred-foot drop. Signals, Patrick sought to make, but who that was likely to receive them could possibly do anything to help him? Black Ewan and his own men from Balruary would be quite helpless, even if he could communicate with them. Shouting was undignified and out of the question—anyway, the noise of the rushing Deveron below would effectively blanket it. He decanted his fire out on to the stone slabbing of the parapet-walk one night, and built up a beacon—but though no doubt it attracted attention and provoked questions, the signaller himself could scarcely see any useful development resulting. Huntly's attentive message next morning, hoping that his guest was warm enough, promising more fuel, but recommending him not to set the castle a-low, confirmed Patrick's own depressed feeling of futility.

His wits, he felt, might not be very bright, but he was at the end of them.

As the days went by with painful tardiness, Daffing Davie became both the younger man's comfort and trial. Visiting him almost every day, as much to gloat perhaps, and to parade his own fine liberty and privilege as out of any charity or fellow-feeling, he was nevertheless someone to talk to, and with his own peculiar and elfin sense of humour—though his gabble was less than easy to listen to, from slack and dribbling lips. But the manner of his delivery in no way implied that what he said was nonsense. In fact, in many ways Davie had a remarkably acute mind, ears that missed nothing, and an insatiable curiosity. No doubt his faculty for finding things

187

out had strengthened his position with Huntly over the years. Certainly, he knew more about what was going on, far and near, than did most—even if the knowledge frequently failed to form any significant pattern in his random mind. Thus it was that by chattering all his crazy mixture of news into Patrick's ear, he kept his hearer informed of how the world wagged in things great and small, and at the same time he all but drove the prisoner frantic at his own powerlessness to take any part in events so vital and in which he was so deeply involved.

It was from Davie, then, as the days lengthened into weeks, that Patrick learned in some measure, winnowing the wheat of worthwhile tidings from the chaff of kitchen and stable talk, how went the affairs of State and of Gordon. Huntly was ever well-informed, and therefore in his own way, so was Davie. Patrick learned that after Darnaway, the Queen's train had spent two nights at Spynie Palace, reducing the over-full coffers of Patrick Hepburn, Bishop of Moray, and then next day pressed on to Findlater. The castle stood above the sea, on a rocky coastline, difficult to invest. The Queen had sent forward trumpeters to summon the captain of the guard to deliver it up but the demand had been rejected with contumely. Without the cannon necessary to reduce it, the royal army had perforce passed on, leaving a covering party of fifty men, the Queen very wrath it was said. She had spent the night at the house of the Laird of Banff, and had then struck inland, by Fyvie, to cut off the hump of Buchan, and so reached Aberdeen in two days' marching. That had been on the 22nd of September.

Since then, events had not stood still. The Lord James was hotter than ever against the Gordons, and had caused to be put out a Proclamation in the Queen's name, revoking Huntly's appointments as Lord High Chancellor of Scotland, and Lieutenant of the North, and demanding tokens of allegiance and submission to the royal authority of all who had been concerned in any way with Gordon, under pain of direst penalties. Aberdeen, occupied and preoccupied, had responded with a hasty compliance—if to the muttering of her citizenry. Spectacles, plays, and loyal demonstrations were put on hurriedly; food, wine, wax and coals were scraped together and proffered, for a projected stay of forty days by the royal household, and a silver-gilt loving-cup filled with five hundred crown pieces presented to the Queen. A number of the nearer-at-hand Gordon Lowland lairds had already made humble duty to the Throne, promising not to support their Chief against it. Others from the Laigh were said to be hurrying south to do likewise—though Huntly had Highland patrols out, to apply suitable dissuasion.

That was only one side of Daffing Davie's picture, of course. All of the North was not flocking to throw itself at Mary Stewart's small feet. Sir John Gordon had made a prompt return raid on the royal covering party outside Findlater Castle, relieving them of fifty arquebuses, all their other weapons, and their captain. He was raiding up and down the Laigh, terrorising all would-be royal supporters into staying at home and guarding their own properties, and had promised to make a torch out of Darnaway Castle—and was said to be coming to Strathbogie here to collect the only cannon in all the North, to help him do it. His brother, the Lord Gordon, was not far away either, sitting with his mixed Highland force in a strategic position amongst the low hills around Rothie Norman, presumably to act as a barrier between his brother and Aberdeen—though some said, the Lord James loudest of all, that he was really there as a pistol aimed at her Grace's heart. And the hill septs were rallying on Strathbogie, from far and near—not on the castle itself, where Patrick could have seen them, but hidden in the glens to the west, for Huntly was temporising with the Queen for time to assemble his fullest force.

Altogether an explosive situation, lively as it was fraught with possibilities—for all except a frustrated and lacerated young man immured in the top of a tower at the very centre of it all.

Fluctuating between furious unreasoning anger, equally unreasoning hope, and sullen despair, Patrick Gordon plumbed his own hell in those days of sunny autumn, the hell of an active and urgent man condemned in a crisis to shamefully comfortable but helpless passivity. In more than his dreams two young women, both of them red-headed, peered in at his inglorious failure with reproachful eyes.

So September passed into October, and no easement of spirit came to Huntly's guest. And the momentum of events increased. The Privy Council sent to the South, to areas where Gordon had little influence, for levies. Also, it sent to Edinburgh for the realm's two most able generals, Kirkcaldy of Grange and the Master of Lindsay. More immediately, it sent Captain Hay, with a small escort directly to Strathbogie to collect the selfsame cannon that John Gordon was interested in, in the Queen's name—for the reduction of Findlater Castle; the only artillery in the North, it stood, suitably, in the courtyard of Strathbogie. Thither the Lord James sent Captain Hay to demand it. Huntly got word of the captain's errand, managed to have the lumbersome object stowed away in a cellar in time, and the remainder of his Highlanders off into the glens and so was able to welcome the envoy with much hospitality, to bewail the fact that the artillery was no longer available, and to send him back to Aberdeen with heartfelt messages that not only the Queen's cannon but the Earl's body and goods were entirely and always hers to command.

This comedy, however, was not appreciated fully by the Privy Council—though the lords were interested to hear that Huntly had apparently obeyed the royal injunction to disperse his forces—at least they were not at Strathbogie and the castle seemed to be held by comparatively few men. This word duly reached Huntly from the Earl of Sutherland, all along his inconspicuous spy and informant at Court. Further word came a few days later, that on the morrow, the 9th of October, three contingents, under Kirkcaldy of Grange, the Master of Lindsay, and the Lord John Stewart of Coldinghame, would converge on Strathbogie, one openly, the others secretly, ostensibly to see if the outlawed Sir John of Findlater had taken refuge there, but in reality to apprehend the Cock o' the North himself—bold men.

190

According to Davie Gordon, chuckling fit to choke himself, Huntly was too wily a bird to take the obvious course and fall upon and demolish these innocents, with his hidden clansmen. That would be only to give the Bastard warning—bigger game was sought than this.

Consequently, the day following, about midday, Patrick from his lofty perch observed the debonair arrival at an all but deserted Strathbogie Castle of Kirkcaldy of Grange and a dozen horsemen, at the main gate, and the almost simultaneous quiet departure of the Earl of Huntly by a postern door down to Deveronside and away. At the same time he was able to watch the gleam of sunlight on steel in various woodlands a mile or so off, where Lindsay and the Prior of Coldinghame imagined fondly that they hid their contingents, to await Grange's signal to descend on the castle. How many thousand pairs of Highland eyes watched this pantomime would have made interesting calculation. The Countess entertained the martial visitors right royally, assured them of her absent husband's entire devotion to the Crown, with an account of her indiscreet son John's mischievous but essentially harmless proclivities since childhood, and sent them away to their waiting and hungry colleagues out-bye with a gift of jewellery for the Queen's Grace. They rode away, with the sunset behind them, with fifty weary miles to cover to Aberdeen and the Lord James's wrath, a somewhat acrimonious and disgruntled company. This sort of thing was no ploy for generals.

Huntly was back in time for supper, the façade of his fine loyalty intact.

These amusements, it might have been thought, would hurt nobody. But, according to Sutherland, the Lord James, Earl of Moray, was as nearly impassioned as his peculiar nature allowed. Hard on Sutherland's report came the official announcement, signed by the Queen; unless Huntly appeared in person before her, and unarmed, to answer for himself and his sons, in two days' time, on the 17th instant he would be put to the horn—outlawed.

Even the jaundiced Patrick laughed at such a conception. The Chief of Clan Gordon, the proudest noble in the kingdom, the Cock o' the North—put to the horn like any thieving cateran! The thing was so unthinkable as to be barely offensive! Strathbogie Castle still echoed to the shouts of laughter when word of a graver sort reached Huntly's well-served ears. The Mackintosh—Lauchlan Mor, Captain of Clan Chattan, had turned back from his successful punitive campaign against the Camerons in Lochaber, and was returning up Loch Laggan-side to the North-East with a force estimated at two thousand men. Seriously this new situation complicated the issue. The Mackintosh had not said that he intended to attack Huntly—indeed, he and his clan were man-rented to Gordon; but Huntly had been the death of his father, and Lauchlan Mor was in the Queen's service in Lochaber . . . as well as his own. Moreover, it would have been the act of a discreet and friendly man to keep himself and his army out of embroilment in this to-do. Huntly feared the worst. Too many of his allies and vassals had links with Clan Chattan. This development required dealing with promptly; a force of two thousand—and Highlanders—at his back, was a different matter from the Bastard's Lowland thousands in front. He would have to talk with Mackintosh, at once—and with the voice of authority. One other factor influenced Huntly in this decision; there had been stirrings and murmurings amongst his lairds and chieftains assembled in the glens. They were being worked on, he believed, by his troublesome son George. A progress into Badenoch on discipline bent, would keep his people occupied, engender a fine aggressive spirit of solidarity, and incidentally tend to fill empty sporrans with the spoil of rich Strathspey—excuses for marching through that delectable fat region were ever welcome. And Macpherson of Cluny, the rat, was known to be with the Queen at Aberdeen, at the old game of striving to keep a foot in both camps.

Huntly, then, had more important things to do than to go presenting himself before the lassie Stewart. On the very day that he was due to give personal account of himself before his sovereign, he set out from Strathbogie westwards, with a force of almost three thousand five hundred broadswords, for

Badenoch. He intended to have five thousand at least with him, when he returned.

He did not find time to say his personal farewells to his honoured guest up aloft, though he sent customary kindly messages—and took with him the twenty men from Balruary.

If the Earl of Huntly took the Queen's summons and threat of outlawry thus lightly, his Countess did not. She was not a Gordon born, of course, being only a Keith, daughter of the Earl Marischal, and so perhaps lacking moral fibre. Her husband had barely turned his back on her, and on the royal command, before she was making preparations to set out for Aberdeen, to make her lord's submissions for him. What male pride and folly might blunder, woman's wit and sanity might redress. She rode south-east, on a jennet, with a small bodyguard, at sun-up on the 19th of October.

Patrick Gordon, from the depths of his despondency, watched her go. Glendoig remained to see to his gaoling.

Lady Huntly got near enough to Aberdeen to actually see it from the high ground next day, when she obtained word that the Queen would not receive her—indeed, that her liberty was in danger. She turned round, and came back to Strathbogie, a harassed and exhausted woman.

Not so exhausted, however, that she was daunted by all the steps and stairs up to Donald's Tower. Barely had she reached home before she was up them all in person, breathless and weary but determined, her coldly-beautiful daughter the Lady Jean at her back, and an agitated and disapproving Glendoig following on with adequate escort, filling the narrow stair-head.

She made no beating about the bush. "Balruary—you have the Queen's ear, I am told?" she panted.

"I *had*, ma'am. Now, I have no one's ear but Daffing Davie's!" Patrick assured her, but sourly.

"She will . . . her Grace will heed you, nevertheless, if you go to her still?"

Though he tried, the prisoner could not keep the lift of hope out of his voice. "I misdoubt it. I have failed her, in being imprisoned here. I cannot think that my name sounds well in her ears, after this."

"It may, yet. I think that she will hear you, at least. I wish you to go to her, Balruary, apace. You must tell her, from me, that Gordon is leal, that my Lord Huntly is the Queen's man, as he has ever been. Tell her this—that the keys of Findlater and Auchindoun shall be delivered to her—I have them here. You yourself shall take them to her. Tell her that my son . . . that Sir John, shall make restitution. I promise it. Tell her that he shall leave the kingdom—that he shall sail for France and trouble her no more. If her Grace will but remit the horning of my Lord, I myself shall be her hostage for his lealty, with this girl Jean here, and my young son Adam. I shall deliver myself into her Grace's hands, when and where she will. . . ."

Patrick, despite himself, was touched. This stern-faced ageing and unattractive woman, that men but followed her husband in showing scant respect to, was prepared to make sacrifice of herself and her children for that same husband. He shook his head.

"What would Huntly say to this, ma'am?" he wondered.

"That is my concern, not yours, sir," the Countess declared. "You will go?"

"Ma'am, ma'am—here is folly!" Glendoig cried, from the doorway. "My Lord's case is not so ill as to merit such methods. You are a-wearied, beside yourself. Huntly has the power of the North in his hands, yet. Never would he agree to such surrender. Would you tie his hands, and him away . . . ?"

"Silence, Glendoig!" The woman's faded eyes flashed. "Would *you* question me in my own house!"

"In my Lord's absence, as his Seneschal, ma'am, I must act for him. . . ."

"In Huntly's absence, as his wife and bearer of his nine sons, *I* act for him!" she cried. "Think you that you know better than I do what is best for my family? Be silent, sir." Lady Huntly turned to Patrick. "You, Balruary—I would have you to leave forthwith."

"Gladly, ma'am. I am not so greatly enamoured of this

cage as not to wish to win out of it. But . . . in this matter, are you not imputing overmuch power to the Queen? Though all is done in the Queen's name, 'tis not her Grace who makes decisions—'tis her brother. I fear ma'am, that whatever you may effect with the Queen, you will not turn the Lord James from his path. And he . . ."

"The Queen, Balruary, is the Queen. Without her sign and hand-of-write James Stewart can do little. Mary of Scotland is stronger than she seems—and wilier. She plays her hand a woman's way—think you I do not see it? As the wife of your Chief, I command that you carry my message to her Grace."

"Your command shall be fulfilled, ma'am."

"Come, then. Myself, I shall see you horsed, provisioned and away." The Countess looked at Glendoig directly, haughtily, but not entirely assuredly, and moved towards the door.

That mans lips moved, but soundlessly, and shrugging, he stood aside, his glance down-bent. Lady Huntly swept past him, Patrick forcing himself to a decent and dignified pace at her heels, and the silent, all but expressionless younger woman bringing up the rear.

In such fashion ended that young man's second incarceration. Undoubtedly women had their uses when it came to opening prison doors.

XV

ALONE, for Black Ewan had been forced to go with the rest and he sought no less trustworthy companion, Patrick rode for Aberdeen, clad once again in the garb of a Mackintosh clansman—and if ever a man gulped the heady wine of restored liberty, that man was Patrick MacRuary Gordon. His throat was hoarse from singing, as he rode through the night—and if there were any to hear, on that long journey, no doubt they crossed themselves heedfully in the dark, for safety's sake.

Unchallenged, unhampered, and scarcely even feeling tired, after all his enforced resting, Patrick rode into Aberdeen, by the Old Toun, on a sunny morning with the nip of early frost in the air and the first powdering of snow visible on the blue mountain peaks to the west. Even the Old Toun, formerly all but deserted, was full of armed men, now, quartered and camped in all the ruined magnificence of the episcopal city. Otherwise, the atmosphere prevailing on Aberdeen was extraordinarily alike that which had greeted him that day, almost two months earlier—the narrow streets and wynds still thronged with idling men-at-arms and their doxies, the retinues of lords great and small beating their loud-tongued way through, everything in a stir and an uproar. The city was enjoying all the favours of harbouring the royal array.

Judiciously leaving his garron at a stable near the walls Patrick slipped as inconspicuously as possible, by back lanes and vennels, towards the town's centre, tholing as best a bare-shanked, red-kneed bog-walloper might the jeers and witticisms that a lone Highlander inevitably provoked amongst the Lowland levies. At least he did not allow himself to become too deeply involved.

The Queen, he learned from a burgess, was again lodged in the Provost's house. And where were her Grace's Mackintosh bodyguard, he wondered—to be informed that they were billeted in the tannery in the wynd behind the Provost's garden.

Thither the traveller made his way, to be treated by a grievously bored company of clansmen to a distinctly mixed reception. Some saw him as returned from the grave, others as a suspicious character indeed, playing a doubtful game. Patrick gave neither reaction much attention. He promptly sought for Donald Gorm, to take him to his mistress—to be told that the gillie was with Mary of Moy in the Provost's house. He would have to wait.

The Gordon had had his fill of waiting. Across the wynd he strode, to the gate in the garden wall, the same out of which he had emerged with the royal banquet party, en route to Black-friars. Outside it now, two Mackintosh stalwarts stood guard. "Gordon of Balruary, to see the Queen's Grace," he said strongly.

They eyed him, and each other, uncertainly.

Even as they hesitated, he heard the liquid notes of a lute, and a skirl of high-pitched women's laughter, from over the wall. Lifting his sword-belt from off his shoulder, he handed it ceremoniously to one of the guards, his dirk to the other, and giving no time for debate, stepped between them, his hand out, to throw open the wooden door and stride within.

No replica of that other garden scene met the man's gaze. The weather was past for pleasant dalliance out-of-doors. Exercise was necessary for warmth—and exercise the Queen of Scots was taking. She was not one who could sit all day in a house, however comfortable, without fretting—and the streets of Protestant Aberdeen were not for her. She was walking up and down the garden paths, with some of her gentlemen, talking animatedly, while over nearer to the house, on the greensward, two or three of her young ladies sought to teach French dancing to laughing gallants, with the aid of Signor Davie Rizzio's lute-playing.

An engaging and pleasing picture.

Patrick's glance slid from the Queen to the group of dancers. There was no red-head amongst them. He stood, for a moment or two, undecided. So far, the Queen had not observed him. Possibly his best course was to walk straight across the garden to the door of the house from which he had emerged on that other memorable occasion—acting the part of one of the Mackintosh clansmen on duty bent. There, he could await his opportunity. Possibly he would not be interfered with. . . .

And then Mary Stewart looked up, saw him, and their eyes met. He saw her start, and falter, momentarily, in her pacing, glance swiftly at the men on either side of her, and then as though rapidly reaching a decision, come on straight towards him. "That man," she said, clear-voiced, "I would have word with him."

She was perhaps a dozen yards from him. Neither of the men who flanked her did Patrick know, he was thankful to note. Nevertheless this drawing direct attention to him was dangerous. Any of Moray's, or the Protestant lords' people present might recognise him, beard and tartan notwithstanding. Involuntarily, he frowned.

The Queen came on.

And then, there was a diversion. A cry rang out, "Patrick!"

And from directly to his right came the sound of hurrying feet and the rustle of skirts. And there was Mary Mackintosh, who had been hidden from him behind a clipped yew tree, coming to him likewise, frankly running.

Right in front of the Queen she ran, ignoring etiquette and humble duty, up to the motionless figure in the torn and stained tartans and ragged shirt. A hand she reached out to grasp him, his wrist, his elbow—almost it seemed that she might throw herself upon him. "Patrick—I thought you . . . I feared you gone! Dead! I . . . oh, Patrick—you are safe! . . ."

Faced with the warm emotion in those sea-blue eyes, the flushed features, the agitation of throat and breast, and all the vivid vital loveliness of her, it took every ounce of the man's will-power and self-control to prevent him from gathering her to him there and then, before them all. He leaned to her, undeniably, his eyes locked with hers.

"*A ghraidh!*" he murmured. "*Mhairi—Mhairi Moytach, mo luaidh!*" His clenched fists quivered with the effort of his restraint.

A voice came to aid him in that—the voice of Mary Stewart, a Queen's voice, cold, level, authoritative. "Mistress Mackintosh! You forget yourself. Think you my ladies may behave thus? Recollect yourself, girl!"

Mary Mackintosh stiffened, bit her red lip, and then drawing back, sketched a not very profound curtsy. "I . . . I crave your Highness's pardon. I was taken by surprise. . . ."

"Evidently so, girl! This fellow may be a clansman of yours—but he is, I conceive, a messenger to me, from—from your father!"

In the pause which followed that, both Patrick and the other girl scanned the Queen's face sharply. Mary Mackintosh parted her lips to speak, and then closed them again. The man inclined his head in something between a bow and a nod of acceptance.

Behind the Queen, Sir James Melville smiled his thin quiet smile.

Mary Stewart went on calmly, assuredly. "You have advices for us, sirrah?"

"*Tha gu dearbh*. Yes, indeed. From my Chief to your Grace," Patrick agreed, endeavouring to make his voice sound humble, and therefore strange.

"*C'est bien*. We shall hear you. But not here." She glanced about her, back towards the house and then forward towards the door in the wall through which Patrick had come. "Over there will serve—in the tannery, amongst my excellent bodyguard. That is best." She turned to Melville. "Sir James—you shall attend us. And Mackintosh—perhaps it is best that you come, also. These are your people, and we may require your facility with the language. *Allons*." And she swept on to the open gate, and through.

The two gentlemen who had been walking with her eyed each other doubtfully, and seemed as though they might follow on, when Sir James Melville waved them back with a veined but imperious hand, and stalked stiffly after the lissom Queen. Mary Mackintosh brought up the rear, and as she came level with him, in the doorway, Patrick fell into step at her side. Close behind her he walked, across that vennel, and beneath the folds of plaid that fell from his shoulder, his hand sought hers, gripped tight, and was gripped in turn. Thus they came to the tannery. The Queen and Melville stood just inside the building, Mary Stewart wrinkling her delicately wrought if just slightly over-long nose at the smell of hides, the interested clansmen leaving a respectful space around her.

"Mackintosh—you—! You fool of love!" she chided, low-voiced. "Would you have your braw Gordon hanging on a rope? Is your dear silly head so turned that he must lose *his*! Think you my good brother will not hear of this—and when he hears, add two to two to make a damning four?"

"I know—oh, I know, your Grace," though it was barely at the Queen that Mary Mackintosh looked as she acknowledged her folly. "It was ill-done, indeed. I . . . I just saw him. I did not think. I was overcome. . . ."

"Yes, yes. But hush you, girl, while still a shred of woman's modesty remains to you! Think of the man standing there, listening to you! Thus was not I taught to handle men—eh, Sir James?" But Mary Stewart was smiling now. "As well for you, Gordon," she declared, "that one woman kept her head . . . and that the new Lord High Chancellor of my realm, whom in my wisdom I have this day appointed, my right trusty and well-beloved Lord of Morton, holds high banquet for his friends in celebration! Else, 'tis like you would have been recognised in the moment this addlepate ran piping your name."

Patrick gestured protestingly. "The blame is my own. I should not have appeared thus, unannounced. But in my guise as a gillie only, I could not have reached your ear. . . ."

Mary Mackintosh was nibbling at her lip again. "I am sorry. Pray God I have not endangered you! I had feared never to look on you, again. . . . The Lord Gordon feared that John o' Findlater must have taken you! And in that man's hands . . . !" She left the rest unsaid.

"The Lord Gordon! How had you word with Seorus Og?" Patrick demanded.

"Well might you ask, Gordon," the Queen said. "When you came not back to us, and the days passed into weeks, nothing would serve but that our Mary must needs go in search of you. With some of these warriors of hers, she rode your Province of Moray, seeking you. She found my Lord of Gordon—and twice all but found his ruffianly brother, Sir

200

John of Findlater! The Lord Gordon told her that you had gone on to deliver my commands to Huntly himself. He made inquiries of his father, but Huntly said that he knew naught of you. So it was feared that you must have fallen into the hands of his brother John, whom the good God punish . . ."

"Huntly said that he knew naught of me!" Patrick interrupted, Queen or none.

"So your Lord Gordon sent us word. Where have you been, Patrick Gordon, all this time?"

"Locked in the topmost tower of Strathbogie Castle, Ma'am. For five grievous weeks—a prisoner!" He turned to Mary Mackintosh. "And you came seeking me? You risked falling into the hands of John o' Findlater!"

"Was that so strange? Her Grace, indeed, all but sent me!"

Patrick looked from one to the other, and shook his head wordlessly.

"But you are well? Unhurt?" the girl demanded.

"Does he puke and pine? I declare that he is fatter than when last we saw him! Use your eyes, Mackintosh," the Queen said. "Huntly has not starved him, at any rate. And now, I ween, the same Huntly having bethought him of some lie or hypocrisy with which to assail our ears, and finding you useful as carrier of it, looses your bonds? Is that it, Gordon?"

"Not so, Ma'am. I come from his lady. She it was who released me. . . ."

"And Huntly looking on?"

"No. Huntly is furth of Strathbogie." Patrick conceived it as no part of his duty to inform the Queen of his Chief's present whereabouts. "In his absence, Lady Huntly sent me with her tidings . . . since your Grace would not receive herself."

Mary Stewart glanced at Melville, and her toe tapped. That grave man inclined his silvery head. "No hurt in hearing what the vixen has to say," he advised. "It could be that the fox's mind will be the more readily read, therefore. You'll mind, your Grace, that myself I was for receiving the Lady Huntly."

"Yes. But . . . very well, Patrick Gordon—say on. How speaks the Countess of Huntly?"

"Fairly, Ma'am. And humbly, as your leal subject . . ."

"Ha! The Gordons ever speak fairly. 'Tis their actions that sound otherwise!"

"She sends you these, in token of her fair speaking." Patrick reached into his sporran, and drew out two keys, handing them to the Queen. "The keys of the castles of Findlater and Auchindoun!"

Mary Stewart stared, they all stared, at those symbols in her slender hands, heavy rusty keys. "What . . . what does this mean?" she faltered.

"Your Grace has asked for these, I understand. They represent Gordon submission to your loyal will. . . ."

"Sir *John* Gordon's?"

Patrick lifted shoulders and brows together. "Not Sir John's, I think—no. But the *House* of Gordon's. Findlater is not Gordon. Lady Huntly bids me assure your Highness that Gordon is leal, that Huntly is your man, as ever he has been. She says that Sir John shall make restitution for his misdeeds—she says that he will be sent to France, to trouble your Grace no more. She says that she, and her youngest son Adam, and the Lady Jean, will be hostage for Gordon, will put themselves in your hands, where and when you will. That is Lady Huntly's message. She pleads with you, in royal mercy, to accept it as true . . . and to remit the horning of her lord."

The Queen was silent, weighing those keys in her hand, as though with them she would weigh the weight and substance of these propositions.

To aid her, Patrick spoke again. "Will not these tidings enable you to act, as you said when you sent me as messenger to Gordon, from Darnaway? Much that you demanded is here conceded, Ma'am."

"Had it come from Huntly, yes. But from his wife, only . . ." She shook her head. "Sir James—how think you?"

Melville pursed his blue lips. " 'Tis little enough to out-face my Lord of Moray with—twa bits of rusty iron, and an auld wife's pleas! You'll need mair, lassie, nor that . . . with John o' Findlater harrying your royal lands o' Garioch but twa days agone!"

202

"Yes. Yes—you are right. I would save the House of Gordon, if I could. But I need more than this to do it. It was Huntly's submission I sought, not his lady's. . . ."

"His wife and bairns in your hands might be useful *towards* that submission, nevertheless," the old man mentioned.

"Mayhap."

"At the price, first, of remission of Huntly's outlawry!" Patrick reminded.

Mary Stewart shook her head again, decisively. "*That* price is not for my paying," she declared. "The Council, it was, that ordained his horning. They will not undo it at such a price, believe me. It is too late for that. You came too late, Patrick Gordon. I fear the die is cast. Huntly has delayed too long. There is no other end to it now, but his full submission." The Queen sighed as she said it, but her tone was final.

"Submission . . . or hanging!" Patrick raised both voice and open hand, unhappily. "It has not escaped your Grace's notice, nor your Privy Council's, that Huntly sees himself in no such desperate case? He still has much of the Catholic North at his back, and many thousands of his own clansmen to hand. He is not on his knees, yet—whatever his lady fears."

"His lady's fears are well founded. My brother has three thousand men here in Aberdeen. There are nigh on a thousand Leslies and Forbeses gathered at the Don crossings. Most of the Gordon lairds in Moray have made submission, and Ormiston has six hundred horse chasing John Gordon in Garioch." The young voice of the Queen, daughter of a hundred kings, rose to the tale of it despite herself. "Two forces of a thousand each are marching north from Angus and Gowrie, equipped with arquebuses and cannon. Argyll has his Campbells hastening across the Mounth to us, and the Captain of Clan Chattan with two thousand broadswords marches from the West. Gordon's days are numbered, I fear."

Patrick's head sank. All that rang a dire knell in Gordon ears. So she knew of Lauchlan Mor and the Clan Chattan's approach! Likely she would know also that Huntly had gone to Badenoch to counter it. The clouds were banking up indeed, and the storm could not long delay in breaking. Whoever won the day, how many of the hill Gordons, his own people, would ever see their glens again?

It was Mary Mackintosh who spoke. "The Lord Gordon will save his clan, if he can. Could he not usurp the power, pull down his father, while there is yet time? For the sake of Gordon, of the North, for all Scotland's sake?"

None could answer that. The Queen shrugged. "Would that he might," she said. "But such is profitless talk—and here is no place for it. The longer I bide here, the more talk there will be to reach my brother's ears—and he has ears and eyes in every place! Time that you were gone, Patrick Gordon—you may not bide in Aberdeen, if you value your life."

Patrick was nodding his acceptance of that, when Mary Mackintosh started forward. "Gone! So soon . . . ?" she exclaimed. "Not . . . not already! Surely he need not . . . ?"

"Would you have my Lord's myrmidons lay hold of him again? Methinks it would not be the Tolbooth *cells* this time, but the Tolbooth parapet for Master Gordon," the Queen declared. "I warrant, already the word of this is in his lordship's ear. Think you not so, Sir James?"

"I think, Ma'am, that this young man would be very unwise to delay his going."

"Yes. But do not fear, *ma pauvre chérie*—you shall not be severed from your precious Gordon." Mary Stewart turned, smiling, to her namesake. "Not for long, at all events. Think you that *you* may remain safe in Aberdeen, when this is bruited to my Lord of Moray? If he conceives that you are leaguing with Gordon, I could not succour you. You must go, likewise. But not now—not in daylight."

"My clansmen shall hold me secure," the Highland girl cried. "They shall keep us both—Patrick Gordon with me. We shall ride forth in their midst, as we rode into Inverness. . . ."

Mary Stewart drew herself up, and in the action was no more the elder sister, the girlish companion, but the Queen of Scots.

"Not so, Mackintosh," she said. "Your clansmen bide with me. They are my shield and buckler, one of the few weapons in my poor armoury. With them, I can talk something bolder to my brother and his lords. Since you brought them, my hand has been strengthened. With me they bide. You hear?"

"Yes. Yes, your Grace. But . . ."

"But nothing, girl." She turned to Patrick. "Master Gordon —get you out of Aberdeen, with dispatch, to lie low where you will, outwith the city. Your mistress shall bide here secure, amongst her warriors, till nightfall. Then come you back, with the dark, for her. I will give you your charges, then. Be here, in this place, at two hours after curfew. I am watched, always, but by then I shall have retired to my chalmer, and can slip out through the window into the garden. You have that—two hours after curfew?"

"I shall be here, Ma'am."

"*C'est bien.* Be off with you, then—minutes may be all that you have. I know my brother, God pity me! Be off."

Patrick bowed, turned for a single urgent glance at Mary Mackintosh, and meeting her gaze, saw that tell-tale rosy flush mount from her throat—and went, with little of the furtive in his swagger.

Mary Stewart's exhalation was half-laugh and half-sigh as she watched him go.

By devious paths Patrick Gordon made his way over to the Old Toun, out through one of the many breaches in its walls, and down across the links to the deserted shore beyond. At a place of rocks, he curled up in a cranny bedded with soft sand, ate the last of his provender from Strathbogie, and wrapping himself in his ragged plaid, slept to the lullaby of the waves.

Twice or thrice he woke, during a day of breeze and scudding clouds, but only to the screaming of sea-birds and the sigh of the tide. His capacity for sleep was one of that man's greatest assets.

The dusk saw him, chilled and cramped, but refreshed and ready for what the night might bring forth—at least, he thought so. He found his way back into the town. It was after curfew, but with the place so overcrowded, and with gentry

205

scarcely amenable to such regulations, the streets nowise could be kept clear at nights. Patrick, affecting a drunken stagger, and occasionally a snatch of song, lurched boldly along the crowns of the causeways, and suffered no challenge. A beckoned invitation he received from one generous citizeness at her dark pend-mouth, but, while her hospitality might well have provided his safest means of passing an hour or so, he sensed himself to be unreceptive to her charms, and amidst a volley of pithy abuse, made for the alternative comforts of St. Nicholas's graveyard instead. There, under a table-topped tombstone, he lay awaiting the Tolbooth clock to chime away his hours for him.

And so, a bare two minutes after the chime of nine, he slipped down the dark vennel behind the Provost's house, and presented himself to the Mackintosh guard at the tannery door.

"Gordon of Balruary," he murmured, and was admitted quick as a mouse into its hole.

In the shadowy ill-lit interior he was surprised to find revelry of a sort in progress, a *ceilidh* or impromptu concert, of piping and song. Blinking, Patrick stood gazing in some wonderment at the scene, the rows of sitting or reclining Highlandmen on the cobbled floor, ranged round the flickering fire of what looked suspiciously like tannery fittings below one of the great vats, the strutting piper, and the tall powerful-voiced chorus-leader who stood with arms a-beat. The abrupt and unexpected change of atmosphere, to say nothing of the stench of the place enhanced by heat and closed doors, momentarily all but overcame the newcomer.

He felt a hand on his arm, and turned to find Mary Mackintosh at his side, bonneted and clad in her long tartan cloak, her face warm in the firelight.

"Thank God that you are safe," she said. "They did not lay hands on you!"

He smiled. Her urgency set him more at ease than did this untimely *ceilidh*. "I'd remind you that the name is Gordon!" he said. "They are almighty merry here tonight, surely?"

"It was my own notion," the girl told him. "This *ceilidh* could serve as excuse for the Queen to have come here, should

her absence from her chamber be noted and told her brother."
And she pointed to the far end of the tannery building where,
illuminated by a lantern and candles, a group stood apart.

Thither they picked their way, amongst the interested singers.

The Queen was there, and Mary Livingstone, Davie Rizzio,
Sir James Melville, and a third man, darkly clad, who held a
little back and apart, in deeper shadow. Also, Donald Gorm,
Mary Mackintosh's gillie.

"You have not hurried, Gordon!" Mary Stewart accused,
but lightly. "Even if you would keep your Queen awaiting,
'tis an ill habit to be late for your wedding—a grievous fore-
taste for your lady!"

"My wedding . . . !" Patrick gasped.

"Assuredly. Do not look so stricken, man! 'Tis worse for
the poor helpless female—I know! Think you that I would
deliver you one of my ladies, this poor lamb placed in my
care by her father—allow you to take her hence alone and
unescorted into the night, into your wild and barbarous hills,
save under the decent state of holy matrimony?" As the man
tried to speak, she raised a be-ringed and mock-imperious
hand. "Hush—would you interrupt your Sovereign? I know
what you would say—that already you have so escorted her.
But just because I have learned something, just a little, *mon
brave*, of what went on on *that* occasion, so must I take
precautions now . . . if it is not too late! Not so, Mackintosh!"

Astounded, the man turned to stare at the other girl. Eyes
downcast, she shook her head, the red firelight no redder than
its tresses. "Her Grace does but jest, Patrick. . . ."

"Jest! Mary of Heaven—I jest not! Father Roche is here to
prove it. Father, come you. . . ."

"I meant the other—about when we travelled before. . . ."

The dark-clad priest had stepped forward a little, a mild
and anxious-seeming man, as well he might be. He was given
scant opportunity for words.

"You said at Inverness, Master Gordon, that you would
sooner be wed by a priest than not at all! Was that no more
than words, sirrah?"

Patrick shook his head. "No. No, but . . ."

"I understood that you had told this chucklehead that she should be your wife?" the Queen charged. "If you did but gull her—if you deceived and betrayed one of my own ladies, Patrick Gordon . . . !"

"Your Grace—this is ill-contrived!" Mary Mackintosh cried. "I told you so, before. 'Tis not seemly. Desist, I prithee. . . ."

"Until your father Lauchlan Mackintosh arrives from the West! And then, will he permit that you wed a Gordon, think you?"

The girl was silent, shaking her head. And then, Patrick was at her side, reaching but to grip her hand. "Bespeak your priest to proceed, Ma'am," he said, strongly. "We are like-minded in this matter."

"Oh, are we so!" Strangely enough, that was the proposed bride's voice, upraised and vigorous. "I shall *not* be taken to wife as a whim, or an expediency, or out of any man's kindness. I shall not! It is not . . ."

"Mother of Mercy, girl—spare us a tantrum at this hour!" Mary Stewart requested. "You were none so backward earlier, I vow!"

Patrick Gordon had his back shamelessly turned to his Queen, now. "It was not as whim or expediency that I said you would be Gordon's wife, at the gate of Inverness Castle, *Mhairi Moytach*," he told her, low-voiced—or what would have been low-voiced had he not had to compete with bagpipes and song; the entire discussion had perforce to be carried on at not far off the shout. "Nor when I plighted you my troth yon morning, above Glen Avon. . . ."

Her eyes rose to his, questioning. "Plighted your troth . . . ? Did you so, Patrick?"

"On the hills of Cromdale, when we had won out of that bog, and you covered in mud. You mind? Then it was that I had to admit to myself that my heart was lost to me."

"Your heart, it is, Patrick?"

"My heart, yes. What else?"

"You have never said so. . . ."

"No? Did I not say so, the very moment that I clapped eyes on you—over in the garden yonder? Did I not vow myself to be your loyal and humble and devoted servant, and yourself my queen!"

She shook her head, wordless.

He smiled, grinned. "My heart that must have been. My head was much too hotly wrathful, thereafter! I' faith—my head would never be allowing me to wed myself to the daughter of Clan Chattan!"

"Nor mine to wed a hillocky Gordon lairdling!" she gave back. She laughed now, too, but it was but a broken and uncertain achievement. "The foolish hearts we must have, the two of us!" she said.

His hand tightened and tightened on hers then, till she should have cried with the pain of it—had she but noticed it. "The two of us!" he repeated, and nodded at the finality of it. Then he turned around. "We are ready, your Grace," he said.

And so they were wed, in the uncertain light of fire and wavering candles, against a background of odoriferous hides, of singing men and wailing pipes, with scouts posted, armed guards at the doors, and the Queen of the Realm assisting. Mary Mackintosh had her clansmen singing mouth-music, something low and chant-like and repetitive, religious-seeming yet that would not arouse suspicion should they be broken in upon. A flaying-bench with two candles and a white cloth, and Father Roche's crucifix upended upon it, served for altar, and Signor Rizzio made most of the responses in his rich tenor. The office was cut to a minimum, and in view of the bridegroom's heretical background, Nuptial Mass dispensed with.

But it was no scamped nor unseemly ceremony—indeed, the extraordinary conditions and the tension only served to enhance the solemnity and validity of the occasion. Patrick Gordon went through it all, with details scarcely registering on his mind but his own adequate anthem and avowal resounding within him. When the need for a ring arose, the Queen herself slipped one off her own finger and into the man's hand. What were the bride's reactions only a woman might know—and be unlikely to tell.

The ending was perhaps a trifle abrupt, owing to a warning

from the guard at the door—but which turned out to be occasioned merely by the passage down the vennel of a group of drunken soldiery. Before this fact was ensured, the bridal party had become only interested spectators of the *ceilidh*, with the groom down on the floor inconspicuous amongst the other singers. Thereafter, it transpired that all the essentials had been completed anyway, and that the principals concerned were now duly and indissolubly man and wife—though it would take some time for the conviction of that to really penetrate, to Patrick Gordon at least.

There was little tendency towards any celebration of the event, save for quick congratulations and good wishes. Signor Rizzio and Father Roche were both obviously on tenter-hooks to be gone, and Sir James Melville was prompt at the Queen's elbow. Mary Stewart fell on the bride's neck, for a brief indulgence in due feminine emotion. Mary Livingstone, somewhat differently affected, kissed Patrick heartily and comprehensively on the mouth—a stage that he had not yet reached with his wife—and while he was still recovering from this, the Queen came to buss him gaily on both cheeks, and to whisper something in French in his ear, the drift of which, unfortunately, he failed to catch. Thereafter, the royal party was making for the door, with the chorus loud in 'Clan Chattan's Wedding March', as accompaniment.

Patrick had to run after the Queen. "What are your charges for me?" he demanded. "You said that I should have them, here. What am I to tell the Lady Huntly?"

Mary Stewart shook her head, "Nothing," she said. "Go you not near the Lady Huntly. I shall send another messenger to Strathbogie. But your Mary knows all—she will tell you what is my will. Go where you may rest safest—to your own Balruary in the hills. There await my word. Methinks I shall have work for you yet. And essay to have speech with George Gordon, on the way. Tell him to seek to hold Gordon back from attacking Clan Chattan. At any cost, see you—any cost! You understand?"

Patrick rubbed his bearded chin, frowning. "Your Grace— Seorus Og will not work his father's hurt. You cannot expect it. Not for any prize . . . nor even for your royal pleasure!"

"Not for the saving of Clan Gordon? Lauchlan Mackintosh—who is now your father-in-law—is new appointed my Deputy Lieutenant of the North. If Huntly attacks him, in Badenoch, as he comes to my command, nothing can save Clan Gordon. Already my brother and the Council would have me horn and proscribe the whole clan of you. If I am to withstand them still, I must have my hand strengthened. If the Captain of Clan Chattan is attacked, then nothing can stem the bloody spate that will follow. Is one man's life worth that price, Patrick Gordon?"

That young man hung his head.

"That is why you were married this night," the Queen went on. "Later might have been *too* late! *Au revoir, mon brave*— and . . . be kind to her!"

Sombrely, the bridegroom watched his monarch's back, as she slipped through the part-open door into the night.

He found his own Mary giving last instructions to the somewhat doubtful leaders of her clansmen. She would return to them, very soon. She was not leaving them for good. And shortly her father, their Chief, would be with them, with the Queen. They must remain here, as her Grace's leal bodyguard, meantime. Donald Gorm would act as link between them. . . .

Donald Gorm, there and then, had three garrons ready saddled, provisioned, and awaiting them in the tannery yard. Thither they were escorted, the piper in attendance—though still the singing went on after a fashion within, as a precaution.

Patrick strode over to one of the horses, and vaulted into the saddle. As the girl started to move towards another, he spoke—his first direct words to his bride. "Mary Gordon!" he said, deep-voiced. "Come, you."

He heard her footsteps hesitate on the cobbles, and then he had his garron urged over beside her. Stooping, he flung his arm around her, and hoisted her up before him, all in the one sweeping movement.

Behind them, as they plunged forward, Donald Gorm scowled blackly, and mounting, took the third horse on lead, and clattered after them into the dark narrow streets of Aberdeen.

XVI

A MAN is entitled to privacy surely on his honeymoon. Let him have it, then. Even if the fact that it *was* a honeymoon took some time to sink in—and produce suitable reactions. But that is no business of ours.

Some things need to be told, however. How, after heedfully reconnoitring the armed camps that held all the Don crossings, the fugitives were forced to go all the way upstream again, through the night, as they had done on that previous occasion, till at length they found the same neglected ford at Nether Coullie, east of Monymusk, and slipped thankfully across. How they came to the Lord Gordon's encampment at Rothie Norman in due course, to discover their bird flown. George Gordon had anticipated the Queen's injunctions—which coincided with his own reading of the situation's requirements—and on hearing of his father's move in force towards Badenoch, had recognised that it was now or never if he was going to seek to dissuade the hill chieftains from actually drawing the sword. Accordingly, leaving approximately two-thirds of his force under Gordon of Glenloy to continue to act as buffer between his brother and the royal forces, he had taken most of his mounted men and set of in Huntly's wake for the mountains of Badenoch, hoping to be in time to prevent a clash between his father and the homing Captain of Clan Chattan.

With the errand done for them, the bridal couple took their inconspicuous way across rolling moors and quiet hill-paths of the Gordon country, to upper Glen Livet, avoiding Strathbogie and as far as possible all other haunts of men— or of women, rather, for most of the men had gone with their Chief. And if, at Balruary by its quiet loch, Patrick's mother was surprised to find her hints about her eventual sup-plantation thus early fulfilled, she did not show it. Indeed, the

212

arrival of the new lady of Balruary might have been just what she was daily looking for—and more, longing for. It seemed that the one thing that the older woman had been seeking all these years was a change of roof; there was a little house a mile or two down the glen, prepared during the period of the unfortunate and hardly-to-be-mentioned Anna of Dalnavert, wherein she was waiting impatiently to be installed. If Mary saw through all this, she did not spoil another woman's manoeuvre. From the first, she and Patrick's mother eyed, assessed, and perceived each other's worth—and came to their prompt conclusions, as women will. Each recognised the value of co-operation. The man had no chance, from the beginning. Theirs was ever the practical sex.

For the rest, the days and the nights of that brief interlude concern us not at all. That they were not compounded of flawless bliss only, may be assumed—but then, such occasions seldom are, whatever the books conspire to suggest. These two young people were essentially and particularly human, not to say wilful, and one at least of them without the fullest preparation for all the implications of matrimony. Moreover, each was affected by considerable preoccupation, mutual and personal, such as might nowise be dismissed for long; the fate of men, of friends and relatives, of clans and armies, even of the realm itself, hung in the precarious balance. Patrick's conflict of loyalties, though resolved, niggled at him yet; and Mary's father and brothers, despite being notably well able to look after themselves, might yet be marching north-east to their doom. Though there was no action that either of them might take that would affect the issue now, the preoccupations persisted in some degree, even when more immediate and personal matters demanded individual attention. Mars and Venus make but trying, if demanding, bedfellows.

Leave them to it, then.

Four days they had, and four nights, and then the summons came. It came to them on the misty morning of the 26th of October in the persons of two weary Mackintosh gillies bearing the Queen's command. Patrick Gordon was to repair to her side at Aberdeen forthwith and in haste. That was all—and enough.

Mary was not named, but even Patrick realised that to seek to prevent her from accompanying him would be worse than profitless.

Within the hour they were mounted and on their way. Though it was with a mutual sigh that they looked back across the still and steaming waters of the lochan to the small grey-stone tower-house that lifted above its cabins under the swelling birch-clad hillside, neither knew either reluctance nor any resentment—almost relief, indeed; they had put their hands to this plough, and the furrow was by no means complete.

A party of five, they rode fast into the morning sun.

By late afternoon they had won out to the edge of the foothills of Bennachie, and were looking out over the wide valley of the Don, awaiting the darkness that would take them across the river once more at Nether Coullie. And as they waited, the last rays of the sun that sank behind all the piled mountains to the west, picked out and glinted on the weapons and armour of a great array far to the south, on the Braes of Midmar, an army on the move, that distance and the dusk soon banished from their view. But not from their minds. Whose, what, and whence was that host? The Mackintosh gillies knew nothing.

It was near to midnight when they slipped discreetly into Old Aberdeen. But no sentry challenged them, no watch inquired their business, no roisterers paraded the streets. And even at this hour, the place itself seemed different, empty; no horse-lines filled the overgrown gardens of the episcopal city, no fires smoked from broken chimneys. Most evidently, the legions of the Protestant lords had gone; that was the royal army that they had viewed on Midmar Braes.

They came without let nor hindrance, through the New Toun, to the tannery in the vennel. There they were told that the Queen had instructed that should they come during the night, they were to be fetched over to her privy chamber in the Provost's house. Thither Patrick and Mary went, across the dark garden, with Mackintosh guards at every door.

Lights shone from the royal apartments, and the travellers were admitted to the Queen's chamber without special secrecy and without delay. Conditions most obviously had changed. Mary Stewart, dressed for bed but with a furred robe draped loosely around her exquisite person, sat beside a fire of blazing logs.

"I thought that it would be the two of you that I should welcome!" she said, smiling. "But welcome you are, both. Tush, Gordon man—do not gape so! You are a married man now— a woman in her night-shift ought not to disturb you so, surely!"

"I . . . ah . . . yes, your Grace."

"Come to me, *ma chérie*, and let me look into your eyes," she ordered, to Mary. "*Oui. Bien.* You are happy. That is well—as well for this Gordon!" She rose, opened her arms, and the two girls embraced—to the further derangement of her attire. Patrick, married man or none, looked up at the painted ceiling.

When he glanced down again, it was to find the Queen's eyes fixed upon him, over his wife's shoulder, and her gaze was strange, unfathomable, disturbing; what it said he knew not—but it was not in the words of a nineteen-year-old girl. It flashed across the man's mind that it could be that the Lord James, her brother, might be deserving of pity, one day.

And then, suddenly she was business-like, and the other girl drew back. "You have come quickly *mes amis*—and that is as well. There is little time to be lost—if it is not too late, already. If you are going to try to save your Chief from complete disaster, Gordon, you will require every moment that *le bon Dieu* offers."

"Huntly . . . ? Disaster, Ma'am?"

"Aye. Folly, knavery, and treachery, to spell disaster, Patrick. As ill a business as is made to stain my honour— and Scotland's. Were Huntly twice as doubtful a servant as he has proved me, still must I needs seek to warn him . . . if there be time."

"Your Grace would have me ride to Badenoch?"

The Queen shook her head. "Not so far as that. Huntly is back on Donside, with Sir John Gordon."

Patrick furrowed his brows. "How comes this, Ma'am? 'Tis but seven days, or eight . . ."

"The way of it, as I am told, was this. Huntly reached Badenoch, and assembled his forces at the narrows of Spey, at some place I have forgot the name of, there to await the Captain of Clan Chattan's army. Your father, *chérie*, must needs pass him there, or turn back down Laggan again. It was a strong position. . . ."

"And have they clashed? Have they fought, Ma'am? My father—what is the outcome, in God's name?" the other girl cried.

"Hush! There has been no clash—yet. Your Lord Gordon seems to have obeyed my word. He has gone to Badenoch and persuaded his fellow Gordons to stay their hands and their swords—at least, against Clan Chattan. His father was like a man possessed, they say. But he could not prevail, it seems. These Gordon hillmen heeded his son. . . ."

"God be praised for Seorus Og!" Patrick exclaimed.

"Amen to that!" the Queen agreed, soberly. "But that is not the end of it. Huntly has sworn that his clansmen shall fight, even if he has to drive them into battle at the sword's point—*John* Gordon's sword! He has ridden back hot-foot to these parts for his son Sir John and his band of bravoes, to impose his will for him on the rest. And on his son George."

"Aye," the young man breathed a long sigh. "Pity Gordon! What now, then? Is it Badenoch for me?"

"No. In Badenoch the Gordons sit about Spey, watching Clan Chattan, and Clan Chattan sits at the head of Loch Laggan watching Clan Gordon. If Huntly returns not thither, there will be no fighting, I think. Which is well. I say that Huntly shall *not* return. So said my brother. And I blessed his enterprise. He is ridden forth from Aberdeen, with the lords, and the levies new arrived from the south, to bar Huntly's return to Badenoch."

"We saw them, I think, at Midmar from across Don." Patrick shook his head. "But, Ma'am—it will take more than the Lord James's lords and levies to prevent Huntly winning back through his own Gordon country, to Badenoch."

216

"Mayhap. But Huntly did not come through Gordon country, it seems. He came by what I am told is the shorter way, if more difficult—over the high mountains, by Feshie, is it and Dee? By the south, anyway. And he goes back the same way—is already on his way, with Sir John and four hundred men. He is in haste, see you."

"M'mmm. That was unwise." The man shrugged. "Still . . . your brother's line must needs be thin stretched, and John o' Findlater's force a sharp enough blade to cut its way through, if need be."

"No. Huntly is even now trapped in the basin between Don and Dee, and the few passes out are stopped, secure. He can not win out, I am assured, turn where he will."

"He can turn back, whence he came, into Gordon country again."

"Not so. The Forbeses let him across Don—but they will not let him back. So my brother arranged it. Huntly thinks that Forbes will not raise his hand to bring him down—and Huntly is wrong."

Patrick thought quickly. The so useful little-known and neglected ford at Nether Coullie . . . ? "What would your Grace have me to do, then?" he asked.

Mary Stewart turned, and looked into the fire, unhappily.

"You have not heard all yet. You have not heard the ill of it. I do not weep that Huntly may not come back to Badenoch—even that he is in a net. But I mislike treachery—and treachery is here. There is a force of mixed clans of these parts—Leslies, Keiths, Forbeses, and Skenes. Seven or eight hundred. They are to offer themselves to Huntly, in his need, as allies—for all their Chiefs have been man-rented to Gordon. And when the due moment arrives, they are to turn and strike him down. That is the plan—my good brother's plan . . . in his Queen's name! Possibly as Huntly seeks to get back across Don again. And I would not leave even my Lord Huntly unwarned of such!"

"But, Ma'am—it is beyond all believing that Forbes and Keith and the rest would yield themselves to this dastardy!" Patrick cried. "Forbes and Gordon may not ever see eye to

217

eye. But never a dirk in the back! And the Keiths—why, the Lady Huntly was daughter to Keith, Earl Marischal!"

"My Lord of Forbes and the Earl Marischal know naught of the business," the Queen assured. "These are broken men— the scouring of the north-east clans. They will wear Huntly's heather as badge in their bonnets. And they will serve. Huntly will not refuse their aid, I think. And afterwards my brother will find the fact that they were Keiths and Forbeses and the like most useful in dealing with their Chiefs. He thinks of everything, does my Lord Earl of Moray!"

The young man muttered something unfit for ladies', even Queens', hearing.

"For George Gordon's sake, and for yours, Patrick . . . and for my own self's esteem, I would warn Huntly. Will you rest till dawn, and be off with the light, to seek him? I think, this once, that you will rest better lacking your bedfellow! She shall be mine, instead."

"My garron shall serve me as bedfellow, Ma'am. I shall do my resting in the saddle," the man returned. "If minutes are precious to Gordon now, this Gordon shall not squander them in a bed."

The Queen nodded. "As you will. I would do likewise myself, I think." She eyed him directly. "I . . . I cannot expect that you will be careful of yourself, Patrick Gordon. But you will recollect, I prithee, that you are not your own man in this business. You are your Queen's man, and your wife's man. Remember it—and see that you come back safely!" And she gave him her hand, at the end of a long bare arm to kiss, and even as his lips met the back of it, turned it over to brush with slender fingers his bearded chin and cheek, in frank but delicate caress. Sighing, she turned back to the fire. "Take him away, girl. I shall await you. And be not overlong about it. *Adieu, mon brave.*"

The other Mary's farewells, if less coherent, took a little longer.

Cold curtains of thin rain delayed the late October daylight. Wrapped in his Mackintosh plaid and hunched in his saddle, the grey day found Patrick Gordon in the level boggy country south of the Loch of Skene, midway between Dee and Don. The two rivers enclosed a great wedge of low-lying territory, dotted with outcropping brown hills of no great height, like leviathans rising out of a green sea, a wedge based on the ramparts of the massive mountains of Monadh Ruadh, out of which both rivers were born, and pointing to the sea at Aberdeen itself, where the two estuaries were but three miles apart. Thirty miles long that wedge might be, with a hill base of a third of that measure, for the western end rose steadily. But the passes out of it were few and far between, and the fords on the deep swift-running rivers scanty and well-guarded. Bridges there were none. Into this great trap Huntly and his son had ridden, and would not ride out again without scathe. The Lord James had waited patiently, and laid his plans well.

Patrick's problem might not seem over difficult; to find his Chief and four hundred men, even in an area so large as this, ought not to be hard. The trouble was that Huntly's was not the only such company therein. The terrain was teeming with armed bands. Much of Protestant Scotland had been scoured for manpower. The Lord James had anything up to seven thousand men in that triangle of land between the rivers, much of the number split up into raiding and scouting and stopping parties, ranging the country or standing guard at strategic points. The local lairds were mobilised to a man—Forbeses, Inneses, Skenes, Keiths—watching their own interests, as well they might in that cauldron of conflicting pressures. And with none did Patrick wish to meet, save only with Huntly's tight group of Gordons. It behoved him to be wary indeed. One party of armed men looks much like another—till it is over-late for mistaken identity.

Where the local people would, or could, answer him, Patrick made careful but constant inquiry as the morning wore on— but sensible folk tended to have gone to ground, and their cattle with them, under the gun-loops of the nearest friendly laird's house, where the inquirer was nowise inclined to follow them. The cabins and cot-houses and farm-touns were apt to be deserted, the able-bodied men had flocked to arms, and the dotards, women and children that still were to be found were less than forthcoming, or for that matter knowledgeable, on military matters.

Time and again the lone wayfarer was nearly into trouble. More times than he could number he was forced to hide himself in woods and thickets and marshland, to avoid roving bands of soldiery. And none looked like Gordon. With wearisome regularity, from high ground, he espied cavalcades of horsemen or standing camps, worked as close as he dared, and withdrew just in time. Again and again, drawn by the billowing smoke of burning clachans and farmsteads, he moved in cautiously to see if this was Huntly's doing—always to find that it was the work of other reformers.

It was noon, with a gleam of watery sunlight behind the smirr of chill rain, before Patrick gained his first clue. He had worked west to the edge of the green Howe of Alford when on the back hill of Corrennie he perceived all the signs that a very large force had passed that way, heading south, but a short time previously, and in a hurry. This was no scouting party—no four hundred Gordons, either. And wherever it was bound, it was on business bent. He turned to follow its all too evident tracks.

Before long, in the neighbourhood of Rinnalloch, he gained confirmation of what he had suspected. This was the mounted contingent of the Lord James's main army. He came on three drunken stragglers, wearing the Red Heart badge of Douglas, emerging uproariously from a pillaged farm-place, faces still flushed and clothing disarranged. What they left behind them within, Patrick did not investigate. But, in answer to his inquiry, they informed him, amongst other things, that he was a knock-kneed Hielant stot, that the women of this country needed their claws a-clipping, that the Bastard Stewart's and their lord's army was in front, heading for yonder accursed bunch of hills—and could head further still, to hell itself, for all they cared; also, that the bare-shanked barbarian was the world's fool indeed to go chasing after it, for the devil-damned Gordons were treed up on that Hill of Fare, and there would be slit weasands and broken pows aplenty before the day was out. Wise men, like themselves, would bide elsewhere.

Acknowledging their kindly consideration, Patrick hastened onwards, nevertheless.

The Hill of Fare rose about four miles away to the south-west, a lumpish land-mass of five or six summits, lifting out of the Midmar braes to no great height but to marked effect, and covering an area of perhaps four miles by three. Was Huntly cornered therein? Was he too late to be of any service to his erring Chief?

Patrick rode fast now, and as the ground rose before him, from one of the great rolling waves of the land he espied the host of the Lord James's cavalry. A vast concourse of riders, they covered the foothill braes, perhaps three miles ahead, the legion of their banners astream in the breeze. Too many banners, perhaps, too many masters, for disciplined handling—but for all that, their numbers would swallow up four hundred many and many a time. This army was in process of working its way around the west side of the Hill of Fare, dropping stopping parties here and there as it went. Patrick perceived that he would have to watch his step hereafter very carefully.

Pulling round, he made for the other side, the eastern flank of the hill. He could see no sign of any large body of men up on the slopes facing him. The place was kidney-shaped, with its back to the north, towards him; presumably Huntly was over on the other face, in the protected hollow. Patrick gave a wide berth to the Forbes castle of Midmar, and picking his way discreetly through scattered woodland wherever possible, made for the distinct corrie of the Gormack Burn that drove deep into the massif. In the very mouth of this, a fair-sized body of horse was ensconced, but the men wore some Lowland lord's livery, and the Gordon had to set his garron to the steep braeside hurriedly to avoid them. A volley of shouts followed him, but that was all. Fools who rode *into* traps could be left to their folly.

Keeping well above the burn Patrick climbed sharply now, making for the high gap between two summits. Well above the tree-level, he was able to see, by the flash of steel and colour and stir of movement, how the entire hill was surrounded. And his heart sank.

He had but little time for his gloomy forebodings. Below the lip of the gap between the crests, he was abruptly halted. Out from a clump of outcropping rocks three caterans leapt, to grasp his garron's head, broadswords levelled at his person.

"What road would you be on, bold man?" one cried.

"A Mackintosh, on his quick road to hell!" another answered for him.

"You are Gordons," Patrick gave back, without argument. "Take me to your leader. I have word for Huntly."

The trio looked doubtful at his tone of authority, uncertain whether they should be incensed or impressed. They were spared a decision. From behind them, amongst the further rocks, a voice hailed. "Here with him. To me." And a tall man beckoned.

"Willie!" Patrick cried. "Willie Gordon, Delmore. Myself, it is—Balruary. Patrick MacRuary, of Balruary!"

The freebooter stared, and then clapped his kilted thigh. "Mother o' God—and it is so, too! A fine Mackintosh you have made of yourself, Balruary! Your own clan is not good enough, eh? Come, you."

"It is on my own clan's business that I come, Willie. You have Huntly here. Take me to him. I bring him urgent word."

"Better than Huntly—I will take you to John o' Findlater. You will gladden his eyes, I warrant, Balruary!"

Patrick frowned. "No! If Gordon means anything to you, Willie, Huntly it is that I must see first. At once. Afterwards, if I must, I shall speak with Findlater. But take me to his father first. It is my right—to see my Chief, first. And all our lives may depend on it."

"Our lives! *Dhia*—our lives depend on the edge of our broadswords and on nothing else—as ever they did! And the edges are sweetly sharp, Patrick MacRuary."

"May be. But four hundred sharp swords will not serve to save Gordon today! You are in the crutch of disaster. . . ."

"Four hundred!" the other scoffed. "Man—there are nigh on a thousand more to aid us, down over the hill yonder.

Keiths and Forbeses and the like. Already the battle may be joined. We but wait, up here, to stop the rear meantime. Any minute the signal to join in the bursting of the bladder may show. We shall drive the Bastard into the bogs down-bye, and make an end of him. And Scotland shall be the sweeter. Does the fool think that he can hold Gordon!"

Patrick groaned. "For the mercy of God—get me to Huntly!" he said.

XVII

OVER the hill Patrick and Willie Gordon rode, and before them the land dropped swiftly into a vast hollow, open to the south and east, and rimmed north and west by the enclosing summits. Down the centre of this green amphitheatre a headlong stream cut its way, to level out and flood the bottom lands with the emerald and black of moss and marsh. And this great basin teemed with men. But not indiscriminately, as an ant-hill teems. Great as were the numbers of men therein, they were tightly concentrated in well-defined and tight-packed groups.

Directly below, and in far the highest position, up near the head of the burn in the arms of the corrie, were clustered the Gordon horse. Away downhill to the south, perhaps half a mile off, and in the lowest position of all, was a much larger body, of mixed horse and foot, in the bonnets and plaids of the North—the Keiths and Forbeses and Skenes and other clansmen of the north-eastern lowlands. And directly across the valley from them, surmounting and overspilling a low flat-topped hill, were ranked the serried cohorts of the royal army, a brave sight of shining armour, glinting weapons, tossing manes and waving standards. While to their right, up a nearby but isolated spur of hill, and considerably higher, a lesser supporting force of Moray's cavalry was strategically situated. The board was set.

Even as Patrick and his escort slanted down towards the Gordon position, the almost unreal and so static pattern of that scene was suddenly broken. From their lofty stance a sizeable squadron of horsemen, perhaps a third of the whole, detached itself, and went galloping eastwards along the contour of the hill, towards that isolated spur whereon the Lord James's flanking troops were sited. And well in front, and easily to be distinguished, was the gallant figure of Sir John

Gordon of Findlater on his magnificent black barbary, sword held high.

"There goes Johnnie, to wipe the Sassenach off yonder side hill!" Willie Gordon cried. "At them, Johnnie! A Gordon! A Gordon!" He would have pulled up, to watch, but Patrick pressed on downhill, however much the stirring assault drew at his eyes.

Their approach to the main body of the Gordon's attracted little or no attention, for all eyes were riveted on the progress of the attacking party, not unnaturally. Patrick, ignoring Willie Delmore, made straight for the figure of his Chief.

Huntly, clad in rich gold-inlaid half-armour, swathed in tartan, his bonnet with the three eagle's feathers of his rank pulled down flat on his round head, sat hunched and glowering on a powerful pure white charger, wispily-bearded chin sunk on his gorget, small red-rimmed eyes following his son's charge from under down-drawn brows. He looked a sick man, and an angry one, his powerful corpulent body slumped wearily in the saddle, his heavy-jowled features lined and sagging, and blotched grey and purple. But the eyes lacked no lustre, and the jaw jutted strongly as ever.

As Patrick cantered up, along the line of far-going horsemen, to draw rein beside the Earl, the other spared him a single irritated glance. "Back man—out o' my way," he growled, and jerked an imperious hand.

A corresponding growl rose from the supporting ranks of Gordon, especially from those whose view the newcomers were impairing.

"Huntly! Cousin George! 'Tis myself—Balruary," Patrick said. "I have urgent tidings for you."

He was allowed a second glance, brief as the first, and keen. "In God's Holy Name—quiet you! Later for you, Patrick MacRuary. Can ye no' see what's to do, man? Wait. Your time will come, I promise ye!" That was grimly said.

"Sir—my tidings brook no waiting!" the younger man exclaimed, desperately. "There is treachery. You must heed me. . . ."

"Silence!" Huntly snarled. "God's death—another word

from ye, fool, and it will be your last! Yonder rides a true Gordon, leading true men. Look, ye—belike 'twill be the last ye'll look on!"

As men grasped at him, Patrick shook his head helplessly, and turned in his saddle to watch whither all were watching.

John Gordon and his dashing company had covered more than half of their mile-long approach around the curve of the hillside. Continuing on their present course would bring them to a slope directly above the drawn-up ranks that held Moray's flank, on the isolated spur, a force at least twice as large as the advancing Gordon's but closely ordered and with little room for manoeuvre. Undoubtedly they had been sent there purely as a threat to encircling movement, not to withstand deliberate assault. Even as the attackers approached, the watchers from afar could observe a stirring and breaking away in the compact ranks, as some moved down from the hilltop into the small dip that separated them from the main hillside rising above them. No doubt, their aim was to break the Gordon's first impetus.

But John Gordon ignored them. All his life he had been ignoring the feints of others. Straight as an arrow he led his hundred-and-fifty, till they were directly above the enemy, crowded on their hillock and spilling down into the dip. Past them, he careered, and had the people in the little hollow streaming this way and that in doubt. And then, at a given signal, he swung his force as a single man, and took it thundering down the steep slope at a tangent, in a full charge.

The watchers could hear the war-cry of "A Gordon! A Gordon!" echoing across the mile of heather, and in their excitement they took it up and threw it back, in encouragement and pride. "A Gordon! A Gordon!"

Their shouting was punctuated, however, by the rattle of a discharge of arquebuses, from dismounted men amongst the horses. Three or four of the Gordon horses were seen to stumble and fall, rolling down that steep face. But the range was over-long as yet, and moreover, the noise of the volley set up such a rearing and alarm amongst the enemy's own horses, close-crowded as they were, that even from a distance it was apparent that the firearm salvo had been a mistake.

Down the Gordons plunged, in a headlong cataract of horse-flesh, shouting men, and thrusting steel, Sir John two lengths in advance. Nothing below could withstand the impact of that charge; sheer gravity would have ensured that. And infinitely more than gravity was here. Driving through the people in the dip like a fist through paper, they swept on up the lift of the hillock beyond.

Now would have been any opportunity there was for the defenders. But instead of hurling themselves down upon the up-climbing Gordons, they stood fast. Perhaps their leaders misunderstood the role of cavalry. Perhaps there were too many leaders—or none. But there they waited, huddled. And with a bare hundred feet to climb out of the dip, the Gordons were up and amongst them, swords flailing, with still some of the impetus of their downward charge unspent. Tight-packed as they were, and unable to make use of either weight or mobility, the Lowland horse wilted under the shock, keeled over like ninepins, and were lost. They probably suffered comparatively few actual casualties, but they broke and scattered and fled.

In less time than it takes to tell, they were streaming down-hill towards the main army, in ragged groups, and Sir John of Findlater's standard flew proudly from their lost position.

Moray's flank was open.

A thunderous cheer rose from the Gordon throats around Patrick, drowning Huntly's chuckled acclaim. Men shook each other by the hand, clapped corseleted backs and grinned wide-mouthed. But there was more than mere congratulation and applause therein; there was self-encouragement and the bracing of nerves and mettle. It was their turn, now.

Gordon of Cocklarachie, a swank and black-avised soldier of fortune, and one of Findlater's boon companions and principal lieutenants, thrust his mount between Patrick and his Chief. "Time for us to put ourselves in order, Huntly," he cried. "When yonder banner of Johnnie's dips, we ride!"

"Aye, Cocklarachie—see you to it," the Earl nodded. "They

all ken the way o' it? We cross the burn half-roads down, by yonder rowan-tree—this side goes down to soft bog that would sink us. Then straight for the enemy, cross the burn again below the big bend, and up at him. The mass o' the Keiths and Forbeses will cross further to our right hand, and assault the hill from the southward. And Sir John will descend on them on our left hand. Assailed from three sides, and with falling ground behind him, the Bastard will neither stand nor reform. He is delivered into our hands. See that the lads know the way o' it, Cocklarachie—there maun be no mistakes. And God be merciful to James Stewart—for I will not!"

" 'Tis done, Huntly—all know the ploy. I will see that all are ready. . . ."

"For blessed mercy's sake—you must hear me, Huntly!" Patrick exclaimed. "Before it is too late. I come from the Queen, to warn you. . ."

"Hush, man—too late it is, now! What time is this for a lassie's warnings?" the Earl said, shaking his head. "I hae listened to ower many such already. We face action now, not talk. Draw your sword, Patrick, if ye're no' feart, and play the man!"

"*Dhia*—if you slay me for it, you shall hear me, Huntly! The Queen would save you, if she may. Those clans down there are false. They are in the Bastard's pay. They will not fight for you, but against you. The Lord James has planned it. . . ."

"You haver, boy!" the older man rasped. "Those men down there are bonded to me—Forbes and Keith and the like. Is Keith no' my ain wife's folk, and a daughter o' mine married to Forbes himself!"

"But the Laird of Forbes and the Marischal come not into this," Patrick asserted. "They know naught of it. These are broken men, the scourings of the North . . ."

"And ye think that they will therefore serve the Bastard, the Southron, rather than me, the Cock o' the North? Even if they hae his money in their pouches!"

"They are sworn to do so. The Queen got word of it and . . ."

228

"Man, man—ye are young and foolish! Do broken men ne'er break their word? If they are what ye say, they will fight on the side that savours o' winning, see you. And that is Gordon. Saw ye not what went on on yonder hill. That will be the way o' it. The Bastard has numbers—but little else. His lords hate and fear each other. Not one in his ramshackly array trusts the other. Yonder is no army, but a score of rabbles itching for each other's throats! Swallow your fears, boy—and your tongue with them! There is no time for chatter and debate. . . ."

"If these, below, fail you, Huntly, you are outnumbered five to one," Patrick persisted doggedly. "Why risk all on such a throw, when your son has opened a way of escape for you over yon hill? Ride thither, and through the gap he has made for you. I will lead you to an unguarded ford over Don, at Nether Coullie . . ."

The older man had turned away from him, listening to Tillyangus and Craigoullie. But he had heard, in some fashion, for he tossed back some reply over his shoulder. "I have trysted to meet my son on the spot where the Bastard now stands! Think you Huntly shall fail him and bolt like a frightened deer?"

"If you rode now, he would perceive your change of plan, and wait," Patrick declared. "For the sake . . ."

"Too late!" Tillyangus cried and pointed. Over on the captured hilltop Findlater's standard that had been clear to be seen by all, had disappeared. Even as they looked, a great shout from its vicinity lifted to give point to its vanishing.

"The signal!" Cocklarachie called, at Huntly's back. "We ride! Gordon rides!" and he tossed his naked broadsword twirling high into the air, to catch it again expertly, laughing.

"A Gordon! A Gordon!" the cry swelled from near three hundred throats behind them, swelled and maintained.

"Huntly . . . !" Patrick exclaimed, despairingly.

"Too late, boy—too late. I shall not fail my fine son this day! Out with your sword, man." Huntly was unhandily tugging at his own. "Forward!" He raised his wheezy wet voice. "For Gordon! Bydand! A Gordon!" The words shrilled and cracked in his throat.

And the roar of voices and the pound of hooves swept them up in its savage fierce refrain.

What followed, was ever a jumbled confusion in Patrick's mind—as are most battles to those who take part in them. How long it lasted, what stages the affray went through, and how the balance swung, were only doubtfully and uncertainly sensed rather than consciously perceived. The fog of war depends not on the smoke of gunpowder so much as on the emotions and limitations of individual men.

Down the hill, parallel with the brawling burn, the Gordon host thundered, the braeside ashake to their going, Cocklarachie and Tillyangus in the lead—Huntly's age, portly figure and heavy charger all unfitting him for such position. Patrick, clinging close to his Chief, no doubt shouted with the rest; certainly, his sword was in his hand, and for the time being he had dispensed with worrying, with thinking even. In this mad gallop, thronged on every side by his straining fellows, thought was at a discount.

But somewhere down that first near-mile's breakneck progress, a corporate perception grew on the charging company, that all was not well. Undoubtedly those in the lead, heading for that point in the burn's course where they had planned to cross, recognised it first, and something in their attitude communicated itself to their less responsible followers, and gradually made its impact. The plan was not working as it should. Though no blow would yet be struck for a time, things were going agley.

It was the great concourse of clansmen down on the low ground. Their orders had been, when they saw the Gordon main body start its charge, to move half-right, cross the burn which here took a great bend southwards, and storm the south face of the rise whereon Moray's army was based. They were on the move now, indeed—but instead of slanting half-right they were moving due left. In a solid phalanx they shifted over, between eight hundred and a thousand men, across the very route that the advancing horsemen had planned to cover.

The move took a little time, of course—time in which the Gordons were hurtling down towards it. Cocklarachie turned in his saddle, to gaze back towards Huntly in doubt and indecision. He was supposed to lead the way across the burn in a hundred yards or so—but once across the stream, they must drive straight into the mass of men. Huntly, staring tight-lipped, plunged on for a moment or two, and then gestured onwards, forwards, on their present course—not to cross the burn. Patrick saw, they all saw, and their shouting died on them, as their voices sank with their hearts.

Huntly had little or no choice; almost certainly he had to take the course he did. Sir John had just commenced his own downwards rush; to have halted the charge now, even if possible, would have been to leave Findlater and his men to their fate. To continue on the chosen course would have meant a headlong collision with the bedevilled Forbeses and Keiths, and the utter break up of his advance. To continue down the open north side of the burn was all that was left to him. The mass further down seemed to be halting at the burnside; even if it surged across, the Gordons would be down there before any large proportion were over. But it was the wrong side of the burn—and the emerald green of bog awaited them, balefully smooth.

It was too late for any other decision now. Down the remainder of the slope the charge proceeded, grimly silent men and snorting pounding horses.

They came level with the first ranks of the clansmen, false or mistaken. They were stationary now, drawn up along the far side of the stream, and silent also. Perhaps Huntly had been right—broken men would break their word to the Bastard just as readily as to himself. They made no hostile gesture, now; just stood in their hundreds, Huntly's heather sprigs in their bonnets, waiting—waiting upon developments. They would strike no blow for either side, until they saw how the battle went. Broken men—with no hearts to break.

Past their treacherous close-ordered ranks the Gordons hurtled, no more than thirty yards distant from the nearest, with only the splashing chuckling burn between—and Gordon lips were not silent then. Some few of them had the grace to drop their eyes before the burning hate and scorn of betrayed men—but nothing could stop their ears to the blistering epithets and potent cursing of men about to die.

On the downward onslaught maintained. Cocklarachie was shouting something now, and pointing here and there with his sword—advising desperately how to take the bog. Patrick, glancing up higher, saw Findlater's force halfway down their slope in gallant style. But his glance was drawn elsewhere. The royal army was on the move, unhurriedly, not charging, it was deliberately advancing down towards them—though leaving a reserve on its plateau to deal with Sir John.

And then, all such observation came to an abrupt closure, as the Gordon horse reached the waterlogged bottom-land, their leaders' arms waving them outwards into wider dispersal. Hillmen all, they knew what to expect. But it was worse, infinitely worse, than their direst forebodings. Cocklarachie, in the front, racing to cover what looked like a slightly more solid causeway of dried peat, proved it to be only the merest skin, had his mount immediately bogged to the belly, to be thrown headlong and all but buried in a fountain of jet-black mud.

Unable to draw up or even to slew round to any extent, owing to their pace and close array, the Gordons came in after him. As their leaders were engulfed in their turn, men endeavoured to swing away to their left, to try to hold to higher firmer ground, to encircle the bog. Patrick and Huntly himself, sought to pull round that way. But the impetus and weight of their going, the treacherous nature of the surface, and the lie of the land, all worked against them. Some few managed to remain on solid ground, others succeeded in floundering in some fashion to more substantial terrain, but the vast majority were swiftly and hopelessly sucked in, foundered, and brought low. Seldom can such a furious charge have come to such a sudden halt, or so fierce a body of experienced fighting-men have met with such complete disaster.

Patrick's garron plunged, sank to its knees, and pitched forward. He was tossed over its outstretched neck, and fell into a spongy bed of moss, his sword wrenched from his hand. Scrabbling, flailing with his arms, he strove to work himself free of the clutching cloying softness. Somehow he got to his feet—and found the mire to come up over his knees. When he sought to move, his legs were anchored, and he fell again. He could feel firm ground beneath his brogues, but there were a couple of feet of peat-broth above it. Rising anew, and standing still, he stared about him.

Unutterable chaos filled that hollow. Fallen men and horses were floundering and sprawling all around him. He looked for Huntly. His white charger was readily distinguishable, lying on its side, its hooves lashing the mud. Its rider, presumably, was one of the bodies struggling on all fours in the mire nearby. Drawing one foot out with great effort, falling forward, and drawing the other after it, Patrick began laboriously to cover the intervening space of a dozen yards.

Somehow he got to Huntly's side, found a fairish stance for his wide-planted feet, and stooped to help to raise the massive obese figure to its feet. His Chief was a sorry sight, bonnet gone, his almost bald head plastered in peat-mud like the rest of him, his face congested, breathing laboured and erratic. He did not answer when Patrick demanded how he fared. He did not speak at all. Respiration alone seemed to be sufficient task for him. With difficulty the younger man held him up, and cast about him with urgent glance for a course of action. If he could but get help, to drag Huntly back to firm ground, at least . . .

Patrick's swift survey revealed three circumstances. The front ranks of Moray's army were drawing near; the wretched clansmen at their back, cause of this astounding débâcle, were beginning to approach across the stream towards them, in little doubt now as to where lay their duty; and up on the hill, John of Findlater had changed the direction of his onset, and was galloping down straight for them in heroic and hopeless support—though that would take him directly across the front of the advancing army.

Everywhere, the bogged and unhorsed Gordons were struggling to win back to solid earth, cursing, all but weeping

233

in their helpless fury. Patrick found two men to aid him with the speechless Huntly. Almost dragging him, they laboured to get him back those dire few yards to rising ground.

And then James Stewart struck. From the further edge of the bog, his arquebusiers dismounted, set their pieces, and fired. Their aim, with these new-fangled weapons, was but doubtful, and their fire ragged—but the range was short and the targets bunched, all but motionless, unable to retaliate or to take cover. It was excellent practice for Kirkcaldy's new levies. Men died, and dug their graves with their own weight. Men, wounded only, not infrequently did likewise.

One of the men aiding Patrick with their Chief was struck at the base of the neck, and died instantly. Patrick himself was grazed down his left forearm with a ball. In front of him, he saw young Glenlogie hit, pitch beside the thrashing hooves of a fallen horse, and be kicked into a bloody pulp. And still the shooting maintained.

But they were to have a respite. As Sir John's company drew closer, with a detachment of the royal army cutting in behind them, the fire of the arquebusiers was lifted from the target in the bog and hurried some way to the flank to deal with the new opportunity, as Findlater cut across part of their front. It was a less rewarding, because more swiftly-moving, mark—but still the execution was considerable. Numbers of men and horses fell. This new kind of warfare was going to demand revised tactics from honest decent fighting-men. In fury, John Gordon swung his squadron through almost a right-angled turn, and charged the arquebusiers, dead in the face of their fire. And in all their waiting ranks, the royal horse moved cheerfully down for the kill.

The hail of shot lifted from them for the moment, Patrick and his colleague succeeded in getting Huntly back on to solid ground. Most of the Gordons who still could move were there already—barely two hundred out of the original three hundred, and not forty of them mounted. But not to stand idle, dress wounds, or recover themselves. The mass of the false clansmen were now across the burn and advancing upon them. They came without any dash or fire, but they came deliberately, their purpose plain. Every bitter wordless Gordon who had sword or dirk and could handle them yet, went grimly to meet them. Here was something that they could do before they died.

Patrick drew his own dirk. The man at Huntly's other side still had his broadsword. He gestured with it back towards the bog and the burn, shaking fist and it together.

"Accursed be the name of Corrichie, from this ill day until the last day of time!" he cried, hoarse and choking. "Corrichie—God Almighty's curse upon it!"

"Cor . . . Cor . . . Corrichie . . . ?" The syllables issued slowly, in a wheezy croak from Huntly's throat.

"Aye, Corrichie—black be the name of it! There flows the Corrichie Burn . . . and Gordon's life-blood!"

"Corrichie! Cor—Cor—" A pause. "Then God—be—merciful—unto me!" the Cock o' the North muttered, and lurched heavily, so that only his two supporters saved him from falling.

Patrick gulped, and knew the icy finger of fear upon him. Whether the other Gordon was aware of the significance of his words, *he* was. All those close to Huntly knew. As a young man, the Earl had been warned by a spae-wife who had no reason to love him, that he would meet his doom at Creighie. At least, Creighie was the name that Huntly had taken her as saying—and the name of a placing lying between Strathbogie and Aberdeen, which the Chief had religiously made a point of avoiding, however he might scoff, and at whatever inconvenience. And now—Corrichie!

Holding up the stricken Earl, Patrick looked desperately around him. The pitifully few mud-stained Gordons were being overwhelmed inevitably, falling where they stood, and killing ferociously as they fell. Behind, across the bog, Sir John and his company had completely disappeared, lost and swallowed up in the tenfold superiority of the royal cohorts. Already Lowland horse were beginning to ride round the rim of the bog towards them. The day was completely and disastrously lost—and much more than the day.

Patrick prepared to do all that remained to him—to save his Chief alive, if might be, and if that was denied him, to sell

235

his own life dearly. The advancing clansmen looked as though they were taking no prisoners. It was debatable as to who would reach them first—their coldly bloodthirsty betrayers or the Lord James's horsemen.

The question was decided, purposely or otherwise, by the sudden reopening of the arquebus fire. Shot came whistling over into the backs of the remaining Gordons—and inevitably, into the faces of the advancing clansmen. Great was the consternation and the roar that went up, and immediately the situation was changed. Almost to a man the north-country foot began to press back instead of forward, amidst enormous confusion. Bewildered Gordons turned, uncertain which way to face. For a few moments the shots continued to fall, and then died away as the first of the royal cavalry swept up.

Further resistance was not only hopeless but inconceivable. Sullenly the few remaining Highlanders stood amongst the dead and dying, the moaning wounded and the lashing horses, their red sword-tips to the trampled ground.

Patrick found a group of four horsemen bearing down on him. He threw down his dirk, setting his brogued foot upon it, and waved to them urgently. "Here is the Earl of Huntly!" he cried. "Hold you! A sick man—and your prisoner."

The riders pulled up. The foremost, a big burly fellow wearing the colours of Douglas, waved a heavy pistol at him. "Huntly, eh? This bag o' carrion?"

"The Earl of Huntly, Lord of Aboyne, Chief of Clan Gordon, and lately Lord High Chancellor of Scotland!" Patrick desperately made the titles sound as momentous as he knew how, to impress this oaf that had immediate power of life and death in his great hands. "An important prisoner, for my Lord of Morton!"

"Eh? Aye—och, aye. Though be damned, he doesna look it! But we'll gey soon find oot, or my name's no' Andra Redpath!" Holding his pistol within a yard of Huntly, he gestured with it. "Come, on, wi' you."

"He is a sick man, I tell you. He cannot walk. . . ."

"Goad's death!" the other grumbled. "Sandy—get doon an' hae him up on your beast, the aul carl. Up wi' him."

But all four horsemen, and Patrick also, were needed to hoist the massive and almost inert body of Huntly up on to the animal. With horror, Patrick saw that he had begun to twitch and jerk, as on that evening at Strathbogie Castle. The face was darkening too. Walking by the horse's flank, and trying to support him in the saddle, the younger man moved forward at the fellow Redpath's command.

Only a hundred or two yards they had gone, around that fateful bog, when the thronging men-at-arms on all sides drew aside hastily and respectfully to give passage to a group of plumed and richly armoured riders. In their midst, clad all in black, with neither weapon nor any of the panoply of war about him, sat James Stewart, Earl of Moray, looking more than ever like an inferior if sanctimonious clerk in holy orders. He halted at sight of them, raising a long arm to point—and all the gorgeous throng with him halted likewise with notable promptitude.

"Is that the outlaw, George Gordon?" he demanded, his fish-like eyes cold, cold.

" 'Tis said to be the Earl o' Huntly, my Lord," Redpath called.

"Aye. The Earl of Huntly that *was*!" Moray grated. "George Gordon—you are delivered into the hands of justice, by the finger of the all-just God Himself, to answer for your sins. Your son, also! God's kingdom upon this earth is the nearer for this day!"

Huntly, a strange jerking figure, his head and neck swelled horribly so that his gorget seemed to choke him, his face almost black, gradually, painfully, raised a wavering arm. Slowly a finger pointed, pointed tremblingly at James Stewart. The thick lips moved, but no sound issued therefrom. And slipping sideways the ungainly body fell, despite Patrick's clutching, and crashed heavily to the ground. When he ran round to him, the younger man knew before he stopped beside his fallen Chief, that the game was played to the bitter end. The Bastard, and apoplexy, had won. George, fourth Earl of Huntly, was dead.

The Lord James's down-turning mouth turned down still

further in distaste. "Too much blood—and all of it bad!" he said, and turned his horse's head round, to move away. "Bring him . . . and tie his son to him. They shall ride the one horse, and make a pretty pair! Come."

That was the Battle of Corrichie.

XVIII

THE victorious army staged a triumphant entry into Aberdeen, with the Gordon vanquished, dead and alive, as an important item therein. The dead were set up on appropriately prominent points in the town, and Huntly was publicly disembowelled outside the Tolbooth. The living would make their suitable contribution to the festivities, in due course. With the latter Patrick trudged, amongst perhaps one hundred and eighty others, Sir John of Findlater, blood-stained but erect, limping at their head. It was a day to be remembered. The Queen and her court were duly escorted to a convenient stance where nothing might be missed. James Stewart proved himself as a showman, to add to his other capabilities.

After a fairly full day, the weary and wounded prisoners were penned into the same burying-ground of St. Nicholas where Patrick had taken refuge from temptation and other forces on the evening of his wedding. The rank and file, that is; John Gordon, Cocklarachie, and such other lairds as had survived, were removed and locked up elsewhere, for greater security.

That night, Aberdeen held high carnival.

Thus it was that when a strong and well-armed party of Mackintoshes of the Queen's bodyguard appeared at the graveyard during the early part of the night, well supplied with the wine of the country, they had not a great deal of difficulty in persuading the celebrating guards that a single errant Mackintosh amongst the prisoners would be most suitably and drastically dealt with by his own loyaler clansmen.

So Patrick was abstracted from the midst of his less fortunate colleagues, with a minimum of upset. He pleaded for one or two of his fellow-captives, particularly the man who had aided him with Huntly. But Donald Gorm, who led the rescue party, had strict orders, and had no intention of infringing them for any Gordon whatsoever.

Through the thronged and noisy streets, then, they came to the tannery. And there the man yielded himself thankfully to the arms, the mothering, even the tears of his fine new wife, content for once that all decisions should be hers. He was tired, tired, and numbed in some essential part of him, and there were corners of his mind into which he dared not look—not yet. Patrick's spirit was as weary and bludgeoned as the rest of him. He wanted only somewhere to hide and rest and salve it. His Mary perceived it, and in her womanly pity something of her knew gladness for it. She took him to her young and generous bosom, actually and metaphorically, and yearned over him, hers as never he had been before.

But she did more than yearn. She dressed as well as kissed his wounded forearm, fed him, found him fresh clothing, and trimmed his beard to a square spade that, with the new gauntness of his cheeks, changed the appearance of him notably. And the vital strength of her was not the least of her gift to that man, who needed it all.

The Queen came to them just before midnight, when at last she had been able to withdraw herself, without exciting suspicion, from the feasting and gaiety with which her Council were celebrating victory and the downfall of the power of Gordon. She was quiet, restrained for her, almost as though she was on the defensive. Perhaps the defensive was becoming second and unlikely nature to that young woman.

"I thank the good God to see you returned safely, Patrick Gordon," she said. "He heard our prayers in that, at least." But she stood at a little distance, and did not offer him her hand to kiss.

Nor was the man any more forthcoming. His voice was not only weary—it was formal, distant. "Your prayers, Ma'am, have need to be effective, and for more than such as myself. There is much evil done in your name!"

She drew breath as though she had been struck. "Think you that I do not know it?" she exclaimed. "Think you the knowledge does not stalk with me by day and share my pillow by night? I tell you . . ." Her voice died away, and she half-shrugged, half-shook her head. "I am the Queen—and that is the Queen's burden, *Sainte Mère* pity me. And more evil is to follow!"

"In that I believe you, Ma'am."

Mary Stewart sighed. "You are bitter, Gordon—and with cause. But your Huntly knew that he played with fire, and his son likewise. Did I not warn them sufficiently? *You* know that I did." And then, in an abruptly changed tone. "John Gordon dies tomorrow."

There was a frozen silence in that shadowy place.

The Queen herself it was who broke it, urgently, at last. "They would not heed me! I besought them—I pleaded with them, for his life. Banishment, forfeiture, imprisonment—anything, save his execution. But there was not one to support me. The lords, the Kirk, and the Burghs—they all demand his head. He dies by the axe at noontide tomorrow."

"Without trial?" Patrick grated, harshly.

"He is a man at the horn—outlawed. Outside the law. When the Council put him to the horn—that was his trial." Mary Stewart bit her lip. "But see you, my good friends—I came not here to discuss John Gordon, but your escape from this place. I had thought that you should go this night . . ."

"No. He is too weary," Mary Gordon broke in. "He must rest. . . ."

"Yes. I see that, plainly."

"Not so," Patrick asserted. But his voice was flat, almost automatic, next to a denial of his words. "I can go, at once."

"No. I have thought of the better way," the Queen declared. "Tonight, with the gates locked and guarded, you might only slip out three or four at most, unseen, for the town is awake and astir. But tomorrow, when all are assembled to watch what will be, you could ride out in the midst of your two-score Mackintoshes, Patrick Gordon here but one amongst them. You could be riding to meet your father, *ma chérie*, as is only dutiful. Moreover, with the country a-move with broken men, you are wise to be strongly escorted."

"But you, your Grace—your bodyguard?" the other girl

pointed out. "Your weapon—would you leave yourself without it, again?"

"I cannot take your hillmen to Edinburgh with me. Already my brother is talking of leaving for the South. His work in the North, and mine it seems, is done. Justice triumphs! No—I must seek for myself now another weapon for my safeguarding. Possibly the husband that George Gordon advises. Perhaps Scotland needs an heir more than she needs her Queen!" Mary Stewart looked away and away. "Would I were you, *ma petite*!"

"I am sorry, your Grace."

The Queen shook her sighs from her, and turned back to Patrick. "There is one last charge that I have to put upon you, my friend. A last message. The Council, when it condemned John of Findlater to the axe, would have put his brother the Lord Gordon, to the horn also. It would have had him die, likewise. But that I did prevent, the Saints be praised. Instead, the lords have forfeited him in his lands and titles, and proclaimed that he is to put himself in ward forthwith, to await trial. My charge is—if you can see George Gordon, tell him that I have sworn in front of all my Council that he is no unfriend of mine, and shall not die. Tell him that is my royal promise, and that I shall keep it."

"He will be vastly relieved, Ma'am!" Patrick said. And his wife looked at him swiftly, anxiously.

The Queen inclined her lovely head. "You may say it, Patrick Gordon—and I cannot find it in my heart to blame you. But, natheless, that is my promise to him. Once he told me 'Trust Gordon!' I know not if it was good advice—but I could not act upon it. Now I say to him 'Trust Mary!' I will save him if I may; restore to him his honours and lands as and when I can. And saving him, save your Clan of Gordon, yet, God helping me! Will you carry this last message, Patrick?"

The man drew himself up to his full height, and reached for her hand to kiss it. "I will, Mary Stewart—and I crave your Grace's forgiveness for a surly dog! I am your man, yet—and to the end of me!"

The Queen's breath caught in her long throat, and for a moment her eyes were misty in the firelight. Then she spoke. "I am content," she said. "I think that I shall not see you again. Tomorrow, I . . . I watch what is done, Heaven aiding me! I say farewell now . . . and I hate farewells. What I do I must do quickly . . . or fail myself. Have you a sword, man?"

He shook his head. The Queen, glancing about her in the shadows, darted to the wall of the place and drew a broadsword from amongst the many that hung there on shoulder-belts. "Kneel," she commanded.

As the man got down on his knees almost on the selfsame spot where he had been wed, she laid the sword-blade first on his right shoulder, then on his left.

"I dub you my true and leal and courtly knight, Patrick Gordon, in the sight of God, and those present. Arise, Sir Patrick, *mon cher ami!*"

Gasping, the man got slowly to his feet. "Your Grace . . . Ma'am . . . I, I cannot . . ."

"Do not say it, man. Do not say it—for I cannot answer it!" she whispered. "Say nothing—save to promise me that in time to come, when you hear of the ill that the Queen has done, you will remember, and think less hardly of me!"

Patrick opened his mouth to speak, and still found no words.

The other eyed him directly, for just a moment, her woman's gaze frank, unflinching, revealing, even in that uncertain light. Then she turned to Mary Gordon, and flung her arms around her. The two girls clung to each other, murmuring incoherencies, till the younger broke loose and went, practically running across the tannery floor to the door, her wide skirts hitched high, uncaring for her royal dignity or the gaze of all the wondering Mackintoshes.

And at the door, Mary of Scotland turned and looked back, a slight and terribly lonely figure in that moment. "Pray for me, tomorrow!" she cried, and was gone into the night.

Patrick, Mary, and Donald Gorm were only three amongst the vast crowd that thronged the Broadgate and all its tributary streets and wynds and alleys. They were inconspicuously clad, the girl with an old plaid over her head and enveloping her person, the men merely ragged Mackintosh clansmen. But in that tightly-packed concourse they could scarcely have been safer, their identity swallowed up and lost in seething humanity. All Aberdeen was there to see Sir John Gordon of Findlater die.

The trio stood at the corner of the vennel and Broadgate, whence they could withdraw back to the tannery when the time came, as would be necessary. The execution was to be staged in the Broadgate, right opposite the Provost's house, by the ever-thoughtful Moray's express command, so that the Queen might view it all conveniently from her window—or perhaps, have no excuse for not viewing it. Thus, the tannery party had no need to go any distance from their refuge, either.

Mary Gordon had no desire whatsoever to observe the final act in the life of the man whom she had detested and feared. But Patrick had dourly insisted that *he* was bound to see the end of this companion of his youth, for various reasons that did not lend themselves readily to explanation, and one that did—that he owed it to his new Chief, the Lord Gordon, to report to him how his brother had died. And since Mary would not allow him to go out of her sight, there they were. At a suitable moment, when all attention was fixedly engaged elsewhere, they would slip away, back to the tannery, where the Mackintosh contingent would be awaiting them, ready horsed for the road.

They could see the open windows of the Provost's lodging, all already filled with watchers, save for one on the first floor, notably empty as yet and reserved undoubtedly for Scotland's Queen. No other window in sight was not fully occupied; even the roofs of the houses were black with people. This was an occasion which the fortunate spectators would retell to children and to children's children.

The chattering excited crowd, swaying this way and that, suddenly was galvanised, with every face turning towards that significant window. It was no longer empty. Two men in black had appeared therein, one in the Geneva gown and bands of the Kirk, the other still more soberly clad. This latter raised a white hand, and gradually the noise of the throng stilled, till only the thin screaming of the gulls and a distant clatter of horses' hooves on cobbles sounded in those thousands of ears.

"Let us worship Almighty God," the voice came, level, flat, cold, but penetrating. "Let us glorify His Name, and thank Him for His Grace towards us His Elect. Let us seek His blessing on what is done this day, for the furtherance of His rule and worship in this *His* Kingdom of Scotland!"

As James Stewart finished speaking, a low murmur rose from the crowd—a murmur to which Sir Patrick Gordon contributed in altogether unsuitable proportion.

"The thrice-damned hypocrite!" he growled, and drew sundry glances, not all of them unsympathetic, as well as Mary's anguished hushing and urgent grip.

Then the other voice arose, harsh, powerful, but sonorous and vibrant—the voice of that same Master Forbes of the Kirk of St. Nicholas who had so ably dealt with their Creator over the matter of grace before meat on the occasion of the banquet at Blackfriars. Now, on this still meatier theme, of the just and inevitable downfall on earth, and everlasting and excruciating punishment elsewhere, of all papists, idolators, recusants, and defilers of the Word, he truly excelled himself. Not all of his hearers prayed with him, no doubt—after all, they had come for other emotional exercise—but none could fail to be affected by what he said. And behind him, deeper in the room and only dimly discernible, stood the slight figure of his Catholic Queen.

Master Forbes went on at some length. The crowd grew a little restive, more especially when the sound of the horses drew near, and a cavalcade was to be observed above the sea of heads, approaching from the Gallowgate.

Unaffected by the praying, probably unconscious of it, the troop came on, and the crowd, opening to give it passage, began to stir and give tongue again. It was perhaps apt enough, even at this pass, that the heretic John Gordon should still interrupt the devotions of the Elect.

For Sir John of Findlater it was, led in the midst of a strong escort under Douglas of Cavers, sitting a mean garron, his hands and arms bound behind him with rope. Somehow, he had managed to spruce himself up, to get rid of the blood and grime of battle and wounds—and always he had been a man with a flair for clothes. His bare head held high, the splendid amber hair in well-combed waves to his wide shoulders, the brilliant glittering eyes looking straight before him in almost humorous disdain, he sat his horse, bound as he was, with the mien and bearing of a king bound for his crowning. And a handsomer man no woman in that great concourse had ever looked upon.

As he came on, the noise of the crowd grew—a strange noise compounded of numerous and conflicting emotions. There was malice in it, and fear, rancour and cruelty; but also, there was admiration and pity and even acclaim.

Master Forbes was where he was because he was a man who knew when to bow to circumstances—a great gift, in clergymen as in others. Accordingly, he wound up while still he could be heard, no doubt crediting the Creator with a like percipience. Gordon and his escort moved up through the press to the wooden scaffold that had been set up overnight in the middle of the Broadgate. Without waiting for aid in his dismounting, he threw his right leg over his saddle and leapt lightly, straight from horse to platform. Guards stationed at the four corners of it took alarm, evidently fearing that he might even now be making a break for freedom amongst the throng, and hastily levelled their halberds at him threateningly.

But scornfully Findlater ignored them, and limped over to inspect the ominous block, sardonic brows raised. Some in the crowd laughed.

The executioner, a lanky figure round-shouldered enough to be an incipient hunchback, climbed up on to the scaffold, to the advice of those nearby. Behind him Master Forbes came, panting a little from his hurried change of stance. He said something inaudible, to the condemned man, who demonstrated complete contempt by turning away to stare whence the divine had come. And all the waiting company turned with him—and a new sound lifted therefrom.

It was as difficult a sound to describe as that which had greeted the prisoner himself. It was more of a sigh than anything else. Certainly it was no cheer—but then, the Scots have never been great cheerers, and besides, the Harlot of Rome was scarcely the subject for discreet townsfolk and engaged mercenaries to applaud.

Mary of Scotland stood at the window, her hands gripping a crucifix, the Earl of Moray close at one shoulder and the Earl of Morton at the other. She was dressed all in white, without ornament of any sort, save for the black crucifix, which stood out sharply—and her face was no less white than the rest of her.

For a long moment Queen and captive stared at each other, eyes unwinking. It was the woman whose glance fell—fell to the cross in her hands. And the crowd's voice rose.

Moray made a quick gesture of his hand. But it was the Douglas, Lord of Morton, who spoke. "John Gordon," he bellowed. "Ye are condemned to die a traitor's death. Ye have taken up arms against your Queen and her Council. Ye have broken ward, led revolt, slain the Queen's servants, and been put to the horn. Ye now meet your just doom—to the rejoice of all true men!"

There was silence, then. Findlater did not so much as raise one of his expressive eyebrows. The throng held its breath.

"Hae ye nothing to say?" Morton barked.

"Not to such as you," the Gordon answered, clear-voiced. And then, in a changed tone, "Madam—your true lover stands before you, to say his farewell." He spoke quietly, sadly, but so distinctly that none failed to hear his words. "I have loved you well . . . but methinks you make but a cruel mistress!"

A curious deepening note came from the watching assemblage, something that was next to a growl, now. And that it was not directed at the speaker would have been obvious to the merest child. Moray and Morton exchanged glances. It was partly for something of this sort that they had forced the Queen to stand there.

Mary Stewart said no word, though she bit her lip.

"You are the loveliest amongst women, Madam—but your

247

heart, I think, is of stone. I embrace death, now, as the warmer lover!"

A tear welled out of the Queen's eye and fell unheeded down on to her tightly-clenched hand. But head up, still she did not speak.

The crowd's growl harshened, a snarl to it plain and not good to hear.

"I have cared naught for states and thrones and honours, Madam—empty words. It is for men . . . and women, that I care. But perhaps you are only a Queen, and no woman?"

The noise grew greater. Fists were shaken—and towards the window, not the scaffold. Epithets were hurled. A seething began amongst the densely packed mass. John Gordon smiled.

At Mary Stewart's back, her half-brother's eyes met those of her Chancellor, and he frowned. This was going too far —there could be danger in it. A crowd's sympathies were fickle. Moray's hand rose and cut the air in front both of himself and the Queen. "Enough," he said, sharply. And to the executioner. "To your duty, man."

"I salute your Grace, and bid you *adieu*," Sir John went on, imperturbably. "Who knows, perhaps we may meet again elsewhere . . . without the benefit of Reformers!"

The headsman tapped him on the shoulder.

Findlater bowed to her deeply, if stiffly, owing to his bonds, looked into her eyes that blinked back the tears, thoughtfully, and then turning about, knelt down and laid his head on the block, without fuss.

The growl of the onlookers altered to a quivering groan.

The headsman ran a thumb along the edge of his axe, grinning his embarrassment. Flexing his muscles, he raised his weapon.

"Tut, man—the other way round," James Stewart's voice cut into the hush. "Have him facing us."

A shudder of suspense ran through the crowd. Shaking his head, an uncomfortable man, the executioner lowered the axe, and jogged Sir John's shoulder with his knee.

Findlater slowly rose to his feet, walked round the block, and round to face that window, his features stern now, as

248

though graven in stone. He stared for a moment, and then knelt once again.

The Queen sobbed in her throat. Then, as once again the axe rose, suddenly she leaned forward, and a wordless cry burst from her lips.

Raising his eyes from the block, John Gordon saw that her arm was outstretched. She held the crucifix out towards him, urgently.

A sudden smile came to soften that graven face. And then the axe fell.

A corporate whimper that swelled to a wail that rose and sank and rose again, broke from a thousand throats.

It was a botched affair. Some said that James Stewart had ordained it so—though it could have been no more than the inefficiency and nervousness of the unpractised headsman. Time and again he had to wield his axe, whilst the crowd whinnied and writhed in its own emotional convulsions. But Patrick Gordon did not see it; his wife had had her head buried in his plaided chest since Findlater had knelt. At the first fall of the axe he turned away, sick, his last picture that of the young Queen, erect still, though gripping the window-jamb as though to hold her up, maintaining the cross high. He could have seen no more, even had he looked, for his eyes failed him.

Grabbing his Mary's hand, he dragged her blindly through the panting press. None heeded them, none even saw them.

XIX

BY Don and Urie and Foudland the Mackintosh party rode into the north-west—and there were no laggards to be urged on; no man amongst them but had seen enough of Aberdeen and the low country. Their own clean hills, a blue rim to the vista, beckoned like a magnet before them. They avoided Strathbogie—for already Moray had dispatched a force for its plunder and burning—and came to Spey by Deveron and Invermarkie and Fiddich, making for Badenoch of the mountains. But at Ballindalloch, just after noon of the second day out, they gained word which abruptly changed the direction and tenor of their going. Only a couple of hours previously the Lord Gordon and a small company had passed this way, riding hard, and had turned up Glen Avon heading for Livet, the Cabrach, and Donside, by the high passes. After them Patrick Gordon turned his party, into his own familiar hills.

Tired as the horses were, he spared them not at all, now. If George Gordon was riding hard, they must ride harder. The early November dusk was draining the colour from golden bracken and brown heather, when near the head of Glen Livet, they spied a group of perhaps a dozen riders on the long slope ahead of them, and hallooing till the outraged hills quivered to the echo, gave chase.

A mile or so from their quarry, Patrick and Mary drew well ahead of their followers, lest there be any doubts in the minds of the pursued. Soon they perceived that the company in front had drawn up, to await them. The Lord Gordon sat his steaming horse upright, silent, and unsmiling, a stiff and sombre man. There were still but two feathers in his bonnet, when there ought to have been three—for he now was Chief of Clan Gordon, by birth. Patrick swallowed, and prayed for words that would not hurt more than they must.

"Greetings, Seorus Og," he cried, and then changed the

designation deliberately from young to great, ". . . Seorus Mor!"

The other nodded acceptance of that. "You make good seeing, Patrick," he declared, calmly. "And you, Mistress Mackintosh. You, at least, look well."

"Gordon, the name is, my Lord," Mary said quietly.

He raised his dark heavy eyebrows. "Ah! Then you are a bold young woman, if not a foolhardy! Methinks 'tis not a name that man would select this day, who might do otherwise!"

" 'Twas . . . 'twas chosen for me, sir, as it were." She smiled faintly, there. "And I make no complaint."

The other inclined his head. "Gordon is honoured," he said briefly, and turned back to her husband, a man with little gift for dalliance. "Whence come you—and on what errand this time, Patrick?"

"From Aberdeen—and with the Queen's word . . . for the last time, as she said it. But, first, Huntly—my loyal duty to my Chief!"

George Gordon shook his head, slowly. "Huntly I am not— since my father was forfeited and horned. And Chief I may be only if the clan conceive me worthy. And I was not my father's choice!"

Patrick stared at his fingernails. "Your brother . . ."

"Yes—my brother. How goes it with John? He was captured, wounded in the leg, I heard . . . ?"

The other moistened dry lips, glancing behind him to where all the Mackintosh clansman had now ridden up and were ranged at his back. "John of Findlater never will be Chief . . . though he died like one," he said.

"Dead!"

"Yes, Seorus Og. To my sorrow."

There was silence over the darkening hillside, save for the weary calling of the curlews in their own sorrow. It seemed as though time stood still, until the inevitable question came.

"How did he die?" The words came harshly.

"By the axe." And swiftly. "But the shame was on those who ordered it, not on him who suffered it!"

251

George Gordon looked through him, through them all, away and away. "Yon bonny head . . ." he said.

No man met his eye.

"A traitor's death . . . for Johnnie! And my father dead in a bog! God's hand is heavy. Is there more to tell, man?"

"Aye. Your brother Robert, too—at Corrichie." Robert Gordon, Huntly's eighth son, had ridden with his father from Badenoch, and had not survived the fatal field.

"And him but a laddie! God rest his soul!" The other drooped his dark head. "And I remain! Methinks, if there was a traitor, here he sits—a traitor to mine own kin!"

"Not so, by God's name!" Patrick cried. "That is folly—false! You sought to save them all—and they would not heed."

"I could have died with them, Patrick MacRuary."

"And whom would that have served—save only the Bastard? Them, or Gordon, or your Queen? Say it not, Seorus Og. Even if your kin would not heed you, you did what Huntly, what the Chief should have done—you saved your clan. Huntly is dead, and many with him—but thanks to you Clan Gordon survives. Think what might have been had you not acted as you did!"

"Aye," the other said, heavily. "It may be so, Patrick. But I think that I know what men will say of me. They will say—where was George Gordon at Corrichie?" He sighed. "But that is of no matter. Only the clan matters, now . . . and her Grace. You say that you have her word, again?"

"Yes. She . . . she is deeply grieved, sore hurt at what is done in her name. But she says, once, you told her to trust Gordon. Now, she tells *you*—trust Mary! The Council would have pronounced your doom, and put you to the horn. But she swore before them all that you are her friend, and should not die. It is her promise, and her word to you is that she will keep it, God willing."

"If she may!" Lord Gordon commented, grimly.

"Aye. But that is her word. You are forfeited, in freedom, land, and titles, and required to place yourself in the royal ward forthwith, by order of the Privy Council. But the Queen is committed to saving you, and to restoring to you your lands

252

and honours as and when she may. And saving you, to save Clan Gordon. That is my message, Seorus Og."

"And I thank you for bearing it, whatever the outcome, Patrick MacRuary. Though belike, it is my death warrant!"

The younger man creased his brows unhappily. "I . . . I deem it could be . . . if you heed it!"

"I shall heed it," the other assured, simply.

"But . . . if you think that she cannot save you—that they will slay you, notwithstanding—then you need not yield yourself up to ward. You may bide here, in your own mountains and all Clan Gordon will protect you."

"And die in the doing of it! Would that not be the way of it? The Bastard would not rest till he had me, the heir of Gordon, in his hands—and all Gordon would suffer. 'Tis one man or many, Patrick. I set out on this course to save Gordon —I shall not fail the clan now."

"The clan, I swear, would liefer have you stay with them, come what may, Seorus Og."

"Mayhap—but that is not the way I see my duty. And I have told all men that I am the Queen's man—I shall obey the Queen's command. I shall yield myself to her Grace. But not here and now, while passions are hot and the Council is flushed with victory. I shall yield myself in the South, in Edinburgh, where the Duke, my gudefather, and his Hamiltons may help to even the Bastard's scales of justice."

Patrick shook his head at all the enclosing hills. "I know not what is best," he said.

"But *I* do, my friend. And I shall perform it, God willing." The other nodded. "As indeed, shall you likewise."

Patrick looked up, hiding swiftly he hoped, the gleam of perturbation in his eyes. "Me? I . . . I am at your service, Seorus Mor. You are Gudeman o' the Bog, now—I await your commands." And he did not let his glance stray near his wife.

A brief flicker of a smile lighted the Lord Gordon's sombre features for an instant. "Yes, Patrick—I know it. And here is your command. Go you home to Balruary, with your woman, and hang up your sword on the wall, and raise you good tall sons for Gordon! That is your best service to me, now—and

Gordon, methinks, shall need them! Ma'am—you will aid me in this?"

Flushing as she was, the girl met his dark and piercing eye. "I will," she said—and said it more strongly than she had made her marriage vows.

"That is well. Now—I think all is said that need be said. Balruary lies yonder, Patrick."

"Yes. But you—will you honour my roof this night . . . ?"

"No. I ride back to Badenoch. I shall act the Chief, and send the clan back to its glens. Pray God that they have kept from blows with Clan Chattan, the while. I shall leave peace in the North, if I may. And I think Lauchlan Mor will aid me in that, this once."

"If you have word with my father, my Lord, will you tell him that his daughter is well content, and will come to him at Moy, one day, in her own time?"

"I shall be your messenger, ma'am. And . . . it comes to me that a good name enough for the first-born of those sons of yours could be George! God-speed, Patrick MacRuary. If it is permitted that Mary Stewart keep her word, we shall meet again. If not—say a prayer to your Protestant God for my soul. Farewell."

And Patrick could answer him no word, as he swung his mount round, waved his followers on, and plunged away downhill.

One man of his party remained behind, unbidden, and came wordlessly to manoeuvre his garron into position at the tail of Patrick's own—Black Ewan Gordon.

When even the vibration of drumming hooves had faded from the hillside, the watchers turned slowly, silently, into the south, where the dark cowls of the night clouds already were drawing around the snow-streaked shoulders of the high mountains. Below them lay the quiet place of Balruary, of the birches and the lochan, where the threads of an old life lay waiting to be picked up, and a new life to be woven into them. Out of the dusk Balruary opened its arms for them.

They rode down through the swishing heather. And the woman's hand reached out and found the man's, and held.

EPILOGUE

THE wheels of justice once a-move turned to good effect. On the same day as Findlater's execution, six Gordon lairds were hanged in the streets of Aberdeen, and the list of those proscribed made wearisome reading.

Strathbogie Castle presented the richest pickings Scotland had ever known, to the Earl of Moray's great content. But the burning proved ineffective, and the masonry hard to ding doun. And so it stood—and stands yet.

The disembowelled body of Huntly, rudely embalmed, was dispatched by sea to Leith, to await due trial in Edinburgh—his apoplectic death being a considerable inconvenience to legal processes. There the corpse was duly set up on its feet, at the bar of Parliament, in the Queen's presence, when it was decreed that George Gordon, former Earl of Huntly, was guilty of treason, that his lands and goods were forfeit, his dignity, name, and memory extinct, his arms cancelled, and that his posterity were thenceforth incapable of office, honour, or dignity within the realm.

The Earl of Sutherland was also condemned to death by Parliament—but by the Queen's influence was not executed, and four years later received pardon.

The Lord Gordon presented himself to the Queen on November 26th, 1562, five days after she herself reached Edinburgh, and was committed to the Castle. He was tried by the Justice Court, found guilty of treason, and condemned to be hanged, drawn, and quartered. But by Mary's intervention he was removed to Dunbar Castle, where he remained in free ward for three years, until, three days after Mary's marriage to Darnley, he was released, pardoned, and eventually reinstated in his lands and honours. He restored Strathbogie, or Huntly, Castle. His son was created first Marquis of Huntly.

With the Queen's marriage, and begetting of an heir to the

throne, much of her half-brother's power slipped out of his hands. How he laboured to regain it, by the dagger, gunpowder, forgery and other ingenuities, till eventually, with the baby King James Sixth in his grip, and Mary in Elizabeth's prison of Fotheringay, he ruled Scotland at last as Regent, is a tale that has been told often enough. He was an efficient blackguard, and consistent; probably, had his esteemed father seen fit to marry his spirited mother, he would have made Scotland one of her strongest and most successful kings.

As for Mary of Scotland, all the world knows her fate. On the day that men cease to dispute her honour, her virtue, her beauty, and her grace—on that day shall disputation have vanished from this earth.